James H. Graff, Edmund Hodgson Yates

The Rock Ahead

a novel

James H. Graff, Edmund Hodgson Yates

The Rock Ahead
a novel

ISBN/EAN: 9783337349417

Printed in Europe, USA, Canada, Australia, Japan

Cover: Foto ©Andreas Hilbeck / pixelio.de

More available books at **www.hansebooks.com**

THE ROCK AHEAD.

A Novel.

BY

EDMUND YATES,

AUTHOR OF

"BLACK SHEEP," "KISSING THE ROD," "THE FORLORN HOPE," ETC.

"The Gods are just; and of our pleasant vices
Make instruments to scourge us."

A NEW EDITION.

LONDON:

TINSLEY BROTHERS, 18, CATHERINE ST., STRAND.

1869.

TO M. E—D. FORGUES.

My dear Sir,

Although I have not the pleasure of your personal acquaintance, I venture to ask you to accept the dedication of this book, in slight acknowledgment of the admirable manner in which you have reproduced two of my previous stories (*Broken to Harness* and *The Forlorn Hope*) in the pages of the *Revue des Deux Mondes*, and of the flattering way in which you have frequently referred to my writings in that excellent periodical.

Faithfully yours,

EDMUND YATES.

London, April, 1868.

CONTENTS.

Book the Second (*continued*)

Book the Third.

THE ROCK AHEAD.

Prologue.

CHAPTER I.

WHISPERED.

HOT in Brighton, very hot. The August sun reflected off white-chalk cliff and red-brick pavement, and the sea shining and sparkling like a sapphire ; the statue of George the Fourth, in its robe of verdigris, looking ou in blighted perspiration at the cabmen at its base, as though imploring a drink ; the cabmen lolling undemonstratively on the boxes of their vehicles, not seeking for employment, and—partly by reason of the heat, but more, perhaps, in consequence of the money received recently at the races —rather annoyed than otherwise when their services were called into requisition. For the Brighton races had just taken place, and the town, always so full, had been more crammed than ever. All the grand hotels had been filled with the upper ten thousand, who moved easily over from Chichester and Worthing and Bognor, where they had been staying for Goodwood, which immediately precedes Brighton ; and all the lodgings had been taken by the betting-men and the turfites,—the " professionals," with whom the whole affair is the strictest matter of business, and to whom it is of no interest whether the race is run at Torquay or Wolverhampton, in blazing sunshine or pouring hailstorm, so long as the right thing " comes off," and they " land the winner."

It was all right for the bookmakers this time at Brighton : the favourites, against which so much money had been staked, had been beaten, and "dark" horses, scarcely heard of, and backed for nothing, had carried off the principal prizes. So it followed that most of the gentry of the betting-ring, instead of hurrying off to the scene of their next trials of fortune, finding themselves with plenty of money in their pockets, at a pleasant place in lovely weather, made up their minds to remain there during the intervening Saturday and Sunday, and to drop business so far as possible until the Monday morning, when they would speed away by the early express-trains.

So far as possible, but not entirely. It is impossible for them to drop business altogether, even on this glorious Sunday afternoon, when the whole face of Nature is blandly smiling. See the broad blue bosom of the sea smooth and sparkling as glass, dotted here and there with white-sailed pleasure-boats ; see far away, beyond the encircling belt of brick and stone, the broad shoulder of the bare and bushless downs, over which the fresh air careering comes away laden with the delicious scents of trodden turf and wild thyme and yellow gorse ; see the brown beach, where under the lee of the fishing-smacks, or making a table of the large flukes of rusty anchors, sit groups of excursionists,—pallid Londoners exulting in the unwonted luxury of escaping from the stony streets, and more excited by the brisk and revivifying sea air than by the contents of the stone bottle which stands in the midst of each group, and whose contents are so perpetually going round from hand to hand in the little footless glass ; see the Esplanade thronged with its hundreds of foot passengers, its scores of flies and carriages ; see the Stock Exchange in all its glory, and the children of Israel gorgeous in long ringlets, thunder-and-lightning neck-ties, and shot-silk parasols ; and see the turf-men standing here and there in little knots, trying to be interested in the scenes passing around them, but ever and again turning to each other with some question of "odds," for some scrap of "intelligence."

The ring is strongly represented this Sunday afternoon on Brighton Parade, both in its highest and its lowest form. The short stout man in the greasy suit of black, with the satin waistcoat frayed round the pockets by the rubbing of his silver watch-guard, who is jotting down memoranda with a fat cedar-pencil in his betting-book, enters freely into conversation and is on an equality with the gentlemanly-looking man whose only visible "horseyness" is expressed in his tightly-cut trousers and his bird's-eye neckerchief with the horseshoe pin. Patrons of the turf, owners of race-horses, commission-agents, book-makers, touts, tipsters, hangers-on of every kind in turf speculations and turf iniquities, are here at Brighton on this lovely Sunday afternoon.

There was one group, consisting of three people, planted on the Esplanade, just in front of the Old Ship Hotel, the three component members of which were recognized and saluted by nearly every one who passed. One of them was a short square-built man, with keen eyes closely set and sunken, small red whiskers, and a sharp-pointed nose. He was dressed in black, with a wonderfully neatly-tied long white cravat, folded quite flat, with a dog's tooth set in gold for a pin; and he wore a low-crowned hat. The other two were young men, dressed in the best style of what is known as "horsey get-up." They had been talking and laughing ever since they had taken up their position, immediately after lunching at the hotel, out of which they had strolled with cigars in their mouths; and it was obvious that any respect which the elder man might receive was not paid to him on account of his age, but rather in acknowledgment of the caustic remarks with which he amused his companions. These remarks seemed at last to have come to an end. There had been a long silence, which was broken by the elder man asking,—

"O, seen anything of Gore—Harvey Gore? Has he gone back, or what?"

"Don't know; haven't seen him since Thursday night," said the taller of the young men.

"Won a pot of money on the Cup," said the other sententiously; "regular hatful."

"What did his pal do?" asked the elder man. "Lloyd I mean. Did he pull through?"

"Dropped his tin, Foxey dear. Held on like grim death to Gaslight, and was put in the hole like the rest of us. He tells me he has been hit for——"

"*He* tells you!" interrupted the elder man; "*he* tells you! I've known Gilbert Lloyd for two or three years, and anything *he* tells me I should take deuced good care not to believe."

" Very good, Foxey dear ! very nice, you sweet old thing ! only don't halloo out *quite* so loud, because here's G. L. coming across the road to speak to us, and he mightn't—— How do, Lloyd, old fellow ? "

The new-comer was a man of about four-and-twenty, a little above the middle height, and slightly but strongly built. His face would generally have been considered handsome, though a physiognomist would have read shiftiness and suspicion in the small and sunken blue eyes, want of geniality in the tightly-closing mouth visible under the slight fair moustache, and determination in the jaw. Though there was a slight trace of the stable in his appearance, he was decidedly more gentlemanly-looking than his companions, having a distinct stamp of birth and breeding which they lacked. He smiled as he approached the group, and waved a small stick which he carried in a jaunty manner ; but Foxey noticed a flushed appearance round his eyes, an eager worn straining round his mouth, and said to his friend who had last spoken, " You're right, Jack ; Lloyd has had it hot and strong this time, and no mistake."

The young man had by this time crossed the road and stood leaning over the railing. In answer to a repetition of their salutes, he said,—

" Not very bright. None of us are always up to the mark, save Foxey here, who is perennial ; and just now I'm worried and bothered. O, not as you fellows imagine," he said hastily, as he saw a smile go round ; and as he said it his face darkened, and the clenching of his jaws gave him a very savage expression,—" not from what I've dropped at this meeting ; that's neither here nor there : lightly come, lightly gone ; but the fact is that Gore, who is living with me over there, is deuced seedy."

" Thought he looked pulled and done on Thursday," said Foxey. " Didn't know whether it was backing Gaslight that had touched him up, or—— "

" No," interrupted Lloyd, hurriedly ; " a good deal of champagne under a tremendously hot sun ; that's the cause, I believe. Harvey has a way of turning up his little finger under excitement, and never will learn to moderate his transports. He's overdone it this time, and I'm afraid is really bad. I must send for a doctor ; and now I'm off to the telegraph-office, to send a message to my wife. Gore was to have cleared out of this early this morning, to spend a day or two with Sandcrack, the vet, at Shoreham ; and my proprietress was coming down here ; but there's no room for her now, and I must put her off."

"Do you think Harvey Gore's really bad ?" asked one of the younger men.

"Well, I *think* he's got something like sunstroke, and I *know* he's a little off his head," responded Lloyd. "He'll pull round, I dare say—I've no doubt. But still he can't be moved just yet, and a woman would only be in the way under such circumstances, let alone it's not being very lively for her ; so I'll just send her a message to keep off. Ta-ta ! I shall look into the smoking-room to-night at the Ship, when Harvey's gone off to sleep." And with a nod and a smile, Gilbert Lloyd started off.

"Queer customer that, Foxey."

"Queer indeed ; which his golden number is Number One !" said Foxey, enigmatically.

"What's his wife like ?"

"Never saw her," said Foxey ; "but I should think she had a pleasant time of it with that youth. It will be an awful disappointment to him, her not coming down, won't it ?"

"Foxey, you are an unbeliever of the deepest dye. Domestic happiness in your eyes is——"

"Bosh ! You never said a truer word. Now, let's have half-a-crown's-worth of fly, and go up the cliff."

A short time after Gilbert Lloyd had left the house in which he had taken lodgings, consisting of the parlour-floor and a bedroom upstairs, Mrs. Bush, the landlady, whose mind was rather troubled, partly because the servant, whose "Sunday out" it was, had not yet returned from the Methodist chapel where she performed her devotions—a delay which her mistress did not impute entirely to the blandishments of the preacher—and partly for other reasons, took up her position in the parlour-window, and began to look up and down the street. Mrs. Bush was not a land-lady of the jolly type ; she was not ruddy of complexion, or thin and trim of ankle, neither did she adorn herself with numerous ribbons of florid hue. On the contrary, she was a pale, anxious-faced woman, who looked as if she had had too much to do, and quite enough to fret about, all her life. And now, as she stood in the parlour-window on a hot Sunday, and contemplated the few loungers who straggled through the street on their way to the sea-shore, she assumed a piteous expression of countenance, and shook her head monotonously.

"I wish I hadn't let 'em the rooms, I'm sure," said Mrs. Bush to herself. "It's like my luck—and in the race-week too. If *he's* able to be up and away from this in a day or two, then *I* know nothing of sickness; and I've seen a good deal of it too in my time. No sign of that girl! But who's this?"

Asking this, under the circumstances, unsatisfactory question, Mrs. Bush drew still closer to the parlour-window, holding the inevitable red-moreen curtain still farther back, and looked with mingled curiosity and helplessness at a cab which stopped unmistakably at the door of her house, and from the window of which a handsome young female head protruded itself. Mrs. Bush could not doubt that the intention of the lady in the cab was to get out of it and come into her house; and that good-for-nothing Betsy had not come in, and there was nobody to open the door but Mrs. Bush—a thing which, though a meek-enough woman in general, she did not like doing. The lady gave her very little time to consider whether she liked it or not; for she descended rapidly from the cab, took a small travelling-bag from the hand of the cabman, paid him, mounted the three steps which led to the door, and knocked and rang with so determined a purpose of being admitted, that Mrs. Bush, without a moment's hesitation,—but with a muttered "Mercy on us! Suppose he'd been asleep now!" which seemed to imply that the lady's vehemence might probably damage somebody's nerves,—crossed the hall and opened the door.

She found herself confronted by a very young lady, a girl of not more, and possibly less, than nineteen years, in whose manner there was a certain confidence strongly suggestive of her entertaining an idea that the house which she was evidently about to enter was her own, and not that of the quiet, but not well-pleased, looking person who asked her civilly enough, yet not with any cordiality of tone, whom she wished to see.

"Is Mr. Lloyd not at home? This is his address, I know," was the enigmatical reply of the young lady.

"A Mr. Lloyd *is* lodging here, miss," returned Mrs. Bush, with a glance of anything but approbation at her questioner, and planting herself rather demonstratively in the doorway; "but he isn't in. Did you wish to see him?"

"I am Mrs. Lloyd," replied the young lady, with a frown, and depositing her little travelling-bag within the threshold; "did you not know I was coming? Let me in, please."

And the next minute—Mrs. Bush could not tell exactly how it happened—she found the hall-door shut, and she was standing in the passage, while the young lady who had announced herself as Mrs. Lloyd was calmly walking into the parlour. Mrs. Bush was confounded by the sudden and unexpected nature of this occurrence; but the only thing she could do was to follow the unlooked-for visitor into the parlour, and she did it. The young lady had already seated herself on a small hard sofa, covered with crimson moreen to match the window-curtains, had put off her very becoming and fashionable bonnet, and was then taking off her gloves. She looked annoyed, but not in the least embarrassed.

"*That* is Mr. Lloyd's room, I presume?" she said, as she pointed to the folding-doors which connected the parlours, and which stood slightly open.

"Yes, m'm; but——"

Mrs. Bush hesitated; but as the young lady rose, took up her bag, and instantly pushed the door she had indicated quite open, and walked into the apartment, Mrs. Bush felt that the case was getting desperate. Though a depressed woman habitually, she was not by any means a timid one, and had fought many scores of highly successful battles with lodgers in her time. But this was quite a novel experience, and Mrs. Bush was greatly at a loss how to act. Something must be done, that was quite clear. Not so what that something was to be; and more than ever did Mrs. Bush resent the tarrying of Betsy's feet on her return from Beulah Chapel.

"*She* would have shut the door in her face, and kept her out until I saw how things really were," thought the aggrieved landlady; but she said boldly enough, as she closely followed the intruder, and glanced at her left hand, on which the symbol of lawful matrimony duly shone,—

"If you please, m'm, you wasn't expected. Mr. Lloyd nor the other gentleman never mentioned that there was a lady coming ; and I don't in general let my parlours to ladies."

"Indeed ! that is very awkward," said the young lady, who had opened her bag, taken out her combs and brushes, and was drawing a chair to the dressing-table ; "but it cannot be helped. Mr. Lloyd quite expected me, I know ; he arranged that I should come down to-morrow before he left town ; but it suited me better to come to-day. I can't think why he did not tell you."

"I suppose he forgot it, m'm," said Mrs. Bush, utterly regardless of the uncomplimentary nature of the suggestion, "on account of the sick gentleman ; but it's rather unfortunate, for I never *do* take in ladies, not in my parlours ; and Mr. Lloyd not having mentioned it, I——"

"Do you mean to say that I cannot remain here with my husband ?" said the young lady, turning an astonished glance upon Mrs. Bush.

"Well, m'm," said the nervous landlady, "as it's for a short time only as Mr. Lloyd has taken the rooms, and as it's Sunday, I shall see, when he comes in. You see, m'm, I've rather particular people in my drawing-rooms, and it's different about ladies ; and——" Here she glanced once more at the light girlish figure, in the well-fitting, fashionable dress, standing before the dressing-table, and at the white hand adorned with the orthodox ring.

"I think I understand you," said the intruder, gravely ; "you did not know Mr. Lloyd was married, and you are not sure that I am his wife. It is a difficulty, and I really don't see how it is to be gotten over. Will you take *his* word ?—at all events, I may remain here until he comes in presently ?"

Something winning, something convincing, in the tone of her voice caused a sudden revulsion of feeling in Mrs. Bush. The good woman—for she was a good woman in the main —began to feel rather ashamed of herself, and she commenced a bungling sort of apology. Of course the lady could stay, but it *was* awkward Mr. Lloyd not having told her ; and there was but one servant, a good-for-nothing

hussy as ever stepped—and over-staying her time now to
that degree, that she expected the "drawing-rooms" would
not have their dinner till ever so late ; but at this point the
young lady interrupted her.

"If I may stay for to-night," she said gently, and with
a very frank smile, which made Mrs. Bush feel indignant
with herself, as well as ashamed, "some other arrangement
can be made to-morrow ; and I require no waiting-on. I
shall give you no trouble, or as little as possible."

Mrs. Bush could not hold out any longer. She told the
young lady she could certainly stay for that day and night,
and as for to-morrow, she would "see about it ; " and then,
at the dreaded summons of the impatient "drawing-rooms,"
bustled away, saying she would return presently, and "see
to " the stranger herself.

Pretty girls in pretty dresses are not rarities in the
lodging-houses of Brighton ; indeed, it would perhaps be
difficult to name any place where they are to be seen more
frequently, or in greater numbers ; but the toilet-glass on
the table in the back bed-room of Mrs. Bush's lodging-house,
a heavy article of furniture, with a preponderance of frame,
had probably reflected few such faces as that of the lady
calling herself Mrs. Lloyd, who looked attentively into it
when she found herself alone, and decided that she was not
so very dusty, considering.

She was rather tall, and her figure was slight and girlish,
but firm and well-developed. She carried her head gracefully ; and something in her attitude and air suggested to
the beholder that she was not more commonplace in character than in appearance. Her complexion was very fair
and clear, but not either rosy or milky ; very young as she
was, she looked as if she had thought too much and lived
too much to retain the ruddiness and whiteness of colouring
which rarely coexist with intellectual activity or sensitive
feelings. Her features were well-formed ; but the face was
one in which a charm existed different from, and superior
to, any which merely lies in regularity of feature. It was
to be found mainly in the eyes and mouth. The eyes were
brown in colour—the soft rich deep brown in which the
pupil confounds itself with the iris ; and the curling lashes
harmonized with both ; eyes not widely opened, but yet
with nothing sly or hidden in their semi-veiled habitual

look—eyes which, when suddenly lifted up, and opened in surprise, pleasure, anger, or any other emotion, instantly convinced the person who received the glance that they were the most beautiful he had ever seen. The eyebrows were dark and arched, and the forehead, of that peculiar formation and width above the brow which phrenologists hold to indicate a talent for music, was framed in rippling bands of dark chestnut hair.

She was a beautiful and yet more a remarkable-looking young woman, girlish in some points of her appearance, and in her light lithe movements, but with something ungirlish, and even hard, in her expression. This something was in the mouth : not small enough to be silly, not large enough to be defective in point of proportion ; the line of the lips was sharp, decisive, and cold ; richly coloured, as befitted her youth, they were not young lips—they did not smile spontaneously, or move above the small white teeth with every thought and fancy, but moved deliberately, opening and closing at her will only. What it was in Mrs. Lloyd's face which contradicted the general expression of youth which it wore would have been seen at once if she had placed her hand across her eyes. The beaming brown eyes, the faintly-tinted rounded cheeks, were the features of a girl—the forehead and the mouth were the features of a woman who had left girlhood a good way behind her, and travelled over some rough roads and winding ways since she had lost sight of it.

When Mrs. Bush returned, she found the stranger in the front parlour, but not standing at the window, looking out for the return of her husband ; on the contrary, she was seated at the prim round table, listlessly turning over some newspapers and railway literature left there by Gilbert Lloyd. Once again Mrs. Bush looked at her with sharp suspicion ; once again she was disarmed by her beauty, her composure, and the sweetness of her smile.

"Mr. Lloyd is not in yet, m'm," began Mrs. Bush, "and you'll be wanting your lunch."

"No, thank you," said Mrs. Lloyd ; "I can wait. I suppose you don't know when he is likely to be in ?"

"He *said* directly," replied Mrs. Bush ; "and I wish he had kept to it, for I can't think the sick gentleman is any better. I've been to look at him, and he seems to me a deal worse since morning."

Mrs. Lloyd looked rather vacantly at Mrs. Bush. "Have you a lodger ill in the house?" she asked. "That makes it still more inconvenient for you to receive me."

Mrs. Bush felt uncomfortable at this question. How very odd that Mrs. Lloyd should not know about her husband's friend! They are evidently queer people, thought the landlady ; and she answered, rather stiffly,—

"The only lodger ill in the house, m'm, is the gentleman as came with Mr. Lloyd ; and, in my opinion, he's very ill indeed."

"Came with Mr. Lloyd?" said the young lady, in a tone of great surprise. "Do you mean Mr. Gore? Can you possibly mean Mr. Gore?"

"Just him," answered Mrs. Bush succinctly. "Didn't you know he was here with Mr. Lloyd?"

"I knew he was coming to Brighton with him, certainly," said Mrs. Lloyd ; "but I understood he was to leave immediately after the races—before I came down. What made him stay?"

Mrs. Bush drew near the table, and, leaning her hands upon it, fell into an easy tone of confidential chat with Mrs. Lloyd. That lady sat still, looking thoughtfully before her, as the landlady began, but after a little resting her head on her hand and covering her eyes.

"He stayed, m'm, because he was very ill, uncommon ill to be sure ; I never saw a gentleman iller, nor more stubborn. His portmanteau was packed and ready when he went to the races, and he told Betsy he shouldn't be five minutes here when he'd come back ; and Mr. Lloyd said to him in my hearing, 'Gore,' said he, 'how your digestion stands the tricks you play with it, I can *not* understand ;' for they'd been breakfasting, and he had eat unwholesome, I can't say otherwise. But when they come from the races, they come in a cab, which wasn't usual ; and, not to offend you, m'm, Mr. Lloyd had had quite enough" (here she paused for an expression of annoyance on the part of her hearer ; but no such manifestation was made) ; "but Mr. Gore, he *was* far gone, and a job we had to get him upstairs without disturbing the drawing-rooms, I can assure you.

And Mr. Lloyd told me he had been very ill all day at the races, and wouldn't come home or let them fetch a doctor—there were ever so many there—or anything, but would go on drinking; and when he put him in a cab, he wanted to take him to a doctor's, but he wouldn't go; and Mr. Lloyd did say, m'm, begging your pardon, that Mr. Gore damned the doctors, and said all the medicine he ever took, or ever would take, was in his portmanteau."

"Was there no doctor sent for, then? Has nothing been done for him?" asked Mrs. Lloyd, with some uneasiness in her tone, removing her hand from her eyes and looking full at Mrs. Bush.

"We've done—Betsy and me and Mr. Lloyd; for no one could be more attentive—all we could; but Mr. Gore was quite sensible, and have a doctor he *would not;* and what could we do? We gave him the medicine out of the case in his portmanteau. I mixed it and all, and he told me how, quite well; and this morning he was ever so much better."

"And is he worse now? Who is with him?" asked Mrs. Lloyd, rising.

"Well, m'm, I think he looks a deal worse; and I wish Mr. Lloyd was come in, because I think he ought to send for a doctor; I don't know what to do."

"Who is with him?" repeated Mrs. Lloyd.

"No one," returned Mrs. Bush. "No one is with him. When Mr. Lloyd went out, he told me Mr. Gore felt inclined to sleep: he had had some tea and was better, and I was not to let him be disturbed. But when I was upstairs just now, I heard him give a moan; and I knew he was not asleep, so I went in: and he looks very bad, and I couldn't get a word out of him but ' Where's Lloyd?' "

"Take me to his room at once," said Mrs. Lloyd, " and send for a doctor instantly. We must not wait for anything."

But the incorrigible Betsy had not yet returned, and Mrs. Bush explained to the stranger that she had no means of sending for a doctor until she could send Betsy.

"Let me see Mr. Gore first for a minute, and then I will fetch the nearest doctor myself," said Mrs. Lloyd; and, passing out of the room as she spoke, she began to ascend the narrow staircase, followed by the landlady, instructing her that the room in which the sick man was to be found was the "two-pair front."

The room in which the sick man lay was airy, and tolerably large. As Gertrude Lloyd softly turned the handle of the door, and entered, the breeze, which bore with it a mingled flavour of the sea and the dust, fluttered the scanty window-curtains of white dimity, and caused the draperies of the bed to flap dismally. The sun streamed into the room, but little impeded by the green blinds, which shed a sickly hue over everything, and lent additional ghastliness to the face, which was turned away from Gertrude when she entered the chamber. The bed, a large structure of extraordinary height, stood in front of one of the windows; the furniture of the room was of the usual lodging-house quality; an open portmanteau, belching forth tumbled shirts and rumpled pocket-handkerchiefs, gaped wide upon the floor; the top of the chest of drawers was covered with bottles, principally of the soda-water pattern, but of which one contained a modicum of brandy, and another some fluid magnesia. Everything in the room was disorderly and uncomfortable; and Gertrude's quick eye took in all this discomfort and its details in a glance, while she stepped lightly across the floor and approached the bed.

The sunlight was shining on Harvey Gore's face, and showed her how worn and livid, how ghastly and distorted, it was. He lay quite still, and took no notice of her presence. Instantly perceiving the effect of the green blind, Gertrude went to the window and pulled it up, then beckoned Mrs. Bush to her side, and once more drew near the bed.

"Mr. Gore," she said, "Mr. Gore! Do you not know me? Can you not look at me? Can you not speak to me? I am Mrs. Lloyd."

The sick man answered her only with a groan. His face was an awful ashen grey; his shoulders were so raised that the head seemed to be sunken upon the chest; and his body lay upon the bed with unnatural weight and stillness. One hand was hidden by the bedclothes, the other clutched a corner of the pillow with cramped and rigid fingers. The two women exchanged looks of alarm.

"Was he looking like this when you saw him last—since

I came ? " said Mrs. Lloyd, speaking in a distinct low tone directed completely into the ear of the listener.

" No, no ; nothing like so bad as he looks now," said Mrs. Bush, whose distended eyes were fixed upon the patient with an expression of unmitigated dismay. " Did you ever see any one die ? " she whispered to Gertrude Lloyd.

" No ; never."

" Then you will see it, and soon."

" Do you really think he is dying ? " and then she leaned over him, shook him very gently by the shoulder, loosened his hold of the pillow, and said again,—

" Mr. Gore ! Mr. Gore ! Do you not know me ? Can you not speak to me ? "

Again he groaned, and then, feebly opening his eyes, so awfully glazed and hollow that Gertrude recoiled with an irrepressible start, made a movement with his head.

" He knows me," whispered Gertrude to Mrs. Bush ; " for God's sake go for a doctor without an instant's delay ! I must stay with him."

The landlady, dreadfully frightened, was only too glad to escape from the room.

For a few moments after she was left alone with the sick man Gertrude stood beside him quite still and silent ; then he moved uneasily, again groaned, and made an ineffectual attempt to sit up in his bed. Gertrude tried to assist him ; she passed her arms round his shoulders, and put all her strength to the effort to raise him, but in vain. The large heavy frame slipped from her hold, and sunk down again with ominous weight and inertness. Looking around in great fear, but still preserving her calmness, she perceived the bottle in which some brandy still remained. In an instant she had filled a wine-glass with the spirit, lifted the sufferer's feeble head, and contrived to pour a small quantity down his throat. The stimulant acted for a little upon the dying man ; he looked at her with eyes in which an intelligent purpose pierced the dull glaze preceding the fast-coming darkness, stretched his hand out to her, and drew her nearer, nearer. Gertrude bent over him until her chestnut hair touched his wan livid temples, and then, when her face was on a level with his own, he whispered in her ear.

*   *

Mrs. Bush had not gone many steps away from her own hall-door when she met Gilbert Lloyd. He was walking slowly, his hands thrust deep into his pockets, his head bent, his eyes frowning and downcast, and his under-lip firmly held by his white, sharp, even teeth. He did not see Mrs. Bush until she came close up to him, and exclaimed,—

"O, Mr. Lloyd, how thankful I am I've met you! The gentleman is very bad indeed—just gone, sir—and I was going for a doctor. There's not a moment to lose."

Gilbert Lloyd's face turned perfectly white.

"Impossible, Mrs. Bush," he said; "you must be mistaken. He was much better when I left him; besides, he was not seriously ill at all."

"I don't know about that, sir, and I can't stay to talk about it: I must get the doctor at once."

"No, no," said Lloyd, rousing himself; "I will do that. Where is the nearest? Tell me, and do you go back to him."

"First turn to the right, second door on the left," said Mrs. Bush, with unusual promptitude. "Dr. Muxky's; he isn't long established, but does a good business."

Gilbert Lloyd hurried away; and Mrs. Bush returned to the house, thinking only when she had reached it, that she had forgotten to mention his wife's arrival to Gilbert Lloyd.

* * * * *

When Lloyd entered the sick man's room, bringing with him Dr. Muxky, as that sandy-haired and youthful general practitioner was called by his not numerous clients, he saw a female figure bending over the bed. It was not that of Mrs. Bush; he had passed her loitering on the stairs— ostensibly that she might conduct the gentlemen to the scene of action, really because she dared not re-enter the room unsupported by a medical presence. The figure did not change its attitude as they entered, and Dr. Muxky approached the patient with a professional gliding step. He was followed by Lloyd; who, however, stopped abruptly on the opposite side of the bed when he met the full unshrinking gaze of his wife's bright, clear, threatening eyes.

"May I trouble you to stand aside for a moment?" said

Dr. Muxky courteously to Gertrude, who instantly moved but only a very little way, and again stood quite still and quite silent. Dr. Muxky stooped over his patient, but only for a few seconds. Then he looked up at Gilbert Lloyd, and said hastily,—

"I have been called in too late, sir; I'm afraid your friend is dead."

"Yes," said Gertrude, quietly, as if the doctor had spoken to her; "he is dead. He has been dead some minutes."

Gilbert Lloyd looked at her, but did not speak; the doctor looked from one to the other, but said nothing. Then Gertrude stretched out her hand and laid her fingers heavily upon the dead man's eyelids, and kept them there for several moments amid the silence. In a little while she steadily withdrew her hand, and without a word left the room.

On the drawing-room landing she found Mrs. Bush. That practised and cautious landlady, mindful of the possible prejudice of her permanent lodgers against serious illness and probable death in their immediate vicinity, raised her finger as a signal that a low tone of voice would be advisable.

"Go upstairs; the doctor wants you," said Gertrude, and passed quickly down to the parlour. A few moments more, and she had put on her bonnet and shawl, opened the hall-door without noise, closed it softly, and was walking swiftly down the street towards the shore.

CHAPTER II.

PONDERED.

THE sandy-haired slim young man, whose name was Muxky, who was a member of the Royal College of Surgeons of England, and who amongst the few poor people of Brighton that knew of his existence enjoyed the brevet-rank of doctor, found himself in anything but a pleasant position. The man to see whom he had been called in was dead; there was no doubt of that. No pulsation in the heart, dropped jaw, fixed eyes—all the usual appearances—

ay, and rather more than the usual appearances : " What we professionally call the *rigor mortis*—the stiffness immediately succeeding death, my dear sir, is in this case *very* peculiarly developed." Mr. Muxky, in the course of his attendance at St. Bartholomew's Hospital, had seen many death-beds, had inspected in an easy and pleasant manner many dead bodies; but he had never seen one which had presented such an extraordinary aspect of rigidity so immediately after death. He approached the bed once more, turned back the sheet which Mrs. Bush had drawn over the face, and, kneeling by the side of the bed, passed his hand over and under the body. As he moved, Gilbert Lloyd moved too, taking up his position close behind him, and watching him narrowly. For an instant a deep look of anxiety played across Gilbert Lloyd's face, the lines round the mouth deepened and darkened, the brows came down over the sunken eyes, and the under jaw, relaxing, lost its aspect of determination ; but as Mr. Muxky turned from the bed and addressed him, Lloyd's glance was perfectly steady, and his face expressed no emotions stronger than those which under the circumstances every man would be expected to feel, and no man would care to hide.

" This is rather an odd experience, my dear sir," said Mr. Muxky ; " called in to see our poor friend, who has, as it were, slipped his cable before my arrival. Our poor friend, now, was a—well—man of the world as you are—you will understand what I mean—our poor friend was a—free liver."

Yes, Gilbert Lloyd thought that he was a man who ate and drank heartily, and never stinted himself in anything.

" Nev-er stinted himself in anything !" repeated Mr. Muxky, who had by this time added many years to his personal appearance, and entirely prevented the bystanders from gleaning any expression from his eyes, by the assumption of a pair of glasses of neutral tint—" nev-er stinted himself in anything ! Ah, a great deal may be ascribed to that, my dear sir ; a great deal may be ascribed to that ! "

" Yes," said Gilbert Lloyd carelessly ; " if a man will take as much lobster-salad and Strasbourg pie as he can eat, with as much champagne and moselle as he can carry ; and if, in spite of the remonstrances of his friends, he will sit without his hat on the top of a drag, with the August sun beating down upon him——"

"Did he do that, my dear sir ?—did he do that ?"

"He did, indeed ! Several of us implored him to be careful ; but you might as well have spoken to the wind as to him, poor dear fellow. We told him that he'd probably have a—a—what do you call it ?"

"General derangement of the system ? Flux of blood to the——"

"No, no ; sunstroke—that's what I mean ; sunstroke. Perigal, who was out in India in the Punjaub business—he was on our drag when poor Harvey was taken bad, and he said it was sunstroke all over—regular case."

"Did he, indeed ?" said Mr. Muxky. "Well, that's odd, very odd ! From the symptoms you have described, I ima-gined that it must have been something of the kind :— brain overdone, system overtaxed. In this railway age, Mr. Lloyd, we live such desperately rapid lives, concen-trate so much mental energy and bodily fibre into a few years, that——"

"I'm glad you're satisfied, Mr. Muxky," said Gilbert Lloyd, pulling out his purse. " It's a satisfaction in these melancholy cases to know that everything has been done, and that there was no chance of saving the poor fellow, even if——"

"I scarcely say that, Mr. Lloyd. A little blood-letting might, if taken at the exact moment—*in tempore veni ;* you recollect the old quotation—might have been of some use. There's a prejudice just now against the use of the lancet, I know ; but still—— For me ?" taking a crisp bank-note which Lloyd handed to him. "O, thank you, thank you ! This is far too munifi——"

"The labourer, Mr. Muxky, is worthy of his hire," said Gilbert Lloyd ; "and it is our fault—not yours—that you were summoned too late. But, as you just now remarked, it is impossible in these cases to know what is impending, or how nigh may be the danger. I was very much struck by that remark. And now good afternoon, Mr. Muxky. I must go out and find my poor wife, who is quite upset by this unfortunate affair. Good afternoon—not another word of thanks, I beg ; and any of the usual formalities in these

matters—I don't know what they are—but certificates, and
that kind of thing, we may look to you to settle! Thanks
again. Good day."

And Gilbert Lloyd shook hands with the overwhelmed
Mr. Muxky, whose eyes gleamed even through the neutral-
tinted glasses, and whose pale face burst into a pleased perspiration, as he crumpled the crisp bank-note into his waist-
coat-pocket, and followed Mrs. Bush down the stairs.

"A sensible man, that, Mrs. Bush," said he when he
reached the first landing; "a very sensible, kind-hearted,
clear-headed man. Under all the circumstances, you're very
lucky in having had such a man in the house. No fuss, no
preposterous excitement—everything quite proper, but
thoroughly business-like."

"You're right, Dr. Muxky," responded the sympathetic
landlady. "When I saw as clear as clear that that poor
creature was going the way of all flesh—which is grass,
and also dust and ashes—and knew I'd got those Miss
Twillows in the drawing-rooms, you might have knocked
me down with a feather. Nervous is nothing to what the
Miss Twillows is; and coming regular from Peckham for
the sea-bathing now five years, regular as the month of July
comes round; and giving no trouble, through bringing their
own maid; and stopping on all September,—without per-
ambulators in the passage, and children's boots, which after
being filled with sand will *not* take the polish,—their leaving
would be a loss to me which——"

Mrs. Bush stopped suddenly in her harangue, as the
drawing-room door, by which they were standing, was cau-
tiously opened, and an elderly female head was slowly
protruded. It was a large head, and yet it had what is
called a "skimpy" character. What little hair there was
on it was of a mixed pepper-and-salt kind of colour, and
gathered into two large roll-curls, one on either side of the
head, in front, and into a thin wisp behind. In this wisp
was stuck a comb, pendent from which was a little bit of
black lace. The features could not be defined, as the lower
part of the face was entirely hidden in a handkerchief held
to the nose, exhaling pungent vinegar. Mr. Muxky stared
a little at this apparition—stared more when the head
wagged and the mouth opened, and the word " Doctor ?"

was uttered in interrogative accent. Then Mr. Muxky, beginning to perceive how the land lay, said in his softest tones : "Yes, my dear madam, I *am* the doctor."

The head dropped again, and again the lips opened. "Fever?" was what they said this time, while a skinny hand at the end of a skinny arm made itself manifest, pointing upwards.

"Fever," repeated Mr. Muxky, "that has removed our poor friend upstairs ?—nothing of the sort, my dear madam, I can assure you ; nothing but——"

"Not smallpox?—don't say it's smallpox!" This from another voice, the owner of which was in the background, unseen. "O, Hannah, does he say it's smallpox?"

"He don't say anything of the kind, Miss Twillow," interposed Mrs. Bush ; "knowing that in the midst of life we are in death, specially sitting in hot suns without our hats on the tops of stage-coaches, and to say nothing of too much to drink. You've never been inconvenienced since you've been in this house, have you, m'm? and you won't be now. It isn't my fault, I'm sure ; nor yet Dr. Muxky's ; and, considering all things, not a great put-out, though doubtless upsetting to the nerves."

"That's just the point, Mrs. Bush," said Mr. Muxky, who was not going to lose the chance ; "nothing to fear ; but yet, some temperaments so constituted that, like the Æolian harp, the—the slightest breath of fright has an effect on them. If my poor services now could be of any use——"

"Yes, now do," said Mrs. Bush, "Miss Twillow, Miss Hannah ; just see the doctor for a minute. You've had a shock, I'll allow, and it's natural you should be upset ; but the doctor will put you right in a minute."

Thus Mr. Muxky secured two new patients ; not a bad day's work.

While these matters were in progress in the house Gertrude had left, and the subdued bustle inevitably attendant upon the necessary care and the unavoidable household disorganization which succeeds a death, even when the dead is only a stranger in the house where the solution of the enigma has come to him,—she was sitting on the shore close by the foamy edge of the waves, and thinking.

Gertrude had gone down to the shore across the broad road, now crowded with people out for the bright summer afternoon ; with carriages and gigs, with vehicles of the highest elegance, and with such as had no pretence to anything but convenience ; with pedestrians of every class, assembled with all sorts of objects, hygiene and flirtation being predominant. She had gone away down the slope, and on to the strip of pebbly sand ; and where one of the wooden barriers marked out a measured space, she sat down on a seaweed-flecked heap of shingle, and began to think. The long line of the horizon, where the blue sea met the blue sky, parted only by a narrow verge of light, broken white clouds, was before her ; between it and her absent, troubled eyes, lay the wide expanse of sea. A short space only parted her from the moving, restless, talking crowd upon the Esplanade ; but her sense of solitude was complete. The ridge of the slope hid her ; the soft plash of the sea, with its monotonous recurrence, soothed her ear, and deadened the sound of wheels and the murmur of voices ; her eyes met only the great waters, across which sometimes a boat glided, on which sometimes a sea-bird's wing rested for an instant. As Gertrude sat there, with her arms extended and her hands tightly clasped together, with her head bent forward and her eyes fixed upon the distant line of the sea and sky, her thoughts obeyed her will, and formed themselves, consecutive, complete, and purposeful. The girl—for she was but a girl, after all—had brought thither a heavy trouble ; to be taken out, looked at, weighed, examined. She had brought there a half-developed purpose, to be thought into maturity, to be fully fashioned and resolved upon. Before she should leave that place she would have done these things ; and when she should leave it, a new phase in her life would have begun. Ineffable sadness was in her brown eyes—grief and dread, which did not seem newly born there, but constant dwellers, only that to-day they had been suddenly awakened once again from temporary repose. If there had been any one to see Gertrude, as she sat by the edge of the waves, and to note her face, with its concentrated and yet varying expression, that person, if an acute observer, would have been struck by the contrast between the eyes and the mouth. The character of the look in the eyes shifted and varied ; there was fear in it, grief, weariness, disgust, sometimes even horror ; and these expressions passed like the lights and shadows over a fair landscape. But the mouth did not vary ; firm, closely shut,—so compressed that its tightness produced a white line above the red of the upper lip,—it expressed power and resolution, when that long process of thinking—too purposeful to be called a reverie—commenced, and it expressed power and resolution when at length Gertrude rose. Hours had passed over her unheeded, as she sat by the sea ; the afternoon had lengthened into the evening ; the crowd of loungers had dispersed. She had heard, but not heeded, the church-bells ringing for evening service ; and now silence was all around her, and the red flush of sunset was upon the sky and the sea. When she had risen from her seat of shingle, Gertrude stood for some minutes and looked along the shore, where her solitary figure seemed doubly lonely. Then she turned and scanned the long line of the houses and the road, on which a few scattered human beings only were moving. A strange reluctance to move possessed her ; but at length she shook it off, and with a slight shudder turned her back upon the sea, fast becoming grey as the sun went down, and walked steadily, though not quickly, back to the lodging-house where she had left her husband.

As she drew near to the house, Gertrude looked up at the window of the room in which she had seen Harvey Gore die. It was open ; but the green blind was closely drawn. Looking upwards at the window, she did not perceive till she was close upon it that the house-door was slightly ajar ; but as she raised her hand to the knocker, the door was opened widely by Mrs. Bush, and Gertrude, going into the passage, found Gilbert Lloyd there. The sudden sight of him caused her to start for an instant, but not perceptibly ; and Mrs. Bush immediately addressed her with voluble questions and regrets.

Where had she been all this time ? She had gone out without her lunch, and had she had nothing to eat ? How uneasy she and Mr. Lloyd had been about her ! (Mr. Lloyd had evidently secured by this time a high place in the good graces of Mrs. Bush.) Mr. Lloyd had been waiting and watching for her ever so long ; and she, Mrs. Bush, as soon as ever the poor dear dead gentleman upstairs had been "put tidy," which was her practical mode of expressing the performance of the toilet of the dead, had been also watching and waiting for Mrs. Lloyd's reappearance. Suspicion and scanty civility had given place in the manner of the worthy landlady—who was infinitely satisfied with the proper sense of what was due to her in the unfortunate position of affairs exhibited by Gilbert Lloyd—to anxiety for the comfort of the young lady whom she had so unwillingly received.

During the colloquy between Mrs. Bush and Gertrude, Gilbert Lloyd had been standing, awkwardly enough, in the passage, but without speaking. But when a pause came, and Gertrude approached the parlour-door, he spoke.

"Where have you been, Gertude?" he asked, sternly.

His wife stood still and answered, but did not look at him.

"I have been sitting by the sea-shore."

"You must be cold and hungry, I should think."

"I am neither."

"I suppose you know you cannot remain here?"

"Why?"

He seemed a little at a loss for an answer; but replied, after a moment's pause,—

"A death in the house is sufficient reason. Mrs. Bush can't attend to a lady-lodger under the circumstances. You can go back to town in the morning; for to-night I shall take you to the nearest hotel."

"Very well."

She never looked at him; not by the most fleeting flicker of an eyelash did she address her face to him, though he looked steadily at her, trying to compel her glance. She went into the parlour, through the folding-door into the bedroom, collected the few articles which she had taken out of her travelling-bag, and returned carrying it in her hand. Evidently all arrangements had been made by Gilbert Lloyd with Mrs. Bush: no more was said. Gertrude took a friendly leave of the landlady, and went out of the house, walking silently by her husband's side. He did not offer her his arm, and not a word was spoken between them until the door of a private sitting-room at the George had closed behind them. Then he turned savagely round upon her, and said, in a thick low voice, "The meaning of this foolery?"

This time she looked at him—looked him straight in the face with the utmost calmness. There was not the least flush of colour in her pale face, not the slightest trembling of her lips, not the smallest flutter of her hands—by which in woman agitation is so often betrayed—as she said calmly, "You are polite, but mysterious. And I suppose the journey, or something, has rendered me a little dull. I don't quite follow you. What 'foolery' are you pleased to ask the meaning of?"

She had the best of it so far. She stood erect, facing the light, her head thrown back, her arm outstretched, with nothing of bravado, but with a good deal of earnestness in her manner and air. Gilbert Lloyd's head was sunk on his breast, his brow was knit over his frowning eyes, his lips tightly set, and his under-jaw was clenched and rigid. His hands were plunged into his pockets, and he had commenced to pace the room; but at his wife's question he stopped, and said, "What foolery! Why, the foolery of your conduct in those lodgings this day; the foolery of your coming down, in the first place, when you weren't wanted, and of your conduct since you came."

"I came," said Gertrude, in a perfectly calm voice, and still looking him steadily in the face, "in pursuance of the arrangement between us. It was your whim, when last I saw you, to wish for my company here; and you settled the time at which I was to come. My 'foolery' so far consists in having exactly obeyed you."

"Your obedience is very charming," said Gilbert Lloyd with a sneer; "and no doubt I should have enjoyed your company as much as I generally do. Few men are blessed with wives embodying all the cardinal virtues. But cir-cumstances have changed since we made that arrangement. I couldn't tell this man was going to die, I suppose?"

She had purposely turned her face away when her husband began to sneer at her, and was pretending to occupy herself with opening her travelling-bag; but as these words fell upon her ear, she drew herself to her full height, and again looking steadily at him, said, "I suppose not."

"You suppose not! Why, of course not! By heavens, it's enough to drive a man to desperation to be tied for life to a white-faced cat like this, who stands opposite him repeating his words, and shows no more interest in him than—— By Jove," he exclaimed, shaking his clenched fist at her, " I feel as if I could knock the life out of you ! "

To have been struck by him would have been no novel experience on Gertrude's part. More than once in these paroxysms of temper he had seized her roughly by the arm or shoulder, leaving the livid imprint of his hand on her delicate flesh ; and she fully expected that he would strike her now. But as he spoke he had been hastily pacing the room ; and it was not until he stopped to menace her that he looked in her face, and saw there an expression such as he had never seen before. Anger, terror, misery, obstinacy, contempt—all these passions he had often seen mirrored in Gertrude's features ; but never the aversion, the horror, the loathing which now appeared there. The look seemed to paralyze him, for in it he divined the feelings of which it was the reflex. His extended arm dropped by his side, and his whole manner changed, as he said, " There ! enough of that ! It was hard enough for me to have the trouble of poor Gore's illness to fight against, without anything else ; and when you did come, Gertrude, I thought—well "— pulling himself together, as it were, he bent forward towards her, and, with a soft look in his eyes and an inexpressible tenderness in his voice, whispered, " I thought you might have brought a word of cheer and comfort and—and love—to your poor old Gilbert, who——"

While speaking he gradually drew near to her, and advanced his hand until it touched her waist. Gertrude no sooner felt his clasp than, with a short sharp cry as if of bodily pain, she withdrew herself from it.

" Don't touch me ! " she exclaimed, in a voice half choked with sobs. Her calmness was gone, and her whole system was quivering with emotion. " For Heaven's sake keep off ! Never lay your touch on me, in kindness or in cruelty, again, or you will find that the ' white-faced cat ' has claws, and can use them."

Gilbert Lloyd stared for an instant in mute astonishment at his wife, who stood confronting him, her eyes sparkling like glowing coals in the midst of her pale face, her hair pushed back off her forehead, her hands tightly clasped behind her head. He was cowed by this sudden transformation, by this first act of overt rebellion on Gertrude's part, and thought it best to temporize. So he said, "Why, Gertrude, darling, my little lady, what's all——"

"No more of that, Gilbert," she interrupted, calming herself by a strong effort, unlocking her hands, and again confronting him. "Those pet names are things of the past now—of the past which must be to us even more dead and more forgotten than it is to most people."

The solemnity of her tone and of her look angered him, and he said shortly, "Don't preach, please. Spare yourself that."

"I am not preaching, Gilbert, and I am not—as you sometimes tell me—acting; but I have something to say which you must hear."

"Must, eh? Well, come down off your stilts and say it."

"Gilbert Lloyd," said Gertrude, "this day you and I part for ever. Don't interrupt me," she said, as he made a hasty gesture; "hear me out. I knew that this would be the end of our hasty and ill-advised marriage; but I did not think the end would come so soon. It *has* come now, and no power on earth would induce me to alter my determination."

"O, that's it, is it?" said Lloyd, after a minute's silence. "And this is my wife, if you please; this is the young lady who promised to love, honour, and obey! This woman, who now coolly talks about our parting for ever, is one who has hung about my neck a thousand times and——"

"No," exclaimed Gertrude, interrupting him, "no! This" (touching herself lightly on the breast) "is your wife indeed—is the woman who bears your name and has borne your caprices; but" (again touching herself) "this is not the woman that left London this morning. I wish to heaven I were—I wish to heaven I were!"

She uttered these last words in a low plaintive tone that was almost a wail, and covered her face with her hands.

"This is mere foolery and nonsense," said Lloyd, after a momentary pause. "You wish you were, indeed! If you're not the same woman, what the devil has changed you?"

"Do you want to know?" she asked suddenly, looking up at him,—not eagerly, boldly, or defiantly, but with the expression of horror and loathing which he had previously noticed.

"No!" he replied with an oath; "why should I waste my time listening to your string of querulous complaints? You want a separation, do you? Well, I am not disposed to say 'no' to any reasonable request; but if I agree to this, mind, it's not to be the usual business."

Finding he paused, Gertrude said, "I scarcely understand you."

"Well, I mean that 'parting for ever' does not mean coming together again next month, to live in a fool's paradise for a week, and then hate each other worse than ever. If we part, we part for ever, which means that we never meet again on earth—or rather, that we begin life afresh, with the recollection of the last few months completely expunged. We have neither of us any relations to worry us with attempts at reconciliation; not half a dozen men know of the fact of my having been married, and none of them have ever seen you. So that on both sides we start entirely free. It is not very likely that we shall ever run across each other's path in the future; but if we do, we meet as entire strangers, and the fact of our having been anything to one another must never be brought forward to prejudice any scheme in which either of us may be engaged. Do you follow me?"

"Perfectly."

"And does what I propose meet your views?"

"Entirely."

"That's right. Curious," said Lloyd, with a short, sharp laugh,—"curious that just as we are about to part, we should begin to agree. However, you're right, I suppose; we could not hit it; we were always having tremendous rows, and now each of us can go our own way; and," he added, under his breath, as he glanced at Gertrude's expressive face and trim figure, "I don't think I've had the worst of the bargain."

After a moment's silence, Lloyd said, "What do you propose to do?"

"I have no schemes at present," Gertrude replied; "and if I had, you have no right to ask about them."

"You've not taken long to shake off your harness, by Jove!" said Lloyd, bitterly. "However, whatever you do

hereafter, you must have something to start with now."
He took out a pocket-book, and counted from it some bank-
notes. " I've not done so badly as people thought," said
he ; " and here are two hundred pounds, all my available
capital. You shall have half of this—here it is." He
pushed a roll of notes towards her. She took it without a
word, and placed it in her travelling-bag. " You'll sleep
here to-night, I suppose ; and had better clear out of this
place early to-morrow. I shall have to stay until after the
funeral. And now, I suppose, that's about all ? "

" All," said Gertrude, taking up her travelling-bag and
moving towards the door.

" Won't you—won't you say ' good-bye ' ? " said Lloyd,
putting out his hand as she passed him.

Gertrude made him no reply ; but she gathered her dress
tightly round her, as though to preserve it from his touch ;
and on glancing at her face Gilbert Lloyd saw there the
same look of horror and loathing which had paralyzed him
even in the midst of his furious rage.

CHAPTER III.

PROPOSED.

WHEN Gertrude left her husband's presence, without
giving him any clue to her intentions for the future,
something like bewilderment fell upon her for a little. It
was not grief—no such sentiment had any place or share in
the tumult of her mind. The arrangement which had been
made, the agreement that had been come to, was a distinct
and positive relief to her. It would have been a relief
even before the late occurrences which had brought things
to a crisis, and Gertrude neither denied nor lost sight of
that fact. It had become a positive necessity, not to be
avoided, not to be deferred ; and it was done. When the
door closed behind her, as she trod the narrow passage
which divided the sitting-room in which their last interview had taken place from the bedroom in which she was
to pass the night, Gertrude knew that she was relieved—
was even in a dull, hardly-ascertained sort of way, glad ;

and yet she was bewildered. There was more horror in her mind than sorrow. For the hope and happiness of her own life, thus early blighted in their first bloom, she had no sentimental pity; she could not afford to think about them, even if she had had time, which she had not. The circumstances of her life had aided the natural disposition and habits of her mind, and brought her to look steadily at facts rather than feelings, at results and actions rather than at influences and illusions of the past. As a matter of fact, her life in all its great meanings was past, and the best thing she could do was to banish it from memory, to dismiss it from contemplation as completely and as rapidly as possible.

Gertrude had been for many hours without food, and had undergone much and various mental agitation. She was conscious that the bewilderment which pervaded her mind was in a great degree referable to physical exhaustion, and she resolved to postpone thought and action until the morning. She rang a bell, ordered a slight meal to be served to her in her room, and having eaten and drank, went to bed so completely overpowered by the fatigue and restrained excitement of the day that she fell asleep immediately. The calm summer night, unvisited by darkness, passed over, and witnessed only her unbroken rest—a grand privilege of her youth.

Gilbert Lloyd remained for some time in the room where Gertrude had left him, walking to and fro before the windows, lost in thought. The passion and excitement of the day had not been without their effect on him also, and certain components mingled with them in his case which had no existence in the sum of Gertrude's suffering—doubt, dread, suspense, uncertainty. What did Gertrude mean? What still remained hidden, after that terrible interview in which so much had been revealed? What was still unexplained, after all that dreary and hopeless explanation? These questions, which he could not answer, which it was his best hope might never be answered, troubled Gilbert Lloyd sorely. That the agreement which had been made between him and his wife was highly satisfactory to him he knew as clearly as Gertrude knew it; but in the way in which it had been brought about, in the manner of its decision, the advantage had been Gertrude's. Gilbert Lloyd did not

like that, though this parting was so utter and so final that
he might well have dismissed all such considerations, and
turned his back upon the past, as he had proposed to do in
reality, and as he did not entertain a doubt that Gertrude
would do in downright real earnest, never bestowing so
much thought or memory on him again as to produce the
smallest practical effect upon her future life. He knew
that he had achieved a great success that day; that this
final separation between himself and Gertrude was an event
in every way desirable, and which he would have hailed
with satisfaction at any period since he had wearied of her
and begun to regard marriage as the very worst and
stupidest of all mistakes;—a mental process which had
commenced surprisingly soon after he had made the blunder.
But, somehow, Gilbert Lloyd did not taste the flavour of
success. It was not sufficiently unmingled for the palate of
a man of despotic self-will, and the ultra intolerance of complete callousness and scoundrelism. At length he checked
himself in his monotonous walk, and muttering, "Yes, I'll
go back; it's safest," he rang the bell.

His summons was not obeyed with remarkable alacrity—
waiters and chambermaids had had a hard time of it at the
George of late; but a waiter did at length present himself.
By this time the news of a "sporting gent's" death in the
immediate vicinity had reached the George; and the man
looked at Lloyd with the irrational curiosity invariably
excited by the sight of any one who has been recently in
close contact with crime, horror, or grief.

"I rang to tell you I shall send my traps down from
Pavilion Place, but I shall not sleep here," said Lloyd; "I
shall come up to breakfast in the morning, though."

"Very good, sir," said the man; and Gilbert Lloyd took
up his hat and walked out. He called for a minute at
Pavilion Place, and spoke a few words to Mrs. Bush, who
gave him a latch-key, then went away again; and the
morning hours were well on when he let himself quietly
into the lodging-house, and threw himself on the bed in the
back parlour.

The window of the "two-pair front" was open, and the
fresh breeze, sea-scented, blew in through the aperture, and
faintly stirred the drapery of the bed. Presently the sun
rose; and before long a bright ray streamed through the

green blind, and a wavering bar of light shimmered fantastically across the sheet which decently veiled the dead man's face.

Gertrude Lloyd went down to the railway-station early on the following morning, and before Gilbert had made his appearance at the George. She had not passed unnoticed at that hostelry. In the first place, she was too young and handsome to pass unnoticed anywhere during a sojourn of sufficient duration to give people time to look at her, if so disposed. In the second place, there was something odd about her. She was evidently the wife of the gentleman who had brought her to the hotel, and had then changed his mind about staying, and gone away so abruptly. Here she was now going away without seeing him, calling for her bill, and paying it "quite independent like," as a chambermaid, with a very proper reverence for masculine superiority, remarked ; setting off alone, perfectly cool and comfortable. "There's been a tiff, that's it, and more's the pity," was the conclusion arrived at by the waiter and the chambermaid, who agreed that Gertrude was very pretty, and "uncommon young, to be sure, to be so very off-handed."

Mrs. Bush, too, did not omit to inquire for the handsome young lady who had got "the better" of her so very decidedly. "She's off to London, first train in the morning," said Lloyd. "There was no good in her staying here for all this sad affair. *I* can't avoid it, of course ; but she is better out of it all." After which explanation, Mrs. Bush thought, sagaciously, that leaving one's husband in an unpleasant position, and getting safe out of it one's self, was not a very affectionate proceeding ; and that Mrs. Lloyd, if she really was very fond of her husband, at all events did not make the fact obtrusively evident.

But Gertrude Lloyd had not gone to London. Her mind had been actively at work from an early hour in the morning ; and, strengthened and refreshed by rest, she had been able to employ it to good purpose. Her first resolve was not to go to the lodgings she and her husband had occupied in London any more. She had no wish to embarrass his proceedings in any way. She desired to carry out their contract in both letter and spirit, and to disappear at once and completely from his life. So she left a note for Gilbert

Lloyd at the George, containing the words, " Please have everything belonging to me sent to Mrs. Bloxam's," and then took her way to the station, and her place in an early train for Worthing. Gertrude was alone in the carriage, and she profited by the circumstance to tear up and throw out of window a letter or two, and sundry bills on which her name, " Mrs. Lloyd," appeared. Her initials only were stamped on her travelling-bag. The letters disposed of, she drew off her wedding-ring, and, without an instant's hesitation for sentimental regret, dropped it on to the rails. Then she sat still, and looked out at the landscape. Her face was quite calm now, but the traces of past agitation were on it. The first person to whom Gertrude Lloyd should speak to-day would not be struck by the contrast between her assured, self-possessed manner and her extreme youth, as Mrs. Bush had been impressed by it only yesterday.

Arrived at Worthing, Gertrude had no difficulty in securing quiet and respectable lodgings, away from the sea, and not far out of the town. It was in a small house, forming one of a row of small houses, with climbing roses about the windows, and common but fragrant flowers in a liliputian strip of garden-plot on either side of the door. On the opposite side of the road was a row of gardens corresponding to the houses, remarkable for numerous arbours of curiously small dimensions, and great variety and ingenuity of construction ; likewise for the profusion and luxuriance with which they grew scarlet-runners and nasturtiums. In one of these houses, Gertrude engaged a sunny parlour and bedroom for a week certain ; and then, having explained to the woman of the house that she was a governess, and was about to enter on a new situation, but was not certain when she would be required to proceed to the house of her employers, she set herself to the carrying out of the plans she had formed that morning, and, as a first step, wrote the following letter :—

" 7, Warwick Place, Worthing,
" Monday.

" MY DEAR MRS. BLOXAM,—You will probably be very much surprised to receive a letter from me, and I am not less astonished to find myself writing to you. Though you were kind to me after a fashion, while I lived at the Vale

House, the circumstances under which I quitted your protection, and the events which have since occurred, were of a nature to render me unwilling to open up any communication with you, and to make it extremely improbable that I should ever be called on to do so. I retain some pleasant and grateful recollections of you and of my childhood, when I was, on the whole, happy ; and I remember in particular, and with especial gratitude, that you put down, with the high hand of authority, the very natural inclination of the other girls to ridicule and oppress me, because I had no relations to give me presents, take me out, and beg half-holidays for all the pupils on the strength of their visits, and because my holidays were always passed at school. You will wonder what I am coming to, and why, if it be anything important, I should recall these seemingly trivial things by the way ; but I do so in order to remind myself, and to gain courage in so doing, of the only protection and friendship I have ever received from a woman,—now, when I need protection and friendship very, very much, and am about to ask you to extend them to me.

"When I left you as I did, and married the man who had induced me to deceive you as I did (do not suppose I want to extenuate my own share in the matter, or throw the blame on him because I mention him thus), you told me, in the only letter you ever addressed to me, that I had made a bad mistake, and should inevitably find it out sooner or later. You were distinctly and unerringly right. I did make a bad mistake—a worse mistake than any one but myself can ever know or guess ; and I have found it out sooner instead of later. I have known it for a long time ; but now circumstances have arisen which oblige me to act on my knowledge, and a separation has taken place between my husband and myself. Not a separation in the ordinary sense, with the tie repudiated and yet retained ; but a separation by which each has undertaken to cease to exist for the other. I have no relations, so far as I know. If I have any, you and you alone are aware of the fact, and know who they are. I have no prejudices to offend, no position to forfeit. Gilbert Lloyd and I have parted never to meet again, as we both hope ; never, under any circumstances, to recognize or interfere with one another. I have no friends, except I may venture to call you a friend ; and to you alone can I now turn for assistance. I would say for advice, but that the time for that is past. There is nothing to be done now but to act upon the resolution which has been taken.

"My plan for the future is this : I have £100, and a voice whose quality you know, and which has improved since I was at the Vale House; so that I know it to be of the best kind, and in the best order, for concert-singing at least, perhaps ultimately for opera. I intend to become a public singer ; but I must have more teaching, and the means of living in the mean time ; so that the small sum in my possession may be expended upon the teaching and training of my voice. From many indications, which I perfectly remember, but need not enter into here, I have reason to believe that I was a profitable pupil to you ; that from some source unknown to me you received sums of money for my maintenance and education of an amount which was very well worth having. I do not say this in any way to disparage the habitual kindness with which you treated me, and which I have always acknowledged gratefully, but because I am about to propose a bargain to you, and wish to assure myself that I have some grounds for doing so, and for counting upon your acquiescence.

"Will you receive me at the Vale House for one year free of charge, in the capacity of a teacher for the junior classes, and giving me sufficient time to enable me to take music-lessons and practise singing? If you will do this, and thus enable me, if I find my voice fulfils my expectations, to earn a livelihood for myself in an independent fashion, I will undertake to repay the cost out of my earnings. Possessing, as you do, the knowledge, if not of my parentage, at least of some person who became voluntarily responsible for my support during several years, you may perhaps be able, unless I am considered to have sacrificed all claim on my unknown connections by my marriage, to procure from them a little more assistance for me ; but you must not make any attempt to do so if such an attempt should involve the revelation of my secret. I presume if any one exists whom it concerned, you made known my marriage. That circumstance is the last to be known about me ; henceforth Gertrude Lloyd has no more existence than Gertrude Keith.

"If you should accede to my request, it will be necessary for me to know whether any of the girls now under your charge were at the Vale House when I left it, also whether you have any servants now likely to recognize me. I shall await your answer with much anxiety. Should it be unfavourable, I must endeavour to devise some other method of carrying out the fixed purpose of my future life; and at present no possible alternative presents itself to my mind. In conclusion, I beg that you will decide quickly. I shall be here only one week; that expired, if you do not answer me, or if you answer me unfavourably, I must face the problem to which just now I see no solution. Address Miss Grace Lambert.—Yours sincerely,

"GERTRUDE LLOYD."

CHAPTER IV

SETTLED.

THE Vale House, Hampstead, was admirably suited in point of size and situation for a boarding-school or "establishment" for young ladies. It stood in its own grounds, which, though not really extensive, had been made the most of, and contrived to look as if there were a great deal more of them than there really was; and it commanded an extensive prospect from the upper windows, well elevated above the jealous walls which guarded the youth and beauty committed to Mrs. Bloxam's charge from contact with the outer world. Occasionally, or at least in one instance, as will presently appear, the security had not been altogether so inviolable as might have been desired; but, on the whole, the "establishment" at Vale House maintained and deserved a high character. A heavy, square, roomy, red-brick mansion, with its windows cased in white stone, and a coat-of-arms sculptured in the same material, but now nearly undecipherable, inserted over the heavy mahogany hall-door, the Vale House belonged to a period of architecture when contract-building was unknown, when the art of "running up" houses was yet undiscovered, and a family mansion among the middle-classes meant a house in which fathers and sons and grandsons intended to live and die, un-beguiled by "splendid opportunities" into constant migra-tions and rapid changes in their style and manner of living.

The Vale House had, however, suffered from the changes and innovations of the age; and the grandson of its last hereditary inhabitant now dwelt in splendour in a west-end "place," forming an "annexe" to a square of ultra-fashion-able pretensions and performances, and looked and spoke as though he had never even heard the name of a locality more northern or more distant from the centre of civilization than the Marble Arch. If the Townleys were oblivious of the Vale House, so was the Vale House of them. Except among such of the inhabitants of Hampstead as were care-ful and religious conservators of tradition, the origin and history of the Vale House had been forgotten; and a general notion prevailed that it had always been a school. The pupils—with the exception of such as were of a romantic turn of mind and given to the association of all old houses having plenty of room in them with the *Orphan of the Forest* and the *Children of the Abbey*—hated the place, and believed that it must always have witnessed the incarceration of unoffending girlhood. The ancient and much-effaced armorial bearings awakened no compassionate respect in the minds of these haughty young creatures, but rather a lively scorn. "Old Bloxam was only a sea-captain, and she was a governess in some old lord's family, and they set her up in the school, and she gives herself airs as if she was a lady," they would remark, under the influence of irri-tation, arising from causes gastronomic or otherwise; and the caricaturing of these armorial bearings was a favourite *jeu d'esprit* among the livelier and cleverer section of Mrs. Bloxam's pupils.

The school at the Vale House had been of late years a very prosperous undertaking. Mrs. Bloxam's connection was among the rich and respectable mercantile community, not the shopkeeping, be it known: she observed with the utmost strictness the distinction between wholesale and retail trades, and especially affected the learned professions. In Gertrude's time, two daughters of a Scotch baronet had effectively represented the real aristocracy; but they were "finished" long since, and had returned to the land of their

birth, having learned to braid their sandy locks, and to tone
down their hereditary freckles, and equally hereditary
accents, to the admiration of all Glen Houlaghan. The real
aristocracy was quite unrepresented at the Vale House, but
the "British-merchant" element flourished there. Mrs.
Bloxam had prospered of late years, and was now in circumstances which permitted her to contemplate retiring from
the labours of school-keeping,—in which she had never pretended to herself to find a congenial occupation,—as a
not impossible, indeed not even a very remote, contingency.

Mrs. Bloxam was not at all like the conventional schoolmistress; she as little resembled the Pinkerton as the
Monflathers type ; and, despite the contemptuous comments
of her pupils, was very ladylike indeed, both in appearance
and manners. She was a tall slight woman, very fair of
hair and complexion, with blue eyes, which were a little hard
in expression, and a little shifty ; with an inexpressive
mouth, a graceful figure, and a good deal of character and
decision in her voice, gestures, and movements. She had
purchased the Vale House from its former proprietor, a
distant relative of her own, and, like herself, a schoolmistress, on highly advantageous terms, when she was a
new-made widow, and a very young woman ; and now she
hoped, after a year or two, to dispose of it on terms by no
means so advantageous to the purchaser. But this hope
Mrs. Bloxam had not spoken of to any one. She was of
silent and secretive temperament, and liked to make up her
mind completely, and in every detail, to any plan of action
which she contemplated before making it known to any
friend or acquaintance. Her man of business was Mrs.
Bloxam's sole confidant, and even he knew no more of her
affairs than was indispensable to their safe and profitable conduct.

Mr. Dexter would have been as ignorant as any mere acquaintance of Mrs. Bloxam's—as any of the young girls asleep
in the white beds, standing in long ranges in the " lofty and
well-ventilated dormitories " which formed so important a
feature in the prospectus that eloquently set forth the
advantages of the Vale House "establishment "—of the
nature of the contents of a bundle of letters which Mrs.
Bloxam set herself to peruse, late on the same evening on
which Gertrude Lloyd's letter reached her well-shaped

hands. Only one individual in the world besides Mrs. Bloxam knew that the letters which she was now engaged in reading had ever been written ; and their writer would probably have been surprised—as they did not contain any guarantees for the payment of money—had he known that they were still in existence.

Gertrude's letter had reached Mrs. Bloxam just at the hour at which the concluding ceremonial of the school-day routine was about to be performed. She laid it aside until prayers and the formal leave-taking for the night insisted upon at the Vale House as essential to the due inculcation of good breeding had been gone through ; and then, in the welcome retirement and solitude of her own sitting-room, seated before her own particular bureau, and with her own particular supper in tempting perspective, Mrs. Bloxam read, not without sympathy mingling with her astonishment, the letter of her quondam pupil.

Mrs. Bloxam read the letter once and laid it down, and thought very profoundly for some minutes. Then she took it up and read it again, and once more fell into a fit of musing. The bureau before which she had seated herself had a number of small drawers at the side. One of these Mrs. Bloxam opened, and selected from among its neatly-arranged contents a packet, tied with green ribbon and docketed, "Lord S——, from 185- to 186-." The parcel contained twenty letters, and Mrs. Bloxam read them all through. The task did not occupy much time ; the writing was large and clear, her sight was strong and quick. When she had read the letters, she replaced them in the order which she had temporarily disturbed, retied the packet, and locked it away in the drawer whence she had taken it. Then she arranged a sheet of paper on the blotting-pad before her, took up a pen, and began to write with a rapid hand what was evidently intended to be a long letter.

But in the middle of the third page Mrs. Bloxam changed her mind. "Safer not, better not," she muttered to herself ; "the written letter remains. Witness these ;" and she inclined her pen-handle towards the drawer in which she had just replaced the packet of letters ; "time will show whether she had better know, or not know."

Then Mrs. Bloxam tore the sheet, the third page of which she had begun to write on, into fragments sufficiently minute to defy the curiosity and the ingenuity of the most prying and ingenious of housemaids, and replaced it by another, on which she wrote the following words :—

> "The Vale House, Hampstead,
> "Tuesday night.

" MY DEAR GERTRUDE,—I have your letter. I accede to your request, and will make arrangements in reference to the proposal which you have submitted to me. None of the girls now here have any recollection of you. There are several younger members of the families whose older girls were here ; but your change of name prevents that being of any consequence. The servants were all changed at the Easter Term. Let me know when it will suit you to come here ; and believe me yours sincerely,
> " ELINOR BLOXAM."

When she had read this brief note over, addressed it to Miss Grace Lambert, and placed it in the appointed spot for all letters to be despatched by the morning post, Mrs. Bloxam sat down to her solitary supper with a well-satisfied expression of countenance.

It was nearly eleven years since Gertrude Keith, a handsome, intelligent, and self-willed child of eight years old, had been confided to the care of Mrs. Bloxam and the advantages, educational and otherwise, of the Vale House. The letters which Mrs. Bloxam had read, that summer night, formed the greater part of all the correspondence which had been addressed to her by the individual who had placed the child under her protection, and whose confidence Mrs. Bloxam had won, and to a certain extent undeniably deserved. It had been stipulated that Gertrude Keith was to be kept in ignorance of her parentage, and of the circumstances under which she had been placed in Mrs. Bloxam's establishment ; and this condition the schoolmistress had conscientiously observed. Gertrude knew nothing of her own origin. She was believed by her companions, and she believed herself, to be an orphan girl, without any living relatives.

Gertrude Keith was the natural daughter of Lord Sandilands, a nobleman whose wild youth had given place to a correct and irreproachable middle age, which stage of life he had now passed, and was beginning the downward descent. He had placed the child under the care of Mrs. Bloxam, who had been formerly a governess in the family of his sister, Lady Marchmont, and who retained the confidence and regard of her former employers, after she had made the adventurous and unsuccessful experiment of matrimony. Certain circumstances connected with the little girl's birth and the early death of her ill-starred mother made Lord Sandilands shrink from seeing her, with strange and strong aversion ; and one of the conditions to which he had required Mrs. Bloxam's consent and adherence was, that his name was never to be spoken to the child, and that, except in the event of her illness or death, he was to be spared all communications respecting her, except at certain stated intervals. These conditions had been scrupulously observed ; and Gertrude's childhood had been as happy as any childhood passed under such exceptional conditions could be. She was a handsome, healthy, brave, independent-spirited child, who did not give much trouble, and who held her own against the envy, hatred, malice, and all uncharitableness of that world in miniature—a girls' boarding-school. As for Mrs. Bloxam, she liked the handsome, sturdy child ; and she liked the stylish, graceful girl, who developed herself so rapidly from that promising childhood. Then Gertrude was not a troublesome, while she was a very lucrative, pupil ; and there was an agreeable certainty about the very liberal payments made on her account by Lord Sandilands, and an equally agreeable uncertainty about the period of the girl's removal from the Vale House, which formed an exception to the rule in general cases ; and Mrs. Bloxam highly appreciated both these advantages. A portion of the correspondence which Mrs. Bloxam had read on the evening on which she had received Gertrude's letter referred to the time when she should have attained to womanhood, and her schooldays should be over. It was Lord Sandilands' wish that the arrangement made for her in her childhood should continue ; that Mrs. Bloxam should act as her protectress ; that the girl should remain with her, until she should feel indisposed to stay at the Vale House any longer, or should decide upon some manner of life for herself. "In any of these cases," said Gertrude's unknown father in one of his letters, "on your communicating the facts to me, I will make the best arrangement for Gertrude within my power."

It was not very long after this had been written, though much before the time at which either her father or Mrs. Bloxam had contemplated the probability of any change in Gertrude's life, or of the girl's taking her destiny into her own hands, that an accident made her acquainted with Gilbert Lloyd. She had not shared any of the early romance and follies of her companions: the "young gentlemen" of Dr. Waggle's "establishment" had had no charm, singly or collectively, for her; the doctor, the chemist, the music and drawing masters, even the Italian signor, who made singing-lessons a delight, and was so fascinating, though he used his hair-brush sparingly, and his nail-brush not at all— each and all were perfectly without attraction or danger for the young girl, who seemed to ignore or despise all the petty flirtations and manoeuverings of her schoolfellows.

Of and for not one of the young girls under her care had Mrs. Bloxam less fear or anxiety. Gertrude was proud and stately, and though tall for her seventeen years, and firm as well as graceful of outline, and though she had made fair progress with her education, and in her musical studies was notably in the van, there was something childlike about her still, something which kept Mrs. Bloxam in a happy condition of unsuspecting tranquillity.

But all Gertrude Keith's childlike peace and passionless calm vanished when she met Gilbert Lloyd, at a house where Mrs. Bloxam was in the habit of visiting during the vacations, and whither she brought Gertrude, in order to avoid leaving her to the portentous solitude of the Vale House, in the absence of her companions. The girl fell in love with the young man—who paid her quiet, stealthy, underhand attentions—with a suddenness and a vehemence which would have alarmed any one who loved her, for the future of a woman endowed with so imaginative, sensitive, and passionate a nature. All the dormant romance, of which no one had suspected the existence in Gertrude's nature, whose awakening no one perceived, when the time came was aroused into force and action, and the girl was transformed. Now was the time at which the instinct, the care, the love, the caution of a mother, would have been needed to guide, direct, and save Gertrude from her own undisciplined fancy, from her own untaught impulses. But Gertrude had no such aid extended to her. Mrs. Bloxam, a good woman in her way, and of more than average intelligence, had no feelings towards the girl which even bordered on the maternal ; and the habitual authority of the schoolmistress was naturally in some degree abrogated by the fact that it was vacation time. She was not of a very confiding or unsuspicious disposition ; but she had, unconsciously to herself, to deal in Gilbert Lloyd with one who knew well how to lull suspicion, and he in his turn found an apt pupil in Gertrude. They met again and again ; the girl's beauty, freshness, and daring had a strong charm for a man like Lloyd ; and for the first time since he had had to calculate life's chances closely, and to rely upon himself for the indulgences and luxuries which alone made life worth having to a man of his temperament, he committed the blunder of gratifying feeling at the expense of prudence. He did not fall in love with Gertrude quite so precipitately or so violently as she fell in love with him, but the second meeting did for him what the first had done for her ; and in Gilbert Lloyd's case to form a desire was to resolve to achieve it, at whatever cost to others, at whatever sacrifice of personal honour, provided it did not entail public disgrace, such gratification might necessitate or involve.

The vacation enjoyed by the pupils, and not less enjoyed by the proprietor, of the Vale House, was within three days of its expiration, when a housemaid belonging to the establishment reported Miss Gertrude Keith " missing ; " and the search and anxiety consequent on the intelligence were terminated by a letter from the fugitive, informing Mrs. Bloxam that she had been married that morning to Gilbert Lloyd by special licence, and was then about to start for a short continental excursion.

Mrs. Bloxam was very much shocked, and very much annoyed, in the first place that the event should have happened at all ; in the second, that Gilbert Lloyd, of whom she knew something, and cordially disapproved what she did know, should be the hero of an affair certain to bring her into discredit with Lord Sandilands, and likely, if she did not contrive to hide it very skilfully, to bring her school into discredit with the public. She had no doubt as to the veracity of Gertrude's story, no doubt that Lloyd had really married her—a copy of the certificate of the marriage was enclosed in her letter; but she bitterly regretted her own blindness and negligence, and, to do her justice, felt not a little for the girl's probable fate.

Mrs. Bloxam rapidly perceived the advantage to be derived from the circumstance that the untoward event of Gertrude's elopement had taken place during the vacation. She summoned all the servants, informed them that Miss Keith had left the Vale House under certain unpleasant circumstances which it was not necessary to explain; that any indiscreet reference to the circumstance made to the other pupils on the reassembling of the school would be visited by condign punishment in the forfeiture of the offender's place; and then dismissed them, to assemble downstairs in their own domain and learn all the particulars from the housemaid, who was in Gertrude's confidence, and had been liberally bribed by Gilbert Lloyd to facilitate and connive at all the preliminary meetings which had resulted in the elopement.

To this proceeding succeeded a period of reflection on the part of Mrs. Bloxam. Should she inform Lord Sandilands of the events that had taken place? Should she tell him how much sooner than she had calculated upon, Gertrude had taken the decision of her fate into her own hands? Should she tell him that the time to which she had looked forward as an eventuality, which might come about in a couple of years, had already taken place, and that now was the opportunity for fulfilling the intentions which he had continuously, if vaguely, expressed in his letters to her? Mrs. Bloxam debated this question with herself, and self-interest loudly and persistently advised her to silence. Lord Sandilands had never seen the girl, had never even hinted at seeing her, had indeed distinctly disclaimed any intention of ever seeing her. Nothing could be more improbable than that he should find out what had occurred. If she should continue to apply to his solicitor for the money which he was authorized to pay her at certain intervals, no suspicion of any change in the state of affairs could arise. And the money would be very welcome to her. By resorting to the simple expedient of holding her tongue, she might avoid scandal, avoid doing herself the injury which she must necessarily inflict upon her school by the admission of an elopement having taken place from within its walls, and secure a sum of money which would be both useful and agreeable. To be sure, the day of reckoning must come, but not yet; and if ever she should have it in her power to do any service or kindness to the poor misguided girl, who would certainly inevitably come, or she (Mrs. Bloxam) was much mistaken in Gilbert Lloyd, to need service and kindness before much time should have gone over her, she pledged herself to herself to show her all the kindness in her power, unreservedly and heartily. Thus did Mrs. Bloxam make the devil's bargain with herself; and very successfully did she pursue the line of conduct which she had determined to follow, from the period of Gertrude Keith's elopement to that evening on which she had received the no longer deluded girl's letter, two years and a half later.

With the fatal facility which results from impunity, Mrs. Bloxam had almost ceased to remember Gertrude, and had quite ceased to feel uneasiness regarding the concealment she had practised towards Lord Sandilands, and the appropriation of the sum of money which he paid to her yearly. But with the perusal of Gertrude's letter the subject again arose in her mind, and, as was Mrs. Bloxam's habit, she faced it steadily and considered it maturely. Gertrude's proposition was not an entirely pleasing one. There was a certain responsibility attaching to assuming the charge of a young woman so strangely situated; and the present acceptation of the trust might involve Mrs. Bloxam in difficulties and dilemmas to which she was by no means blind or insensible. But, on the other hand, she saw in Gertrude's return a perfect security against the divulgement of her decidedly unpleasant secret. Should Lord Sandilands now make any inquiry about Gertrude, she should experience no difficulty in satisfying him or any representative he might send. Even should the change of name become known—a contingency which a little well-timed manœuvering might prevent—Mrs. Bloxam could afford to trust to her own ingenuity to find a reason for that proceeding which should satisfy all querists. Gertrude's own interest and safety were now concerned in preserving the secret of her elopement, her marriage, and the duration of her absence from the Vale House; while the offer of her services as teacher to the junior classes was sufficiently valuable to leave Mrs. Bloxam still a gainer to the full extent of the annual stipend, even when Gertrude's maintenance and needful expenses should be taken into account—a calculation which Mrs. Bloxam made very accurately and minutely, and which was very much in her line.

The result of the cogitations to which Mrs. Bloxam gave herself up after she had read Gertrude's letter has already appeared. On the following day she received from Mrs. Lloyd a few brief lines of acknowledgment and thanks ; and the Saturday of the week which had begun with the death of Harvey Gore and the final parting between Gilbert Lloyd and his young wife witnessed the installation of a new inmate, holding an anomalous position—partly parlour-boarder and partly pupil-teacher—at the Vale House. This new inmate was known to her companions and pupils, in short to all concerned, as Miss Grace Lambert.

END OF THE PROLOGUE.

Book the First.

—

CHAPTER I.

ROWLEY COURT.

THE traveller of thirty years ago, whom pleasure or business took through the heart of Gloucestershire, and who had the satisfaction of enjoying the box-seat of the admirably-appointed mail-coach which ran through that district,—if he had an eye for the picturesque and a proper appreciation of the beauties of nature, exhibiting themselves in the freshest turf, the oldest trees, the loveliest natural landscape-gardening combination of grassy upland, wooded knoll, and silver stream,—seldom refrained from inquiring the name of the owner of the property which was skirted by the well-kept road along which they were bowling, and was invariably informed by the coachman that all belonged "to the Challoners, of whom you've doubtless heerd ; the Challoners of Rowley Court." By his phrase, "of whom you've doubtless heerd," the coachman expressed literally what he meant. He and his compeers, born and bred in the county, were so impressed with the seignorial dignities of the Challoners of Rowley Court, that they ignored the possibility of the position of the family being unknown throughout the length and breadth of the land. That they were not what they had been was indeed admitted, that the grand old estate had somewhat diminished, that the family revenues had decreased, that the present members of it were to a certain extent impoverished, that the hand of poverty was one of the many objectionable hands which had an unpleasant grip upon the old Squire,—all these were facts which were tacitly admitted in privileged regions— such as the servants'-hall at the Court, or the snuggery at the Challoners' Arms—but which were never hinted at to passing strangers. So jealous, indeed, of the honour of the

family were its retainers—among whom the mail-driver was
to be classed, as he was doubtless connected with the
tenantry by family or marriage—that if " the box "
ventured to comment on the evident want of attention to
the property, manifested in broken hedges, unmended thatch,
in undrained fen or unreclaimed common, he received but
a short answer, conveying an intimation that they knew
pretty well what was right down in those parts, the
Challoners did ; at all events, as well as most cockneys : the
biting sarcasm conveyed in this retort having generally
the effect of closing the conversation, and reducing the fee
given to the driver at the journey's end to one-half the sum
originally intended.

There are no mail-coaches now, and the traveller by rail
has no chance of getting a glimpse of Rowley Court, save
a momentary one in the short interval between a cutting
and a tunnel which are on the extreme border of the park.
The Court itself stands towards the centre of the park, on
low ground encircled by wooded hills, towards which, in the
good old times, avenues of stately oak, elm, and lime trees
extended in long vistas. But under the dire pressure of necessity the woodman's axe has been frequently at work
lately in these " cool colonnades," and the avenues are consequently much shorn of their fair proportions. The house
is a big incongruous mass of two distinct styles of
architecture—a grafting of Inigo Jones's plain façade and
Corinthian pillars on a red-brick Elizabethan foundation,
with projecting mullioned windows, octagonal turrets,
quaintly-carved cornices, and ornamental doorways. Round
the house runs a broad stone terrace bounded by a low
balustrade, and flanked at each of the corners by a large
stone vase, which, in the time of prosperity, had contained
choice flowers varying with the season, but which were
now full of cracks and fissures, and were overgrown with
creeping weeds and common parasites. The very stones of
the terrace were chipped, moss-edged, and grass-fringed ;
the black-faced old clock in the stable-turret had lost one
of its hands, while several of its gilt numerals had become
effaced by time and tempest ; the vane above it had only
two points of the compass remaining for the brass fox,
whose bushy tail had gone in the universal wreck, to point
at ; the pump in the stable-yard was dry ; the trough in

front of it warped and blistered; a piece of dirty oilcloth
had been roughly nailed over the kennel, in front of which
the big old mastiff lay blinking in the sunshine; and a
couple of cart-horses, a pair of superannuated carriage-
horses, the Squire's old roan cob, and "the pony" (a strong,
rough, undersized, Welsh-bred brute, with untiring energy
and no mouth), were the sole tenants of the stables which
had once been occupied by the best-bred hacks and hunters
of the county.

They were bad times now for the Challoners of Rowley
Court—bad times enough, Heaven knew; but they had
been great people, and that was some consolation for Mark
Challoner, the old Squire, as he stiffly returned the bow of
Sir Thomas Walbrook, ex-Lord Mayor of London, carpet-
maker, and millionaire, who had recently built an Italian
villa and laid out an Italian garden on a three-hundred acre
"lot" which he had purchased from the Challoner estate.
They had been the great lords of all that district. Queen
Elizabeth had lodged for some time at Rowley Court on
one of her progresses; and Charles I. and Henrietta Maria
had slept there, the royal pair finding "all the highways
strewed with roses and all manner of sweet flowers," as
was recorded in a worm-eaten parchment manuscript kept
among the archives in the old oak-chest in the library.
There was no sign then of the evil days in store—evil days
which began in 1643, when Colonel Sands' troopers pillaged
the Court, and sent off five waggons loaded with spoil to
London.

It is the custom of the Challoners to say that then began
that decadence which has continued for ever since; and in
truth, though there have been many vicissitudes of fortune
undergone by the old family, the tendency has been for
ever downward. The final blow to their fortunes was
dealt by Mark Challoner's immediate predecessor, his
brother Howard, who was one of the ornaments of the
Prince Regent's court, and who gambled and drank and
diced and drabbed with the very finest of those fine gentlemen. It was in his time that the axe was laid to the root
of the tree; that Sir Thomas Walbrook's father, the old
carpet-maker, made the first money advances which resulted in his ultimate purchase on easy terms of the three
hundred acres; and that ultimate ruin began decidedly to

establish and proclaim itself at Rowley Court. When providence removed Howard Challoner from this world by a timely attack of gout in the stomach, long after his beloved king and patron had been gathered to his fathers, it was felt that there was every chance of a beneficial change in the family fortunes. The godless old bachelor was succeeded by his brother Mark, then a clear-headed, energetic man in the prime of life, a widower with two remarkably promising boys—the elder a frank, free-hearted, jovial fellow, fond of country sports, a good shot, a bold rider, " a downright Englishman," as the tenantry delighted to call him ; the younger a retiring, shy lad, wanting in the attributes of popularity, but said to be wondrous clever " with his head," and to know more than people double his age, which in itself was something bordering on the miraculous to the simple Gloucestershire folk. And, for a time, all went very well. Mark Challoner was his own steward, and almost his own bailiff ; at all events, he allowed no one on the property to be more thoroughly master of its details than he. Without any undue amount of niggardliness he devised and carried out unsparing retrenchments ; thriftless tenants, after warning, were got rid of, and energetic men introduced in their places ; a better style of farming was suggested, and all who adopted it were helped by their landlord. The estate improved so greatly and so rapidly that vacant farms were largely competed for, and rents were rising, when suddenly Mark Challoner withdrew himself from the life into which he had plunged with such eagerness, and in which he had succeeded so well, and became a confirmed recluse, a querulous, moody, silent man, loving solitude, hating companionship, shutting out from him all human interest.

A sudden change this, and one which did not happen without exciting remarks from all the little world round Rowley Court, both high and low. The Walbrooks and their set (for during the few later years there had been frequent irruptions of the plutocracy into the old county families, and the Walbrooks were now the shining centre of a circle of people with almost as much money and as little breeding as themselves)—the Walbrooks and their set shook their heads and shrugged their shoulders, and secretly rejoiced that the old man from whom they never received

anything but the sternest courtesy, and who so pertina-
ciously repelled all attempts at familiar intercourse from
them, had at last come upon the evil days in store for him,
and would no longer twit them by his aristocratic presence
and frigid behaviour. The more humble classes—the old
tenantry, who had been rejoicing at the better turn which
things on the estate had undoubtedly taken, and who were
looking forward to a long career of good management under
the reign of Mark Challoner and his sons—were wofully dis-
appointed at the change, and expressed their disappointment
loudly amongst themselves, while taking due care that it
should never reach the master's ear.   No one, however,
either among the neighbours or the dependents, seemed to
notice that the change in Mark Challoner's life—that his
fading from the hearty English squire into the premature
old man, that his abnegating the exercise of his tastes and
pleasures, and giving up everything in which he had hitherto
felt the keenest interest—was contemporaneous with the
departure of his younger son, Geoffrey, from the paternal
roof.   In that act there was nothing to create surprise : it
had always been known that Master Geoffrey's talents were
destined to find exercise in the great arena of London, and
now that he was eighteen years of age, it was natural
that he should wish to bring those talents into play ; and
though nothing had been said in or out of the house about
his going, until one morning when he told the coachman
to bring round the dog-cart and to come with him to the
station, there was no expression of surprise on the part of
any of the household—beings to whom the expression of
anything they might feel was of the rarest occurrence. The
old butler, indeed, a relic of the past, who had been Howard
Challoner's body-servant in his later years, and who was
almost superannuated, remarked that the Squire sent
for his eldest son immediately after his youngest son's departure ; that the two were closeted together for full two
hours (a most unusual thing at Rowley Court, where, in
general, all matters were discussed before the servants,
or, indeed, before any one that might be present) ; and that
" Master Miles " came out with pallid cheeks and red eyes,
and in a state which the narrator described as one of
" flustration."
    Seven years had passed since Geoffrey Challoner's depar-

ture,—seven years, during which his name had never been mentioned by his father or his brother ; seven years, during which the old man, wrapped in the reserve, the silence, and the moodiness which had become his second nature, had been gradually but surely breaking in health, and wending his way towards the trysting-place where the Shadow, cloaked from head to foot, was in waiting for him. That meeting was very close at hand just now. So thought the servants, as from the ivy-covered windows of the office they peered occasionally at their master, propped up by pillows in his bath-chair, which had been wheeled into a corner of the stone terrace where the light spring sunshine fell fullest ; so thought Dr. Barford, the brightest, cheeriest, rosiest little medico, on whom all within the Cotswold district pinned their faith ungrudgingly, and who had just sent his dark green gig, drawn by that flea-bitten grey mare, which was known within a circuit of fifty miles round, to the stables, and who approached the invalid with a brisk step and an inquiring, pleasant smile.

"Sitting in the sunshine," said the Doctor aloud (having previously said, *sotto voce*, " Hem !—hem ! much changed, by George ! ")—" sitting in the sunshine, my dear old friend ! And quite right too :

> The sunshine, broken in the rill,
> Though turned astray, is sunshine still,

as somebody says. Well, and how do we feel to-day ? "

" Badly enough, Doctor ; badly enough !" replied the Squire, in a low thick voice. " I'm running down very fast, and there's very little more sunshine for me——" here an attack of coughing interrupted him for a moment ; " so I'm making the most of it."

" O, you mustn't say that," said Dr. Barford cheerily. "While there's life there's hope, you know ; and you've gone through some baddish bouts since we've known each other."

" None so bad as this," said Mark Challoner. " Your skill, under Providence, has kept me alive hitherto ; but though you're as skilful as ever, and as kind—God bless you for it !—you've not got Providence working with you now. I'm doomed, and I know it. What's more, I don't repine, only I want to make the most of the time that's left me ; and, above all, I want to see Miles again."

"Miles ?   O, ay !   He's staying in town, is he not ? "

"Yes, with my old friend Sandilands, who loves him as if he were his own son.   Poor Miles, it's a shame to drag him away from his enjoyment to come down to a poor, dull, dying old man."

"You would not hurt his feelings by saying that before him," said the Doctor shortly, "and you've no right to say it now.   Has he been sent for ? "

"Yes, they telegraphed for him this morning."

"Well, there can be no harm in that, though I won't have you give way to this feeling of lowness that is coming over you."

"Coming over me ! " the old man repeated wearily. "Ah, Barford, my dear friend, you know how long it is since the light died out of my life, and left me the mere shell and husk of man that I have been since ; you know, Doctor, how long it is ago, though you don't know the cause of it."

"Nor ever sought to know it, Squire ; bear me witness of that," said the little Doctor.   "It's no part of my business or of my nature to seek confidences ; and though perhaps if I had been aware of what was troubling you—and at the first I knew perfectly well that *animo magis quam corpore* was the seat of your illness—and though, being unable to ' minister to a mind diseased,' as somebody says, I was labouring, as it were, at a disadvantage,—you will do me the justice to say that I never for a moment hinted that —hum ! you understand ? "   And Dr. Barford, who would have given the results of a week's practice to know really what had first worked the change in the old man, stopped short and looked at him with a confidence-inviting glance.

"Perfectly," said the Squire ; "but it could never have been.   My secret must die with me ; and when after my death the closet is broken open, and people find the skeleton in it, they will merely come upon a lot of old bones jumbled together, and, not having got the key of the puzzle to fit them together, will wonder what I can have been afraid of.   Why do you stare so earnestly ? "

"A skeleton, my dear Squire ! " said the little Doctor,

on tiptoe with eagerness ; "you said a skeleton in a closet, and a lot of old bones jumbled together——"

A smile, the first seen for many a day, passed across Mark Challoner's wan face as he said, "I was speaking metaphorically, Barford ; that is all. No belated traveller was ever robbed and murdered at Rowley Court—in my time at least, believe me."

Dr. Barford laughed a short laugh, and shrugged his shoulders as though deprecating a pursuance of the subject, but he evidently did not place entire credence on his friend's assertion. However, he plunged at once into a series of medical questions, and shortly afterwards took his leave. As 'he passed the hall-door, which was open, on his way to the stables, he saw a neatly-dressed middle-aged woman pacing quietly up and down the hall ; and recognizing her as the nurse from London, who for some time past had been in nightly attendance on the old man, he beckoned her to him.

"Coming out to get a little breath of fresh air, nurse ? " he said pleasantly, as she approached. " You must need it, I should think."

"Well, sir, it is warm and close in the Squire's room now, there's no denying ; and what it'll be when the summer comes on I often dread to think."

"No you don't, nurse," said the Doctor, eyeing her keenly. " You know better than that, with all the practice· and experience you've had. No summer for the Squire, poor fellow, this side the grave."

" You think not, sir ? "

" I *know* it, nurse, and so do you, if you only chose to say so. However, he's gone down so very rapidly since I was here last, and his tone is altogether so very low and depressed, that I imagine the end to be very close upon us ; so close that I think you had better tell Mr. Miles—the son that has been telegraphed for, you know, and who will probably be down to-night—that if he has anything special to say to his father he had better do so very shortly after his arrival. What's that ? " he asked, as a dull sound fell upon his ear.

" That's the Squire knocking for Barnard to fetch his chair, sir ; see, Barnard has heard, and is going to him."

" O, all right ! Poor old Squire ! poor good old fellow !

Don't forget about Mr. Miles, nurse. Good night ; " and the little Doctor, casting a kindly look towards the spot where the figure of the old man in the chair loomed hazily in the dim distance, hurried away.

When Mark Challoner's servant had reached his master's chair, and, obedient to the signal he had received, was about to wheel it towards the house, he found that the old man had changed his intention, and was desirous of remaining out on the terrace yet a few minutes. On receiving this order, Barnard looked over his shoulder at the nurse, who was still standing at the hall-door ; and as she made no sign to him to hasten his movements, he concluded that his master's wish might be obeyed, and so, after touching his hat respectfully, he returned to the genial society of the gardener and the stable-lad. And Mark Challoner was once more left alone. The fact in its broadest significance seemed to become patent to him as he watched the retreating figure of his servant, and two tears coursed down his wan cheeks. Mark Challoner knew that his last illness was then upon him ; for weeks he had felt that he should never again shake off the lassitude and weakness so stealthily yet so surely creeping over him ; but now, within the last few minutes, the conviction had flashed across him that the end was close at hand—that he had arrived at the final remnant of that originally grand strength and vitality which, slowly decaying, had enabled him to make head against disease so long, and that he was taking his last look at the fair fields which he had inherited, and in the improvement of which he had at one time—ah, how long ago !—found his delight. It was this thought that made him dismiss Barnard. The old man, with the new-born consciousness of his approaching end fresh in him, wanted to gaze once more at his diminished possessions ; and for the last time to experience the old associations which a contemplation of them never failed to revive. There, with the westering sun just gilding its topmost branches, was the Home Copse, where he had shot his first pheasant, to his old father's loudly-expressed delight. Just below it lay the Black Pool, out of which, at the risk of his own life, he had pulled Charles Gammock, a rosy-faced boy with fair hair—Charles Gammock ! ay, ay, they buried him a year ago, and his grandson now holds the land. There, bare and attenuated now, but as he first

remembered it young and strong and full of promise, was
the Regent's Plantation, so called in honour of the illustrious
personage who, staying for the night with Howard Challoner, had honoured him by planting the first tree in it.
Beyond it, Dirck's land, now—and as that thought crossed
him the Squire's brow became furrowed, and his wan colour
deepened into a leaden hue, for Dirck was one of the
moneyed interest, one of the manufacturers who had come
in Sir Thomas Walbrook's wake, and were bent on the
acquisition of all the county property which might come
into the market. Beyond it lay Thurston Gap, the surest
place for finding a fox in the whole country, old Tom
Horniblow used to say. Old Tom Horniblow! Why,
there had been three or four huntsmen to the Cotswold
since him: he must have been dead these forty years,
during which time the Squire had not thought of him a
dozen times; and yet then, at that moment, the stout figure
of the old huntsman mounted on his famous black horse, just
as he had seen him at the cover-side half a century ago, rose
before his eyes. This reminiscence turned Mark Challoner's
thoughts from places to people; and though his glance still
rested on the landscape, his mind was busy recalling the
ghosts of the past. His father, a squire indeed of the old
type—hearty, boisterous, and hot-headed : it was well—and
a faint smile dawned on Mark Challoner's cheek as the
thought crossed his mind—it was as well that his father had
died before the irruption of the Walbrooks, Dircks, and
such-like ; it would have been too much for him. His
brother, the dandy with the high cravat and the buckskin
breeches and Hessian boots, ridiculed by his country neighbours, and regarding his estate but as a means to supply his
town dissipation. His wife—she seemed more dim and
ghost-like to him than any of the others ; he had known her
so short a time, so much of his life had been passed since her
death ; since the gentle little woman, whose wedding-ring he
had worn on his little finger until it had eaten into the
flesh, glided out of the world after having given birth to her
second son. And, with the train of thought awakened by
the reminiscence of the career of that second son, from his
birth until the morning of his abrupt departure from the
ancestral home, surging round him, the old man's head sunk
upon his breast, a fresh access of feebleness seemed to come

over him ; and when the watchful Barnard sallied from his
retreat and advanced towards the chair, he found his master
in a state bordering on collapse, and made the utmost haste
to get him to his room, and place him under the professional
care of the nurse.

In the course of a very few minutes, however, the Squire,
aided by stimulants, revived; and his senses rapidly returning, he ordered his desk to be brought to the side of the
bed into which he had been moved, and commenced listlessly sorting the papers therein. They were few and unimportant; the old man's illness had not been sudden; he
had always been a thoroughly methodical man, and he had
had plenty of time and opportunity to attend to his correspondence. Propped up by the pillows, he was leisurely
looking through the orderly bundles of letters, neatly tied
together and scrupulously docketed, when the sound of a
horse's hoofs on the gravel outside, the grating of wheels, the
barking of the dogs in the stable-yard, and the almost
simultaneous ringing of the house-bell, gave warning of an
arrival. Mark Challoner had scarcely time to note these
various occurrences when the room-door was thrown open,
and in the next instant the old man's wavering and unsteady hands were fast in the grasp of his son Miles.

A tall man, over six feet in height, with a bright red-
and-white complexion, large brown eyes, a straight nose too
big for his face, a large mouth full of sound white teeth,
with dark brown hair curling crisply at the sides of his head
and over his poll, with long moustache and flowing brown
beard, with a strongly-knit but somewhat ungainly figure,
dressed in a well-made but loosely-fitting grey suit, and with
large, well-shaped, brown hands, which, after releasing the
first grip of the Squire's fingers, joined themselves together
and kept working in tortuous lissom twists : this was Miles
Challoner. A faint smile, half of pleasure, half of amusement—something odd in Miles had always been remarked
by his father—flitted over the Squire's face, as he said, after
the first greeting, " You've come in time, Miles : you received the telegram ? "

" And started off at once, sir. All I could do to prevent
his lordship from coming with me—wanted to come immensely ; but I told him I thought he'd better not. Even

such an old friend as he is in the way when one's seedy—
don't you think I'm right, sir?"

"You're right enough, Miles; more especially when, as
in the present case, it's a question of something more than
'seediness,' as you call it. My time," continued the Squire,
in tones a little thickened by emotion,—" my time has come,
my boy. I'm only waiting for you, before, like Hezekiah,
I should 'turn my face unto the wall.' I have, I hope,
'set my house in order,' and I know that now 'I shall die,
and not live;' but I wanted to see you before—before I
go."

The young man leaned quickly forward and looked
earnestly in his father's face, as he heard these words; then
with a gesture of inquiry elevated his eyebrows at the nurse,
who was standing just inside the door. Receiving for
answer an affirmative nod, Miles Challoner's cheek for an
instant turned as pale as that of the invalid; but he speedily
recovered himself, and said in a voice which lacked the
cheery ring that should have accompanied the words:
" You're a little down, sir, and that's natural enough, considering your illness; but you'll make head against it now,
and we shall soon have you about as usual. It was only
yesterday Lord Sandilands was saying that though he's
some quarter of a century your junior, he should be very
sorry to back himself against you at 'anything British,' as
he expressed it—anything where strength and bottom were
required."

The old man smiled again as he said: "Sandilands has
been a townman for so long that he's lost all condition, and
has ruined his health for want of air and exercise. But at
least he lives; while I—I've vegetated for the last few
years, and now there's an end even to that."

" Why didn't you send for me before, sir? If I'd had
any idea you thought yourself so ill, I'd have come long
since."

" I know that, my dear boy, and that's the very reason
why I didn't send. Why should I fetch you from your
friends and your gaiety to potter about an old man's bedside? I would not have sent for you even now, save that I
have that inward feeling which is unmistakable, and which
tells me that I can't last many days, many hours more, and

I wanted, selfishly enough, to have you near me at the last."
The old man spoke these words with indescribable affection,
and, half involuntarily as it seemed, threw his arm round his
son's neck. The big strong frame of the young man shook
with ill-repressed emotion as he took the thin hand hanging
round his shoulder, and pressed it reverently to his lips.
"Father!" he said; and as he said it, both the men felt
how many years had passed since he had chanced to use the
term "Father!"

"True, my boy," said Mark Challoner, quietly, "it is a
pleasure, though, I fear, a selfish one. 'On some fond breast
the parting soul relies,' you know, Miles; and you're all
that's left to me in the world. Besides, the tie between us
has been such a happy one; as long as I can recollect we've
had no difference,—we were more like brothers than father
and son, Miles."

Miles answered only by a pressure of his father's hand.
He dared not trust himself to speak, he knew that his
voice was thick and choked with tears. His father looked
at him for an instant, and then said: "Now, boy, go and
get some dinner. How thoughtless of me to keep you so
long fasting after your journey!—Nurse, take Mr. Miles
away, and see that he is properly attended to. Be as careful
of him as you are of me, that's all I ask;" and the old man,
half-exhausted, sank back on his pillow.

Miles Challoner left the room with the nurse, and when
they were alone, he took the first opportunity of asking
her real opinion as to his father's state. This she gave him
frankly and fully, telling him moreover what Dr. Barford
had said as to the necessity of not delaying anything which
he might have to say to the Squire. Miles thanked her,
and then sat down to his cheerless meal. His thoughts were
preoccupied, and he ate and drank but little, pausing every
now and then, bestriding the room, reseating himself, and
leaning his head on his hand with a helpless puzzled air, as
one to whom the process of thought was unfamiliar. He
could scarcely realise the fact that the presiding spirit of the
place, the man whose will had been law ever since he could
recollect, "the Squire," who, with diminished possessions
and failing fortunes, had commanded, partly through his
own style and manner, partly through the prestige attaching to the family, more respect and esteem than all the

members of the invading calicocracy put together,—he could scarcely realise that this rural autocrat's power was ebbing, and that he himself lay on his death-bed. On his death-bed!—that was a curious thought : Miles Challoner had never attempted to realise the position, and now, when vaguely he attempted it, he failed. Only one thing came out clearly to him after his attempted examination of the subject, and that was that it would be most desirable to be at peace with all the world, and that any enmity cherished to the last would probably have a most disturbing and uncomfortable effect. Pondering all this he returned to the sick-room. During his absence the curtains had been closed and the night-lamp lighted. The nurse sat nodding in a large easy-chair by the bed-side, and the Squire lay in a dozing state, half waking now and again as his head slipped off the high pillow on which it rested, or when the heaviness of his breathing became specially oppressive. Miles seated himself on a couch at the foot of the bed, and fatigued by his journey, soon fell asleep. He seemed to have been unconscious only a few minutes, but in reality had slept nearly an hour, when he was awakened by a touch on the shoulder, and opening his eyes, saw the nurse standing by him. "The Squire's calling for you," she said, adding in a whisper, "he's going fast!" Miles roused himself, and crept silently to the head of the bed, where he found his father gasping for breath. The Squire's dim eyes recognised his son, and between the paroxysms of laboured respiration he again threw his arm round Miles's neck and touched the bowed forehead with his lips. Then the thoughts that had been fermenting in Miles Challoner's heart for so many years, and which had caused him such mental disturbance that night, at length found vent in words. With his father's arm around him, and with his face close to the old man's, Miles said, "Father! one word, only one! You hear and understand me?" A pressure of the hand on his cheeks— O, such a feeble pressure, but still a recognition—answered him. "Father, what of Geoffrey?" A low moan escaped the old man's lips ; other sign made he none. "What of Geoffrey?" continued Miles,—"years ago you forbade me ever to ask what had become of him, why he had left us, even to mention his name. I have obeyed you, as you know : but now, father, now—"

"Never!" said the old man, in dull, low accents. "Your brother Geoffrey is, and must be for ever, dead to you. Miles, my boy, my own boy, listen! Should you ever meet him, as you may do, shun him, I urge, I command you! Think of what I say to you now, here, as I am—shun him, fly from him, let nothing earthly induce you to know him or acknowledge him."

"But, father, you will surely tell me why——"

The nurse touched Miles on the shoulder as he spoke, and pointed to the Squire, whose swooning had been noticed by her observant eyes. When he recovered himself he essayed again to speak, but his strength failing him he laid his hand in his son's, and so peacefully passed away.

CHAPTER II.

IN POSSESSION.

"REALLY, hardly sooner than I expected, my dear sir," said Dr. Barford, when he came to pay his accustomed daily visit at Rowley Court, and found his occupation gone. "A little accelerated by nervousness about your coming home, but very little ; not more than a few hours. I quite expected the event ; told the nurse as much yesterday, in fact. Ah, well, my dear sir, it is what we must all come to. He was a fine old gentleman, a very fine old gentleman—has not left many like him in Gloucestershire ; more's the pity ;" and Dr. Barford continued to talk on with smooth professional glibness, by no means unconscious of the fact that he was not listened to by Miles Challoner with even a show of attention.

Old Mark Challoner's death was emphatically a "bad business" for Dr. Barford, and he said so (to himself) quite frankly. The Squire had been a very profitable and by no means a troublesome or exacting patient to the worthy doctor for a considerable time, and it was not pleasant to him to know that the attendance which brought much that was agreeable with it, in addition to liberal and regularly-paid fees, was at an end. Dr. Barford looked at Miles Challoner, and a mild despondency possessed itself of his

soul. Miles was a model of health and strength ; his complexion indicated unconsciousness of the presence of bile in
his system, and he looked as little like a man troubled, or
likely to be troubled, with nerves, or fancied ailments of
any kind, as need be. So Dr. Barford felt his footing at
Rowley Court was a thing of the past, and mentally bade it
farewell with a plaintive sigh. He was an honest little
man, and kind-hearted too, though he did think of the
event, as we all think of every event in which we are concerned, from a selfish standpoint ; and he was frankly,
genuinely sorry for his old friend ; and Miles recognised the
sincerity of feeling in him, and threw off his absence of
mind, and shook hands with him over again, thanking him
for the skill and care that had availed so long, none the less
warmly that it could avail no longer.

Miles Challoner's grief for his father was very deep and
poignant. His nature was acutely sensitive, and he had the
power of feeling sorrow more intensely than most men, while
he lacked the faculty for shaking it off, and betaking himself
to the way of life which had been his before the trouble came
upon him, which most men possess, and find very useful in a
world which affords little time and has not much toleration
for sentiment. Loneliness fell heavily upon him, and the
society, which in the winter would have been within his
reach, was not available now. The season was well on in
London, and most of the people who formed the not very
extensive neighbourhood of Rowley Court, were in town ; so
that Miles Challoner was all uncheered by neighbourly kindness, and his evenings were especially solitary.

Incidental to his position as sole heir to the diminished
but still respectable possessions of the Challoners, a great
deal of business had to be gone through which was particularly distasteful to Miles. The family lawyer lived in
London, of course, but his personal services had not been
needed. Old Mark Challoner had set his house very
thoroughly in order ; no rents were in arrear, the debts
were few, and the tenants were orderly and well-behaved.
They had liked their old landlord well enough, and had
been somewhat afraid of him. They were not quite sure
whether they should approve altogether so much of the new
one. Not that Miles had done anything to offend his
father's people ; not that he had saliently departed from, or

violently transgressed, the traditions of conduct of the foregone Challoners. Not that there was the slightest suspicion of milksopism attaching to Miles; but there was an uneasy notion abroad that Miles did not take much interest in the old place, that he cared over-much for books and "Lunnon," and was rather degenerately ignorant in matters appertaining to agriculture. On the whole, though there was no disaffection among the Rowley Court tenantry, there was not much enthusiasm. Men who would have thought it a desperate hardship, an entirely unnatural and unheard-of slight indeed, if they had not been, whenever they desired it, immediately admitted to an interview with old Mark Challoner, were perfectly satisfied to transact their business with Mr. Styles, the steward, and displayed to the deputy very little curiosity respecting his principal. They talked about Miles a little among themselves, wondering whether he would not marry soon, and supposing, in rather depreciatory accents, that he would bring a lady from "Lunnon."

"Glo'ster won't do for *him*, depend on it," said farmer Bewlay to the buxom wife of farmer Oliver; "he'll be having a fine madam, what'll want to be six months among the furriners, and save all she can at home the other six. Times have changed since the old Squire brought his pretty little wife home, and she shook hands with us all in the churchyard, after morning prayers, her first Sunday here, and told us how she knew us all already, from her husband's talk."

"I don't remember it myself," said farmer Oliver's buxom wife; "but I've heard Tummas talk of it, and how she looked up at the old Squire when she said, 'my husband,' and smiled just like a summer morning."

"Ay, indeed she did," assented farmer Bewlay; "but he wasn't the old Squire then, but a brave and good-looking gentleman; and she was a pretty girl was madam, when she came to Rowley Court, and pretty up to the time they carried her out of it. I helped in that job; and the Squire had nowt but his little boys left."

"Has anybody heerd tell anything about Master Geoffrey?" said farmer Oliver's wife, dropping her voice, and looking round her, as people look who are talking of things which are not, or should not be, generally mentioned.

"Does Mr. Styles say anything about him? Does Mr. Styles know where he is?"

"Mr. Styles never mentions him. I don't believe he knows any more than we do where he is, or what has become of him. A handsome child he was, and a handsome boy, though small and sly and cruel in his ways, and no more like the Squire, nor madam neither, than I am. You remember Master Geoffrey, surely?"

"O yes, I remember him. How the Squire changed after he went away! He ran away to sea, didn't he?"

"Some folk said so; but for my part I don't believe it. The sea, from all I've ever heard tell of it, ain't an easy life, nor a gay life, for the matter o' that; and wherever Master Geoffrey run to—and it's certain sure he ran somewheres—it wasn't to sea in my opinion. I don't know; I only have my own thoughts about it; and I ha'n't no means of knowin'. Anyhow, he went, and Squire was never the same man after; he were always good, and fond of the place, and that he were to the last; but he never had the same smile again, and I never see him talking to the children about, or patting them on the head, or doing anything like what he used."

The honest dark eyes of Polly Oliver filled with tears. "It's all true," she said, "and more than that. When our Johnny were lying in the measles, and very near his end, the Squire came down one day along with Dr. Barford, the physician, you know. He thought there ought to be someone beside the doctor to see the child; and when Dr. Barford told us—very kind and feeling like, I must say—as the child couldn't be left with us any longer, and I began to cry, as was only natural, and made no difference to me who was there, Squire or no Squire, he says to me, quiet like, but I can hear the words now, 'You won't believe me, Mrs. Oliver, and it would be hard to expect you should: but there are worse things in life than seeing your boy die;' and then he went away. And when Johnny was buried, and I had time to think of anything else, I thought of the Squire's words; and many a time I wondered what was the meaning that was in them, and knew it must be Master Geoffrey's doing somehow, but how I did not know, and I suppose no one knows."

"I don't know about that," said farmer Bewlay; "it's

likely as Mr. Miles knows, and Mr. Geoffrey; but I'm sure
Styles doesn't; and outside them two, and the Squire in his
grave, I daresay nobody in this world knows the rights of
the story."

While the people over whom Miles Challoner had come
to reign in the course of nature thus curiously, but not un-
kindly or with any lack of feeling, discussed the actualities
and the probabilities of his life, and raked up the memory
of that mysterious family secret, strongly suspected to be of
a calamitous nature, which had long been hidden by the
impenetrable silence of the Squire, and now lay buried in
his grave, Miles Challoner himself was much occupied with
the selfsame subject. The unanswered question which he
had asked his father in his last moments,—the unsolved
enigma which had disturbed his mind for years, which
haunted him now, and made all his life seem unreal, wrong,
and out of joint,—rose up before him, and engaged his
thoughts constantly, almost to the exclusion of every other
matter for reflection except his father's death. The two
linked themselves together in a strong bond of pain, and
held him in their withes. This time was a very heavy one
to the new master of Rowley Court.

His position was irksome to him. The privileges of proprietorship had no charms for Miles Challoner. He disliked the
business details in which it involved him; he shrunk from the
keenly painful associations it produced; he suffered much from
his loneliness,—from the loneliness of the Court generally.
Hitherto, whenever he had been away, he had returned to
enjoy the tranquillity—tranquillity which, when it was tasted
as a change, he appreciated very highly, but which as the
normal state of things wearied him rapidly and excessively.
He had had much companionship, in and since his boyhood,
with his father, and the blank left by the old Squire's
death was indeed complete. Miles Challoner, without
deserving precisely the appellation of a student, was fond
of books. He was well-educated, not in a very profound,
but in a tolerably extensive and various sense; and his taste
took a literary turn early in life, which, wholly unshared by
his father, had been encouraged, fostered, and directed by
his father's friend, Lord Sandilands. Miles was a man of
few intimacies. He liked society; but no one would ever
have called him sociable: he had much more the air of

frequenting general, in order to keep clear of particular, society; and this really was the case. Upon his sensitive disposition the family secret, concerning which he had vainly questioned his father on his death-bed, weighed heavily. It set him apart, and kept him apart from anything like intimacy with young men of his own age, because he felt that they too would be always trying to find out that of which he himself was ignorant; and he was not at ease with the older people, his father's contemporaries and neighbours, because he was not sure whether they had any inkling or certain knowledge of the family secret,—whether they were all in a conspiracy to keep him in the darkness to which his father had condemned him from the period of his brother's disappearance. Would Mark Challoner have at last confided the truth to his son, had a little more life, a little longer time been accorded to him? This was the vain question which Miles asked himself as he sat moodily in the library after his solitary dinner, and watched the sun go down in a sea of gold and azure behind the grand old woods of Rowley Court, or strolled about the terrace listlessly, until the night fell. He could never answer it —no one could ever answer it; but this did not keep Miles Challoner from pondering upon it. He felt quite certain that there was but one man in the world who could resolve his doubts, who could tell him the worst,—might it not rather be the best?—of this matter, which so sorely perplexed him. That man was Lord Sandilands. If anyone knew the truth, it was he; but whether Miles would ever hear it from him depended, as he felt, entirely on the terms on which the communication had been made, if it had been made at all, by his father to Lord Sandilands. That the family lawyer knew nothing of it, Miles felt confident; that Mr. Styles, the steward, was as ignorant and as curious, if not as anxious, as himself, he had no doubt whatever. There was no one to share, no one to aid his mental inquietude. Was his brother living, or was he the only—the last—one bearing the old name left?

Very shortly after Mark Challoner's funeral had taken place, his son had instituted the strictest possible search among the documents of all kinds which the house contained, for any letters or papers bearing upon the mysterious occurrences which had changed the aspect of affairs at

Rowley Court while the old Squire's sons were yet boys, and had shut the younger out from his father's house into banishment and oblivion. This search, which Miles had conducted quite alone, and had been careful to keep from the knowledge of the servants, had been entirely unrewarded by success, and had only revealed to Miles a circumstance which still further deepened the mystery which tormented him, and increased its distressing effect. Not only did there not exist among the Squire's papers any memoranda, letters, or documents of any description bearing upon, or having any reference to, the period at which Geoffrey Challoner had left Rowley Court, but none existed in any way, directly or indirectly, relating to him. Not a scrap of his writing as a child, though Miles found his own little letters to his father and mother carefully treasured up, with the correct dates noted upon each packet ; and his portrait, as a baby of three years old, hung over the mantlepiece of his father's bedroom. But there was no likeness of Geoffrey. By an effort of memory Miles recalled the taking of that little portrait ; he remembered how he had sat upon his father's knee, and played with the heavy gold hunting-watch, which was his especial delight—it was ticking away still in a watch-stand in the library—while the artist did his work. He remembered how his hair had been additionally brushed aud curled for the occasion ; and—yes, now he distinctly remembered that Geoffrey's portrait had also been painted. Where was it ? What had been done with it ?

All the circumstances returned to Miles Challoner's memory. The two pictures had hung side by side for years. Where was that of the younger son ? The Squire had gone abroad for a short time, and the brothers had remained at Rowley Court under the care of their tutor. They had both written regularly to their father ; and Miles found all his own letters of that period carefully preserved, arranged according to their dates, and indorsed, in his father's hand, "My Son's Letters, 18—." But there was no scrap of Geoffrey's writing, there was no trace that he had ever lived, to be found within the walls of Rowley Court. Only when Miles went into the room which had been the brothers' study, only when he entered and looked round the long-unused apartments which had been their nursery and play-room, could he realize that there had been two in that stately old house eleven years ago. The room which had been his wife's had always been occupied by the Squire after her death; otherwise Miles would have hoped to find some little memento of his brother there,—there, where he could dimly remember—or was it fancy, and not memory?—a gentle pale face turned wistfully towards him when, a very little child, he was brought to see the fading mother who had been early and mercifully taken away from the evil to come. From evil indeed, from terrible and irremediable evil Miles Challoner felt it must have been; else why the hopeless banishment, why the impenetrable silence, why the apparently complete oblivion? He brooded upon these things in the solitude to which the first few weeks of his proprietorship of Rowley Court were devoted, almost to the exclusion of every other subject of thought; and Mr. Styles found him singularly inattentive and indifferent to the details of his property and his squirearchical duties, as that experienced person laid them before him.

"I can't make him out, and that's the truth," Mr. Styles remarked to Dr. Barford one day that the steward met the doctor taking his gig by a short cut through a lane which formed the boundary of Rowley Court on one side,—"I really can't make him out. He cares for nothing; and it is not natural for a young gentleman like him. I was talking to him this morning about the likely look of the turnips on the Lea Farm, and I'm blessed if he heard one word in ten; and when I asked him a question, just to rouse him up like, he said, 'O, ah! turnips, I think you said? Of course do as you think best;' which was altogether complete nonsense. Of course he's cut up about the Squire; and very natural and right it is he should be so; but it ain't natural and it ain't right to go on as he's going. And it's my belief," said Mr. Styles, as he removed his hat, took his checked pocket-handkerchief out of the crown, gave his face a desponding wipe with it, and replaced it,— "it's my belief as he don't know the difference between turnips and pine-apples; and there's a fine promise too, such as a man might look to getting some credit along of."

"That's bad, Styles; that's bad," said Dr. Barford; "I don't like to hear that my old friend's son is taking to moping. I'll call up at the Court and see him to-morrow. Good-day, Styles;" and the doctor drove on, thinking gravely of the changes he had seen at Rowley Court, though he knew as little of their origin as everybody else knew.

On the following day, as Miles Challoner and the doctor walked together on the stone terrace, Miles stopped on the very spot whence his father had taken his last look at the lands which had called him master so long; and, looking full and earnestly at his companion, asked him: "Dr. Barford, do you know why my brother left his home? Do you know what that grief was which my father had on his mind while he lived, and when he died?"

Dr. Barford hesitated for a moment before he replied to Miles Challoner's question, but his hesitation arose from surprise, not from uncertainty. There was not the least tone of doubt or reserve in his voice and manner as he answered: "No, Mr. Challoner, your question surprises me very much; but I can assure you most positively I know nothing of the matter."

"Did my father never mention it to you? Never, even at the last, when he knew—for he told me so—he was dying?"

"Never," said Dr. Barford; then he added, after a momentary pause, "he did say something to me, on the last occasion when I had any talk with him, which may have had some reference to your brother; but if it had any, it was only incidental, and quite unexplained. He said something about his sharing in the common lot—having a skeleton in the cupboard; but that was all. Nothing more explicit ever passed his lips to me."

"Then, or at any time?" asked Miles.

"Then, or at any time, Mr. Challoner," repeated Dr. Barford gravely; and the two fell into silence, which lasted for several minutes.

At length Miles spoke:

"You really advise me to leave Rowley Court?" he said.

"Certainly I do; if not as a physician—in which capacity you do not require my services, happily—as a friend. You are not naturally of a very active temperament; and moping about here, in a place which is necessarily gloomy just now, and where you have no congenial occupation, will not improve you in that respect. Go up to town for the remainder of the season, and then go abroad for a few months; and you will find that you will come back wonderfully reconciled to being master of Rowley Court."

"I like your advice," said Miles with unusual briskness of tone; "and I think I will take it; at least I will take it so far as going up to town is concerned. As for the rest——"

"As for the rest, you can think of it when the time comes," said the doctor. "And now I must bid you good-bye, and be off. I have to call at Dale and Stourton before I go home to dinner."

As Dr. Barford drove down the wide smooth avenue, between the ranks of tall stately elms which bordered the well-kept road, he thought: "That's a fine young fellow, but of rather a gloomy turn of mind. I hope he may fall in love and marry up in London, and bring a new mistress to the Court."

Miles walked up and down the terrace long after the doctor had left him, and his face wore a brighter and more serene expression than it had been used to wear of late. He had remained at Rowley Court long enough; he knew how his affairs stood now; he had really nothing to keep him there. He could only learn what he most desired to know, if indeed it were possible to learn it at all, from Lord Sandilands, who was just then at his house in London. He would go and stay with Lord Sandilands. Having come to this decision, he turned into the house with a brisker step, and felt the evening which ensued the least dreary through which he had lived since the Squire died.

Had Mark Challoner been of a less autocratic disposition it would have been very difficult, if not impossible, for him to have carried into execution the absolute taboo under which he had placed the subject of Geoffrey's disappearance. But the Squire had been a man of inexorable determination of character; and as he was not at all capricious, and exerted this resolution only when and where it was necessary, he had never met with rebellion on the part of his elder son. What the story of the younger had been, no one knew; no one had any certain indication by which to guess. The tutor to whom the education of the two boys had been intrusted was absent from Rowley Court when the separation intended by Mark Challoner, and destined by Providence, to be final, had taken place; and there was no reason to suppose that Mr. Mordaunt had ever received any information concerning his former pupil from the Squire. Had Miles

Challoner been either older or younger at the time of the occurrence, he might have been unable to observe his father's peremptory command with the reluctant obedience he had manifested until the end, when his pent-up anxiety had found vent in his useless appeal to the dying Squire. But he had outlived the restless irrepressible curiosity of the child, and he had not reached the calm deliberative reasoning of the man. Now that the latter mode of thought had fully come to him, he suffered keenly, as only such sensitive natures have the gift to suffer, from his helpless ignorance of his brother's fate. The thought haunted him. As children, he and Geoffrey had loved each other well enough, after the childish fashion which includes any amount of quarrelling and making-up again; but as boys they had never got on very well together. They were essentially different, with the difference which makes discord, not with the contrast which produces harmony. Miles had always had an unacknowledged consciousness that Geoffrey cared very little about him, and this had had its influence upon the sensitive boy, an influence even stronger than that of the want of accord in the tastes and pursuits of the brothers. As Miles had advanced into manhood, he had come to understand all the appalling gravity of such a sentence as that which his father had passed upon his brother when he forbade the mention of his name in the house where he had been born and bred. With this comprehension came an intense yearning to know the meaning of the sentence,— to be enabled to estimate its justice; a kind of revolt on behalf of the banished brother, in which affection had less share than an abstract love of right, happily strong in the nature of the young man. And now there was no means of satisfying this yearning; the secret had to all appearance died with the Squire, but its consequences remained, to become an almost intolerable burden to Miles Challoner.

Lord Sandilands received his young friend's letter with sincere pleasure. He liked Miles; he liked his ideas and "ways;" he liked his society. The young man had a happy faculty for creating this kind of liking among his fellows. He was large-minded and unselfish, and so he did not neglect or trample upon the feelings of other people, or try their tempers much or often. He was not a brilliant person, and therefore could afford to be good-natured and unaffected;

and though he possessed rather more than an average amount
of information upon most subjects of general interest and importance, there were few men less inclined to display their
knowledge than Miles Challoner. He was disposed to
accord to everybody his or her fair share of conversation,
and had an acquiescent uncritical way with him which made
friends for him, particularly among women. Without being
in the least deserving of that truly opprobrious epithet, a
lady's man, Miles had strong partizans among " the conflict-
ing gender;" and women who found him a very impracticable
subject for flirtation were ready to acknowledge that his
notions of friendship were peculiarly exalted and practical.
People who knew him, but had never troubled themselves
to think about him particularly, would nevertheless have
answered promptly to any question respecting him, that he
was a fine honourably-minded fellow, and rather clever than
otherwise ; and the few who knew him well would have
said substantially the same thing in more numerous and
perhaps stronger words. The truth is, it was about all that
could be said of Miles Challoner at the important period of
his life which witnessed his father's death and his own
succession to the family property, with its penalties and
privileges of squiredom. He had reached man's estate some
years before ; but there had been nothing in the course and
manner of his life previously to develop his character
strongly,—to bring its good or evil traits into prominence.
It had been an even, prosperous, happy life, on which he had
entered with all the advantages of high animal spirits and
unblemished health. Whether he had in him the stuff
which either defies or moulds destiny, the courage which is
matured in suffering, the truth and steadfastness of character
which are at once weapons and armour in the strife of
human existence, it was for time to tell.

Time did tell.

" I'm uncommonly glad you have made up your mind to
come to town," wrote Lord Sandilands to Miles Challoner ;
" it is the best thing you can do ; and so far from being
disrespectful to your father's memory, it is your best way of
avoiding what might even appear disrespectful to those
who are no doubt watching you pretty closely. You have
not a taste for the things the Squire (God bless him !)
delighted in, and you cannot affect to have ; because, in the

first place, it is not in you to affect, and, in the second, you would certainly be found out by Mr. Styles. (Ceres and Pomona! shall I ever forget a dialogue between your father and him about the best crop for the Bayhamsfields?) You will offend your new people much less by absence than by indifference, depend upon it. Then you can thoroughly depend on Styles; and you can always put agricultural enthusiasm on paper. So come up, my dear boy; and the sooner the better."

Miles Challoner went to London, and very soon after he arrived there "time" began "to tell."

<hr>

CHAPTER III.

CARABAS HOUSE.

CARABAS HOUSE is in Beaumanoir Square, as most people know. Long before the smart stuccoed residences—with their plate-glass windows, their conservatoried balconies, their roomy porticoes—sprung up, like Aladdin's palaces, at the command of the great wizard-builder, Compo, who so recently died a baronet and a millionaire; when the ground on which Beaumanoir Square now stands was a dreary swamp, across which our great-grandmothers, in fear of their lives, were carried to Ranelagh, Carabas House stood, a big, rambling, red-bricked mansion, surrounded on all sides by a high wall, and looking something between a workhouse, a lunatic asylum, and a gaol. To the Marquis of Carabas of those days it mattered little what was the aspect of his ancestral home, as he, from the time of his accession, had resolutely declined to see it, or any other part of the domain whence his title and estates were derived, preferring to spend his life on the Continent of Europe, in the society of agreeable men and women, and in the acquisition of a splendid collection of pictures, statues, and other *objets d'art*, which at his lordship's lamented demise were sold in Paris at a world-famous sale extending over many days, the pecuniary result of which was hailed with the greatest satisfaction by his lordship's heir. For Mr. Purrington, his lordship's cousin, who succeeded to the title and estates, wanted money very badly indeed, he had been speculating for a very long time on the chances of his succession, and he had to pay very dearly for these speculations. He had contested his county in the Tory interest four separate times, at a cost known only to himself, his wife, and his head agent. He had married the daughter of an Irish peer ; a lovely woman, full of talent, affectionate, loyal, energetic, and thoroughly understanding her position as a county member's wife, but with a number of impecunious relations, all of whom looked for assistance to the heir to an English marquisate. He was a crack shot, and always paired about the 25th of July for the remainder of the session, having, according to his own account, the great luck of having one of the best Scotch moors "lent to him" for three weeks from the 12th. He was a capital judge of a horse, a keen rider to hounds, and the invariable occupant of a little box near Egerton Lodge, with a stud sufficient to see him "out" four days a week ; but this, as he pathetically put it, was his "only expense." In the season Lady Fanny had her Wednesday-evening receptions, when a perpetual stream of fashionables, political people, and the usual ruck of young men who are met everywhere, would filter from ten till one through her little drawing-rooms in Clarges Street ; and her Saturday dinners of eight, which were very good and very enjoyable, and where pleasant people in various social circles met together without the dread of seeing their names announced in the fashionable journals. But all these things cost a great deal of money ; and when Mr. Purrington became the Marquis of Carabas, he was very nearly at the end of his tether.

The marquisate of Carabas, however, was by no means an empty title, a grand position lacking means to support its proper state, than which it is impossible to fancy anything more painful. During the late lord's lifetime the revenue had very far exceeded the expenditure, and the Parisian, sale had left a very large balance at Coutts's ; so that the new people entered upon their estate with great comfort, and were enabled to carry out their peculiarly extensive views of life without embarrassing themselves in the slightest degree. It was shortly after their accession that the big brick screen-wall was replaced by a light and elegant bronze railing ; that the rambling red-bricked mansion was trans-

formed into a modern stone house ; that the Marchioness of
Carabas took her position as a leader of *ton*, and in Carabas
House, so long black and desolate and abandoned, chimneys
smoked, and lights blazed, and music resounded, and the
best people in London found themselves gathered together
three times a week.

The best people ?   The very best.

It was the fashion in certain circles to talk of " the
mixture " which you met at Carabas House ; and the young
Duchess of Taffington (whose father was old Bloomer the banker
of Lombard-street, and whose grandfather was old Blöom
the money-lender and diamond-merchant of Amsterdam)
and old Lady Clanronald, with whom her husband, then the
Hon. Ulick Strabane, fell in love, from seeing her looking
over the blind in her father's (the apothecary's) window in
Drogheda,—both these great ladies shrugged their very
different pairs of shoulders whenever the Marchioness's
receptions were alluded to before them ; but neither of these
leaders of fashion could deny that princes of the blood, royal
dukes, stars and garters, ambassadors, belles of the season,
Foreign-Office clerks, and all the great creatures of the day,
were blocked together, week after week, on the staircase at
Carabas House ; or that the Marchioness herself took *pas*
and precedence, according to her rank, and was one of the
most distinguished and most highly-thought-of guests
wherever she chose to go.

" That's so ! " as Jack Hawkes, of the F. O., would
remark to his familiars; " neither the Duchess nor old
Clanronald can get over that, and that's what makes them
so wild ; and as to the mixture they talk about, that's lions.
She's in great form, don't you know, Lady Carabas is, and
quite fit, but her weakness is lions ; and I'm bound to say
that you meet some people at Carabas House who are quite
out of the hunt.   If any fellow gets talked about, no matter
what he is—writing fellow, painting fellow, fiddling fellow
—I'll lay odds you'll find him there.   There's what's his
name ?—Burkinyoung : man who made a stir last year with
his poems ; they had him down there, sir, at their place on
the river—Weir Lodge—and he used to sit on the lawn
under the trees with Lady Carabas pouring eau-de-cologne
on his head, and some of her lot—Maude Allingham, and
Agnes Creswell, and that lot, don't you know ?—fanning

him and keeping the flies off while he composed ; no one was allowed to come near for fear of disturbing him. Give you my honour, heard it first-hand from Chinny Middleton of the Blues, who pulled up from Windsor in his canoe, and was going to land, as usual, and got warned off, by George, as though he'd got the plague on board ! "

There was a good deal of truth in Mr. Hawkes's remarks, Lady Carabas being Mrs. Leo Hunter on a very superior scale. Her passion was that every one distinguished not merely in her own rank in life but in every other should be seen in her rooms ; and from her position and by her fascinating manner she generally managed to attain her object. The pilot of the state ship, at a period when opposition winds were howling loud and the political horizon was black with threatened storm, would find time to pass a few minutes at one of Lady Carabas's receptions, however haggard his looks, however burning his brain. The right honourable gentleman the leader of the Opposition, who for the last month had been gathering himself together for a tiger-like spring on the state pilot, might have been seen, on the night before he made his grand onslaught, jammed into a corner of the staircase at Carabas House, looking like the Sphinx in evening dress, and pleasantly bantering Mr. Mulvaney, the celebrated " special correspondent " of the *Statesman*. Any one talked of in any way ; the *belles* of the season ; pretty women, presentable of course, but quite out of the Carabas set ; dawning lights in politics, no matter of what party ; artists, young and old—of every one whom you saw at Carabas House you would learn that they had done something special ; indeed Jack Hawkes, an invaluable *cicerone*, could talk for two hours on a grand night, and not get through his list. " Who are all these strange people that one sees nowhere else ? Well, everybody's somebody, and it's difficult to know where to begin. Let's see. That short, stout, common-looking man is Vireduc, the great engineer and contractor—builds bridges, railroads, and those kind of things, don't you know ?— horrible fellow, who's always telling you he came to London with eightpence in his pocket, and rose from nothing, as though one couldn't see that. Woman sitting this side the ottoman is Mrs. Goodchild ; writes novels—pretty good, they say. I don't read ; I haven't any time. Her husband's somewhere about ; but he's nobody—only asked because of his wife. The little man talking to her is Bistry the surgeon—have your leg off before you can say 'knife ;' and the brown-faced man, who looks so bored, is Sir Alan Tulwar, Indian army man, made K.C.B. for something he did out there—Punjaub, don't you know ? The little man with the big head is Polaski, the flute-player ; and the fat man with the red face is Ethelred Jinks, the Queen's Counsel. That pretty little fair girl is Miss Wren, who shot the burglar down in Hampshire three years ago ; and the little boy in black, as you call him, is Jules Brissot, the Red Republican, who was blown off a barricade on the 4th of December, and settled down here as a—what do you call it ?—tutor."

This will suffice as a specimen of Mr. Hawkes's conversation, which, on such occasions, had the singular merit of having a substratum of truth.

But though lions of all kinds were to be found roaring during the season at Carabas House, none were so welcome as the musical lions, both native and foreign. In her younger days, Lady Carabas had had a pretty little voice herself, and even in Clarges Street she had always managed to secure some of the best professional talent at a very much less expense than any of her friends ; and when once Lord Carabas had succeeded, "musical mossoo," as Jack Hawkes was accustomed to call all foreigners who played or sung professionally, had his head-quarters in Beaumanoir Square. Heinrich Katzenjammer, who, being a native of Emmerich on the Lower Rhine, thought proper to advertise in the English newspapers in the French language, had not been "de retour" many hours before his limp glazed card was on the hall-table at Carabas House. Baton, the *chef d'orchestre*, would as soon have thought of being absent from his conductor's stool on a Saturday night as from Lady Carabas's luncheon-table on a Sunday afternoon. There the most promising pupils of the Academy of Music made their *débuts* in cantatas or operettas, written by distinguished amateurs, and thereby considered themselves entitled ever after to describe themselves as " of the nobility's concerts ; " and there, on festival nights, could you check off the principal singers and players whom London delighted to honour, with the amateurs, the *dilettanti*, and the *cognoscienti*, who always follow in their wake.

It was a soft bright night in early summer, and Beaumanoir Square was filled with flashing lamps, and whirling carriages, and stamping horses, and excited drivers, and roaring linkmen. It was a grand night at Carabas House, and all London was expected there. The police had enough to do to make the vehicles keep in line ; and when some of tho royal carriages familiarly used the royal privilege and dashed through here and cut in there, the confusion increased a thousandfold ; and it was with the greatest difficulty that the crowd surging round the door were thrust back right and left to allow the visitors to enter, or were prevented from casting themselves under the wheels of the carriages as they drew up, with the recklessness of Juggernaut victims. Halfway down the line was a perfectly-appointed brougham, in which sat Miles Challoner and the friend with whom he was staying. Lord Sandilands was in every respect a remarkable-looking man ; tall and upright, with a polished bald head slightly fringed with snow-white soft hair ; thin clean-cut features ; grey eyes, from which most of the fire had faded ; and small carefully-trimmed grey whiskers. His appearance and manners were those of a past age ; now in his evening dress he wore a high stiff white muslin cravat, an elaborately got-up cambric shirt frill, a blue coat with brass buttons, white waistcoat, black trousers fitting tightly round the ankles, silk stockings and shoes. His voice was particularly soft and clear, as replying to some remark of his companion, he said : " No, indeed ; I think both you and I are perfectly right ; you in consenting to come, I in having persuaded you ; besides, I should have scarcely dared to present myself to Lady Carabas without you. Her ladyship's dictum is that you require rousing, and to-night is to be the first experiment in rousing you."

" Her ladyship is very kind to interest herself in me," said Miles. " I have no claim upon her thoughts."

" My dear fellow," said Lord Sandilands, " you will very soon see that Lady Carabas interests herself about everybody and everything. That is her *métier*. She will talk to the Bishop of Boscastle about the Additional Curates' Fund, and to Sir Charles Chifney about his chance for the Leger. She knows what price Scumble got for his Academy picture ; and can tell you the plot of Spofforth's five-act play, which is as yet unwritten. She could tell you what the Duke of Brentford said to Tom Forbes, who arrived late on escort-duty at the last Drawing-room—she couldn't quote the Duke's exact words, which were full-flavoured; and could give you the heads of the charge which Judge Minos will deliver on the great libel case ; and with all that she dresses as well as Lady Capisbury herself, and bears the whole weight of that household on her own shoulders. There's no estate in Britain better managed than Carabas, and her ladyship is her own agent, steward, bailiff—everything."

" She must be a wonderful woman."

" Wonderful ! there's nothing like her ! Lord Carabas thinks of nothing but shooting and fishing. Her eldest son, the Earl of Booterstown, is a religious monomaniac ; and her youngest, Lord Grey de Malkin, is one of your political new lights, lecturing at mechanics' institutes, and making speeches to working-men. You know the kind of fellow. Now, here we are !—Tell Fisher to wait, James,"—to the footman,—" we sha'n't stay very long."

The hall was filled with people, all of whom the old gentleman seemed to know, and greeted with somewhat stately courtesy. " A regular Carabas crush," whispered he to Miles, as they commenced the ascent of the staircase. " Everybody here. The Lord Chancellor next to you, and the Bishop of Boscastle coming down the stairs. He has evidently dined here, sweet old thing ; and is going away before the worldly music begins.—How do you do, my lord ? I trust Mrs. Shum is well !—Deuced fine woman, by the way, is Mrs. Shum, my dear Miles.—Ha, Ellenbogen ! you in London, and I've not seen you ? Only arrived last night, eh ? Come to me to-morrow, eh ? *Au revoir !*—That is the famous German violinist ; nothing like his touch in the world—so crisp, so perfectly sympathetic. There's Lady Carabas at her post, of course. Brave woman, breasting this surging ocean of visitors. Gad, how glad she must be when it's all over ! "

Following his friend's glance, Miles looked up and saw Lady Carabas stationed at the head of the staircase. A tall handsome woman of fifty, with all the look and bearing of a *grande dame,* a little softened by the frank geniality of her manner. She received Miles Challoner, on his presentation to her, with something more than mere graciousness

—with cordiality ; then, turning to Lord Sandilands, said, " She's here."

"Is she, indeed ? " said the old gentleman with equal earnestness.

" Yes, and in excellent spirits : I have not the least doubt of her success."

" That is delightful ; " and they passed on. When they had gone a few steps, Miles asked his friend who was the lady of whom he and Lady Carabas were speaking.

" My dear fellow," said Lord Sandilands with a little chuckle, " I haven't the remotest notion. Dear Lady Carabas is always giving one half-confidences about people she's interested in, and 'pon my life I'm too old to open my heart indiscriminately, and make myself partaker of the joys and sorrows of half the world. So, as she's a dear good creature, and I would not offend her for the world, I nod my head, and grin, and pretend I know all about it ; and I find that answers very well."

Miles laughed at the old gentleman's evident satisfaction, and they entered the rooms. A large movable platform, so slightly raised as to give the performers sufficient altitude above the spectators without disconcerting them by any pretensions to a stage, occupied one end of the spacious apartment, a recent erection built specially for concert-giving purposes, and with all the latest acoustic improvements. Opposite the platform, bristling with seats for the instrumentalists, stood the conductor's desk. To the right of this were a few benches for the most distinguished guests, and behind it were the seats for the general company. All the seats were unoccupied at present, and the company were grouped together about the room, chatting freely. It was early in the season at present ; and that frightful lack of conversation which necessarily falls on people who have naturally very little to say, and who, having seen each other every night for three months, have exhausted that little, had not as yet made itself felt. Miles Challoner, as he looked round on the beautiful women so exquisitely dressed, the brightly-lighted room, the inexpressible air of luxury and elegance which pervaded the entire scene, as he thought that for the future he might, if he so chose, have similar pleasant resorts at his command, felt the oppressive thoughts, the dull, dead level of world-weariness and vapidity, gradually slipping from him.   His eyes brightened, he looked round him eagerly, and his whole demeanour was so fresh and spirited and youthful as to seriously annoy several *blasé* young men of two or three-and-twenty, who had long since used up all signs of youth, and who inquired of each other who was the rustic, gushing person that old Sandilands had brought with him.

Lord Sandilands had himself noticed the change in his friend's manner, and was about to rally him on it, when the musicians came trooping into the room and took their places. Sir Purcell Arne, the well-known amateur composer, who was to conduct, rapped the desk in front of him; the foreign professionals who had settled themselves modestly in the back rows, uttered profound sounds of " Hsh—sh ! " and the company generally seated themselves.   Lord Sandilands and Miles were proceeding with the rest, when the former saw himself beckoned by Lady Carabas to the place of distinction by her side, and he took his young friend with him.

The overture ought to have been very well played, for it was very much applauded at its conclusion, though, as Jack Hawkes remarked to the young lady sitting next to him, that might possibly have been because they were so glad it was over.   It is certain that during the performance several of the more excitable foreigners ground their teeth, and covered their ears with their hands, while at its close Sir Purcell Arne addressed two recreant members of the orchestra—the second cornet and the first clarionet, being respectively a young gentleman in the Coldstreams, and an old gentleman in the India Office—in terms of the strongest opprobrium.   Sir Purcell's good temper was restored after his son, a favourite pupil of Ellenbogen's, had played a solo on the violin ; and during the applause consequent thereon, he crossed over to Lady Carabas's seat, and whispered, "She's quite ready; shall I bring her in ? "   Lady Carabas, too much excited to speak, gave him an affirmative nod ; and the enthusiasm had scarcely subsided, to be renewed with tenfold force as Sir Purcell returned leading by the hand a young lady, whom, with one of his best bows, he left facing the audience, while he went back to his conductor's desk.

The young lady stood perfectly unmoved by the storm of

applause which hailed her arrival, the only sign of emotion which she betrayed being a slight contraction of her thin decisive lips ; and this was only momentary. She was a decidedly pretty girl, Miles thought ; with rich brown eyes, and well-formed features, and slight though rounded figure. In her dark chestnut hair, which was banded close round her head, and gathered into a large knot behind, she wore one white rose, and another in the front of her plain white-silk dress. Other ornament had she none, save a gold locket with a horse-shoe in turquoises on her neck, and a bracelet, a band of plain gold, on one arm. Who was this handsome and distinguished-looking girl who was received with so much *empressement* ? Miles Challoner took up a perfumed programme that lay beside him, and read her name—Miss Grace Lambert.

CHAPTER   IV

BREAKING COVER.

MISS GRACE LAMBERT ! Who was she ? The programme, of course, told nothing but her name, and when Miles Challoner turned to his companion for the purpose of inquiring further, he saw that his brows were knit, and his lips tightly clenched. Miles looked at Lord Sandilands in surprise, but forbore to question him. It was evident that the people in his immediate vicinity were equally unable to assuage his curiosity, as they were all talking and chattering together, and throwing glances towards the occupant of the platform, who stood totally unmoved. Then Sir Purcell Arne, looking round with a half-anxious, half-triumphant air, gave the customary three taps on his desk, and with a wave of his baton led the orchestra into the prelude. It was a simple English air— very simple—with a pathetic *refrain*, and out from the harmonious *ensemble* of the musicians came a soft sweet bird-like voice, beginning mellowly and low, then rising into a clear pure treble, a volume of lark-like utterance, a continuous ripple of sound, such as is seldom heard in human voice. Few notes had been uttered before their effect became visible on the whole assemblage—amongst the foreigners first ; on the back benches, where were gathered the hirsute professionals honoured with the *entrée* to Lady Carabas' concerts, there was an immediate movement, a simultaneous pricking of ears and elevation of eyebrows, culminating into a general impossible-to-be-suppressed " A—h ! " of intense delight. Then the enthusiasm spread. Impressible young girls, with the *nil-admirari* breeding scarcely yet habitual to them, looked timidly towards their *chaperones*, as though pleading, " For Heaven's sake, let us for one moment be natural, and give vent to the delight with which this girl has inspired us." Said *chaperones*, with some faint reminiscence of nature unbusked and unsteeled by conventionality, sought relief in faintly tapping their kidded palms with their fans. Old boys, dragged away from after-dinner naps, or cosy house-dinners at the clubs, to do family duty, and expecting nothing but driest musical classicalities, expressed their gratitude in strident "bravas." Even the gilded youth of the period, surprised out of its usual inanity into a feeble semblance of life and earnestness, condescended to express its opinion of the singer, that she was not " half bad, don't you know ? " And its component members inquired of each other, " who the devil is she ? " On Lady Carabas' handsome face the hard-set look of anxiety had softened into the blandest smile of triumph ; old Sir Purcell Arne's blond moustache bristled with delight ; and at the conclusion of the ballad, when the singer, rising to the occasion, had sent a flood of melody surging through the room, now dying away in softest trills and most harmonious cadences, the enthusiasm could no longer be restrained, and amidst sonorous applause breaking forth from every side, the amateur instrumentalists leading the van, and Lady Carabas herself, regardless of appearances or of the value of three-buttoned gloves, clapping her hands with the ardour of the most zealous member of a professional *claque*,—Miss Grace Lambert, perfectly composed, and with the slightest bow in recognition of her triumph, laid her fingers daintily on Sir Purcell Arne's tremblingly-proffered arm, and disappeared from public view. Ten minutes' interval now, much needed. Impossible, after such a display, to keep the coterie quiet, and it breaks up at once into twenty little knots, all with the same *refrain* of praise, differently expressed : " *Das ist aber 'was Schönes !*" " *Tiens, tiens, Jules ! v'là donc un rossignol charmant !*" "That's what I call good singing, for an Englishwoman, that is, Veluti ! *Capisco, signor !*" "Tell you what it is, old fella ; since poor Bosio, you know, never heard anything like that, don't you know? It's A 1, don't you know ?" Frank testimonies these, from the male sex ; chiming in with "Dearest Lady Carabas, O, how I congratulate you ! Where did you find such a treasure; Charmin', quite charmin' ; so lady-like, and all that kind of thing. Quite a nice-looking person, too !" from the female portion of the audience.

She had vanished, and Miles Challoner remained mute and dazed. Of beauty he had always had a keen appreciation—that is, beauty as he understood it—showing itself in tolerable regularity of feature, in grace and aristocratic *tournure*. Red-and-white women, were they duchesses or dairymaids—and it must be owned that when Nature alone is depended upon they are generally the latter—found no favour in Miles's eyes. He used to say he liked a "bred"-looking woman ; and here was one who, so far as appearance went, might have been a Plantagenet. And her voice —good Heavens !—was there ever heard anything so completely enthralling ! The blood yet danced in his veins with the delight excited when that low tremulous utterance, gradually rising into trills of lark-like melody, first stole upon his ear. No wonder that all in the room were talking loudly in her praise. All ? No. Rapt in his own delight, Miles had forgotten to speak to Lord Sandilands, to whom he partly owed the pleasure he had just experienced, and he turned to repair his neglect.

Lord Sandilands was sitting "quiet as a stone." He had recovered his gloves, and his long shapely white hands were tightly clasped together on his knee. Despite the tight clasp, the hands twitched nervously, and on the old man's well-cut features Miles noticed a worn pinched look, such as he had never before observed. Lord Sandilands' eyes, too, were downcast, and he did not raise them even when Miles addressed him.

"Was there ever anything so charming as that young lady ?"

"She has a very sweet voice."

"Sweet! it is perfectly entrancing! I had no idea such sounds could be produced by human throat; and then her appearance so thoroughly lady-like, and such an exquisite profile! Why, even you, who go in so strictly for the classical, must have been satisfied with the profile!"

"I scarcely observed her."

"Scarcely observed her! Why, my dear old friend, that is very unlike your usual habit when a pretty woman is in question, unless, indeed, you were so enthralled by her voice that you cared for nothing else."

"Ye-es; that was it, I suppose—I—"

The conversation was interrupted by the return of the other guests, who, summoned by Sir Purcell Arne's preliminary taps, came back to their seats to hear the rest of the concert. All rustle and talk and chatter still. "Never was anything like it. I'm sure I can't tell where you pick up these wonderful people, dear Lady Carabas. And what comes next, dear Lady Carabas? O, now we're to have Mr. Wisk's operetta—for the first time; never was played anywhere before. You know Ferdinand Wisk? clever creature! there he is, comin' to conduct it himself. Sh—h!"

That clever creature, Mr. Ferdinand Wisk, who was supposed to be a scion of the aristocracy, but whose real mission in life seemed to be to devote himself to the affairs, public and private, of every member of the musical world, English or foreign, advanced rapidly through the room, and took the baton which Sir Purcell handed to him amidst general applause. Mr. Wisk's operetta needs but little mention here. It was bright and sparkling, and would have been more original if the overture had not been cribbed from Auber, and the concerted pieces from Offenbach; but as it was, it did remarkably well, affording opportunities for two young ladies and two young gentlemen to sing very much out of tune; for the funny man of the company to convulse the audience with his drolleries; and for the audience generally to repay themselves for their silence during Miss Grace Lambert's ballad, by chatting without stint. Perhaps the only two persons in the room who did not avail themselves of this opportunity were Lord Sandilands and Miles Challoner. The former, having glanced at the programme, and noticed that Miss Lambert's name did not appear again therein, made a half-muttered apology to Lady Carabas about the "heat," and left the room very shortly after the commencement of Mr. Wisk's performance; while the latter could not shake off the spell which held him, and which, during all the comic gentleman's funniments and all the others' bad singing, gave but Grace Lambert's voice to his ears, her face and figure to his eyes.

To supper now, foreigners first—making great running, and leaving every one else far behind; leaping on to edibles and dashing at potables with such vigour as to cause one to think they had not dined, as indeed many of them had not. And now, more congratulation amongst visitors, more "Did you evers?" a perfect whirlwind of "Don't you knows?" and "only to think of dear Lady Carabas being so fortunate, and such a wonderful acquisition even to *her* set!" Ferdinand Wisk, a little depressed at being thrown into the background by the superior attractions of Miss Lambert; and the funny man of the company feeling himself not sufficiently appreciated, and thirsting for Miss Lambert's blood—both, however, consoled by old Piccolo, the fashionable music-master, who is popularly supposed to have been allied with Auber and Offenbach in writing Mr. Wisk's operetta, and who tells them that Miss Lambert's triumph is a mere *succès d'estime*, and that she will "go out like that—pouf!" Piccolo snapping his fingers and blowing out an imaginary candle in explanation. Foreigners having been fed, and a proper quantity of champagne and seltzer-water having been duly drunk, it enters into the minds of some of the younger guests that dancing would be a pleasant pastime for the remainder of the night, such exercise being sometimes permitted at the concerts, when Lady Carabas is in especially good temper, which is the case to-night apparently; for servants are instructed to clear the concert-room, a band is improvised, and the floor is soon covered with whirling couples.

On these dancers Miles Challoner stood gazing with an abstracted air. At the conclusion of the concert he had moved with the rest, and on passing Lady Carabas had addressed to her a few words of compliment on the success of her evening; words which, although Miles did not remark it, were pleasantly received; for though Lady Carabas had come to that time of life when she was called an "old thing" by very young ladies, the epithet having "dear" or "horrid," according to the speaker's tastes, attached to it, she still delighted in the admiration of men, if they were clever or handsome, and purred under their praises with ineffable satisfaction. Whether Miles Challoner was clever, Lady Carabas had yet to learn; but she knew that he was undeniably handsome, and that he was a credit to her evening. Many other people in the rooms had thought so too; and though strange faces were more frequently seen at Carabas House than in any other frequented by the same set, Miles's tall figure and frank face had excited a certain amount of languid curiosity, and the "new importation," as he was called by people who had been twice to the house, made a very favourable first impression.

He was not the least conscious of it, though, nor, had he been, would he have particularly cared. When Lord Sandilands' brougham drew up under the portico of Carabas House, when Miles, after climbing up the staircase—a unit in the throng of pretty women and distinguished men—was presented to Lady Carabas, the young man felt that he was entering on a new and entrancing sphere of life, in which he was henceforth to move; and his thoughts in the little time he allowed himself for thinking, were of a roseate hue. He had sufficient money to live easily with those people amongst whom Lord Sandilands' introduction would give him position, and place him at his ease. Emerging from the dull country-squire life to which he at first had imagined himself relegated, he should now mix on excellent footing with that society which he had always thought of with envy, but never thoroughly comprehended. In a word, when Sir Purcell Arne left the room for the purpose of fetching the new singer, there was not in England, perhaps, at that moment, a more thoroughly happy young man than Miles Challoner. But ever since Grace Lambert's voice had fallen on his ear, he had been a different man. As he listened to her, as he gazed upon her handsome face and elegant figure, he sat enthralled, spell-bound by her charm. And when she had gone, her voice remained ringing in his ears, her face and figure remained before his eyes, while a total change, to him entirely unaccountable, had come over his thoughts. What had sent his mind wandering back to the early days of his childhood? What had suddenly brought to his recollection his brother Geoffrey as he last saw him, a bright, bold, daring boy, persistent in carrying through whatever might be uppermost in his mind, and undeterred by fear of his tutor, or even of his stern father? He had just decided with delight upon the course of life which he would pursue in future; but now he wondered whether he had decided rightly. Ought he not, in his position as head of the Challoner family, to live down at the old place, as all his forefathers, save his uncle Howard, who was universally hated, had done? Was it not his bounden duty to be there, ready, when called upon, to give advice and assistance to his tenantry and poorer neighbours? And that thought of Geoffrey! Ought he not, even in spite of all his father had said, to have taken some steps to trace his brother's career from the time of his leaving home, at all events to endeavour to ascertain the reason of the fatal sentence of banishment which had been pronounced against him? Ought he not—and then he found himself wondering what connection Miss Grace Lambert's voice and face had with these thoughts, and then he roused himself from the reverie into which he had fallen, and things material took their proper shapes and forms to his eyes: he returned from the dim past to the bright present, from the play-room at Rowley Court to the ball-room of Carabas House.

It was getting rather late now for the outer world and common people in general, but not for Carabas House, where the meaning of the word was unknown. The great hall-porter in his younger and slimmer days must have served his apprenticeship as boots at a railway hotel, the only position in which he could have acquired his faculty of sleeplessness. Men constantly spent what they were pleased to call the early part of the evening at Carabas House, went on to other balls, which they "saw out," and returned, certain to find "some one left." The latest lounger at Pratt's, the most devoted attendant at the Raleigh, knew that during the season he should always be able to get his glass of sherry and seltzer in Beaumanoir Square, no matter what time of night it might be. The linkman, whose light had long since paled its ineffectual fire and gone out, seldom left before the milkman arrived; and the pair interchanged confidence about the house and its owners, as is the custom of such people.

The dancing was not quite so animated as when Miles had last looked at it. Careful men who called themselves seven-and-twenty, and who were really five-and-thirty, mindful of all the outing they had before them during the season, had gone home to bed. Those who remained were very young men and very determined girls, whose wearing *chaperones* sat blinking round the room, or solaced themselves with stabbing each other, and tearing to pieces the reputation of their common friends, on the landing. But Lady Carabas was not with these ; she was standing at the far end of the room, surrounded by half a dozen men, with whom she was holding an animated conversation. One of them, to whom she appeared to pay particular attention, had his back turned to Miles, but seemed to be young, and of a slight wiry figure. Miles noticed this man specially, partly from the evident enjoyment which Lady Carabas took in his conversation, and partly from a peculiarity in his appearance, so far as it could be gathered from a back view, in the horsey cut of his clothes, and the slang attitude, rounded shoulders, and hands plunged deep into his trousers pockets, in which he stood conversing with his hostess. Miles had not noticed this gentleman before, and was wondering who he was, when a valsing couple, looking tired and out of breath, stopped immediately in front of him.

" That was a grand spin," said the gentleman ; " the room's splendid just now. Got rid of all those awful people who can't dance a bit, don't you know ? and do nothing but get in your way. You're in great feather to-night, Miss Grenville."

" Thanks, very much," said the young lady, smiling ; " a compliment from you is quite the most charming thing possible—perhaps because it's so rare, Mr. Ashleigh."

" 'Gad, I don't know ! " replied the gentleman, who was two-and-twenty years of age, and who might have been two-and-sixty for calm self-possession and *savoir faire.* " I'm rather a good hand at saying nice things, I think."

" When you don't mean them, perhaps ? "

" No, no. Now you are down upon me too sharp, Miss Grenville ; 'pon my word you are ; and I can never say anything, nice or not nice, at this time of night. Let's finish the *valse*."

" I'm afraid I must not stay any longer, Mr. Ashleigh ! Really, it's quite too cruel to poor mamma ; and we've two dances to-morrow night that we must go to. Besides, Lady Carabas is dying to get rid of us."

" Don't look as if she was, does she, Miss Grenville ? Laughing away ; look at her. Wonderful woman, Lady Carabas ! "

" Who is the gentleman she is talking to ? "

" That ? O, that's a man that's everywhere about."

" I'm as wise as I was before.   What is his name ? where does he come from ? "

" His name ! 'pon my word, Miss Grenville, I forget. I'll go and ask him, if you like. Ah, I know, he's a great friend of Ticehurst's.   You know Ticehurst ? "

" I have met Lord Ticehurst."

" Met him !   O ah, yes ; always know what ladies mean when they say they've 'met' anybody ; mean they hate 'em. Well, if you don't like Ticehurst, I don't think you'd like that man ; they're very much alike, specially Pompey, don't you know ?   Bad egg, and that kind of thing."

" You are enigmatic, but sufficiently expressive, Mr. Ashleigh.   I think I comprehend you, at least.   But if he is that kind of person, why is he admitted here ? "

" Dear Miss Grenville, it's exactly because he is that kind of person that they are glad to see him here.   He's somebody in his line, don't you know ; though it's a bad line. His name, which I forget, is always mentioned in *Bell* and the sporting-papers, and that kind of thing ; and he's a— what do you call it ?—notoriety on the turf.   By Jove ! Coote is just going to make those fellows leave off. Do let's finish the *valse*."

The couple whirled away to the last bars of the music ; and Miles, who had perforce overheard this conversation, glanced across the room at the subject of it, who was still standing with his face averted, talking to Lady Carabas.   " A pleasant man that, if all my dancing friend said of him is true," said Miles to himself.   " I wonder what Lord Sandilands would think of him ?   Pshaw ! he'd take it like a man of the world ; and—eh ? there is the old gentleman, making his way over here; where can he have been all the evening?"

Whatever doubts Miles Challoner may have felt as to the line of conduct which Lord Sandilands would adopt towards the gentleman on whom Miles had bestowed so much observation, they were destined to be speedily set at rest. As Lord Sandilands passed the group at the other end of the room, Lady Carabas beckoned to him; and by the way in which he and the unknown bowed to each other, Miles easily divined that the ceremony of introduction had taken place. With a half-smile at the incongruity just perpetrated, Miles was making his way across the room, when a servant came up to him and said, "I beg your pardon, sir, are you Mr. Lloyd?" Miles had scarcely time to reply in the negative, when the groom of the chambers, a very solemn-looking personage, who was passing at the moment, and who heard the inquiry, said, "That is Mr. Lloyd talking to her ladyship, James. What is wanted?"

"Only Lord Ticehurst, sir, told me to tell Mr. Lloyd he couldn't wait any longer;" and the man proceeded on his mission. Meanwhile Lady Carabas' quick eye had spied Miles approaching, and she advanced to meet him. "Mr. Challoner," said she, with a gracious smile, "I'm afraid you've had a horribly dull evening; been dreadfully bored, and all that kind of thing. O, don't deny it; I'm sure of it. But the fact is, I thought Lord Sandilands would tell you who people were, and introduce you, and all that; and now I find he has been poked away in the library all night, looking at some horrid old political caricatures. Ridiculous of him, I tell him, to strain his eyes over such nonsense. He looks quite pale and worn. You must come and help me to scold him. By the way, I must introduce you to a very charming friend of mine, who fortunately is still here —Mr. Lloyd," touching him with her fan, "let me introduce Mr. Challoner."

The young man addressed wheeled round when he felt the touch on his arm, and before the last words were uttered he confronted Miles Challoner as Lady Carabas pronounced the name; and at that instant the light died out of his small and sunken blue eyes, his cheeks became colourless, and his thin lips closed tightly under his long fair moustache. Simultaneously a bright scarlet flush overspread Miles

Challoner's face. Both then bowed slightly, but neither spoke ; and immediately afterwards Miles turned sharply on his heel, and wishing Lady Carabas a formal "good night," hurried from the room.

"My dear boy," said Lord Sandilands—they were in the brougham going home—"you must pardon my saying that your treatment of Mr.—Mr. Lloyd was *brusque* to a degree. Supposing him even to be a highly objectionable person, the fact that you were introduced to him by Lady Carabas should have assured him—well, a more gracious reception, to say the least of it. You—why, what the deuce is the matter, Miles? you're dead-white, and your hand shakes ?"

"Nothing, dear old friend. I shall be all right again directly. That man—was I rude to him ? I scarcely knew what I said or did. That man is one whom it was my father's most urgent wish I should never meet or know."

CHAPTER V.

MEMORY-HAUNTED.

HAD Lord Sandilands been less preoccupied by certain thoughts, and less disturbed by certain associations and recollections, suddenly aroused by the incidents which had just taken place, and of a painful and distracting kind, he would have been more strongly moved by Miles Challoner's abrupt and extraordinary communication. But the old nobleman's mood just then was a strange one ; and the scene which had passed before his eyes, the words which his young friend had spoken, affected him but slightly and vaguely. There had been some unpleasantness for Miles in the meeting with that clever-looking fellow, Lloyd ; and he was sorry for it. That was all. Old Mark has desired Miles to avoid this man, had he ? The Squire had been very odd latterly, and had taken strong dislikes, and entertained strong prejudices all his life, but especially since that bad business about his son ; and in the midst of his personal preoccupation and abstraction, Lord Sandilands had time for a shudder at the thought of his old friend's great grief, and a sort of pang of thankfulness that it had come to an end, even though a life he valued dearly was finished with it. But his mind was full of his own concerns, and before he had reached the seclusion of his own particular sanctum —a small room within the library—he had almost forgotten the occurrence.

Lord Sandilands sighed heavily as he sat down in a deep leather chair by the window, which opened into a small verandah, with trellised walls well clothed with creeping plants, and tiled with cool quaint-patterned porcelain. A light iron staircase led thence to the garden, which, though unavoidably towny, was cool, pretty, and well-cared for. The summer air passed lightly over the flowers, and carried their fresh morning breath to the old man. But he did not meet its perfume gladly ; it had no soothing, no refreshing influence for him. He moved uneasily, as though some painful association had come to him with the scented breeze ; then rose impatiently, and shut the window down, and paced the room from end to end. " A wonderful likeness," he muttered ; " quite too close for accident. There is more expression, more power in the face, but just the same beauty. Yes, it must be so ; but why have I not been told ?" He stopped before a table, and tapped it with his fingers. " And yet, why should I have been told ? I made the conditions, I defined the rules myself; and why should I wonder that they have not been broken ? What beauty and what talent ! Who would have thought it of poor Gerty's child !—for her child and mine, Grace Lambert is! I am certain. What a strange sudden shock it was to me ! I wonder if anyone perceived it—thought I was ill, perhaps. The room was hot and over-crowded, as usual ; and Lady Carabas cackled more unbearably than ever ; still, I hope I did not make a fool of myself; I hope I did not look upset."

Thus, Lord Sandilands, true to the ruling principles of his order and his age, was disturbed in the midst of greater and deeper disturbance, and even diverted from his thoughts of it, by the dread so touchingly proper to every British mind, that he had been betrayed into emotion, into any departure from the unruffled and impassive calm which British society demands.

At this stage of his soliloquy Lord Sandilands looked at

himself in the chimney-glass, passed his aristocratically slender fingers through his aristocratically fine silver hair, and assured himself that his outward man had not suffered from the internal perturbation and surprise which he had experienced. This critical examination concluded, he resumed his walk and his soliloquy, which we need not follow in form. Its matter was as follows :

In Grace Lambert, Lord Sandilands had recognised so strong a likeness to the mother of the little girl whom he had placed under Mrs. Bloxam's care, and towards whom he had never displayed any fatherly affection beyond that implied by the punctual and uninterrupted discharge of the pecuniary obligations which he had contracted towards that lady, that he entertained no doubt whatever of her identity with Gertrude Keith. This discovery had agitated him less by reason of any present significance which it possessed —the girl was clever, and had achieved in his presence a success of a kind which was undeniably desirable in such a position as hers—than because it had touched long-silent chords, and touched them to utterances full of pain for the old man, who had been so thoroughly of the world, and whom the world had, on the whole, treated remarkably well. But Lord Sandilands was growing old, and was naturally beginning to yield just a little to the inevitable feeling of being rather tired of it all, which comes with age, to the best-treated among the sons of men, and had come perceptibly to him, since Mark Challoner's death had done away with the last of the old landmarks. Things might have been so different ; he had often thought so, and then put the thought from him hurriedly and resolutely. He thought so to-day, and he could not put the thought from him ; it would not go ; but, as he paced the room, it grew stronger and stronger, and came closer and closer to him, and at last looked him sternly and threateningly in the face, demanding harbour and reply; and Lord Sandilands gave it both—no more expelling it, but taking counsel with himself, and repeating to himself an old story of the past which, with a different ending, might have set all his present in another key ;—which story was not very different from many that have been told, and not difficult to tell.

Lord Sandilands had not succeeded early in life to his old title and respectable but not magnificent estates. The

Honourable John Borlase was much more clever, agreeable, and fascinating than rich, when, having left the University of Oxford after a very creditable career, he began to lead the kind of life which is ordinarily led by young men who have only to wait for fortune and title, and who possess sufficient means to fill up the interval comfortably, and sufficient intellect to occupy it with tolerable rationality. The dilettanteism which was one of Lord Sandilands' characteristics developed itself later in life ; while he was a young man, his tastes were more active, and he had devoted himself to sporting and travel. In the pursuit of the first he had made Mark Challoner's acquaintance : and the *camaraderie* of the hunting-field had strengthened into a strong and congenial tie of friendship, which had been broken only by the Squire's death. In the pursuit of the second, John Borlase had encountered many adventures, and made more than one acquaintance destined to influence his future, either sensibly or insensibly ; and among the many was one with whom we have to do, for a brief interval of retrospection.

John Borlase did not affect " Bohemianism " (the phrase had not then been invented, but the thing existed) ; but he liked character, and he liked Art,—liked it better than he understood it, selected the society of those who knew more about it than he did ; and though he by no means restricted himself to the society of artists, he certainly frequented them more than any other class. It was at Berlin that he fell in with Etienne Gautier, an eccentric and very clever Frenchman, exiled by the cruelty of fortune from his native paradise, Paris, and employed by the French Government in some mysterious commission connected with the Galleries of Painting and Sculpture at Berlin,—a city which he never ceased to depreciate, but where he nevertheless appeared to enjoy himself thoroughly. Etienne Gautier was a dark, active, restless man ; vivacious of speech ; highly informed on all matters appertaining to Art a liberal in politics and religion—of a degree of liberalism very unusual at that period, though it would not be regarded as particularly "advanced" at present ; an oddity in his manners ; evidently in poor circumstances, which he treated with that perfect absence of disguise and affectation which is so difficult for English people to comprehend, so impossible for them to imitate ; and devotedly, though injudiciously, attached to his beautiful daughter, Gertrude. The girl's mother, an Englishwoman, had died at her birth, and her father had brought her up after a completely unconventional fashion, and one which would have horrified his own countrymen in particular. She was allowed as much freedom as "bird on branch," and her education was of the most desultory description. Gertrude Gautier was very handsome, very wilful, and totally destitute of knowledge of the world. She was her father's companion in all places and at all times ; and when the Hon. John Borlase made Etienne Gautier's acquaintance and took to frequenting his society, he found that it included that of one of the handsomest, cleverest, and most spirited girls he had ever met. John Borlase was not quite a free man when he first saw Gertrude Gautier. Had her position in life been such as to render his marrying her a wise and suitable proceeding, he could not have offered to do so with honour, though the engagement, if so it could be called, which bound him to the Lady Lucy Beecher, was of a cool and vague description, and much more the doing of their respective families than their own. But he had carried the not unpleasant obligation cheerfully for a year or more ; and it was only when he fully and freely acknowledged to himself that he had fallen in love with Gertrude Gautier, and felt a delightful though embarrassing consciousness that she had fallen in love with him, that he grumbled at his engagement, and persuaded himself that but for its existence he would certainly have married Gertrude, and boldly set the opinions and wishes of his family at defiance. It was a pleasing delusion : there never existed a man less likely to have done anything of the kind than John Borlase ; but he cherished the belief, which nothing in his former life tended to justify. He was a proud man in a totally unaffected way ; and only his fancy—not for a moment his real practical self—regarded the possibility of the elevation into a future British peeress of a girl whose father was a painter, of the Bohemian order, and in whose maternal ancestry the most noteworthy "illustration" was a wholesale grocer. As for Gertrude, she loved him, and that was enough for her. The untaught, undisciplined, passionate girl thought of nothing beyond ; and her father, who was as blind as fathers usually are to the fact that his daughter was no longer a child, but with all the charm and beauty of womanhood had entered upon all its dangers, gave the matter no consideration whatever. This state of things lasted for several months, and then came a crisis. Etienne Gautier fell from a height, in one of the Berlin galleries, and died of the injuries he had received, after recovering consciousness for just sufficient time to commend his daughter to the care and kindness of John Borlase.

"Send her to Leamington," said the dying man; " her mother's uncle lives there. She knows his name."

There is little need to pursue the story of Gertrude Gautier further. She never went to Leamington; she never saw the prosperous grocer, her mother's uncle. The story is not a new one, but at least it ended better than many a one like it has ended. Gertrude was happy; she had no scruples; she knew no better. She had no friends to forfeit; she had no position to lose. Her lover was true to her, and all the more devoted that he had many stings of conscience of which she had no suspicion, in which she never shared. He brought her to England, and the girl was happy in her pretty suburban house, with her birds, her flowers, and his society. But a time came in which John Borlase had the chance of testing his own sincerity; and he applied the test, and recognised its failure. When the institution of the suburban house was a year old, and when he had frequently congratulated himself upon the successful secrecy which had been maintained, John Borlase found a letter to his address awaiting him at his father's town-house. The letter was from Lady Lucy Beecher, and it contained the intelligence of her marriage. "I knew you did not care for me," said the fair and frank writer, " in any sense which would give us a chance of being happy together; but I did not make a fuss about the family arrangement before it became necessary to do so. That necessity arose when I found myself deliberately preferring another man to you. I do so prefer Hugh Wybrant, and I have married him. My people are very angry, of course— perhaps yours will be so also; but you will not care much about that; and I am sure you will heartily thank me for what I have done. We shall always be good friends, I

hope; and if we had married, we could never have been
more, and might easily—indeed should very certainly, I am
convinced—have been less." John Borlase was much relieved by the intelligence contained in this characteristic
letter. Lady Lucy had troubled his mind, had been a
difficulty to him. Under the circumstances he would not
have married, he would not have done so doubly dis-
honourable an action; but he was very glad the ostensible
breach was of her making and not his. He derived a
pleasant self-congratulatory conviction that he was rather
a lucky fellow from this fortunate occurrence; and he
answered Lady Lucy's flippant letter by one which was full
of kindliness and good-humour, and accompanied by a
set of Neapolitan coral.

Then came the question which would make itself heard.
Should he marry Gertrude? He could do so without risk
of her antecedents being discovered; the only odium he
would have to bear would be that of her foreign birth and
insignificant, indefinite origin. The girl's own feelings,
strange to say, counted but little with John Borlase, in the
discussion he held with himself, and which need not be
pursued further. If he had decided in her favour, he felt
that a first and important preliminary would be that he
should explain to her the degradation of her present position, and the immense advantages to her of the compensation
which he should offer her by marrying her. Their life would be
changed, of course; and what had such a change to give him?
He reasoned entirely as a man of the world; and the upshot
of his deliberations was that he did not marry Gertrude
Gautier. It made no difference to her; she did not know
that the subject had ever occupied him; she had never
heard Lady Lucy's name. Her calm, happy, guilty love-
dream went on for a little longer, and then it ended. The
doom of her mother was on Gertrude; and John Borlase
came home one day, as Etienne Gautier had come home, to
find a dead woman and a helpless infant where he had left
youth and health and beauty in the morning. The blow
fell heavily upon John Borlase, and remorse as well as
sorrow was for a long time busy at his heart. During this
period he was extremely restless, and the world was quite
concerned and edified to see how much he had taken Lady
Lucy's defection to heart. Who would have thought a man

could possess so much feeling? And then the generosity with which he acted, the pains he had taken to show how completely he was *sans rancune;* how could Lady Lucy have done such a thing! But everybody flocked to see Lady Lucy, for all that; and as for Captain Wybrant, never was there anyone so charming. John Borlase did not hear all the talk, or if he did, he did not heed it. He was not a sentimental man, and he was sufficiently unscrupulous; but Gertrude's death was more than a racking grief and loss to him. Alongside of her shrouded figure he saw her father's; and now, too late, he was haunted by the unfulfilled trust bequeathed him by the dead. Deceiving himself again, he tried to persuade himself that only the suddenness of Gertrude's death had prevented his marrying her; he tried to throw the blame, which he could not ignore, on circumstances. At first he succeeded, to a certain extent, in this—succeeded sufficiently to deaden the acuteness of the pain he could not escape from. Then, after a time, he knew better; he no longer indulged in self-deception; he acknowledged that the wrong was irreparable, and the self-reproach lifelong; and he bowed to the stern truth. John Borlase was never afterwards talked of as a marrying man; and Lady Lucy Wybrant, whose sources of social success were numerous and various, enjoyed that one in addition, that the inexorable celibacy of Lord Sandilands was ascribed to his chivalrous fidelity to her. She knew that this was a fiction, as well as he knew it; but as it was a gleam of additional glorification for her, and such a supposition saved him a great deal of trouble, and preserved him from match-making mammas, each acquiesced in the view which society chose to adopt, with most amiable affability. Captain Wybrant laughed at the theory of Sandilands' celibacy, as he laughed at most other theories; and said (and believed) that if a man must be fool enough to wear the willow for any woman, his Lucy was the best worth wearing it for, of all the women in the world. And though the whole thing was a myth, Lord Sandilands never cordially liked jolly Hugh Wybrant—perhaps no man ever yet did cordially like the individual in whose favour he had been jilted, though he may not have cared a straw for the fickle fair one, but have honestly regarded her inconstancy as a delightful circumstance, demanding ardent gratitude.

For several years after Gertrude Gautier's death, the
Hon. John Borlase indulged in frequent and extensive
foreign travel ; and during this period the infant girl, who
had inherited her beauty, apparently without her delicacy
of constitution, was well cared for. The child's father cared
little for her, beyond scrupulously providing for her
physical welfare. She was an embodied reproach to him,
though he never said so to himself, but persuaded himself
his indifference to the little girl whom he saw but rarely
and at long intervals, arose from his not naturally caring
about children. When she was eight years old, and the
memory of her mother had almost died out, though the
indelible effect of the sad and guilty episode in his life with
which she was connected remained impressed upon him,
Lord Sandilands placed the little girl under Mrs. Bloxam's
care, with the conditions already stated, and the results
already partially developed. He had provided ample funds
to meet the exigencies of her education ; he had made due
arrangements for their safe and punctual transmission to
Mrs. Bloxam ; he had but vague notions concerning the
requirements and the risks of girlhood : his dominant idea
was, that in a respectable boarding-school the girl must be
safe ; he did not want to see her ; she must not know
him as her father ; and he had no fancy for playing any
part, undertaking any personation—in short, having any
trouble unrepresented by money—about her. John Borlase
had been unscrupulous, and a trifle hard in his nature ; and
despite the conflict in his breast which had ensued on
Gertrude Gautier's death, and which for all his impassive
bearing had been fierce and long, Lord Sandilands was not
much more scrupulous, and was decidedly harder. If the
girl married or if she died, he should be made acquainted
with the circumstance ; and as a matter of fact—fact, not
sentiment, being the real consideration in this matter—
either was all he need know. As time went on, this frame
of mind about his unknown daughter became habitual to
Lord Sandilands ; and of late he had never remembered
Gertrude's existence, except when an entry in his accounts,
under a certain appointed formula, recalled the fact to his
mind.

These were the circumstances on which Lord Sandilands
mused, as he paced his room in the early morning, after he

had seen Grace Lambert at Lady Carabas's concert. The girl's face had risen up before him like a ghost—not only her mother's, but that of his own youth ; and in the proud, assured, but not bold glance of her splendid brown eyes a story which had no successor in the old man's lonely life was written. This beautiful, gifted girl was his daughter. She might have been the pride of his life, the darling, the ornament of his home, the light of his declining years, the inheritor of his fortune, if—if he had done right instead of wrong, if he had repaired the injury he had done to her, whose grave lay henceforth and for ever between him and the possibility of reparation.

"How very handsome she is !" he thought ; "and how fine and highly cultivated her voice ! If I had known she possessed such a talent as that !" And then he thought how that talent might have been displayed in society, in which the possessor might have mixed on equal terms. A long train of images and fancies, of vain and bitter regrets, came up with the strong impression of the girl's grace, beauty, and gifts. Of her identity there could be no doubt. As Gertrude Gautier had looked out from the garden-gate, where she had bidden him the fond and smiling farewell destined to be their last, so this girl, as beautiful as his lost Gertrude, and with something of grandeur in her look, which Gertrude had not, and which was the grace added by genius, had looked that night, as she calmly, smilingly received the applause of her audience. As he recalled that look, and dwelt on it in his memory with the full assurance that his conviction was correct, an idea struck him. He was a known connoisseur in music, a known patron of musical art ; everyone who was anyone in the musical world sought an introduction to Lord Sandilands. In the case of Miss Grace Lambert, his generally extended patronage had been especially requested by Lady Carabas for her *protégée.* Here was a fair and legitimate expedient within his reach for securing access to Miss Lambert, without the slightest risk of awakening suspicion, either in her mind or in that of sharp-sighted observers, that he was actuated by any particular motive in this instance. He must see her, he must know her ! How bitterly he lamented now, and con-demned himself for the indifference which had kept him for so many years contented that his child should be a stranger to

him! How ready he was, now that he saw her beautiful
and gifted, to accord credence and attention to the
voice of nature, in which he had never before believed,
and which under other circumstances would have found him
just as deaf as usual! Then he resolved that he would
write to Mrs. Bloxam, and prepare her for a long-deferred
visit to her charge, stipulating in his letter that Gertrude
should know nothing of the intended visit, and that Mrs.
Bloxam should receive him alone. "She shall tell me my
child's history," he said ; " at least it has been a bright and
happy story hitherto." And Lord Sandilands sighed, and
his face looked old and worn, as he arranged his note-paper,
and dipped his pen in the ink, and then hesitated and
pondered long before he commenced his letter to Mrs.
Bloxam.

The letter consisted of but a few lines, and Lord Sandilands put it in another cover, addressed to Mr. Plowden,
his solicitor, and the medium of his payments to Mrs.
Bloxam. It was not until he had retired to rest, after sunrise, and had been for some time vainly trying to sleep, that
his thoughts reverted to Miles Challoner and the incident
which had taken place just before they parted.

Miles Challoner, also wakeful, was thinking of it too, and
debating with himself whether he should mention the
matter again to Lord Sandilands. He shrank from reviving a
subject so full of pain. The man whom he had met evidently
had an object in concealing his identity, or he would not have
been so reticent by a first impulse. They were not likely
to meet again. So Miles Challoner took a resolution to
keep his own counsel ; and acted upon it.

CHAPTER VI.

LLOYD'S LUCK.

WE have found Gilbert Lloyd the centre of an amused
circle at Carabas House. Let us see what has been
his career since he parted with his wife at the George Inn
at Brighton.

He was free ! That was his first thought when he began

to ponder over the probable results of the step he had taken,—free to come and go as he liked, to do as he listed, without the chance of incurring black looks or reproaches. Not that he had had either from Gertrude for a very long time. When her faith in her husband was first shattered; when she first begun to perceive that the man whom in her girlish fancy she had regarded as a hero of romance—a creature bright, glorious, and rare—was formed of very ordinary clay, Gertrude was vexed and annoyed by the discovery. She was young, too, and had a young woman's belief in the efficacy of tears and sulks; so that when Gilbert stayed out late, or brought home companions to whom she objected, or went away on business tours for several days together, Gertrude at first met him with sharp reproaches, dissolving into passionate fits of weeping, or varied with sufficiently feeble attempts at dignity. But Gilbert laughed these last to scorn, and either took no notice of the reproaches, or with an oath bade them cease. And then, the glamour having utterly died out, and the selfishness and brutality of her husband being fully known to her, Gertrude's manner had entirely changed. No sighs were ever heard by Gilbert Lloyd, no red eyelids, no cheeks swollen by traces of recent tears were ever seen by him. If the cold cynical expression on his wife's face had not been sufficient, the bitter mocking tones of her voice never failed to tell him of the contempt she felt for him. That she was no longer his dupe; that she bitterly despised herself for ever having been fooled by him; that she had gauged the depth of his knavery and the shallowness of his pretensions —all this was recognizable in her every look, in her every word. No brutality on her husband's part—and his brutality sometimes found other vent than language—no intermittent fits of softness towards her, such as would occasionally come over him, had the smallest effect on her face or on her voice. She bore his blows silently, his caresses shudderingly, and when they were over she looked up at him with the cold cynical face, and replied to him with the bitter mocking voice.

Gilbert Lloyd's friends—by which expression is meant the men of the set in which he regularly lived—saw little of Mrs. Lloyd, who was popularly supposed by them to be next to a nonentity, Lloyd being a man who "always had his own way." And, indeed, so far as those words were ordinarily understood, Gilbert Lloyd's acquaintances were right. For months and months his comings and goings, his long absences, his conduct while at home, had been uncommented upon by Gertrude, save in the expression of her face and in the tone of her voice. But these, even at such rare intervals as he was subjected to them, were quite enough to goad a man of his temperament, by nature irritable, and rendered doubly petulant by the exciting life he led; and the knowledge that he was free from them for ever came to him with immense relief. He was "on his own hook" now, and had the world before him as much as he had before he committed the ridiculous error of letting his passion get the better of his prudence, and so binding a burden on to his back. A burden! yes, she had been a burden—a useless, helpless dead-weight—even when his fleeting passion for her began to wane, he had hopes that after all he had not done such a bad thing in marrying her. To a man who looked for his prey amongst the young and inexperienced, a pretty woman would always prove a useful assistant; and Gilbert Lloyd at one time thought of using his wife as a lure and a bait. But any hopes of this nature which he may have entertained were speedily uprooted. "Right-thinking" Gertrude Lloyd certainly was not; of mental obliquity in the matter of distinguishing between good and evil, she had her full share; but she was as proud as Lucifer, and her pride stepped in to her aid where better qualities might not have interfered. Her natural quickness enabled her at once to see through her husband's designs, and she told him plainly and promptly that he must seek elsewhere for a confederate; nay more, when Lloyd would have insisted on her presiding at his table, and making herself agreeable to his friends, her resistance, hitherto passive, became active; she threatened to make known some of his proceedings, which would have seriously compromised him in the eyes of persons with whom he wished to stand well; and neither entreaties nor commands could alter her resolution.

She had been a burden, and he was rid of her. The more he thought it over the more he congratulated himself on the step which he had taken, and felt that he had the best of the arrangement just concluded. He had never loved any one ; and the *caprice*, for it was nothing more, which he had once felt for Gertrude, had long since died away. He was free now to pursue his own career, and he determined that his future should be brighter and more ambitious than he had hitherto hoped. Now was his chance, and he would take advantage of it. Heretofore he had lived almost entirely in the society of the Ring-men— among them, but not of them—despising his associates, and using them merely as a means to an end. He had had more than enough of such companionship, and would shake it off for ever. Not that Gilbert Lloyd intended quitting the turf and giving up his career as a betting-man. Such a thought never occurred to him ; he knew no other way by which he could so easily earn so much money, while its Bohemianism, and even its chicanery, were by no means unpleasant ingredients to his fallen nature. All he wished was to take higher rank, and live with a different section of the fraternity. There were betting-men and betting-men ; and Gilbert Lloyd knew that his birth and education fitted him more for the society of the "swells" who looked languidly on from the tops of drags, or moved quietly about the Ring, than for the companionship of the professionals and welchers who drove what was literally a "roaring" trade outside the enclosure. There was, moreover, con- siderably more money to be made amongst the former than the latter. Opportunity alone had been wanting ; now he thought that had come, and Gilbert Lloyd determined on trying his luck, and going for a great *coup*.

He had a hundred pounds in hand and a capital book for Doncaster, so he made up his mind to leave the last to the manipulation of an intimate friend, who would watch the alterations in the market, and report them to him at Baden, whither he started at once. Here he established himself in a pleasant little bedchamber in the bachelor's wing of the Badischer Hof, and proceeded to commence operations. The language, the appearance, the manners of the regular turfite he at once discarded, though an occa- sional hint dropped in conversation at the *table d'hôte* or in the Kursaal, at both of which places he soon made many promiscuous acquaintances, conveyed a notion that the *arcana* of the Ring were, or had been, sufficiently familiar to him. At the tables he played nightly, with varying fortune it was thought, though those who watched him closely averred that he was a considerable winner. His pecuniary success, however, affected him very slightly ; he was glad, of course, to have been able to live luxuriously during a month, and to leave the place with more money than he took into it ; but Gilbert Lloyd had done far better than merely winning a few hundred louis—he had made his *coup.*

He made it thus. Staying at the Badischer Hof was the Earl of Ticehurst, a young English nobleman who had recently succeeded to his title and estate, and who, during the previous year, had caused a great deal of talk in London. He was a big, heavy-looking young man, with a huge jowl and a bull neck, coarse features, and small sunken eyes. At Eton he had been principally noticeable for his cruelty to animals and his power of beer-drinking. At Oxford these charming qualities were more freely developed, but whereas they had been called by their proper names by Viscount Etchingham's school-fellows, they became known as " high spirits " to the college dons and the tuft-hunting tutors. It is probable, however, that even these long-suffering individuals would have had to take notice of his lordship's vivacious proceedings, had not his father died during his first year of residence ; and on succeeding to the earldom of Ticehurst, Lord Etchingham at once left the University and entered upon London life. This means different things to different people. To the nobleman just interred in the family vault at Etchingham, in the presence of the Premier and half the Cabinet, it had signified the commencement of a brilliant political career. To his son, who had succeeded him, it meant the acquisition of a stud of racers, the sovereignty of the coffee-room at Rummer's, the well-known sporting hotel, and the obsequious homage of some of the greatest scoundrels in London. The young man delighted in his position, and felt that he had really come into his kingdom. His name was in every one's mouth, and people who scarcely could distinguish a racer from a towel-horse had heard of young Lord Ticehurst. The names of the horses which he owned were familiar in the mouths of the most general of the " general public," the amount of the bets which he won or lost was talked of in all classes of society, and by the " sporting world " he was looked upon

as the great revivalist of those pastimes which are always
described by the epithets "old" and "British." The
fighting of mains of cocks, the drawing of badgers, the
patronage of the rat-pit and the P.R. ("that glorious institution which, while it exists among us and is fostered by
the genial support of such true Corinthians as the E— of
T—, will prevent Englishmen from having recourse to the
dastardly use of the knife," as it was prettily described by
Snish, the fistic reporter of the *Life*), the frequent fuddling
of himself with ardent spirits, the constant attendance at
night-saloons, and the never going home till morning—
came into this category. Elderly Haymarket publicans and
night-cabmen began to think that the glorious days of their
youth had returned, when they witnessed or listened to the
pranks of Lord Ticehurst ; and in his first London season
he had established a reputation for gentlemanly black-
guardism and dare-devilry quite equal to any in the records
of the Bow-street Police-court.

Needless to say that with Lord Ticehurst's reputation
Gilbert Lloyd was perfectly familiar, and that he had long
and ardently desired the opportunity of making the acquaintance of that distinguished nobleman. To use his own
language, he had "done all he knew" to carry out this
desirable result ; but in vain. There are hawks and hawks ;
and the birds of prey who hovered round Lord Ticehurst
were far too clever and too hungry to allow any of the inferior kind to interfere with their spoil. Not that Gilbert
Lloyd was inferior in any sense, save that of mixing with
an inferior class. Lord Ticehurst knew several men of
Lloyd's set—knew them sufficiently to speak to them in a
manner varying from the *de haut en bas* style which he
used to his valet to the vulgar familiarity with which he
addressed his trainer ; but it would not have suited Gilbert
Lloyd to have been thrown in his way, and he had carefully avoided being presented or becoming known to Lord
Ticehurst in an inferior position.

When Gilbert arrived at the Badischer Hof, the first
person he saw at the late *table d'hôte* was Lord Ticehurst ; the
second was Plater Dobbs, who acted as his lordship's hench-
man, Mentor, and confidential upper servant. A stout
short man, Plater Dobbs (his real name was George, and he
was supposed once to have been a major in something, the

nickname "Plater" attaching to him from the quality of the racehorses he bred and backed), with a red face, the blood strangled into it by his tight bird's-eye choker, a moist eye, a pendulous under lip, a short gray whisker and stubbly moustache of the same colour, a bell-shaped curly-brimmed hat, and a wonderful vocabulary of oaths. Plater Dobbs was one of the old school in everything—one of the hard-drinking, hard-riding, hard-swearing, five-o'clock-in-the-morning old boys. A sportsman of the old school, with many recollections of Pea-green Hayne, and Colonel Berkeley, and the Golden Ball, and other lights of other days ; a godless abandoned old profligate, illiterate and debauched, but with a certain old-fashioned knowledge of horse-flesh, an unlimited power of drinking without being harmed by what he drank, and a belief in and an adherence to "the code of honour" as then understood amongst gentlemen, as he had proved in person on various occasions at home and abroad. He had taken entire sway over Lord Ticehurst, bought racers with the young nobleman's money, and trained and ran them when he chose ; went with him everywhere ; and was alternately his Mentor and his butt—acting in either capacity with the greatest equanimity.

Now, above all other men in the world, Lloyd hated Plater Dobbs. He had long envied the position which the " vulgar old cad," as he called him, had held in regard to Lord Ticehurst ; and when he saw them together at Baden, his rage was extreme, and a desire to supplant the elderly Mentor at once rose in his breast. Not that Gilbert had any feeling that the counsels or the example given and shown to Lord Ticehurst by Plater Dobbs were wrong or immoral. All he felt about them was that they were *rococo*, old-fashioned, and behind the mark of the present day. The appointment of "confederate" to such a man as Ticehurst, was one of the most splendid chances of a lifetime ; and it had now fallen to the lot of a senile debauchee, who was neither doing good for himself nor obtaining credit for his pupil. If Ticehurst were only in *his* hands, what would not Gilbert Lloyd do for him and for himself? Ticehurst should be in his hands, but how ? That was the problem which Lloyd set himself to solve. That was the thought which haunted him day and night, which dulled his palate to M. Rheinbolt's choicest *plats*, which even made him sometimes inattentive to the monotonous cry of the *croupiers*. To secure Plater Dobbs' position would be to land a greater stake than could be gained by the most un-expected fluke at *trente et quarante*. Let him only hook Ticehurst, and *rien ne va plus !*

An ordinary sharper would have taken advantage of the frequent opportunities afforded by the *table d'hôte* and continental life, generally, have spoken to Lord Ticehurst, and managed to secure a speaking acquaintanceship with him. But Gilbert Lloyd was not an ordinary sharper, and he saw clearly enough how little that course would tend to the end he had in view. He foresaw that Plater Dobbs' jealousy would be at once aroused; and that while the ac-quaintance with the bear was ripening, the bear-leader would have ample opportunity of vilifying his would-be rival. He put it to himself clearly that success was only to be gained by adventitious chance, and that chance came thus.

Among the frequenters of the Kursaal was a French gentleman of some thirty-five years of age, black-bearded, bright-eyed, and thin-waisted. André de Prailles was this gentleman's name, Paris was his nation, and, to carry out the old rhyme, the degradation of England and her children was apparently his vocation. In private and in public he took every opportunity of saying unpleasant things about *la perfide Albion,* and the traitors, native and domiciled, nourished by her. He had, for a Frenchman, an extraordi-nary knowledge of English ways and manners of life—of life of a certain kind—which he amused himself and certain of his immediate friends by turning into the greatest ridicule. He played but little at the tables; indeed, those who had watched him narrowly avowed that there was a certain understanding between him and the *croupiers*, who dis-couraged his attendance; but be this as it might, he frequented the promenade and the baths, lived in very fair style at the Hotel Victoria, and was a " feature " in the society of the place. M. de Prailles' Anglophobia had con-tented itself with disdainful glances at the representatives of the land which he detested, and with muttering with bated breath at all they said and did, until the arrival at Baden of Mdlle. de Merouville, the celebrated *ingénue* of the Vaudeville, with whom M. de Prailles had an acquaintance, and for whom he professed an adoration.

Mdlle. de Meronville was a bright lithe little woman, with large black eyes, an olive complexion, and what Lord Ticehurst called a " fuzzy " head of jet-black hair ; a pleasant good-natured little woman, fond of admiration and *bonbons* and good dinners and plenty of champagne ; a little woman who played constantly at the tables, screaming with delight when she won, and using "strange oaths" when she lost— who smoked cigarettes on the promenade, and gesticulated wildly, and beat her companions with her parasol, and, in fact, behaved herself as unlike a British female as is possible to be imagined. Perhaps it was the entire novelty of her style and conduct that gave her such a charm in the eyes of Lord Ticehurst, for charm she undoubtedly had. A devotion to the opposite sex had never hitherto been classed among the weaknesses of that amiable nobleman ; but he was so completely overcome by the fascinations of Eugénie de Meronville, that no youth ever suffered more severely from " calf-love " than this reckless roisterer. He followed her about like her shadow ; when in her company, after he had obtained an introduction to her, he would address to her the most flowery compliments in a curious *mélange* of tongues ; and when absent from her he would sit and puff his cigar in moody silence, obstinately rejecting all efforts to withdraw him from his sentimental abstraction. Plater Dobbs regarded this new phase in his pupil's character with unspeakable horror, and was at his wits' end to know how to put a stop to it. He endeavoured to lead Lord Ticehurst into deeper play ; but unless Mdlle. de Meronville were at the tables the young man would not go near them. He organized a little supper-party, at which were present two newly-arrived and most distinguished beauties : an English grass-widow whose husband was in India, and a Russian lady, who regarded the fact of her liege lord's being ruined, and sinking from a position of affluence into that of a hotel-keeper, as quite enough to excuse her leaving him for ever. But Ticehurst sulked through the banquet, and the ladies agreed in voting him *bête* and *mauvais ton.* The fact was that the man was madly in love with Eugénie de Meronville, and cared for nothing but her society.

What one does and where one goes and with whom one

passes one's time is, of course, very easily known in a small coterie such as that assembled in the autumn at Baden ; and it is not to be wondered at that M. André de Prailles suffered many a bad quarter of an hour as he witnessed and heard of the amicable relations between his fair compatriot and one of the leading representatives of that nation which he detested. What added to M. de Prailles' anger was the fact that whereas in Paris, where he was known to be the friend of certain *feuilletonistes* with whom it was well for every actress to be on good terms, he had had cause for believing himself to be well thought of by the *ingénue* of the Vaudeville, at Baden, where no such inducement existed, he had been completely snubbed by Eugénie, and treated with a *hauteur* which set his blood boiling in his veins. M. de Prailles resented this after his own fashion. First, he addressed a passionate letter to his idol, reproaching her for her perfidy. To this he received a very short, and, to tell truth, a very ill-spelt answer, in which the goddess replied that it was not his "*afair*," and that she would behave herself "*come je voulai*" wheresoever and with whomsoever she pleased. Then he took to a more open course of defiance— following on the trail of Mdlle. de Meronville and Lord Ticehurst, standing behind them at the table, occupying adjacent seats to theirs in the Kursaal or on the promenade, and enunciating, in by no means a hushed voice, his opinion on Englishmen in general and Lord Ticehurst in particular. But Lord Ticehurst's comprehension of the French language was limited, his comprehension of the English language, as spoken by M. de Prailles, was still more limited ; and the strongest comment with which he favoured his opponent's ravings was a muttered inquiry as to what " that d—d little Frenchman was jabbering about."

At last, one night, the long-threatened explosion took place. A sudden storm of wind and rain swept down from the Black Forest, and the curious vehicle attached to the Hôtel d'Angleterre was sent for to convey Mdlle. de Meronville from the Kursaal to her rooms. The little actress had been playing with great ill-luck, and had been duly waited upon by Lord Ticehurst ; but at the moment when the arrival of the droschky was notified to her, he had been called into another part of the room by Plater Dobbs, and only arrived in time to see her, mortified and angry,

being conducted to the carriage on the arm of M. de
Prailles. Rushing forward to make his excuses, Lord
Ticehurst caught his foot in the train of Mdlle. de Meronville's gown, and, amid a suppressed burst of laughter from
the bystanders, pulled her backwards and fell forward
himself. He had scarcely recovered himself when the roll
of the departing vehicle was in his ears, and M. de Prailles
was standing before him fuming.

"An accident? nothing of the sort! *Exprès! tout à
fait exprès!*"

A crowd gathered at the ominous words and at the tone
of voice in which they were uttered: Plater Dobbs and
Gilbert Lloyd foremost among the concurrents, the one
flushed and excited, the other cool and collected; Lord
Ticehurst, very pale, and with an odd twitching in the
muscles of his mouth.

"It was no accident, that tumble!" shrieked M. de
Prailles. "It was a studied insult offered to a lady by a
barbarian! *Exprès, entendez-vous, messieurs, exprès?*"

Then, seeing that his opponent stood motionless, the little
Frenchman drew himself on tiptoes, and hissed out,

"*Et il ne dit rien? Décidément, milor, vous êtes un
lâche!*" and he made a movement as though he would have
struck Lord Ticehurst with his open hand.

But Plater Dobbs, who had been puffing and fuming and
grasping for breath, caught the angry Frenchman by the
arm, and called out,

"Holla, none of that! We'll produce our man when
he's wanted. We don't want any rough-and-tumble here!
Ally, party, mossoo!"

"*Au diable, ivrogne!*" was all the response which M. de
Prailles chose to make to this elegant appeal; but he
turned to some of his compatriots, and said, "*Regardez donc
la figure de ce milor là!*" And in truth Lord Ticehurst
was almost livid, and the chair against which he was
leaning trembled in his grasp. At that moment Gilbert
Lloyd stepped forward.

"There's no question of producing any man on this
occasion, except a *gensdarme*," said he, addressing Plater
Dobbs.

A hush fell on the little crowd—the Englishmen silenced
by what they heard, the foreigners by the effect which they

saw the words had produced. Only Dobbs spoke, and he said, " What the devil do you mean ? "

"What I say," replied Lloyd ; "it's impossible for Lord Ticehurst to fight this fellow," with a contemptuous wave of the hand at De Prailles. " I've long thought I recognised him ; now I'm sure of it. I don't know what he calls himself now, but he used to answer to the name of Louis three years ago, when he was a billiard-marker at the rooms over the Tennis Court, just out of the Haymarket."

" *Tu mens, canaille !* " screamed M. de Prailles, rushing at him ; but Gilbert Lloyd caught his adversary by the throat, and with every nerve in his lithe frame strung to its tightest pitch, shook him to and fro.

" Drop that ! " he said ; " drop that, or by the Lord I'll fling you out of the window ! You know the height you'd have to fall ! " and with one parting shake he threw the Frenchman from him. " I'm glad my memory served me so well ; it would have been impossible for your lordship to have gone out with such a fellow."

M. André de Prailles left Baden very early the next morning, but the events of that night affected more than him. Although he was not of a grateful or recognisant nature, Lord Ticehurst felt keenly the material assistance which Gilbert Lloyd afforded him at what, in his inmost heart, his lordship knew to have been a most critical and unpleasant time, and he showed at once that he appreciated this assistance at its proper value. He made immediate advances of friendship to Gilbert, which advances Gilbert received with sufficient *nonchalance* to cause them to be repeated with double ardour. At the same time he by no means declined the acquaintance which Lord Ticehurst offered him, and in the course of various colloquies contrived to indoctrinate his lordship with a notion of his extraordinary 'cuteness in things in general, and in matters pertaining to the turf and to society in particular. The world, as viewed through Gilbert Lloyd's glasses, had to Lord Ticehurst quite a different aspect from that under which he had hitherto seen it ; and he raged against opportunities missed and stupid courses taken while under the tutelage of Plater Dobbs. To rid himself of that worthy's companionship and to instal Gilbert Lloyd in his place, was a task which Lord

Ticehurst set himself at once, and carried out with great speed and success. He found little opposition from the Plater. That worldly-wise old person had seen how matters stood—"how the cat jumped," as he phrased it—from the first, and was perfectly prepared to receive his *congé*. Nor, indeed, was he altogether displeased at the arrangement. His good qualities were few enough ; but among them was the possession of personal pluck and courage, and a horror of any one in whom these were lacking. "I always knew Etchingham was a duffer, sir," he would say in after-days— "a pig-headed, obstinate, mean duffer—but I never thought he was a cur until that night. He was in a blue funk, I tell you—in a blue funk of a d—d little Frenchman that he could have swallowed whole ! I don't complain, sir. He hasn't behaved badly to me, and I hope he'll find he's done right in holding on to Master Lloyd. A devilish slippery customer that, sir. But him and me couldn't have been the same after I saw he funked that Frenchman, and so perhaps it's better as it is." So Major Plater Dobbs retired on an allowance of three hundred a year from his ex-pupil to the cheerful city of York, and this history knows him no more.

When Gilbert Lloyd returned to England in time to accompany his patron to Doncaster, where they witnessed the shameful defeat of all Lord Ticehurst's horses, which had been trained under the Dobbs' *régime*, he felt that he had made his *coup* ; but he did not anticipate such success as fell to his lot. By an excellent system of tactics, the mainspring of which was to make himself sought instead of to seek, and to speak his mind unreservedly upon all points on which he was consulted, taking care never to interfere in cases where his opinion was not asked, he obtained a complete ascendancy over the young man, who, after a very short time, made him overseer, not merely of his stable, but of his house, his establishment, and his estates. And excellently did Lloyd perform the functions then allotted to him. He had a clear head for business, and a keen eye for "a good thing ; " and as a large portion of all Lord Ticehurst's luck and success was shared by his "confederate," it was not surprising that Lloyd employed his time and brains in planning and achieving successes. Not a little of his good fortune Lloyd owed to keeping in with his former allies the Ring-men, who were treated by him with a frank cordiality which stood him in excellent stead, and who were delighted to find that one of their own order, as they judged him, could climb to such a height without becoming stuck-up or spiteful. The old trainer, the jockeys, and all the Dobbs' satellites were swept away as soon as Gilbert Lloyd came into power, and were so well replaced that Lord Ticehurst's stud, which had previously been the laughing-stock of Tattersall's, now contained several animals of excellent repute, and one or two from which the greatest things were expected.

Nor was the change less remarkable in Lord Ticehurst himself. Of course his new Mentor would have lacked the inclination, even if he had had the power, to withdraw his pupil from turf-life ; but to a certain extent he made him understand the meaning and the value of the saying, "*Noblesse oblige.*" It was understood that henceforward Lord Ticehurst's horses were run "on the square," and that there was to be no more "pulling," or "roping," or any other chicanery. And after a good deal of patience and persuasion, Gilbert Lloyd succeeded in indoctrinating his patron with the notion that it was scarcely worth while keeping up the reputation of being "British" with a small portion of the community at the expense of disgusting all the rest ; that if one had no original taste in the matter of costume, and needs must copy some one else, there were styles not simpler, perhaps, but at all events as becoming as those of the groom ; and that all the literary homage of the *Life* scarcely repaid a gentleman for having to associate with such blackguards as he met in his patronage of the prize-ring, the cock-pit, and the rat-hunt. The young man, who being young was impressionable, was brought to see the force of these various arguments ; more easily, doubtless, because they were put to him in a remarkably skilful way, without dictation and without deference—simply as the suggestions of a man of the world to another worldling, the force of which he, from his worldly knowledge, would perfectly understand and appreciate. And so, within a year after submitting himself to Gilbert Lloyd's tutelage, Lord Ticehurst, who had been universally regarded as a "cub" and a "tiger," was admitted to be a "doosid good fellow," and his friends laid all the improvement to Gilbert Lloyd.

Amongst those friends, perhaps the warmest of Lloyd's supporters was Lord Ticehurst's aunt, Lady Carabas. Lady Carabas had always delighted to have it thought that she was a *femme incomprise;* that while she was looked upon as the mere worldling, the mere butterfly of fashion, she had a soul—not the immortal part of her system which she took notice of once a week in St. Barnabas's Church, but such a soul as poets and metaphysical writers spell with a large S, —a Soul for poetry, romance, love, and all those other things which are never heard of in polite neighbourhoods. The Marquis of Carabas was quite unaware of the existence of this portion of his wife's attributes, and if he had known of it, it is probable it would have made very little difference to him : it was nothing to eat, nothing to be shot at or angled for, at least with a gun or a rod, so had no interest for his lordship. But there was always some one sufficiently intimate with Lady Carabas to be intrusted with the secret of the existence of this Soul, and to be permitted to share in its aspirations. Lady Carabas had married very early in life, and although she had two large and whiskered sons, she was yet a remarkably handsome woman ; so handsome, so genial, and so winning, that there were few men who would not have been gratified by her notice. And here let it be said, that all her friendships—she had many, though never more than one at the same time—were perfectly platonic in their nature. She pined to be understood —she wanted nothing else, she said ; but people remarked that those whom she allowed to understand her were always distinguished either by rank, good looks, or intellect. The immediate predecessor of Gilbert Lloyd in dominion over Lady Carabas' Soul, was an Italian singer with a straight nose, a curling brown beard, and a pair of luminous gray eyes ; and he in his turn had supplanted a Prince of the Blood. Gilbert Lloyd was prime favourite now, and was treated accordingly by the " regulars" in Beaumanoir-square. It was Lady Carabas' boast that she could be " all things to all men." Thus while her Soul had gushed with the regal romance of Arthur and Guinevere in its outpourings to the Prince—an honest gentleman of limited intellect and conversation restricted to the utterance of an occasional " Hum, haw, Jove ! "—it had burned with republican ardour in its eonference with the exiled Italian ; and was now imbued with the spirit of Ruff, *Bell*, Bailey, and other leading turf-guides, in its lighter dalliance with Gilbert Lloyd. And this kind of thing suited Lloyd very well, and tended to secure his position with Lord Ticehurst.

At the time of Gilbert Lloyd's introduction to Miles Challoner at Carabas House, that position was settled and secured. Not merely was Lord Ticehurst, to all appearance, utterly dependent on his Mentor for aid and advice in every action of his life, but Lloyd's supremacy in the Ticehurst household was recognised and acquiesced in by all friends and members of the family. It was so recognised, so apparently secure, and withal so pleasant, that Lloyd had put aside any doubt of the possibility of its ever being done away with ; and the first idea of such a catastrophe came to him as the old name, so long unheard, sounded once more in his ears, and as in the handsome man before him he recognised his elder brother. Miles Challoner, as we have seen, sought safety in flight. Gilbert Lloyd, the younger man, but by far the older worldling, soon recovered from his temporary disquietude, so far as his looks were concerned, and gazed after the vanishing figure of his brother with eyebrows uplifted in apparent wonderment at his *gaucherie*. But in the solitude of his chamber, before he went to bed that morning, he faced the subject manfully, and thought it out under all its various aspects.

Would Miles betray him ? That was the chief point. The blood surged up in his pale face, and the beating of his heart was plainly audible to himself as he thought of that contingency, and foresaw the unalterable and immediate result. Exposure ! proved to have been living for years under an assumed name and in a false position—A slight ray of hope here. The real name and the real position were incomparably better than those he had assumed. Had he not rather lost than gained by—Dashed out at once ? Why did he hide his name and position ? Forced to. Why ? O, that story must never be given up, or he would be lost indeed. And then his thoughts digressed, and he found himself picturing in his memory that last night in the old house—that farewell of Rowley Court. Good God ! how he recollected it all !—the drive in the dog-cart through the

long lanes redolent of May ; the puzzled face of the old
coachman, who knew young Master was going away, and yet
could not make out why old Master, and Master Miles, and
the household had not turned out to wish him " God speed ;"
the last glimpse which, as he stood at the station-door, he
caught of the dog-cart thridding its way homewards through
the lanes, almost every inch of which he knew. Would
Miles betray him ? No, he thought not—at least wilfully
and intentionally. If the Miles of to-day had the same
characteristics as he remembered in the boy, he had an
amount of pride which would render it impossible for him
to move in the matter. Impossible ! Yes, because to move
in it would be to announce to the world that he, the Squire
of Rowley Court, was the brother of Mr. Lloyd the turfite,
the " confederate" of Lord Ticehurst, the—and Gilbert
cursed the pride which would make his brother look down
upon him, even though to that pride he principally looked
for his own safety. But might not Miles unintentionally
blunder and blurt out the secret ? He had been hot-headed
and violent of speech as a boy, and his conduct at Carabas
House on the introduction had proved that he had no command over his feelings. This was what it was to have to do
with fools. And then Gilbert Lloyd recollected that, on the
only other occasion in his life when the chance of compromising his future was in the hands of another person, it was
his wife to whom the chance was allotted ; and he remembered the perfect security which he felt in her sense and
discretion. His wife ! He had not thought of her for a
very long time. He wondered where she was and what she
was doing. He wondered whether she had altered in personal appearance, whether anyone else had—pshaw ! what
the deuce did it matter to him? Nevertheless, he angrily
quickened the step with which he was pacing the room as
the thought crossed his mind. O no, Miles would not betray
him ! There were other reasons why he should not. Did
he not—perhaps it was a mistake after all his having broken
with Gertrude in that manner? She would have been in
his way here and there, perhaps ; but she was wonderfully
accommodating, even in letting him have his own way so far
as coming and going were concerned ; and how shrewd and
clear-headed she was ! So good-looking, too ! He found
himself idly tracing her profile with his finger on the table

in front of him. Strange girl—what an odd light there was
on her face that—that night when they parted! And
Harvey Gore—O, good Lord! what had started that vein
of thought? That confounded meeting with Miles had
upset him entirely. Harvey Gore!—did Gertrude suspect?
—she knew. He was certain she knew, and that was what
—It was for the best that he had got rid of her; for the
best that he was on his own hook—only himself to consult
and rely upon, and no one else with a chance of selling him.
All women were unreliable, and interfered with business.
By the way, what was that Ticehurst was saying as they
came away in the brougham about some woman who had
sung in the early part of the evening, before he got to
Carabas House? Ticehurst was wonderfully enthusiastic
for him—such a face, such a figure, such a lovely voice!
These raptures meant nothing serious, Gilbert supposed; at
all events he intended to take care that they should mean
nothing serious. That affair of Eugénie de Meronville, when
Ticehurst's admiration very nearly brought him under an
infuriated Frenchman's fire, had been of infinite service,
Gilbert reflected with a grin, in cooling his lordship's love
ardour, and indeed had kept him very much aloof from the
sex. It was better so; if Lord Ticehurst married, more than
half Gilbert Lloyd's influence would be gone, if indeed the
turf were not abandoned, and the " confederate " chasséd;
and any other arrangement in which a woman might be
concerned would be equally unsatisfactory. Fancy his
having seen Miles, and heard the old name too! How much
did Miles know? He turned on his heel as if——and yet
the old man would never have told him. His pride would
have prevented that; at all events nothing could be gained
by keeping awake now. He had thought it out, and decided
that, for several reasons, his brother would not betray him;
and so Gilbert Lloyd turned into bed, and slept as peacefully
and as easily as the darkest schemers often do, despite all
the romancists say to the contrary.

Next day he was walking through the Park with his
patron, on their way to Tattersall's, when just as they
crossed the Drive, a brougham dashed rapidly by them.
Lord Ticehurst clutched his companion's arm, and said
eagerly, " Look, Gilbert—quick! there she is." Gilbert
Lloyd looked round, and said in a tone of irritation,

"What? Who?" "The girl who sung last night at Carabas's. The stunner I told you of." "Then I wish the stunner had gone some other way," said Lloyd. "I didn't even have the satisfaction of seeing her; and I was just totting-up how we stood on the Ascot Cup, and you've startled all the figures out of my head."

CHAPTER VII.

THE LINNET'S CAGE.

MRS. BLOXAM had had no reason to regret the assent which she had given to the proposition made to her by her ex-pupil Gertrude Lloyd. The arrangement had turned out successfully, and the far-seeing astute lady, who had had quite enough of schoolkeeping considerably before she saw her way to the abandonment of that uncongenial occupation, soon began to see visions and dream dreams of a very different and much more enjoyable kind of life in the future. For a calm person, not to be taken in by appearances, and habitually distrustful of first impressions, Mrs. Bloxam may be said to have been astonished when she beheld her former pupil, after the lapse of two years and a half, during which Gertrude had been learning experience in a school which, though always severe, was sufficiently varied; and Mrs. Bloxam, when she remembered the girl at all, thought of her only as the clever and handsome pupil, who had outwitted her indeed (but that was a feat which she was not likely to overrate—she never imposed any magnified notion of her own vigilance upon herself), but who was not likely to turn out in any way remarkable. Gertrude's letter had struck her rather forcibly as being out of the common way; apart from the unusual nature of the circumstances which had given rise to it, its coolness, firmness, and business-like precision were not common in the schoolmistress's experience of feminine correspondence; and there was nothing in her previous knowledge of Gertrude's intellect and character which would have naturally led her to take such a manifestation of those qualities for granted. Mrs. Bloxam thought a good deal about Gertrude's letter in the interval between the receipt of it and the arrival of its writer. It occurred to her that the girl who took her life into her own management, after the clear, cool-headed fashion in which it was plain that Gertrude was acting, must have been rather a difficult wife to manage, and not a particularly safe one to deceive and injure. From thinking of Gertrude as the wife and the enemy of Gilbert Lloyd, it was an easy transition to think of Gertrude as possibly her (Mrs. Bloxam's) enemy—easy, not pleasant—and significantly encouraging to that lady, in the resolution she had formed, to treat Gertrude in all respects well, and with loyalty. Mrs. Bloxam conceived, in the course of her cogitations, a very reasonable certainty that Gertrude had developed into a kind of person, who, if she made up her mind to discover the secret of her birth, parentage, and previous position, would inevitably do so, or make herself extremely disagreeable in the process of failure. When this notion associated itself with the recollection of the comfortable sums of money which she had continued to receive for Gertrude's benefit, when Gertrude was absent and her fate unknown, Mrs. Bloxam congratulated herself on the course she had adopted, and made such virtuous resolutions that she would advance Gertrude's interests in every way within her power, that she soon succeeded in compounding with her conscience for the—indiscretion.

When Gertrude made her appearance at the Vale House, Mrs. Bloxam's anticipations were more than fulfilled. The young woman's easy and assured grace of manner, the calmness with which she inducted herself into the place which she had assigned to herself in the establishment, and the conviction with which she inspired Mrs. Bloxam that, if she desired to possess her confidence, she must patiently await the time and manner of her accordance of it, at her own will, were simply inimitable. The schoolmistress contemplated the girl with wonder and secret admiration. She had seen so much of the vapidity, the frivolity, the dependence, and the littleness of feminine human nature, that (as she did not care for Gertrude sufficiently to be alarmed by the dangerous side of her complex character) it was a positive pleasure to her to observe a disposition so exceptional. In person she was also changed and much improved, though Mrs. Bloxam was not slow to notice the discordant expression which occasionally deprived her face of its youthfulness by lending it an intensity beyond her years.

Gertrude Lloyd had been settled at the Vale House for more than a week, and had entered on her duties with a grave alacrity which surprised Mrs. Bloxam, whose recollection of her as a desultory pupil had left her unprepared to find the girl an active and conscientious teacher, before she accorded to Mrs. Bloxam any more confidence than that which her letter had conveyed. When so much time had elapsed, she informed Mrs. Bloxam that she intended to commence her singing-lessons, and invited that lady to be present at the trial of her voice. The masters who attended at the Vale House were all of a superior class, and Gertrude was satisfied to abide by the opinion which Signor da Capo should express concerning her musical capacity. The testimony of that dark-eyed and sentimental exile was most reassuring ; he had rarely heard such a voice as Miss Lambert's, and it was perfectly fresh and uninjured, susceptible of the highest training. He could conscientiously assure Miss Lambert no concert-singer in London possessed a finer organ, not even Mademoiselle Roulade, who was just then making such a sensation at the private concerts of the nobility—she was quite the rage at Carabas House in particular.

Miss Grace Lambert was not interested in Mademoiselle Roulade, and cut the worthy signor's raptures rather unceremoniously short ; but he produced a second edition of them for the benefit of Mrs. Bloxam, when Miss Lambert had left the room, and evinced so much curiosity concerning Miss Lambert's future plans, throwing out hints of the advantage to be derived from the judicious promulgation of reports as *avant-coureurs* of a *débutante*, that Mrs. Bloxam felt convinced of his sincerity, and forthwith began to form a pleasant scheme for the future in her fancy.

On the same evening Gertrude requested audience of Mrs. Bloxam in her private sitting-room ; and having been cordially welcomed, briefly expressed her appreciation of the kindness with which she had been received at the Vale House, and asked Mrs. Bloxam's opinion of what Signor da Capo had said. Mrs. Bloxam thought nothing could be

more satisfactory, nothing more encouraging; and if
Gertrude really intended to become a public singer——

"I do intend it," interrupted Gertrude, with a slight
expressive frown; "understand this once for all, Mrs.
Bloxam, my mind is quite made up. I may succeed, I may
fail; but at least I will make the attempt; and I feel that
I *shall* succeed. I am confident this will not be a losing
speculation for you."

"My dear girl," said Mrs. Bloxam—and she said it quite
sincerely, with true interest: there had been a fascination
for her about the girl since her return, a charm partly
arising from the uncommonness of her disposition and
manners, and partly from the elder woman's dim perception
of the pitifulness of her story—"I am not thinking about
that. I am thinking about you, and of what you must
have suffered, to have made you turn your back so resolutely on your past life. You are so young, Gertrude."

"Grace, if you please," said the younger woman, and
she touched Mrs. Bloxam's hand for a moment. In the
slight caress there was a little softening, and the other took
advantage of it.

"You may trust me, my dear, you may indeed," she
said. "I don't pretend to be disinterested in many of the
occurrences of my life; I could not afford to be so—no
woman can who has her bread to earn—and I have not
acted disinterestedly towards you; but I will if you will
trust me."

An unusual expression of gentleness was in Mrs. Bloxam's
face, and her shallow shifty blue eyes grew almost deep and
almost steady under the influence of unwonted feeling.

Gertrude sat still before her, with downcast eyes. A
little interval of silence passed, and then she looked up, and
spoke.

"I will trust you, Mrs. Bloxam, as much as I can ever
trust any one in this world. I am separated for ever, of my
own free will, by my own irrevocable decision, from my
husband. I cannot tell you why in more than general
terms. Gilbert Lloyd is a bad man—I am not a particularly
good woman; but I could not live with him, and I trust I
may never see him again. My life is at my own disposal
now; I have no friend but you."

There was no tremor in her voice, no quiver through her

slight frame, as this young girl gave so terrible an account of herself.

"But if he claims you?" said Mrs. Bloxam.

"He will never claim me," replied Gertrude; and there was that in her voice and in her look which carried conviction to her hearer's mind. "He is more than dead to me—he is as though he had never lived."

"My poor child, how wretched you must be!" exclaimed Mrs. Bloxam, almost involuntarily.

"I am not wretched," said Gertrude; and again she frowned slightly, and again her face looked old, and her voice sounded hard. "I feel that there has been a chapter of misery and of degradation in the story of my life; but I have closed it for ever. I will never speak of it again, I will never think of it again, if by any effort of my will I can keep my mind clear of it. I am young, strong, clever, and ambitious; and I am not the first woman who has made a tremendous mistake, and incurred a dreadful penalty, in the outset of her life; but I daresay few, if any, have had such a chance of escape from the consequences as I have. I will take the fullest advantage of it. And now, Mrs. Bloxam, we will talk of this no more. Let that man's name be as dead to you and me as all feeling about him is dead in my heart for ever; and help me to make a new line in life for myself."

Mrs. Bloxam looked at her silently, and sighed. Then she said:

"You are a strange young woman, and have suffered some great wrongs, I am sure. It shall be as you wish, my dear, and I will try to forget that you ever were anything but Grace Lambert. And now let us talk of affairs—yours and mine, if you like; for I have something to tell you, and to consult you about."

Gertrude looked round her, and smiled. The scene of their interview and its associations were strangely familiar to her. It seemed as though it were only the other day she had sat in that same room, summoned to a consultation with Mrs. Bloxam about the expenditure of her quarter's allowance, and the fashion of her summer costume. The same bureau lay open, disclosing a collection of tradesmen's books and bills of well-known aspect. Gertrude knew in which of the little drawers the reserve of prospectuses, in which the innumerable and incomparable advantages of the Vale House were set forth, was kept. A low chair, with a straight, upright, uncompromising back, whereon a very frosty-looking bunch of yellow dahlias had been worked in harsh worsted by a grateful pupil, stood in the position it had always occupied within Gertrude's memory, beside the bureau. It was known as "the client's chair." Moved by a familiar impulse, Gertrude rose and seated herself in this chair, and looked up at Mrs. Bloxam, with the old look so completely banished from her face, with so exactly the same girlish smile which she remembered, that Mrs. Bloxam started.

"You might have never gone away," she said, "for all the change there is in you now. What a chameleon you are, Gertrude—"

"Grace!" said Gertrude once more; and then the consultation, whose details there is no need to follow, as they will be made plain by their results, proceeded without interruption.

*   *   *   *   *

Signor da Capo was right in his judgment of Miss Lambert's voice. Her industry in the study of her art, her unflinching labour, and her great talent were alike conspicuous. After the interview with Mrs. Bloxam, Miss Lambert did not make her appearance very often in the school-room, and it was rumoured that she was not going to be exactly a teacher. This report proved to be correct. She gave a few occasional lessons, but only in a casual way; and it was understood among the pupils that not only did Miss Lambert receive lessons of preternatural duration from Signor da Capo, but that she went very often into London, and took instruction from a still more eminent professor of music, a beatified creature, glorious on the boards of the Italian Opera. It was even said, and with truth, that Miss Lambert's singing was beginning to be talked of outside the precincts of the Vale House; and that great ladies with coronets on their carriages and pocket-handkerchiefs had questioned Signor da Capo about his gifted pupil, and even called on Mrs. Bloxam. When these rumours had been for some time in circulation, and Grace Lambert's appearance in the school-room had become an event so rare as not to be looked for more than once in ten days or so, another report, and one of a startling nature, disturbed the small world of the Establishment for Young Ladies. This tremendous *on dit* foretold an event of no less moment than the relinquishment of the " Establishment " by Mrs. Bloxam, and that lady's retirement into the genteel tranquillity of private life. The Vale House had been disposed of ; so ran the rumour ; and Mrs. Bloxam was communicating with the " parents and guardians," and making over her interest and "connection" to her successor. The announcement would be made at breaking-up time. Much excitement prevailed. Most of the young ladies entertained a lively hope that their parents would not feel unreserved confidence in the successor, and that thus they should gain an indeterminate addition to the vacation. Those who had no such hope rather liked the novelty of the substitution. They "didn't mind old Bloxam ; "—but anything new must be welcome. For once rumour was not mistaken. When breaking-up time came, Mrs. Bloxam took leave of her dear young charges in a touching speech, and consigned them, with many expressions of interest, to the care of the Misses Toppit, who were henceforth to preside over the Vale House.

It was generally understood that Mrs. Bloxam's retirement had taken place under pecuniary conditions of a satisfactory character, and that Mr. Dexter had acted in the matter with becoming zeal for the interests of his client. A few days after the departure of her " dear young friends " for their several homes, Mrs. Bloxam left the Vale House She was accompanied by Grace Lambert, who remarked, as they drove away, " It must be painful to you, after all, to leave a place where you have lived so long."

" No," said Mrs. Bloxam, " it is not. *I* feel what the girls *fancy* about it : I have had too much work and too little play there, to be able to regret the Vale House."

*　　　　*　　　　*　　　　*

The carriage placed at her disposal by the Marchioness of Carabas whirled Miss Grace Lambert, after her brilliantly successful first appearance at Carabas House, to a small but remarkably pretty villa at Bayswater. The detached house, intensely modern and white, with the largest possible windows for its size, and the prettiest possible ornamentation about it—of carved wood in the Swiss style, and curly iron railings and posts and verandahs in the Birmingham style, with neat flower-beds, the colours all *en suite*, in the miniature Tuileries style—was very pretty and very comfortable. Mrs. Bloxam interested herself in every detail of the small establishment, which she had not found any difficulty in " starting " with her own funds, and which she fully expected to be able to maintain most creditably with those which should accrue from the success of Miss Grace Lambert, about which she was assured by competent authorities no reasonable doubt could be entertained.

And now that success seemed to be assured indeed. The little coterie which was wont to assemble almost daily at the villa would rejoice hugely on the morrow of the grand concert at Carabas House, and the grand Carabas Marchioness would no doubt speed the fame of her *protégée's* success far and wide in the most profitable directions.

The Marchioness had " taken up " Signor da Capo's favourite pupil, concerning whom the gushing Italian was wont to tell wonderful things, while he was pretending to administer instruction to the Lady Angelica, the beautiful and accomplished daughter of the most noble the Marchioness, who had a remarkably pretty throat, which the singing attitude exhibited in a favourable light, but who possessed about as much talent for music, or indeed for anything, as the favourite Persian cat of the most noble. Signor da Capo was very good-looking, and was one of those who, at a respectable distance, and in a modified sense, " understood " the Marchioness, and she responded to his gushing communications about Miss Lambert's talents and attractions, and the inevitable *furore* which she was indubitably to create, by a vehemently-expressed desire to befriend that young lady, and an amiable determination to bring her out at Carabas House, and so at once serve Miss Lambert, and prevent Lady Lowndes, who was her intimate enemy, and a rival patroness of genius, art, literature, and fashionable religion, from " getting hold of" the promising young *débutante*. The pleasure of the honest signor—who was truly interested in his young friend, and who religiously believed every word he had said in her favour—when Lady

Carabas announced her intention of making Miss Lambert's acquaintance, was genuine and demonstrative, and he readily gave the pledge which she exacted from him, that he would not let Lady Lowndes know of the existence of this un-sunned treasure.

"I cannot answer for the discretion of M—, my lady," said the signor; he knows Miss Lambert's genius as well as I do, and he goes to Lady Lowndes' oftener than I do; but there is always the chance for us that M— never thinks, and seldom talks of, anybody but himself."

The acquaintance made under such favourable auspices ripened rapidly into intimacy, very flattering, and likely to prove very profitable, to Miss Lambert. The Marchioness was almost as much delighted with the girl as she professed to be; and Miss Lambert, who "understood" the *grande dame* in quite a different sense from that in which she was in the habit of using the word, was quite alive to the profit and the pleasure to be derived from such exalted patronage. The calmness, the reserve, the unbending self respect of the girl had a powerful effect on Lady Carabas. They excited her curiosity, and awakened her interest. She had a good deal of the former in her disposition, apropos of everything, and particularly apropos of the love affairs of her friends and acquaintances, and she naturally felt strong curiosity on this subject as regarded Grace Lambert. She arrived, as she thought, at a tolerably accurate knowledge of who Miss Lambert saw, and where Miss Lambert went; but she never came upon the traces of the slightest "tendre."

"How very charming!" said the Marchioness of Carabas to herself, a day or two before the grand concert at Carabas House; "this young creature's heart has evidently never spoken. She will be a *débutante* in every sense."

The heart of the most noble had spoken so frequently, that it might fairly be supposed to be a little hoarse. Hence her admiration of the inarticulatism of that organ in the case of Grace Lambert. As she drove in the park that day, she actually meditated upon the expediency of introducing to the special notice of her charming *protégée* a delightful man in the Blues, who had up to a late period "understood" her, but who had had the misfortune to bore her lately, and the bad taste to take his dismissal in dudgeon.

"He knows about music," thought her ladyship; "yes,

that will do;" and then she pulled the check-string, and gave the order "home," and had scribbled half a dozen notes of invitation to a little dinner *en petit comité* on the following Sunday, before post-hour. One of the half-dozen notes was addressed to Lord Sandilands, a second to the man in the Blues, and a third to Miss Grace Lambert. The destination of the other three is no concern of ours.

When Miss Lambert's page brought her the much-monogramed note which contained Lady Carabas' invitation, she observed that a second missive lay on the salver. It was addressed to Mrs. Bloxam, who was sitting in the same room, at a little distance from the piano before which Grace was seated. The page crossed the room, and held the salver towards Mrs. Bloxam, who took the letter, and as she glanced at the superscription, turned deadly pale. She held the letter in her hand unopened, and glanced with a strange uneasiness in her usually placid face towards Grace. But Grace had thrown the note she had just read on the floor beside her, and her fingers were scampering over the keys, and her voice was pouring out volumes of sound; she seemed unconscious even of Mrs. Bloxam's presence. Seeing which that lady rose and went to her own room. Having reached that sanctum, and carefully bolted the door, she broke the seal of the letter which had caused her to experience so much emotion, and found, as she expected, that it came from Lord Sandilands. Its contents were brief and business-like. Mrs. Bloxam knew his lordship's style of old. He told her that he wished to see her alone, for a reason which he would explain in person, should he be so fortunate as to procure the desired interview, on calling at the villa on the following day, at three o'clock in the afternoon. He would take his chance of finding her at home, and, if he should be unsuccessful, would call again.

The receipt of this letter threw Mrs. Bloxam, who had been prevented by indisposition from accompanying Grace Lambert to Carabas House, and was therefore unaware that Lord Sandilands had been present at the concert, into a state of the utmost perturbation. She dreaded she knew not what. It was in vain she asked herself what had she to fear. If, indeed, the design of Lord Sandilands in coming to see her were to inquire after his daughter, he would find her in the care to which he had committed her.

With regard to the career which she had chosen, he certainly could not possess the right, nor could she imagine his having the inclination, to interfere. Was he coming to destroy the long-maintained *incognito*, to make himself known to his daughter? Was he coming to demand from her, to whose care he had committed the child, a stern account of her stewardship? Had he any suspicion of the truth? Had any rumour of Gertrude's miserable marriage reached her father? Was he coming in anger, or in curiosity, or in an access of newly-awakened conscience, of newly-born feeling? She could not tell, and yet she was forced to ask herself these questions, vain though they were; and Mrs. Bloxam acknowledged to herself afterwards that she had seldom passed through more miserable hours than those which elapsed between the receipt of Lord Sandilands' letter, and the page's announcement that Lord Sandilands was awaiting her presence in the drawing-room, on the afternoon of the same day.

At the hour which he had named Lord Sandilands presented himself at the villa. Mrs. Bloxam was alone, and received him with much more composure than she really felt, while he, in his turn, did not betray any symptoms of the unaccustomed mental perturbation which had led him to seek her presence. Years had elapsed since Mrs. Bloxam had last seen Lord Sandilands; years had changed him from a hale middle-aged man to one on whom the burden of age was beginning to tell. Those years had made less alteration in her; and the first desultory thought that occurred to her when she saw him was, how completely the likeness she had formerly traced in his features to those of Gertrude had ceased to exist. Lord Sandilands entered at once on the business of his visit.

"I have come to ask you, Mrs. Bloxam," he said, "whether I am not right in supposing that the young lady whom I saw at Carabas House two nights ago is the same whom I placed with you under the name of Gertrude Keith?"

"Miss Lambert is that young lady," replied Mrs. Bloxam.

"I thought I could not be mistaken. I have never seen her since her childhood, as you know, and did not purpose to see her. But I have changed my mind. She is very handsome and very clever, Mrs. Bloxam;" and Lord Sandilands' voice took almost a pleading tone. "She is a girl who would do credit to such a position as—as I cannot give her now; but I should like to serve her in any way that is open to me; and I have come to you to ask your advice as to how this is to be done."

"Miss Lambert is in the house now," said Mrs. Bloxam; "but I have not mentioned your name to her, or your intended visit. I fancied you might have some such purpose as you tell me of in coming, and thought it better to wait until I should know more."

"You did very right, Mrs. Bloxam," said Lord Sandilands. "I think it is better I should not see Gertrude now; and I do not think she ought ever to know the truth—to know that I am her father. It could do no good to her or to me; there is no undoing the past; but I see no objection, if you have none, to my being introduced to her in the character of an old friend of yours, interested in her because you are, and anxious to serve her. Do you see any reason why this should not be, Mrs. Bloxam?"

"Certainly not, my lord," replied Gertrude's friend; "it requires little consideration, I think, and I shall be happy to carry out your wishes now as formerly."

Mrs. Bloxam spoke with her usual fluent composure. It had forsaken her for a little while after Lord Sandilands' appearance, but now it was perfectly restored. Things were taking the best possible turn. Lord Sandilands was putting himself into the position of her debtor, making a compact of positive friendship with her. What an escape from the danger she dreaded, the risk she felt she had so duly incurred! He had no suspicion—not the slightest— the terrible episode of Gertrude's disastrous marriage was, then, safely concealed from the only human being whom, beside herself and her husband, it concerned! With steady serenity she turned her attention to what Lord Sandilands had to say to her. Their interview was long and uninterrupted, until, a few minutes after they had heard the sound of carriage-wheels in the little avenue, Grace Lambert entered the room abruptly. She was looking handsome, and in high spirits, and came in, saying,—

"I beg your pardon—I thought you were alone."

"This is Lord Sandilands, my dear," said Mrs. Bloxam,

as the old nobleman rose and bowed. "Lord Sandilands,
Miss Lambert. His Lordship saw you the other night at
Carabas House, Grace."

"Indeed!" said Grace, with a perfectly unembarrassed
smile. "I am going there now—Lady Carabas has sent the
carriage for me—so I came to tell you." Then, with a
gesture of leave-taking, she said to Lord Sandilands, "Ah,
yes, I remember now, quite well. You were in the front
seats, next to a tall young man with a very thick dark
beard."

CHAPTER VIII.

THE LINNET'S FIRST FLIGHT.

THERE were many phases of this life in which Lord
Sandilands enjoyed a singular and an extensive popularity, many varieties of the social scale in which his name
was mentioned with respect, and not a few in which he was
regarded with far more than ordinary interest. In the first
place, he was a man well born and well bred, and did
honour to his position by his appearance, his manners, and
the constant decorum which pervaded and formed part of
his life. City merchants, members of parliament, who,
having swept out their own counting-houses, of course
became rigidest Conservatives, when by those wonderful
gradations which are known to the reverent as "honest
perseverance," and to the irreverent as "lucky flukes," they
rose to be heads of the firm, felt immensely honoured by
being permitted to play in the same rubber at the Portland
with the calm, quiet, self-possessed, bald-headed, silver-
fringed old nobleman, who was a model of courtesy throughout the game, but who never missed a point or gave a
chance. Young men imbued with slang, as are the young
men of the present day, dropped the metaphor of the prize-
ring, music-hall, and the *demi-monde* villa in the presence
of the "high-dried old boy," of whose position there could
not be the smallest doubt, and who, on occasion, had shown
that he owned a tongue which could make itself felt
"doosid unpleasantly, don't you know!—kind of rough side

of it, and all that sort of thing, you know!" To women he was always scrupulously attentive, and was in consequence in the greatest favour amongst them. The fact of his wearing the willow for his old love, Lady Lucy Beecher, was *répandu* from Belgrave to Grosvenor Squares; and the story, which had won for him such affectionate interest amongst those who were young at the time when, as all supposed, he was jilted by the fair one, and bore his jilting so manfully, yet lived amongst their descendants, and caused Lord Sandilands to be regarded as "a sweet old thing," who had suffered in Love's cause, by *débutantes* who were unborn when John Borlase first won Gertrude Gautier's childish heart.

And yet Lord Sandilands was by no means a representative man. For politics he cared little or nothing. On special occasions he went down to the House and voted with his party, but in that was comprised his whole Parliamentary career. He never spoke and never intrigued; the Custom House and the Inland Revenue enrolled no members who had obtained their appointments at his instance; his personal appearance was unknown to the private secretary of the Postmaster-General; nor was his handwriting to be found in the bulging pigeon-holes of the Treasury. Many years had elapsed since he had arrayed himself in the charming court-costume which intelligence has retained from the customs of the dark ages, and presented himself at the levees of his sovereign. At flower-shows and races, at afternoon Park or morning Row, at garden parties or *fêtes champêtres*, at none of those gatherings where pleasant Frivolity rules, was Lord Sandilands known—at none, rather, save one— the Opera. There he was *facile princeps;* there he was king of the place. The check-takers and the box-keepers knew him as well as they knew the lessee, and stood in as much awe of him. The principal librarians, Messrs. Ivory, MacBone, and Déloge, prostrated themselves before him, and were always most anxious to learn his opinion of any novelty, as on that opinion they were accustomed to base their calculation of profit or loss. With Schrink, the critic of the *Statesman*—a cynical, hump-backed man, who had a spite against mankind, and "took it out" in writing venomous articles abusive of the world in general, and the musical world in particular—Lord Sandilands was the only man who had the smallest weight; and many a neophyte has owed the touch of oil which she received, instead of the pickling which threatened her, to a kind word dropped by his lordship in the seclusion of that box on the pit tier to which he alone was admitted, where Schrink sat nursing his leg, biting his nails, and glowering with fury alike at singers and audience. Behind the scenes his popularity was equally great; the sulky tenors gave up sucking their cough-lozenges and grinding their teeth at his approach, and welcomed him with courteous salutations; the basso roused himself from his stertorous sleep; the prima donna gave up that shrill altercation with her snuffy old mother; the property-men and the scene-shifters, who dashed indiscriminately against the gilded youth who roamed vacantly about, took special care to steer clear of Lord Sandilands, and touched their paper caps to him as he passed by; and the little ballet-women and chorus-singers dropped deepest curtsies to his lordship, and felt that so long as he was satisfied with them their pound a week was safe.

Had he any interest in the management? That was a moot point. Ever since the publication of the bankrupt's schedule made patent the fact that a well-known advertising teacher of languages was identical with an even more notorious agricultural implement maker, one has been afraid to give any positive opinion as to who is who in this most extraordinary world of ours. Mr. Boulderson Munns was the responsible lessee of the Grand Opera, and held the reins of management; but whose was the money embarked in the speculation it was impossible to say. Young Jeffcock, the China merchant (Jeffcock Brothers, of Shanghai), used to attend all the rehearsals, had boxes always at his command, and was treated with great deference by Mr. Boulderson Munns; but in all these respects he was equalled by Jack Clayton of the Coldstreams, who was notoriously impecunious, who owed even for his button-hole bouquets, and who spent all his ready-money in hansom cabs and sprat-suppers for the *corps de ballet.* Tommy Toshington, who knew most things, declared that Lord Sandilands had no monetary interest in the house, but that his position gave him greater influence with Mr. Boulderson Munns than was enjoyed by any of the others. "Sandilands, sir," Tommy would say, when he had dined well at somebody else's expense,—"Sandilands is the man to give a stamp to a thing of that sort !   Don't know what there is in him, but there's something that when he says a musical thing's all right, it's safe to go.   Why, when that old grey horse and green brougham of his are seen at the door of Canzonet's shop, as they are day after day in the season, it's worth a fortune to Sam Canzonet—he told me so himself.   Money ? Not a sixpence, not a sous.   When he was John Borlase he was a regular screw, and he's not improved with age ; but it is not money Munns wants out of him.   Jeffcock ? nonsense !   Jack Clayton ? bah !   The real capitalist there, sir, is——" and here Mr. Toshington whispered in your ear the name of a well-known Evangelical M.P., whom you would have as soon accredited with Mormonism as with connection with theatrical affairs ; and having made his point, hobbles off chuckling.

There was truth in this, although it was said by Tommy Toshington.   There was no doubt that Lord Sandilands had powerful interest in all the ramifications of the musical world ; and though this fact must for a long time have been patent to him, he never thought of it, never, at least, felt it so strongly as when he was turning over in his mind the curious chance which had brought him face to face with his daughter, and had been casting about as to how he best could serve her.   That the girl had musical talent he was certain.   He had served too long an apprenticeship, all amateur though it was, to his favourite science not to be thoroughly convinced of that ; and he knew perfectly well that Grace Lambert's voice and style were both far beyond those possessed by most of the gifted pupils of the Academy of Music : for the most part delightful young persons, who came out with a gush, and went in with a run ; who gave immense delight to their personal friends at the few concerts at which they sung gratuitously ; and who may, according to the orthodox ending of the children's tales, " have lived happy ever after," but who, at all events, passed the remainder of their lives in obscurity, and were never heard of again.

No : Grace Lambert—what the deuce had made her assume so unromantic a name ?   Gertrude Keith was fifty times as pretty—Grace Lambert was not to be measured by the usual bushel.   Her voice, as Lord Sandilands recollected it at Carabas House, was one of the sweetest, the most *traînante* and bewitching which, in all his great experience, he had ever listened to ; and there was something about her personal appearance, her hair and *tournure*, which completely lifted her out of the common.   " Psht ! " said the old gentleman to himself, as he lay back in his easy-chair, revolving all these things in his mind—" how many of 'em have I seen ?   There was Miss Lavrock—charmin' voice she had, bright and shrill, like a bird's pipe—a little fat, dumpy body, that made the plank in the *Sonnambula* creak beneath the weight of her ten stone, and looked more like a cook than Lucia ; and there was Miss Greenwood—Miss Bellenden Greenwood, I beg her pardon—with her saucy black eyes, and her red-and-white complexion, and her corkscrew ringlets—gad, how horrible !   But this child is marvellously *distinguée* and bred-looking ; the way her head is set on her shoulders, the shape of her head, the curve of her nostrils, and the delicacy of her hands—I'm always telling myself that blood's all bosh, as they say in their modern slang ; but 'pon my word, one finds there's something in it after all ! "

Lord Sandilands was a constant visitor now at the pretty Bayswater villa, and had conducted himself with such courtesy and kindness as to render his presence anything but disagreeable to Grace.   The time during which she had lived with her husband, short though it had been, had been quite long enough to give her an unconquerable aversion for slanginess and bad taste, and enable her to appreciate the spirit of the gentleman, which showed itself in every action, in every word of the old nobleman.   Nor did Lord Sandilands, after a little time, care to conceal the great interest which he took in Miss. Lambert's career.   While carefully veiling everything which might show the relationship in which he stood to the young girl, and while never ceasing to impress on Mrs. Bloxam—much to that worthy woman's secret annoyance, for was she not the possessor of a secret even more mysterious and more compromising in connection with Gertrude ?—the necessity of reticence, Lord Sandilands confessed to Miss Lambert that, actuated by the purest and most honourable motives, he wished to place himself at her service in advancing her interests in the profession which she had chosen, and in which she was evidently destined to take a high position, and in being of use to her in society.

And in both these ways the old nobleman was of the greatest assistance to the *débutante*. As has been before said, his verdict in musical matters was immensely thought of; while, though it must be acknowledged that the open and avowed support of many elderly noblemen would be anything but fortunate in securing the interests of a young musical lady with the members of her own sex, that of such a known Galahad as Lord Sandilands had due weight, and his *protégée*, duly escorted by Mrs. Bloxam, "went everywhere." "Everywhere" included Lady Lowndes'; and the Marchioness of Carabas knew of this, as how could she do otherwise? being a diligent student of the *Morning Post*, in addition to having it told her by seven of her dearest and most intimate friends, who called for the express purpose of startling her with the information during the next afternoon. But the Marchioness knew of Miss Lambert's appearance at Lady Lowndes' house, and yet received her the next day with a welcome which had in it even more than the usual *empressement*. Why? impossible to say, save that people were beginning to talk more and more of Miss Grace Lambert's voice and appearance, and specially of her manners. "Something odd about her, don't you know?—frigid, unimpressionable, something-which-one-can't-make-out sort of thing, you know!" the ladies said; while the delightful creature in the Blues, to whom she had been specially introduced with the view of eliciting the speaking of her heart, declared she was "doosid hard nut to crack," and something which had beaten him, the delightful creature in the Blues, "by chalks." So that Lady Carabas, carefully noting all the phases of society, felt more bound than ever to "keep in" with the *protégée* whom she had introduced; and the ambrosial footmen with the powdered locks went more frequently than ever between the halls of Carabas and the Bayswater villa, and the much-monogramed notes which they conveyed were warmer than ever in their expressions of admiration and attachment, and hopes of speedily seeing their most charming, &c.; and more than ever was Lady Carabas Miss Grace Lambert's dearest friend. But Lady Carabas was a very woman after all, and as such her friendship for her dearest friend stopped at a certain point; she brooked no interference in matters where her Soul (with the big S) was concerned. Other

women, not possessing so much worldly knowledge, might
have given their dearest friends opportunity for intimacy
with the temporary possessor of the Soul, and then
quarrelled with them for causing the Soul to be depressed
with the pangs of jealousy and distrust. Lady Carabas
knew better than that. He whose image the Soul, however
temporarily, enshrined must be kept sacred and apart, so
far as it was possible to keep him, and must be troubled
with no temptation. Hence it happened that Gilbert Lloyd,
then regnant over Lady Carabas' Soul, was never permitted
to meet, or scarcely even to hear of, the young lady in
whom he would have recognised his wife.

Of Miles Challoner, however, Miss Grace Lambert saw a
great deal ; not, indeed, at Carabas House. Ever since the
eventful evening of his introduction to Mr. Gilbert Lloyd,
Miles had crossed the threshold of Lady Carabas' mansion
as seldom as social decency, in deference to the Marchioness's
constantly renewed invitations, would permit him. The
invitations were constantly renewed ; for Lady Carabas had
taken a liking to the young man, and, indeed, the idea had
crossed her ladyship's mind that when Gilbert Lloyd's time
of office had expired—and his tenure had been already more
than the average—she could scarcely do better than intrust
Miles Challoner with the secret of the existence of her Soul,
and permit him to share in its aspiration. There was a
freshness, she thought, about him which would suit her admirably ; a something so different from those *fades* and
jaded worldlings among whom her life was passed. But
though the invitations were constant, the response to them
was very limited indeed, and only on one or two occasions
subsequent to his introduction did Miles avail himself of the
hospitality of Carabas House. On none of these occasions
did he meet Mr. Gilbert Lloyd. The same reason which
induced Lady Carabas to manœuvre in keeping her friend
for the time being from meeting her handsome *protégée*
suggested to her the expediency of preventing any possible
collision between the actual and the intended sharers of her
Soul ; collision, as Lady Carabas thought, by no means unlikely to occur, as she was a shrewd observant woman of the
world, and had noticed the odd behaviour of both gentlemen at the time of their introduction.

But Lord Sandilands, loving Miles Challoner for his own

and for his father's sake, and noticing the strong impression which Miss Lambert's voice and beauty had made upon the young man, had taken him to the Bayswater villa, and formally introduced him; and both Mrs. Bloxam and Grace had "hoped they should see more of him." He was a gentleman. You could not say much more of him than that; but what an immense amount is implied in that word! He was not very bright; he never said clever or smart things—consequently he kept himself from evil-speaking, lying, and slandering; he had no facility for gossip—consequently he never intruded on the ladies the latest news of the *demi-monde* heroines, nor the backstairs' sweepings of the Court; he was earnest and manly, and full of youthful fervour on various subjects, which he discussed in a bright, modest way, which won Mrs. Bloxam's by no means impulsive heart, and at the same time made that impulsive heart beat quickly with its knowledge of Gertrude's secret: a secret with which the unexpressed but impossible-to-be-mistaken admiration of this young man might interfere.

Impossible-to-be-mistaken admiration? Quite impossible. Lord Sandilands—though years had gone by since he had been a proficient in that peculiar vocabulary, whose expressions are undefined and untranslatable—recognized it in an instant, and scarcely knew whether to be pleased or vexed as the idea flashed upon him. He loved Miles like his own son, believed in all his good qualities, recognized and admitted that the young man had all in him requisite to make a good, loving husband; his social status, too, was such as would be most desirable for a girl in Gertrude's position. But Lord Sandilands knew that any question of his natural daughter's marriage would entail the disclosure of the relation in which he stood to her; and he dreaded the ridicule of the world, dreaded the banter of the club, dreaded more than all the elucidation of the fact that the *répandu* notion of his wearing the willow for Lady Lucy Beecher had been all nonsense, and that he had consoled himself for her ladyship's defalcation by an intrigue of a very different calibre.

"I should be laughed at all over town," the old gentleman said to himself; "and though it must come, by George, it's best to put off the evil day as long as possible. I don't know. I'm an old fellow now, and have not as keen an eye for these things as I had ; but *I* don't perceive any sign of a *tendresse* on Gertrude's part ; and, all things considered, I'm glad of it."

And Lord Sandilands was right. There was not the smallest sign of any feeling for Miles Challoner in Grace Lambert. Had she had the least spark of such a feeling kindling in her heart, it is very doubtful whether she would have permitted it to be remarked in her outward manner ; but her heart was thoroughly free from any such sentiment. She liked Miles Challoner—liked his frank bearing, and was touched, after her fashion, by the respect which he showed her. It was something quite new to her, this old-fashioned courtesy from this young man. Of course, during her schooldays she had seen nothing of mankind, save as exemplified in the foreign professors of languages and music, whose courtesy was for the most part of the organ-monkey order—full of bows and grins. After her marriage, the set in which she was thrown—though to a certain extent kept in order by the feeling that Gilbert Lloyd was " a swell," and had peculiar notions as to how his wife should be treated—never had scrupled to talk to her without removing their hats, or to smoke in her presence. And though the gentlemen she had met at Carabas House had been guilty of neither of these solecisms, there had been a certain *laissez-aller* air about them, which Grace Lambert had ascribed to a *tant soit peu* disdain of her artistic position ; the real fact being that to assume a vice if he have it not, and to heap as much mud as possible on that state of life into which it has pleased Providence to call him, is the chosen and favourite occupation of a high-born and wealthy young man of the present day. So Grace Lambert recognized Miles Challoner as a gentleman *pur sang*, and appreciated him accordingly ; had a bright glance and a kindly word of welcome for him when he appeared at the Bayswater villa, made him at home by continuing her singing-practice while he remained, made him happy by asking him when he was coming again as he said his adieux ; but as to having what Lord Sandilands called a *tendresse* for the man, as to being in love with him—Love came into Gertrude Keith's heart three months before she walked out of the laundry-window over the roof of the schoolroom, and stepped down on to the driving-seat of the hansom cab, in which Gilbert Lloyd was waiting to take her off to the church and make her his wife. Love died out of Gertrude Lloyd's heart within three months of that marriage-day; and as for Grace Lambert, she never had known and never intended to know what the sentiment meant. So, so far, Lord Sandilands was right; and the more he watched the conduct of the two young people when alone towards each other—and he watched it narrowly enough—the more he took occasion to congratulate himself on his own perspicacity and knowledge of the world. But at the same time he reflected that the life which Miss Grace Lambert was leading was but a dull one, that she took but little interest in these society successes; and he took occasion to glean from her what he knew before—that her heart and soul were bound up in her profession, and that she was by no means satisfied by the hitherto limited opportunities afforded her of showing what she really could do therein. This ambition of the girl's to make for herself name and fame in the musical world by no means jarred against the ideas of the old nobleman. He should have to acknowledge her as his daughter some day or other, that he saw clearly enough; and it would be infinitely preferable to him, and would render him infinitely less ridiculous in the eyes of that infernal bantering club-world of which he stood so much in awe, if he could point to a distinguished artist of whom all the world was talking in praise, and say, " This is my child," than if he had to bear the brunt of the parentage of a commonplace and unknown person. There were half-a-dozen other ladies occupying a somewhat similar position to Miss Lambert's in society, as queens of amateur singing sets; and though she was acknowledged by all disinterested people to be far and away the best of them, it was necessary that she should have some public ratification of her merits, or, at all events, that some professional opinion, independent of that of Da Capo or her other singing-master, who would naturally be biassed, should be given. The other ladies were daughters and wives of rich men, who sang a little for their friends' and a great deal for their own amusement; but Miss Lambert's career was to be strictly professional, and a touchstone of a very different kind was to be applied to her merits.

That was a happy time for Miles Challoner, perhaps really the happiest in his life. His first love, at least the first passion really deserving that name, was nascent within him, and all the environing circumstances of his life were tinged with the roseate hue which is the necessary "local colour" of the situation. Moreover, his feelings towards Gertrude were at present in that early stage of love in which they could be borne and indulged in without worrying and making him miserable. She was the nicest woman he had ever seen, and there was something marvellously attractive about her, something which he could not explain, but the magnetic influence of which he knew it impossible to resist. So he abandoned himself to the enjoyment of this pleasant feeling, enjoying it doubly perhaps, because up to this point it had been, and seemed to promise to continue to be, a mild and equable flame; not scorching and withering everything round it, but burning with a pleasant, steady heat. You see, at present Mr. Challoner had not seen much, if anything, of Miss Lambert alone; his admiration sprung from observation of her under the most commonplace circumstances, and his passion had never been quickened and stung into fiercer action by the thought of rivalry. True, that whenever Miss Lambert went into society she was always surrounded by a bragging crowd of representatives of the gilded youth of the period, who did their best to flatter and amuse her; attempts in which, if her grave face and formal manner might be accepted in evidence, they invariably and signally failed. And at the Bayswater villa he might be said to have her entirely to himself, he being the only young man admitted there, with the exception occasionally of some musical professor, native or foreign; the delightful creature in the Blues, and other delightful creatures who had made Miss Lambert's acquaintance in society, having tried to obtain the *entrée* in vain.

So Miles went on pleasantly in a happy dream, which was very shortly to come to an end; for Lord Sandilands, thinking it full time that some definite steps should be taken in regard to Gertrude's professional future, arrived one morning at the Bayswater villa, and was closeted with the young lady for more than two hours. During this interview, the old gentleman, without betraying his relationship with her, told Gertrude that, far beyond anything else, he had her interests at heart; that he had perceived her desire for professional distinction; and that, as he saw it was impossible to combat it, he was ready then and there to advance it to the best of his ability. Only, as the training was somewhat different, it was necessary that she should make up her mind whether she would prosecute her career in the concert-room or on the operatic stage.

It was a pity Miles Challoner was not present to mark the brilliant flush which lit up Gertrude's usually pale cheeks, the fire which flashed in her eyes, and the proud curl of her small lips, as this proposition was made to her. For a few moments she hesitated, a thousand thoughts rushed through her mind—thoughts of her real position, retrospect of her past life—a wild, feverish vision of future triumph, where she, the put-aside and rejected of Gilbert Lloyd, the pupil-teacher of the suburban boarding-school, should be queen-regnant, and have some of the greatest and highest in the kingdom for her slaves. As *prima donna* of the Opera, what position might she not assume, or where should her sway stop, if ambition were to be gratified? And then the old cynical spirit arose within her; and she thought of the tinsel and the sham, the gas and the gew-gaws; and the light died out of her eyes, and her cheeks resumed their usual pallor, and it was a perfectly cold hand which she placed in Lord Sandilands', as she said to him, without the smallest tremor in her voice, "You have indeed proved yourself a perfectly disinterested friend, my lord; how could I do better than leave the decision on my future career in your hands?"

Lord Sandilands was rather unprepared for this speech, and a little put out by it. He had an objection to accepting responsibility in general; and in this instance, where he really felt deeply, he thought naturally that Gertrude would scarcely think of him with much gratitude if his choice did not eventuate so happily for her as he intended. However, there was nothing else to be done; so he raised the cold hand to his lips with old-fashioned gallantry, and promised to "think the matter over," and see her again on the following day. With many people, to think a matter over means to discuss it with some one else. Lord Sandilands was of this class; and though he accepted the commission so glibly from Gertrude, he never had the smallest intention of deciding upon it without taking excellent advice. That advice he sought at the hands of Mr. Déloge, the "librarian" of Jasmin Street.

An odd man, Mr. Déloge—a character worth a passing study. His father, who had been a "librarian" before him, had amassed a large sum of money in those good old days when speculations in opera-boxes and stall-tickets were highly remunerative to those who knew how to work them, had given his son an excellent education abroad, and had hoped to see him take a superior position in life. But, to his parent's disappointment, young Déloge, returning from the Continent with a knowledge of several languages, and an acquaintance with life and the world which serves any one possessing it better than any other knowledge whatsoever, determined to follow the family business, adding to it and grafting on to it such other operations as seemed to be analogous. These operations were so admirably selected and so well conducted, that before the old man died he had quite acquiesced in his son's decision, and at the time of our story there was no more thriving man in London. The old-fashioned shop in Jasmin Street bore the name over the door still ; but that name was now widely known throughout England and Europe. No Secretary of State was harder worked than Mr. Déloge, who yet found time to hunt once or twice a week, to live at Maidenhead during the summer, and at Brighton during the autumn, and generally to enjoy life. In person he was a tall thin man, with an excellently-made wig and iron-grey whiskers, always calm and staid in demeanour, and always irreproachably dressed after the quietest style. He looked like a middle-aged nobleman whose life had been passed in diplomacy ; and people who asked who he was—and most people did, so striking was his appearance—were surprised to hear that he was only "the man who sells the stalls, don't you know ?" in Jasmin Street. Nothing pleased him more than to observe this astonishment, and he used to delight in telling a story against himself in illustration of it. One day, in the course of business, he had occasion to wait on a very great lady, one of his customers. He drove to the house in his perfectly-appointed brougham, and the door was opened by a strange footman, to whom he gave his card for transmission to her grace.

The footman led the way into the library, poked the fire, wheeled the largest arm-chair in front of it, and placed the *Morning Post* in the visitor's hands. Mr. Déloge had scarcely finished smiling at the extreme *empressement* of the man's manner, when the door was opened, and the same servant pushed his head in. "Her grace don't want no hop'ra-box to-night," were his charming words, delivered in his most offensive manner. The scales had fallen from his eyes, and the great creature found he had deceived himself into being civil to a " person in business."

Mr. Déloge had gone through what to many men would have been an entire day's business in the morning before Lord Sandilands called upon him. He had read through an enormous mass of letters, and glanced over several news-papers—had pencilled hints for answers on some, and dictated replies to others at full length. His business seemed to have ramifications everywhere : in Australia, where he had an agent travelling with the celebrated Italian Opera *troupe*—the soprano, basso, tenor, and baritone, who were a little used up and bygone in England, but who were the greatest creatures that had ever visited Australia—so at least said the *Wong-Wong Kangaroo*, a copy of which the agent forwarded with his letter; in America, where Schlick's opera, in which Mr. Déloge possessed as much copyright as the large-souled American music-sellers could not pillage him of, was a great success; in India, whence he had that morning received a large order for pianos—for Mr. Déloge is not above the manu-facture and exportation of musical instruments, and indeed realizes a handsome yearly revenue from that source alone. Before eleven o'clock he had come to terms, and signed and sealed an agreement with Mr. McManus, the eminent tragedian, for a series of readings and recitations through-out the provinces, thus giving the " serious " people who objected to costume and gas a quasi-theatrical entertain-ment which they swallowed eagerly ; he had sent a cheque for ten pounds to Tom Lillibullero, who was solacing his imprisonment in Whitecross Street by translating a French libretto for the house of Déloge ; he had given one of his clerks a list of a few friends to be asked down to Maidenhead the next Sunday—all art people, writers, painters, singers, who would have a remarkably jolly day, and enjoy themselves, as they always do, more than any other set of people in the world; and he had written half a dozen private notes—one among the rest addressed to the Marchioness of Carabas, telling her that as her ladyship particularly wished it he should be happy to purchase and publish Mr. Ferdinand Wisk's operetta, which had been performed with such success at Carabas House; but that he must stipulate that the operetta must be dedicated to her ladyship, and that each *morceau* must have a vignette from her ladyship's portrait on the cover.

Mr. Déloge had not half completed his business for the day when he was informed, through the snake-like elastic pipe that lay at the right-hand of his writing-table, that Lord Sandilands was in the shop and asking to see him, but he gave orders that his visitor should at once be admitted. He was far too recognisant of the old nobleman's position in the musical world to have kept him waiting or allowed him to feel the smallest slight, if indeed there had not been, as there was, a feeling of respect between the two men, which, had they been on the same social footing, would have been strong friendship.

"How d'ye do, Déloge?" said Lord Sandilands, walking up and heartily shaking hands; "this is very kind of you, my good fellow, to allow me to come and bother you when you're over head and ears in business, as you always are—very kind indeed."

"I don't want to say a pretty thing, my dear lord," said Mr. Déloge, "but when I can't find leisure from my business to attend to you when you want to see me, I'd better give that business up."

"Thanks, very much. Well, what's the news? Been to Tenterden-street lately? Any very promising talent making itself heard up there, eh?"

"No, my lord, none indeed, I'm glad to say," replied Déloge with a laugh.

"Glad to say! eh, Déloge? that's not very patriotic, is it?"

"O, I did not mean to confine my gladness to the dearth of native talent. If you only knew, my dear lord, how I'm hunted out of life by promising talent, or by talent which considers itself promising and wants to perform, you would know fully how to appreciate, as I do, good steady-going mediocrity."

"By Jove, Déloge! this is not very encouraging for me! I came to ask your advice on the question of bringing out a young lady of unquestionable genius."

"Unless her genius is quite unquestionable I should advise you to let the young lady remain in. Why, think for yourself, my dear lord; you know these things as well as I do, and have every singer for the past quarter of a century in your mind. Run over the list and tell me which of them—always excepting Miss Lavrock—has made anything like a success."

"Ha!" said Lord Sandilands, "yes, the Lavrock— what a voice, what a charming trill! not but that I think Miss Lambert——"

"Is it a question of Miss Lambert—Miss Grace Lambert?"

"It is. Miss Lambert has decided upon adopting the musical profession, and my object in coming here was to consult you as to the best means to give effect to her wishes."

"That's quite another affair. I have only heard Miss Lambert once. I was engaged by Lady Lowndes to pilot Miramella and Jacowski to one of her ladyship's wonderful gatherings, and after they had finished their duet we went to the dining-room to get some of that curious refreshment which is always provided there for the artists. They had scarcely begun to eat when the whole house rang with a trill of melody so clear and bird-like that the Miramella only drank half her glass of sherry, and Jacowski put down his sandwich—I don't wonder at it—untasted. We all rushed up stairs, and found that the singer was Miss Grace Lambert. She sang so exquisitely, and produced such an immense effect, that Madame Miramella was seized with one of her violent headaches, and was obliged to be taken home."

Lord Sandilands was delighted. "Poor Miramella!" said he, chuckling quietly, "and Ger——and Miss Lambert was successful?"

"Successful! I have not heard such a combination of voice and style for years! But I thought she was merely an amateur, and had no idea she intended to take to the profession."

"Yes, she is determined to do so; and as I take the greatest interest in her, I have come to ask your advice. Now, should she select the concert-room or the stage as her arena?"

"The stage! the stage!" cried Déloge excitedly; "there can be no question about it, my dear lord! With that personal appearance and that voice, she must have the whole world at her feet and make her fortune in a very few years. Any dumpy little woman who can sing tolerably in tune and face an audience without the music in her hand visibly trembling, will do for a concert-room; but this young lady has qualities which—Good heavens! fancy the effect she'd make in Opera, with that head and that charming figure!"

"My good friend!" said the delighted old nobleman, "you are becoming positively enthusiastic. In these days of total suppression of feelings, it does one good to hear you. I am charmed to see you think so highly of my *protégé*. Now tell me, what's the first step to be taken towards bringing her out?"

"I should let Munns hear her," said Mr. Déloge.

And Lord Sandilands' face fell, and he looked very grave. Why? Well, the mention of Mr. Munns' name was the first thing that had jarred disagreeably on Lord Sandilands' ears and feelings in connection with Gertrude's intended adoption of the musical profession; and it *did* jar. Why, Lord Sandilands knew perfectly, but could scarcely express.

Who was Mr. Boulderson Munns? You might have asked the question in a dozen different sets of society, and received a different answer in each. What was his birth or parentage no one, even the veriest club scandal-monger, ever assumed to know; and as to his education, he had none. He had been so long "before the public" that people had forgotten whence he came, or in what capacity his *début* was made. Only a very few men remembered, or cared to remember, that when Peponelli's management of the Grand Scandinavian Opera came to smash disastrously, by reason of Miramella, Jacowski, Courtasson, and Herzogenbusch, the celebrated singers, revolting and going over in a body to the Regent Theatre, the opposition house, Messrs.

Mossop and Isaacson, of Thavies' Inn, put themselves in communication with the agents of the Earl of Haremarch, the ground landlord, and proposed their client, Mr. Boulderson Munns, as tenant. Lord Haremarch's agent, old Mr. Finchingfield, of New Square, Lincoln's Inn, looked askance through his double eye-glass at Messrs. Mossop and Isaacson's letter. He had heard of those gentlemen, truly, and knew them to be in a very large way of business, connected generally with people "in trouble"—criminals and bankrupts. Of Mr. Boulderson Munns, the gentleman proposed as tenant, Mr. Finchingfield had never heard ; but on consulting with Mr. Leader, his articled clerk, a young gentleman who saw a good deal of "life," he learned that Mr. Munns had been for some time lessee of the Tivoli Gardens over the water, and was supposed to be a shrewd, clever, not too scrupulous man, who knew his business and attended to it. Mr. Finchingfield was a man of the world. "I don't know anything about such kind of speculations, and indeed it is strongly against my advice that my Lord Haremarch permits himself to be mixed up in such matters," he said. "But I should imagine that from a person tendering for a theatre, you do not require a certificate of character from the clergyman of his parish ; and if Mr. Munns is prepared to deposit a year's rent in advance, and to enter into the requisite sureties for the due performance of the various covenants of the lease, I see no reason why I should not recommend my lord to accept him as his tenant." And Mr. Leader, remembering this conversation, made a point of letting Mr. Munns know as soon as possible that if he, Mr. Munns, should get the theatre, it would be owing entirely to his, Mr. Leader's representations—a statement made by Mr. Leader with a view to the future acquisition of gratuitous private boxes, and that much-coveted *entrée* known as "going behind."

So Mr. Boulderson Munns became the tenant of the Grand Scandinavian Opera House, and took up his position in society, which at once began to pick holes in his garments, and to say all the unpleasant things it could against him. Some people said his name was not Boulderson at all, nor Munns much ; that his real appellation was Muntz, and that he was the son of a German Jew sugar-baker in St. George's-in-the East. People who professed to know said that Mr. Munns commenced his career in the useful though not-much-thought-of profession of a chiropodist, which they called a corn-cutter, in which capacity he took in hand the feet of Polesco Il Diavolo, the gentleman who made a rushing descent down a rope with fireworks in his heels at the Tivoli Gardens ; and that by these means the youthful Muntz was brought into relations with Waddle, who then owned the gardens, and to whom Muntz lent some of the money he had inherited from the parental sugar-baker, at enormous interest. When Waddle collapsed, Muntz first appeared as Munns, and undertook the management of the gardens, which he carried on for several years with great success to himself and gratification to the public—more especially to the members of the press, who were always free of the grounds, and many of whom were entertained at suppers—at which champagne—known to Mr. Munns by the name of "sham"—flowed freely. He was a genial, hospitable, vulgar dog, given, as are the members of his nation, to the wearing of rich-coloured velvet coats and waistcoats, and jewelry of a large and florid pattern, to the smoking of very big cigars, the driving of horses in highly-plated harness in mail-phaetons with wheels vividly picked out with red, to the swearing of loud and full-flavoured oaths, and to Richmond dinners on the Sunday. When he entered on the lesseeship of the Grand Scandinavian Opera House, he continued all these eccentricities of pleasure, but mixed with them some excellent business habits. On the secession of Miramella, Jacowski, and all the rest, the public pronounced the Scandinavian Opera to be utterly dead and done for ; but after the first few weeks of his season Mr. Munns produced Fraulein Brödchen, from the Stockholm Theatre, who fairly routed everyone else off their legs, and took London by storm. Never had been known such a triumph as that achieved by the Brödchen ; boxes and stalls fetched a fabulous price, and were taken weeks in advance. It began to be perceived that the right thing was that Norma should have bright red hair ; and people wondered how they had for so long endured any representative of Lucrezia without a turn-up nose. Miramella of the classic profile and the raven locks was nowhere. Jacowski the organ-voiced bellowed in vain. The swells of the Young-England party—guardsmen and impecunious youths, who were on the free list at the Regent—tried to get up an opposition ; but Munns ran over to Barcelona, and came back with the Señorita Ciaja, whose celebrated back-movement in the Cachuca finished the business. The people who really understood and cared for music were delighted with the Brödchen ; the occupants of the stalls and of the omnibus-box—crabbed age and youth, who, despite the old song, manage to live together sometimes, and on each other a good deal—revelled in the Ciaja, and the trick was done. Mr. Munns realised an enormous sum of money, and was spoken of everywhere as " a marvellous fellow ! a cad, sir, but a genius ! "

He was a cad, there was no doubt of that. The Earl of Haremarch, who, with all his eccentricities, was a highly-polished gentleman, suffered for days after an interview with his tenant, who would receive him in his managerial room with open bottles of " sham," and " My lord " him until the wine had done its work, when he would call him " Haremarch, old fellar ! " with amiable frankness. He always addressed the foreign artists in English ; told them he didn't understand their d—d palaver, and poked them in the ribs, and slapped them on the back, until they ground their teeth and stamped their feet in inarticulate fury ; but his money was always ready when due, and his salaries were liberal, as well as promptly paid. The *corps de ballet* adored him, admired his velvet waistcoats, and screamed at his full-flavoured jokes. In person Mr. Munns was a short stout man, with an enormous chest, a handsome Hebraic face, with dyed beard and whiskers, and small keen eyes.

To such a man as this Lord Sandilands, the polished old nobleman, had naturally a strong antipathy ; and yet Lord Sandilands was almost the only man of his *clientèle* to whom Mr. Munns showed anything like real respect. " There's something about that old buffer," he would say, " which licks me ; " and he could not have paid a greater compliment. The Brödchen had retired into private life before this, and the Ciaja had gone to America on a starring tour ; but Mr. Munns had replaced them with other attractions, had well maintained his ground : and when Mr. Déloge told Lord Sandilands that from Mr. Munns it would be best to obtain the information and the opinion he sought, the old nobleman knew that the librarian was right ; though he hated Mr. Munns from the bottom of his heart, yet he made up his mind to get the great *impresario* to hear Miss Grace Lambert, and determined to abide by his advice.

So, one fine afternoon, the little road in which the pretty Bayswater villa was situated was thrown into a state of the greatest excitement by the arrival of the dashing phaeton with the prancing horses in their plated harness; and Mr. Boulderson Munns alighting therefrom, was received by Lord Sandilands and duly presented to Miss Lambert. After partaking somewhat freely—for he was a convivial soul—of luncheon and dry sherry—which wine he was pleased to compliment highly, asking the " figure " which it cost, and the name of the vendor—the great *impresario* was ushered into the drawing-room, where Signor Da Capo seated himself at the piano, and Gertrude, without the smallest affectation or hesitation, proceeded to sing. Mr. Munns, who had been present at many such inaugural attempts, seated himself near Lord Sandilands with a re-signed countenance; but after a very few notes the aspect of his face entirely changed; he listened with the greatest attention; he beat time with his little podgy diamond-ringed fingers, and with his varnished boots; and at the conclusion of the song, after a strident cry of " Brava ! brava ! " he winked calmly at the radiant nobleman, laid his finger alongside his nose, and whispered, " Damme, that'll do ! "

After a further hearing the great *impresario* expressed himself more fully, after his own symbolic fashion.

" That's the right thing," said he ; " the right thing, and no flies ! or rather it will be the right thing a few months hence.—My dear," he continued, laying his hand on Ger-trude's arm, and keeping it there, though she shrank from his touch, " no offence, my dear ; you've got the right stuff in you ! No doubt of that ! Now what we've got to do is to bring it out of you. Don't you make any mistake about it ; it's there, but it wants forcing. What's to force it ? why, a mellower air and a few lessons reg'larly given by some one who knows all about it. No offence again to Da Capo here, who's a very good fellow—him and me un-derstand each other ; but this young lady wants some one bigger than him, and quiet and rest and freedom from London ways and manners. Let her go to Italy and stop there for nine months; meanwhile, you and me, my lord, the Marsh'ness Carabas, and the rest of us, will work the oracle, and then she shall come back and come out at the Grand Scandinavian Opera House; and if she ain't a success, I'll swallow my Lincoln and Bennett!"

There was a pause for a minute, and then Lord Sandilands said,—"Do you mean that Miss Lambert should make her *début* on the Italian stage?"

"Not a bit of it," shrieked Mr. Munns; "keep her *début* for here! A gal like that, who can walk up to the piano and sing away before me, won't have any stage-fright, I'll pound it! Let her go to Florence, to old Papadaggi—which you know him well, my lord, and can make it all square there; let her take lessons of him, and make her *début* with me. I'm a man of my word, as you know, and I see my way."

Within a fortnight from that time Miles Challoner, who had been out of town, called at the Bayswater villa, found it in charge of a policeman and his wife, learned that Miss Lambert and Mrs. Bloxam had gone to Hit'ly for some months, and—went away lamenting.

CHAPTER IX.

SOARING.

THE novelty of her life in Italy was full of charm for Gertrude. She was still so young that she could escape, in any momentary emotion of pleasure, from the hardening influence of the past, and the entire change of scene had almost an intoxicating effect upon her. Here was no association with anything in the past which could pain, or in the present which might have the power to disconcert her. Her husband's foot had never trodden the paths in which she wandered daily, with all the pleasure of a stranger and all the appreciation of natural beauty which formed a portion of her artistic temperament. He had never gazed upon the classic waters of the Arno, or roamed through the picture-galleries which afforded her such intense delight, and would have been almost without a charm for his cynical materialistic nature. At least, if he had ever visited Italy, Gertrude did not know it ; and with all her very real indifference, despite the wonderfully thorough enfranchisement of her mind and heart from the trammels of her dead-and-gone relation to him, Gertrude, with true womanly inconsistency, still occasionally associated him sufficiently with her present life to feel that distance from Gilbert Lloyd, that the strangeness of the unfamiliar places with which he was wholly unassociated, added to the reality of her sense of freedom, gave it zest and flavour. She understood this inconsistency. "If I go on like this," she would think, "it will never do. I am much too near hating him at present to be comfortable. So long as he is not absolutely nothing to me, I am not quite free ; so long as I prefer the sense of the impossibility of my seeing him by any accident—so long as I am more glad to know that he is staying with Lord Ticehurst, and Lord Ticehurst's reputable friends, than I should be to know that he was in the next house on the promenade—so long as either circumstance has the smallest appreciable interest or importance for me—I am not free. I must regard him as so utterly nothing, that if I were to meet him to-morrow at the Cascine, or passing my door, it could have no importance, no meaning for me. I don't mean only in the external sense, of not appearing to agitate or concern me, but in the interior convictions of my own inmost heart. Such freedom I am quite resolved to have. It will come, I am sure, but not just yet. I am far too near to hating him yet."

Gertrude had unusual power in the distribution of the subjects on which she chose to exercise her thinking faculty, and in the absolute and sustained expulsion from her mind of such topics as she chose to discard. This faculty was very useful to her now. There were certain phases and incidents of her life with Gilbert Lloyd which she never thought about. She deliberately put them out of her mind, and kept them out of it. Among these were the occurrences which had immediately preceded the strange bargain which had been made between her and her husband. Of that bargain herself she thought with ever-growing satisfaction, remembering with complacent content the obscurity in which she had lived, which rendered such an arrangement possible, without risk of detection. But she never travelled farther back in memory than the making of that bargain. So then she determined to carry it out to the fullest, to have all the satisfaction out of it she possibly could. "I am determined I will bring myself to such freedom that the sight of him could not give me even an unpleasant sensation—that the sound of his name announced in the room with me should have no more meaning for me than any other sound devoid of interest."

Gertrude was more happily circumstanced now for the carrying out of this determination. All her surroundings were delightful and novel, she was in high health and spirits, and her prospects for the future were bright and near. The climate was enchanting, the hours and the ways of foreign life suited her ; and her masters pronounced her voice all that could be desired in the case of a daughter of sunny Italy, and something altogether admirable and extraordinary in the case of a daughter of foggy Albion. She worked very hard. She kept her ambition, her purpose steadily before her, and her efforts to obtain the power of gratifying it were unrelaxing.

Hitherto Gertrude's experiences had been those only of a school-girl and a woman married to an unscrupulous man who lived by his wits. She had never been out of England before ; and the interval of her life at the villa, under the beneficial influence of the Carabas patronage, though very much pleasanter than anything she had before experienced, had not tended much to the enlargement and cultivation of her mind or the expansion of her feelings. But this foreign life did tend to both. She was entirely unfettered, and the sole obligation laid upon her was the vigilant precaution it was necessary she should observe against taking cold. It was in Gertrude's nature to prize highly this newly-acquired sense of personal freedom, and to enter with avidity into all that was strange in her life abroad. Her enjoyment of the difference between the habits and customs of Italy and those of England was unintelligible to Mrs. Bloxam, who had also never before been out of England, and who carried all the true British prejudice in favour of everything English with her. She could not be induced to admit the superiority of foreign parts, even in those lesser and superfluous respects to which it is generally conceded. "I cannot see," she remarked to a sympathizing soul, whose acquaintance she had made shortly after her arrival—a lady held in foreign bondage by a tyrannical brother and his wife addicted to travel—" I cannot see, Miss Tyroll, that the new milk can be so much better. Just look at the cows ! I'm sure I've seen some at Hampstead twice the size ; and as for condition ! And then the bread again : how can we tell what stuff they put into it to make it white ? At home, we know there's alum in it ; and that's the worst of it, and all about it. But here, I never dare think about it. Miss Lambert is quite foolish about violets ; and I don't deny it is very nice indeed to have them when you certainly could not in England, and I like them as well as any one ; but I don't know that it makes so much difference after all, in one's comfort, in the long run."

" Certainly not," replied Miss Tyroll, who was a person of decisive mind and manners. " Foreign countries are much the best places for having things which you can very well do without ; but, for my part, I like England best. Don't you get very tired of marble and pillars and church-bells ? I do."

" So do I," assented Mrs. Bloxam ; "and all the places one is obliged to go to are so large and bare." And then the two ladies discussed the subject just started at great length. Even the climate had little merit in the prejudiced estimation of Mrs. Bloxam. She had felt it quite as cold by the Arno as ever she had felt it by the Thames; and she thought the *tramontana* was only a piercing wind with a pretty name. She had felt very much the same sort of thing in London, where she could take refuge from it in a snug room with warm curtains and a coal fire. She had no fancy for sitting with her feet baking over *braise,* and she had seen at Dulwich and Hampton Court pictures enough to satisfy all her aspirations after art. There was something educational in the way in which visitors to Florence—and, indeed, Gertrude herself—did the churches and the galleries which was rather oppressive to Mrs. Bloxam. She hated all that reminded her of the life of sordid toil she had lived through and freed herself from ; she did not like to learn anything, because she could not get rid of the feeling that by doing so she was exposing herself to the danger of having to teach it again. But all her personal discontent did not interfere with Mrs. Bloxam's interest in Gertrude, and did not render her an unpleasant companion. She was not sympathetic ; but Gertrude had been little used to sympathy, and she did not greatly care about it—it never interfered with her enjoyment of anything, that she had to enjoy it alone. She did all in her power to make Mrs. Bloxam's life comfortable and happy, and she never interrupted or withheld her assent from the frequent reminiscences of Bayswater in which her friend indulged ; but she liked her life in Italy, and she entertained a strong conviction that, as she had never been so happy before (for she had come to regard the brief period of her love for Lloyd as an interval of hallucination), so the future could hardly bring her anything better. She had no doubts, no fears about success in her adopted profession. The favourable opinions which had been pronounced by competent judges in England were confirmed and strengthened by those to which she attached most value in Italy, and her progress was surprising to herself and her instructors.

The correspondence between Mrs. Bloxam and Lord Sandilands was frequent and *suivie*. Mrs. Bloxam was a clever letter-writer, and the recipient of her epistles found in them a source of interest which life had long lacked for him. If the young lady in whom he had discovered Gertrude Gautier's daughter had been merely handsome, he would have been pleased with her, doubtless would have taken a kindly interest in her ; had she been only clever he would have felt a secret pride in her talent, and watched its manifestations with a hidden interest : but she was both handsome and clever, and highly gifted ; and all the feelings which, but for his own fault, he might once have declared and indulged openly, had been gratified to the fullest extent.

As time went on, the " working of the oracle " was done in London by the *impresario* and his assistants in a masterly fashion. The higher branch of the same industry was also conducted by the Marchioness of Carabas with all the success to which her ladyship was so well accustomed in her social manœuvrings. To such members of her coterie as understood her passionate devotion to art, her untiring exertions in its interest, and to its professors, she spoke in raptures of her " dear Grace Lambert," carefully avoiding the distant precision of the " Miss " and the too fond familiarity of the " Grace ; " she read what she called " pet bits" of her young *protégée's* letters, which were neither numerous nor lengthy; predicted the future value of those precious autographs, and contrived to keep a flickering flame of interest in Grace Lambert alive, which her appearance would readily blow into a blaze. The steadiness of dear Lady Carabas to this "fancy," as her friends called it, created some astonishment among her circle. She was more remarkable for the vehemence than for the duration of her attachments. It had happened to many aspirants for fame, or for social success, or some other of the many objects which people think worth attainment, even if a little self-respect has to be sacrificed in the process, to find themselves somehow unaccountably set aside by Lady Carabas after a certain season of favour—happily, sometimes, long enough to have enabled them to extract from it all the profit they desired: not "dropped"—that is a rude proceeding, wanting in finesse, quite unworthy of the Carabas *savoir faire*—but calmly, imperceptibly set aside; whereat the wise among the number were amused, and the foolish were savage. But Grace Lambert held her place even during her absence. There was something captivating to the fancy in the idea of the cultivation in "seclusion" of that great talent of which the world had got an inkling, under the auspices of Lady Carabas, and which would inevitably be a splendid testimony in the future to her judgment and taste. Thus, the way for her appearance and success in London being made plainer, easier, and pleasanter for her day by day, and the purpose of her sojourn in Italy fulfilled in a like ratio, time slipped away, and the period named for the return of Grace Lambert and Mrs. Bloxam—who hailed it with delight, and who now positively pined for Bayswater—drew near.

There had not been seen such a house at the Grand Scandinavian Opera for years; there had not been heard such long-continued thunders of applause, such rounds of cheering, since the Brödchen's *début*. Lady Carabas and Mr. Munns had each "worked the oracle," according to their lights; but the discrimination of her ladyship's friends rendered the managerial *claque* quite unnecessary. The opera was the *Trovatore*, and Gertrude's entrance as Leonora was the signal for a subdued murmur of applause. People were too anxious to see and hear her to give vent to any loud expression of their feelings; but when, with perfect composure, and without the smallest trace of nervousness in face or voice, the girl burst into the lovely "Tacea la notte," the connoisseurs knew that her success was accomplished; and long before the enthusiastic roar surged forth at the conclusion of the air Mr. Boulderson Munns, who had been nervously playing with the ends of his dyed moustache, shut up his opera-glass, and said to his treasurer and alter-ego, Mr. William Duff, "By ——, Billy, she'll smash the other shop!"

The lobbies and the refreshment-room were emptying of the crowds which had been raving to each other after the first act of the beauty and talent of the *débutante*, when Lord Ticehurst, who had been among the loudest demonstrators in the omnibus-box, whither he was returning, met Gilbert Lloyd quietly ascending the stairs.

"Only just come in?" asked his lordship.

"Only this instant; straight from Arlington Street; it's all right about Charon."

"O, d—n Charon!" said Lord Ticehurst; "you've missed the most splendid reception—Miss Grace Lambert, you know!"

"My dear fellow, I know nothing—except that Lady Carabas insisted on my going to her box to-night, to hear a new singer."

"There never was such a cold-blooded fish as you, Gilbert! Now be quick, and you'll be in time to see her come on in the second act!"

Gilbert Lloyd walked very leisurely to Lady Carabas' box on the grand tier, and received his snubbing for being late with due submission. When the roar of applause announced the reappearance of the evening's heroine, he looked up still leisurely; but the next instant his glass was fixed to his eyes, and then his hand shook and his cheeks were even whiter than usual, and his nether-lip was firmly held by his teeth, as in Miss Grace Lambert, the successful *débutante*, he recognized his wife.

———

𝕭ook the 𝕾econd.

CHAPTER I.

PROGRESS.

MR. BOULDERSON MUNNS was right in the remark which he made to his treasurer and *fidus Achates*, Mr. William Duff, in regard to Miss Grace Lambert's success, and to the effect which it would have on the future of the opposition opera-house. That very night the triumph was achieved. Ladies who "looked in for a minute" at various balls and receptions after the opera talked to each other of no one but the new singer ; the smoking-rooms of the clubs rang with her praises. Schrink, the humpbacked critic of the *Statesman*, went off straight to the Albion in Drury Lane ; called for some hot brandy-and-water and a pen and ink ; seated himself in his accustomed box, into which no one else dared intrude, and dashed off something which, when it appeared in print the next morning, proved to be an elaborate and scholarly eulogy of the new singer. The other journals were equally laudatory, and the result of the general commendation was soon proved. The box-office was besieged from morning till night ; boxes and stalls were taken for weeks in advance ; crowds began to collect round the pit and gallery doors at three o'clock in the afternoon, and remained there, increasing in size and turbulence, until the doors were opened ; while the fugitive Miramella and the recreant Jacowski were singing away for dear life at the Regent Theatre, to empty benches. The fact of Miss Lambert's being an Englishwoman was with many people a great thing in her favour. Old people who recollected Miss Paton, and middle-aged people who still raved about Miss Adelaide Kemble, hurried off to see the young lady who had succeeded to the laurels erst won so gallantly and worn so gracefully by these two great English singers, and came back loud in her praise. The *Mirror*—the weekly journal of theatricals and music—uplifted its honest, ungrammatical, kindly voice in favour of the *débutante*, and gossipped pleasantly of Kitty Stephens, Vestris, and the few other Englishwomen who have ever sung in time and tune. The *Illustrated News* published Miss Lambert's portrait on the same page with the portrait of the trowel with which the Mayor of Mudfog had laid the foundation-stone of the Mudfog Infirmary; and the *Penny Woodcutter* reproduced the engraving which had previously done duty as Warawaki, Queen of the Tonongo Islands, and subscribed Miss Lambert's name to it. A very gorgeous red-and-white engraving of the new singer figured also on the "Grace Valse," inscribed to her by her obedient humble servant Luigi Vasconi, who was leader of the orchestra of Mr. Munns' establishment, and who played first fiddle under the renowned conductor, Signor Cocco; while the enterprising hosier in the Arcade under the opera-house produced a new style of neck-tie which he christened "The Lambert," and of which he would probably have sold more had the Arcade been anything of a thoroughfare. As it was, the young man who kept the books of Messrs. Octave and Finings, the wine merchants, and who was known to have plunged madly into love with the new singer when he went in once with a gallery order, sported a "Lambert," and led the fashionable world of Lamb's Conduit Street in consequence.

Was this fame? It was notoriety, at all events. To have your portrait in all the photograph-shops and the illustrated journals; to see your name blazing in large type. in every newspaper, and on every hoarding and dead wall of London; to read constant encomiastic mention of yourself in what are called, or miscalled, the organs of public opinion; to be pointed out by admiring friends to other admiring friends in the streets; to be the cynosure of crowds; to be the butt of the *Scarifier*—when some artist or contributor to that eminent journal has seen you on horseback while he was on foot, or seen you clean while he was dirty, or heard you praised while he was unnoticed—these are the recognitions of popularity received by art-workers, be they writers, or painters, or actors. Not very great, not very ennobling,

perhaps, but pleasant—confess it, O my sisters and brethren
in art! Pleasanter to earn hundreds by the novel, or the
picture, or the acting—imperfect though each may be in its
way—which shall cause thousands to think kindly of us,
than to receive two guineas for verbal vitriol-throwing in
the *Scarifier*; pleasanter than to stand up, earning nothing
at all, to be howled at night after night by the vinous
members of the opposite political party, and to be switched
morning after morning by their press-organs; pleasanter
than to go for forty years for six hours a day to the Tin-tax
Office, and at last to arrive at six hundred a year, with the
chance of receiving a pension of two-thirds of the amount,
if you prove by medical certificate that you are thoroughly
worn out! That worn, grey old gentleman going in to
enjoy the joint, and the table, and a pint of sherry at the
Senior United, lost his youth and his hopes and his liver in
India, and in a few years may perhaps get—just in time to
leave it to his heir—the prize-money which he won a quarter
of a century ago; that Irish gentleman with a chin-tuft
has sold the last of his paternal acres to carry him through
his third election, and may possibly obtain from the Government, which he has always earnestly supported, a commis-
sionership of five hundred a year. We can do better than
that, we others! So, let us say, with the French actress,
" *Qu'on leur donne des grimaces pour leur argent et vivons
heureux!*" and in a modified and anglicized sense, " *Vive la
vie de Bohème!*"

Did Gertrude care much for this kind of cheap incense
burnt in her honour? Truth to tell, she cared for it very
little indeed. When she accepted the stage instead of the
concert-room for her career, she was influenced, as we have
seen, by an idea of the brilliancy of her triumph, should she
succeed; but that triumph once secured, there was an end
to such feeling in the matter, so far as she was personally
concerned. She took it all in a perfectly business-like manner; it was good, she supposed, for the theatre that she had
succeeded. Gratified? O yes, of course, she was gratified;
but when people came and told her there had never been
anything heard like her, she was compelled to show them
that, in accepting professional singing for her livelihood, she
had not quite abnegated any pretension to common sense.
With the exception of devoting the necessary time to re-

hearsals and study, her time was spent very much as it was before her departure to Italy. The drawing-room of the little Bayswater villa was gorgeous and fragrant with anonymous bouquets, offerings left the previous night at the stage-door; but Miss Lambert had not made one single new acquaintance since the night of her *début*. Occasionally on "off-nights" she would be seen at Carabas House, or at one or two of the other houses which she had been in the habit of visiting before the commencement of her professional career; but though she was inundated with invitations, she steadfastly refused to increase her visiting-list; and the lion-hunters, male and female, in vain sought to get her to their houses, and equally in vain sought admittance to hers.

To none was she a greater enigma than to her manager, Mr. Boulderson Munns. Proud of her success, and disposed in his open-hearted vulgarity to testify to her his appreciation of it, that liberal gentleman purchased a gaudy and expensive diamond-bracelet, had an appropriate inscription in gilt letters put on to its morocco-leather case, and sent it to Miss Grace Lambert. The next morning, bracelet, case and all were laid on the managerial table, with a little note from Miss Lambert, thanking Mr. Munns very sincerely for his kindness, but declining the present on the grounds that Miss Lambert was doing no more than fulfilling the terms of her engagement, and adding, that if Mr. Munns had found that engagement profitable, the time to show his appreciation of it would be when they came to settle terms for the next season. There was a combination of independence and business in this reply, which tickled Mr. Munns exceedingly. At first he was annoyed at the note, read it with a portentous frown, and strode up and down his room, plucking at the dyed whiskers wrathfully. But by the time Mr. Duff arrived with his usual budget of letters to be read, bills to be paid, questions to be asked, &c., the great *impresario* had softened down wonderfully, and had forgotten his rage at what he at first imagined the slight put upon him by his new singer in his impossibility to comprehend her.

"I can't make her out, Billy," said he, "and that's the fact. I've known 'em of all kinds; but she licks the lot. Look here at her letter! She won't have that bracelet,

Billy—just shove it into the strong-box, will you? we can get the inscription altered, and it'll do for somebody else—and talks about fresh terms for next season. Reg'lar knowing little shot, ain't she? Quiet little devil, too; wouldn't come down to my garden-party at Teddington, on Wednesday, though I had the Dook and Sir George, and a whole lot of 'em dyin' to be introduced to her. 'No go, your Grace!' I said, 'she won't come; but when Venus is bashful let's stick to Bacchus, who's always our friend.' I haven't had a classical education, Billy, but I think that was rather neat; and so they did, and punished the 'sham' awfully. However, it's all good for trade. She and that old cat, her aunt—not her aunt? well, Bloxam; you know who I mean —go about to Lady Carabas', and all the right sort of people, and the more she won't know the wrong sort of people, the more they want to know her, and the 'let's' tremendous. The other shop's done up, sir; chawed up, smashed! Mac-Bone and Ivory and Déloge, and the rest of 'em tell me they can't sell a stall for the Regent; and I hear that Miramella threatened Jacowski with a fork at dinner the other day, because he spoke of Miss Lambert, and swore she'd go to America. Best thing she could do, stupid old fool!"

Although this feeling in regard to Miss Lambert was perhaps nowhere expressed in language so strongly symbolical as that used by Mr. Munns, there is no doubt that it was generally felt. There is a certain class of artist-patronizing society which has the *mot d'ordre* of the *siffleur's* box, and revels in the gossip of the *coulisses*. These worthy persons were in the habit of talking to each other constantly of the new *prima donna*—how she came in "a regular fly, my dear;" how she was always dressed in black silk, "made quite plain, and rather dowdy;" how she was always accompanied by the same old lady, who, whether at rehearsal or in the evening, never left her side; and how, with the exception of Lord Sandilands, with whom she seemed to be very intimate, she entered into conversation with no one during the performance;—in all which things Miss Grace Lambert differed very much from Madame Miramella, who —depending on the kind of temper in which she might happen to be—alternated between the most gorgeous garments and the most miserable *chiffons*; between a coroneted brougham with a five-hundred-guinea pair of horses, and a four-wheeler cab ; between the loveliest com-plexion, and the most battered old parchment mask ; be-tween the most queenlike courtesy to all around her in the theatre, and the use of French and Italian *argot*-abuse, which fortunately was incomprehensible to those to whom it was addressed.   In this society Lord Sandilands was far too well-known for the smallest breath of scandal ever to attach to Miss Lambert's name by reason of his intimacy with her.   People remembered how devoted he had been to the Rossignol—who died, poor lady, in the height of her success—who had the voice of an angel, and the face of a little sheep ; how he had fought an uphill fight for Miss Laverock until he had seen her properly ranked in her pro-fession ; how he had always been the kind and disinterested friend of musical talent.   They wondered that somebody else did not arrive, some English duke, some Italian prince, some *millionaire*, and bear her away as Madame Sontag, Miss Chester, Miss Stephens, and Madame Duvernay had been borne away before her.   She was " thoroughly proper, my dear," they told each other in confidence ; and the obvious result of propriety being marriage, they waited for that result with great impatience.

The successful *début* of the young lady whom the world re-garded as his *protégée*, but whom he in his secret soul acknow-ledged as his daughter, had given Lord Sandilands unmiti-gated satisfaction.   Unmitigated, because his worldly know-ledge had given him sufficient insight into Gertrude's character to enable him to perceive that she could ride in safety over billows and through tempests in which a less evenly-ballasted bark would inevitably suffer shipwreck ; to perceive that the triumph which she had achieved would leave her head unturned ; while in the position which she had gained, her heart would be just as much at her command as it was when she first surprised society in the drawing-room of Carabas House.   So, thoroughly happy, the old nobleman permeated society, listening with eager ears to all comments on Miss Grace Lambert.   He heard them everywhere. Steady old boys at the Portland had heard of the new singer from their " people," and intended, the first evening they had to spare, to make one in the family-box, and hear her. Fast men, young and old, at the Arlington, relaxing their great minds—*neque arcum semper tendit Apollo*—between

turf-talk and whist-playing, spoke of her in exaggerated
laudation. In many of the houses where he had formerly
been accustomed to drop in with tolerable regularity, he
had renewed the habit since Gertrude's arrival in London ;
pleasant, genial, hospitable houses, all the more genial that
neither frisky matrons, nor foolish virgins, nor gilded youth,
were to be reckoned among the component parts of the
society to be found in them ; and there he found that Miss
Lambert was universally popular. A very great lady, indeed—one who held herself, and, truth to tell, was generally
held, far above the Carabas set, or any other of the kind —
no less a lady than the Dowager Duchess of Broadwater—
wrote to Lord Sandilands, saying that she had heard very
much of Miss Lambert, and hoping that through Lord
Sandilands' influence the young lady might be induced to
come and see an old woman who never went out. If you
have studied polite society and its Bible—the Peerage—you
will know that the dowager duchess is the widow of that
good, kind duke who was nothing more than the best
landlord, and the most perfectly representative English
nobleman of his time ; who reduced the rents of his tenants,
and built model cottages for his labourers, and loved music
next to his wife, and composed pretty little pieces, which
were played with much applause at the Ancient Concerts.
A stately gentleman, tall, clean shaven, with his white hair
daintily arranged, with his blue coat, buff waistcoat, and
tight grey trousers in the morning ; his *culotte courte*, black
silk stockings, and buckled shoes in evening attire. His
son, the present duke, wears a rough red beard, buys his
frieze shooting-coat and sixteen-shilling trousers from a
cheap tailor, smokes a short pipe, and talks like a stable-
man. His mother, who adores him—he adores her, let us
confess, and is as soft and docile with her as when he was
a child—looks at him wonderingly ; she is of the *vieille
cour*, and cannot understand the " lowering " tone of the
present day. *Grande dame* as she is, she relaxes always
towards the professors of that art which her husband so
loved ; and when Miss Lambert was brought to her by
Lord Sandilands, and sang two little convent airs which the
old lady recollected having heard, ah, how many years ago !
she drew the girl towards her, and with streaming eyes
kissed her forehead, and bade her thank God for the great

talent which He had bestowed upon her, and which ought always to be used in His service. After that interview, Gertrude saw a great deal of the old duchess, who always received her with the greatest affection, and introduced her to the small circle of intimate acquaintances by which she was surrounded.

And Lady Carabas, who was necessarily apprised of all that happened in Grace Lambert's life, was by no means annoyed at, or jealous of her *protégée's* introduction to the Dowager Duchess of Broadwater, of whom, in truth, her ladyship stood somewhat in awe ; not that she ever confessed this for an instant, speaking of her always as a "most charming person," and "quite the nicest old lady of the day ;" but having at the same time an inward feeling that the "charming person," though always perfectly polite, did not reciprocate the respect which Lady Carabas professed, and, indeed, really felt for her. The dowager duchess's society was as rigidly exclusive as Lady Carabas' was decidedly mixed ; and the platonic *liaisons* into which the Marchioness's Soul was always leading her were regarded with very stony glances from under very rigid eyebrows by the Broadwater faction. Lady Carabas had somewhat more than a dim idea of all this, and had quite sufficient sense of the fitness of things to be aware that it was more politic in her to accept the position than to fight against it—to know that for a recognized *protégée* of hers to be received by the Broadwater clique tacitly reflected credit on her ; and so, while she shrugged her shoulders when she heard of Lady Lowndes, and undisguisedly expressed her scorn at the attempts made by other lion-hunters to get hold of Gertrude, she warmly congratulated Lord Sandilands on the Broadwater connection, and redoubled her praises of Miss Lambert's voice and virtues. These laudations, skilfully served, as a woman of Lady Carabas' worldly experience alone knows how to express them, were always well received by the old nobleman, who could not hear too much in Gertrude's favour, and who day by day felt himself growing fonder of her, and more thoroughly associated with her plans and her welfare.

And there was one other person to whom this lady was equally enchanting, who never wanted the song pitched in any other key, who listened in rapt delight so long as he was allowed to listen, and gaze, and dream—Miles Challoner, who had left town so soon as he found the pretty Bayswater villa deserted, on Gertrude's departure for Italy. He had no further tie to London, and cared not to remain haunting the neighbourhood of the nest whence his "bird with the shining head" had fled. He became suddenly convinced of the utter emptiness of metropolitan existence, and expatiated thereon to Lord Sandilands in a way which greatly amused the old nobleman. He declared that these nineteenth-century views of life were false and wrongly based ; that half the vices and shortcomings of the provincial poor and the labouring classes were due to the absenteeism of the landlords, who by example should lead their inferiors. The holder of an estate, Miles said, be it small or large, had duties which should keep him among his people. He felt that he had neglected these duties ; and though he was not specially cut for a country gentleman's life, he knew that he ought to go down to Rowley Court, and do his best to get on in that sphere of life to which he had been called. The young man said all this with great earnestness, for at the moment he really believed it ; and he was half inclined to be angry when Lord Sandilands, who had listened to the rhapsody with a grave and attentive face, could contain himself no longer, but broke into a smile as he said that he thought Miles perfectly right, " particularly as the shooting season was coming on." So Miles left London, and went to his old ancestral home. The bright bountiful beauty of summer still decked the woods and fields ; the old servants and the villagers vied with each other in welcoming the young squire ; and Miles felt that he had done rightly in following what he was pleased to call the dictates of his conscience, in coming back. The small sum of money which he had expended on the estate had been judiciously laid out, and improvement was manifest everywhere—in heavy crops, mended fences, and common land drained and reclaimed ; in repaired outhouses, and shooting properly preserved ; and, better than all, in a higher class of tenantry, and larger rents. Miles Challoner had never felt the pleasant sense of proprietorship until this visit to his home. He walked round his fields, he stood on little vantage points and surveyed his estate, with an inward feeling of pride which he did not care to check. It *was* something to be an English country gentleman, after all. He had been nothing and no one in London, a hanger-on, a unit in the great social stream—no better than a dancing barrister, or a flirting clerk in a government office ; two-thirds of the people he visited knowing his name, and that he had been properly introduced to them by some account-able person, but nothing more. While here he was the young squire ; as he passed, the "hat was plucked from the slavish villager's head ; " everybody knew him, and was anxious to be seen by him ; he was the man of the place, and—yes it would not be difficult to make out one's life in that position ; not as a bachelor, of course, but provided he had some one with him. Some one ? No difficulty in finding her ! If he knew the language of laughing eyes, Emily Walbrook would not object to become the mistress of Rowley Court. And with her father Sir Thomas's money what might not be done ? The old place might be re-habilitated, the lost lands recovered, the old dignity of the family restored.

But Miles Challoner, being a gentleman and not an adventurer, told himself, after very little self-examination, that he did not care for Miss Walbrook, and that he never could care for her, consequently that he would be a scoun-drel to think of proposing for her hand ; told himself further that he only did care and only had cared—apart from some boyish follies which had not done him nor any one else any harm—for one person in the world, Grace Lambert. Did she care for him ? He did not know ; but, honestly, he thought she did not. And if she did, should he bring her there, to Rowley Court, as his wife ? Did he care for her sufficiently to suffer the universal inquiries as to who she was, the generally uplifted eyebrows and super-cilious remarks when the reply was given ? At present she was only known as a young lady received in excellent society on account of her musical talents ; but if this report was true—this report that she had gone to Italy with the intention of perfecting herself as a singer on the operatic stage ? A singer ? The stage ? The general and only notion of the stage in the neigh-bourhood of Rowley Court was founded on reminiscences of the travelling troupe of mummers who had once or twice come to Bleakholme Fair ; poor half-starved creatures, who had performed a dismal tragedy in an empty barn, by the light of a hoop of guttering tallow candles. How could he prepare the Bœotian mind of Gloucestershire to receive as his wife a woman who would bring with her such associations as these? What would be said by the old county neighbours, by whom the old Challoner name was yet held in the highest respect and regard? What by the wealthy new-comers, whose influence was day by day increasing, and who gave themselves airs of pride and position and exclusiveness far more intolerable than the loftiest hauteur of the real territorial *seigneurie?* Poor Miles! and after all—even if he had made up his mind to brave all the outcry that might arise ; to say, " I love this woman, and I bestow on her my rank and my position ; accept her as my wife, or leave her alone ; think as you please, talk as you please, and go to the deuce !"—he was by no means certain that Miss Grace Lambert would see the magnitude of the sacrifice he was making for her, or, indeed, that she would have anything to say to him.

That was a dull winter for Miles Challoner, that duty season when he steadfastly went through the character of the English country gentleman, to the tolerable satisfaction of his neighbours and his tenants, but to his own intense disgust. He hunted twice a week, he shot constantly ; he attended church regularly, and kept rigidly awake during the dear old vicar's dull sermons ; he gave two or three dull bachelor dinners, where the vicar, the curate, little Dr. Barford, and two or three neighbouring fox-hunting squires, ate and drank, and prosed wearily for three or four hours ; and he went out occasionally. He dined with Lord Boscastle, the lord-lieutenant and principal grandee of the county, where he met all " the best people," but where his attention was principally concentrated on his hostess ; for Lady Boscastle was *née* Amelia Milliken, and, as Amelia Milliken, had been the great attraction for two seasons at the Theatre Royal, Hatton Garden, during the lesseeship of the great Wuff. Miles could hardly realize to himself that the mild, elegant, dried-up, farinaceous-looking old lady had been the incomparable actress who, as he had heard his father relate, entered so thoroughly into her art that she would shed real scalding tears upon the stage ; and whose Juliet yet remained in the memory of old playgoers as the most perfect impersonation ever witnessed. She was an actress when Lord Boscastle married her; and see her now, with a cabinet minister on her right hand, and the best families of the county honoured by her inter- course! Why could not he do the same with Grace Lambert? And then Miles recollected that he was not so great a man as Lord Boscastle, had not the same weight and *prestige;* remembered also that he had heard his father say that Lady Boscastle made her way very slowly into the county society; that she had an immense number of disagreeables to contend with at first; and that it was only the sweetness of her disposition, and her wonderful patience and forbearance, that carried her through. And though Miles Challoner was undoubtedly in love with Miss Lambert, he scarcely thought that sweetness of disposition, patience, and long-suffering were the virtues in which she specially excelled. Miles also dined with Sir Thomas Walbrook, where there was much more display and formality than at Lord Boscastle's—only that the display was in bad taste, and the formality betokened ill-breeding; and he went to a hunt-ball, and tried to attend the weekly meetings of a whist-club, but broke down in the attempt. In the daytime he did not fare so badly; for he was full of life and health, and the love for field-sports which had distinguished him when a boy came back renewed when he again joined in those sports; but in the long evenings he moped and moaned, and was dreadfully bored.

The fact is that, however much he endeavoured to per- suade himself to the contrary, he was in love with Miss Grace Lambert; and the more persistently he turned his thoughts from that young lady, the more he found himself taking interest in persons and things associated with her. He corresponded regularly with Lord Sandilands, and his every letter contained some inquiry after or allusion to "your young friend in Italy." The old nobleman chuckled over the frequency and the tone of these letters, but replied to them regularly, and invariably said something about Grace; something, too, which he thought would please the recipient of the letter, for he loved Miles with fatherly affection; and, if Gertrude saw fit, nothing would have pleased him better than that the two young people should make a match of it. That, however, was entirely for Gertrude to determine ; and nothing could come of it yet at all events, as she had the stage career before her. Meantime, there was no reason why pleasant reports of her progress should not go down to Rowley Court. And when Miles received the letters, he ran his eye over them huriedly to see where *the* name appeared, and read those bits first, and re-read them, and then dropped very coolly and leisurely into the perusal of his old friend's gossip.

He was a queer, odd fellow, though, this Miles Challoner, full of that dogged determination which we call " British," and are extremely proud of (though, like the man who " treated resolution," in the end we often do the thing which we have so stubbornly refused to do) ; and although he knew that Miss Lambert had returned, and was about making her *début* in public, he remained stationary at Rowley Court. He received letters regularly from Lord Sandilands, but none of them ever contained a hint or suggestion that he should come up to town ; indeed, Miles guessed that Miss Lambert would be far too much occupied to admit of his seeing her, and he had said he would "give that up "—" that " being the guiding motive of his life, and he would hold to it. So Miles Challoner was not in the Grand Scandinavian Opera-house on the night when Gertrude made her triumphal entry into theatrical life. But when, the next day, he read the flaming accounts of her success in the newspapers ; when he received letters from Lord Sandilands and other friends, filled with ravings about her voice, her beauty, and her elegance; when he felt that this fresh flame would enormously increase the circle of her admirers, many of whom might have the chance— which they would not neglect as he was neglecting it—of personal acquaintance with her—he could withstand the influence no longer, but made immediate arrangements for returning to London.

His old friend received him with his accustomed warmth, talked about the length of time he had been away, and rallied him on the probable cause of his detention. " I know, my dear boy ! " said Lord Sandilands ; " I know all about what you're going to tell me,—the pleasure a man feels in his own *terre ;* the delightful days you used to have with Sir Peter's pack ; the unequalled cover-shooting, and all the rest of it. Those things don't keep a young man down in the country, leading that frightful dead-alive existence which we try to think pleasant. I know all about it; and I know that there's nothing more horrible. There must be *beaux yeux* somewhere, when a man voluntarily accepts that kind of life; and, by Jove! it's a kind of life to make one find the most ordinary eyes *beaux*. That confounded country life has produced more *mésalliances*, and more—hem! What are you going to do with yourself to-day?" The old nobleman stopped his discourse abruptly, with the reflection, perhaps, that *mésalliances* scarcely fitted him for a theme. Answering him, Miles said that he had nothing to do, and that he was entirely at his friend's disposal.

"Then," said Lord Sandilands, "suppose we stroll out Bayswater way? You have not seen Miss Lambert for a long time now, though you know—for I wrote to you, and you must have heard in a hundred other places—of her success. Really, the greatest thing for years. Everybody enchanted; and, best of all, has not made the smallest difference in her; just the same unaffected, quiet, unpretending girl as when we met her that first night—don't you recollect?—at Carabas House."

They walked across Kensington Gardens and speedily reached the by-road in which Miss Lambert's pretty villa was situated. Up and down this road, fretting against the slowness of the pace allowed them, stepping grandly, and sending the foam in flying flakes around them, were a pair of horses in a handsome mail-phaeton, driven by a correctly-appointed groom.

"Mr. Munns here!" said Lord Sandilands, testily, as this sight broke upon him. "Horribly vexing, when we hoped to have the young lady all to ourselves, eh, Miles? A worthy man, Mr. Munns, but a dreadful vulgarian. Tell me, is it my short-sightedness, or has this fellow really mounted a cockade in his man's hat?"

"There certainly is a cockade in the man's hat," said Miles, with a smile which died away as, on a nearer approach, he added, "and a coronet on the harness."

"A coronet? Why, the man can never have been ass enough to—eh? O dear me, impossible! Whose phaeton's that, sir, eh?"

" Earl of Ticehurst's, my lord ! " said the groom, touching his hat ; " lordship's in there, my lord," pointing to the villa with his whip, " with her ladyship."

" With her ladyship ! " echoed Lord Sandilands in bewilderment. " Let us go in, Miles, and see what it all means."

They saw what it all meant when they found Lady Carabas talking about education to Mrs. Bloxam in the drawing-room, and saw Lord Ticehurst walking with Miss Lambert round the little garden. Lord Sandilands frowned very gloomily, but Lady Carabas made straight at him. She had been dying to see dear Miss Lambert ; she wanted so to see how she bore her success—ah, what a success !—and how charming she is over it all ! not changed in the smallest degree. And her own horses were regularly knocked up with all their work just now ; and as it was such a long way (fashionable people think anything west of Apsley House or north of Park Lane quite out of bounds), she had asked her nephew Etchingham to drive her over. Lord Sandilands bowed very grimly, and Miles Challoner then came forward. Lady Carabas was enchanted to see him ; rallied him on his absence on the night of the *début ;* hoped to have him constantly at Carabas House, and was overwhelmingly gracious. Then Lord Ticehurst and Gertrude came in, and after a few conventional remarks, the young patrician, after a casual glance out of the window, informed his aunt that "the chestnuts had already stamped up the road into a regular ploughed field, by Jove ! and that, as the parish would probably send in the paving-bill, perhaps the best thing they could do was to be off ; " and accordingly he and Lady Carabas retired, with many adieux.

When they were gone, Lord Sandilands approached Gertrude and congratulated her with mock solemnity on her new acquaintance. " You have achieved an earl, my dear child, and there is no saying now what you may not aspire. Charles the Fifth picking up Titian's pencil will be equalled by Lord Ticehurst's turning over the leaves of your music-book for you. Or in time we might get a duke to——"

" We want no higher member of the peerage than a baron, apparently, to render his order ridiculous," said Gertrude, turning upon him with a sarcastic bow and a little *moue.* " Don't be angry, dear friend," she continued ; " but I own

I cannot stand raillery where Lord Ticehurst is concerned.
I have no doubt he means well—I am sure of it; all he
says is genuine, and, so far as he can make it, polite; but
he is very silly and very slangy, and—I can't endure him.
—And now, Mr. Challoner, tell me of all your doings during
your long absence in the country."

Lord Sandilands had a great deal to say to Mrs. Bloxam
on the subject of any future visits which Lord Ticehurst
might wish to pay to the Bayswater villa, and said it
pointedly, and without circumlocution.   When he rejoined
the young people, he found them deep in conversation, and
Miles, at least, looking very happy.

———————

CHAPTER II.

INTEGRATIO AMORIS.

WHEN Gilbert Lloyd satisfied himself that the new
opera-singer, at whose most successful *début* he had
"assisted," was none other than his wife, the momentary
agitation which had so shaken him passed away, and he sat
himself down at the back of Lady Carabas' box—not in the
chair usually reserved for the controller for the time being
of the Soul, but in a more retired position—and gave himself
up, as any uninterested auditor might have done, to listening
to the singing.   He had never been particularly fond of
music, and though he had always known that his wife possessed a fine voice, and had even at one time taken into consideration the probable profits which would accrue were he
to *exploiter* her musical talent, he had never imagined the
possibility of her taking such a position as that in which he
now found her.   Gilbert Lloyd was a man who believed
thoroughly in the truth of that axiom which tells us that
"there is a time for everything;" it would be quite time enough
for him to analyze the new light which had been let into his
life, to weigh and balance the pros and cons connected with
the appearance of Gertrude on a scene which he was accustomed to tread, mixed up with people with whom he was to
a certain extent familiar; it would be time enough for him
to enter into those business details on the next morning,

when his brain would be fresh and clear, and he would be recruited by his night's rest, and able more clearly to see his way, and arrive at a more accurate decision as to the advisability of steps to be taken. Meanwhile, he would listen with the rest ; and he did listen, with great pleasure, joining heartily in the applause, and delighting Lady Carabas by the warmth of his outspoken admiration of her favourite. And he escorted her ladyship to her carriage ; and went to the club, and played half-a-dozen rubbers with admirable coolness and self-possession. It was one of Gilbert Lloyd's strongest points that he could put aside anything unpleasant that might be pressing upon him, no matter how urgently, and defer it for future consideration. In the midst of trouble of all kinds—pecuniary complications, turf anxieties, on the issue of which his position in life depended—he would, after looking at them vigorously with all his power, turn into bed and sleep as calmly as though his mind were entirely free, rising the next morning with renewed health and courage to tackle the difficulties again. Just at this period of Miss Lambert's *début*, Lloyd happened to be particularly busy ; the Derby—on which he and his party were even more than usually interested—was close at hand, and all Gilbert's time was absorbed in " squaring " Lord Ticehurst's book and his own. But he knew that he need be under no alarm from the new element in his life which had just cropped out : though he had seen Gertrude, she had not seen him ; there was no reason as yet why they should be thrown together ; and even if they were, he was too fully aware of her coldness and her pride to imagine she would for an instant attempt to thrust herself upon him, or even acknowledge him. So Gilbert Lloyd made no difference in his life, beyond noting the name under which his wife was charming the public, and paying attention whenever that name was pronounced in his presence. He heard all that— as we know—people said about her ; but as that all was praise of her public performance, and astonishment at the quietude of her private life, it caused him very little emotion, and that little of no pleasurable kind.

It was the intervening week between Epsom and Ascot, and the season was at its height. The Ticehurst party, thanks to the astute generalship of Gilbert Lloyd, had pulled through the Derby very well. Lord Ticehurst's horse had not won—no one had ever imagined that possible —but it had been brought up to such a position in the betting as to secure the money for the stable, and save its owner's credit with the public. Matters for the future looked promising. To be sure, Lord Ticehurst had not taken so much interest of late in his turf speculations; but that did not particularly affect Mr. Lloyd. So long as his patron kept up his stud, and left the entire management of everything to him, that gentleman was content. It was not unnatural that a man of Lord Ticehurst's youth and health and position should wish to enjoy himself in society; and Gilbert rather encouraged his pupil's new notions on this point. It was not that Orson was endowed with reason, but rather that Orson had found out some *jeux innocens* for himself, of which he did not require his keeper's constant supervision.

One morning in the above-named week, Gilbert Lloyd was sitting in his own room in Lord Ticehurst's bachelor-house in Hill Street. It was a pleasant room on the first floor, and was furnished in a manner half substantial and half pretty. The large oak writing-table in the centre, the two or three japanned deed-boxes on the floor, the handful of auctioneers' bills pinned to the wall, announcing property to be disposed of at forthcoming sales—all these looked like business; but they were diametrically contradicted by the cigar-boxes, the pipe-rack, the Reynolds proofs, and the Pompeian photographs on the walls; the ivory statuettes and the china monsters on the chimney-piece; the deer-skins and the tiger-skins, the heavy bronzes, the velvet *portières*, and the luxurious chairs and ottomans; all of which indicated the possession of good taste and the means of gratifying it. Gilbert Lloyd had chosen these rooms —his bedchamber adjoined his sitting-room—when the *ménage* was first transplanted to Hill Street from Limmer's —where, during the reign of Plater Dobbs, Lord Ticehurst had resided—and had kept them ever since. He had chosen them because they were pleasant and airy, and so far out of the way, that the ribald friends of the real proprietor—who were dropping into their companion's rooms on the ground floor at all hours of the day and night—never thought of ascending to them. Trainers and jockeys made their way up the stairs with much muttered cursing, hating the ascent, which was troublesome to their short legs, and hating the business which brought them there; for Mr. Lloyd had a sharp tongue, and knew how to use it; and if his orders were not carried out to the letter, so much the worse for those who had to obey them. And latterly, a different class of visitors found their way to Gilbert's room, demure attorneys and portly land-agents; for Mr. Lloyd was now recognized as Lord Ticehurst's factotum; and all matters connected with the estates, whether as regards sale, purchase, or mortgage, passed through his hands.

It was twelve o'clock in the day, and Gilbert was seated at the oak writing-table. A banker's pass-book lay open at his right hand, and he was busied with calculations on a paper before him, when there was a knock at the door, and upon the cry "come in," Lord Ticehurst entered the room. Gilbert looked up from his writing, and on seeing who was his visitor, gave a short laugh.

"Won't you send up a servant with your name, next time?" said he; "the idea of a man knocking at a door in his own house—at least when that isn't the door of his wife's room! Then, I've heard it's advisable to knock or cough outside, or something of that sort, just to keep all straight you know!"

"Funny dog!" said Lord Ticehurst, indolently dropping into an easy chair and puffing at his cigar. "How are you?"

"Well, but worried," answered Gilbert.

"That goes without saying," said his lordship; "you always are worried, or you would never be well!"

"Look here, Etchingham," exclaimed Gilbert Lloyd, with a mock air of intense interest, "you mustn't do this, 'pon my soul you mustn't, or you'll hurt yourself. I've noticed lately a distinct tendency on your part to be epigrammatic; you weren't intended for it, and it won't agree with you. Take a friend's advice, and cut it."

"Considerate old boy! Tell me the news."

"Tell *you* the news?—I like that. Tell the news to a man whose life is passed in what the newspaper fellows call the 'vortex of fashion;' who is so much engaged that his humble servant here can't get five minutes with him on business, when it's most particularly wanted. Tell *you* the news, indeed!"

"No.   But I say, you know what I mean, Gilbert. How are we getting on ?   Ascot, you know, and all that ?"

"O, business !   Well, Bosjesman will win the Trial Stakes, and Plume will be beaten like a sack for the Cup; both of which facts are good for us.   We shall get Dumfunk's Derby money, or most of it; he's come to terms— nice terms—with that discount company at Shrewsbury; and little Jim Potter's shoulder's better, and he'll be able to ride."

"And what about the house ?"

"What house ?   Parliament ?   Does your lordship intend to put me in for Etchingham ?   I'm as fit as a fiddle for that work, and could roll them speeches off the reel——"

"Don't be an ass, Gilbert !   I mean the house for the week—at Ascot ?"

"O, I see !   Yes, that's all settled.   I couldn't get anything nearer than Windsor ; but I've got a very pretty little box there.   Charley Chesterton rents it for the year—he's there with the Blues, you know; but Mrs. Chesterton's going away, and Charley will go into barracks for the week, and we can have the house.   It's a stiffish figure, but they can get any amount that week, you know."

"O yes, of course, that don't matter.   And it's a nice house, you say ?"

"Very pretty little place indeed—do very well for us."

"Yes.   And Mrs. Chesterton's been living there ?   She's a nice woman, ain't she ?"

"Yes, she's nice enough, as women go.   But what has she to do with it ?"

"Well—I mean to say, it's a sort of crib that—don't you know—one could ask a lady to stop in ?"

"O—h !" exclaimed Gilbert Lloyd, with a very long face —"that's it, is it ?"

"No, no, 'pon my soul, you don't understand what I mean," said Lord Ticehurst hurriedly.   "Fact of the matter is, Lady Carabas wants to come down for the Cup-day ; and she'll bring a friend, of course ; and I told her about my having a house somewhere in the neighbourhood for the week, and thought she and the other lady, and their maids and people, could—don't you see ?—stay.   What do you think ?"

"My dear Etchingham, whatever you wish, of course

shall be carried out. It is not for me to teach etiquette to any lady, especially to Lady Carabas, who despises conventionality, and who, besides, is quite old enough to take care of herself. I should have thought that for a lady to come to a bachelor's house—however, of course she'll have her maid and her footman, and some one to act as her *âme damneé*—her sheep-dog." Who is the sheep-dog, by the way ?"

"I don't know about sheep-dog," said Lord Ticehurst, flushing very red ; "but Lady Carabas said the lady she proposed to do me the honour to bring to my house was—was Miss Grace Lambert."

Gilbert Lloyd looked up without the smallest trace of perturbation, and said, "Miss Grace Lambert ? O, the—the celebrated singer ! O, indeed !"

"Yes," said Lord Ticehurst ; "there's a chance of her getting a holiday on Thursday night—town will be very empty, you know, and I think I shall be able to square it with Munns—and then she might come down to the races, and she and Lady Carabas could come over here afterwards. She's a most charming person, Gilbert."

"Is she ?" said Gilbert Lloyd very slowly. "I have not—what you seem to have—the pleasure of her acquaintance. Have you known her long ? "

"O, ever so long ; ever since she first came out at a concert at Carabas House one night. Don't you recollect my pointing out to you a very stunning girl in a brougham, just as we were turning into Tatt's one day ? "

"My dear fellow, you've pointed me out so many stunning girls when we've been turning into Tatt's, or elsewhere, that I really cannot distinguish that bright particular star. But I've seen Miss Lambert at the Opera."

"And she's a stunner, ain't she ? "

"She seemed to be perfectly good-looking and lady-like on the stage. But these people are so different in private life."

"My dear Gilbert, I've seen her in private life, as you call it, a dozen times, and she's awfully nice."

"O, and she's awfully nice, eh ? "

"What a queer fish you are ! Of course she's awfully nice ; and this place of Charley Chesterton's will do for these ladies to come to ? "

"Yes, I should think so. Mrs. Chesterton is a woman accustomed to have the right thing about her; and it's good enough for her, so I presume it will 'do' for Miss Lambert and Lady Carabas."

"I hate you when you've got this sneering fit on you, Gilbert," said his lordship sulkily; and Gilbert Lloyd saw that he had gone far enough. His patron was wonderfully good-tempered, but, like all good-tempered men, when once put out, he "cut up rough" for a very long time.

"Don't be angry, Etchingham;" and Lloyd rose and crossed the room, and put his hand on the young man's shoulder. "I was only chaffing; and I was a little annoyed, perhaps, because you seemed doubtful whether this house that I have got, and only got after a great deal of trouble, would suit you. You might have depended on me. Well, and so you have made this young lady's acquaintance, and you find her charming?"

"Quite charmin'," said Lord Ticehurst, his good-humour being restored. "I've been with Lady Carabas several times to see her at a pretty little place she's got out Bayswater way, where she lives with an old tabby—by the way, I'll bet odds that old tabby don't let her come here without her."

"Well, there's room for the old tabby," said Gilbert. "But, see, Etchingham; do I really understand that you— that you care for this girl?"

"D——n it, Gilbert, you press a fellow home! Well, then, I'm not given to this sort of thing, as you know very well; but this time it's an awful case of spoons."

"Ah!" said Gilbert, smiling quietly, "your expression is slangy, but vigorous. And what are your views with regard to her?"

"Jove!" said Lord Ticehurst, "only one way there, my dear fellow! Wouldn't stand any nonsense; any of 'em, I mean,—Lady Carabas and all that lot. Besides, she's a lady, you know—educated, and all that sort of thing; and as to looks and breedin', she could hold her own with any of 'em—eh?"

"Of course she could. Besides, chaff apart, when the Earl of Ticehurst chooses to marry, his countess—however, there's time enough to talk about that. Now run along,

for I must write off at once about this Windsor house ; and
I've a heap of things to do to-day."

Lord Ticehurst left his Mentor, after shaking hands
warmly with him, and took his departure in a very happy
frame of mind. It was a great comfort to him to have
made Lloyd aware of the state of his feelings towards Miss
Lambert, immature as those feelings were, for Mentor had
such a hold over the young man that he never felt comfortable while he was keeping anything back from him.
But when he was gone, Gilbert Lloyd did not begin to
write the letter to Windsor, or settle to any of the " heap
of work " which he had mentioned as in store for him. He
got up and opened a drawer full of cigars, selected one
carefully, lit it, and threw himself into a low easy chair,
with his legs crossed, and his hands clasped behind his head.
At first he puffed angrily at his cigar, but after a little time
he gradually began to smoke more quietly, and then he un-
clasped his hands and rested his elbows on his knees, and
his chin on his hands.

"That's it !" he said aloud, "that's the line of country !
Fancy my never having given a thought to where this
fellow was going so often, never wondering at the sudden
fancy he had taken to his aunt's society ; and then discovering from his own lips that he has been paying visits to
my wife ! More than that—that he is confoundedly in
love with her, and wants to marry her ! Wants to marry
my wife ! There's something deuced funny in that. I
wonder whether any other fellow ever had a man come to
him and tell him he wanted to marry his wife. I should
think not ! Not that I should care in the least if any one
married Gertrude—any one, that is to say, except this youth
downstairs. I have not done with him yet, and a wife
would interfere horribly with me and my plans. Yes,
that's the right notion. There is no reason why Etchingham
should not be encouraged in this new fancy. It will keep
him from dangling after any other woman, and it can come
to nothing. I know her ladyship of Carabas rather too
well to credit her with any desire for Miss Lambert the
opera-singer as a relative ; as a plaything, an amusement,
she's well enough : but Lady Carabas cries '*Halte là !*' and
a hint from me to her would make her speak the word.

Besides, *I* am not dead yet, and I might have something to say about my wife's second marriage—that is, of course, supposing that second marriage did not suit my views. But there will be no question of that for some time. Now that I know the state of affairs, I can keep myself *au courant* to all that goes on through Lady Carabas : I shall make her ladyship induce her charming nephew to moderate his transports so far as any question of proposing is concerned ; but he may be 'awful spoons,' as he charmingly phrases it, as long as he pleases. As for this Windsor notion, that must be knocked on the head at once. I don't intend to give up the Cup-day at Ascot myself, and I certainly could not well be there, if Gertrude were to be of the party. I'll settle that with Lady Carabas."

Here behold Gilbert Lloyd's philosophy and views of life. Affection for the woman whom he had wedded, and from whom he had separated, he had not one scrap ; nor even care as to what she did, what course of life she pursued, whence she obtained the means of livelihood. Any interest in that he had abnegated when he accepted the terms which she dictated for their separation,—terms which meant oblivion of the past and *insouciance* for the future, terms which he had indorsed when they were proposed, and which he was ready to hold to still. But when his knowledge of his wife's previous life—of the thrall from which she had actually, but not legally, escaped—gave him the mastery over her actions, or the actions of those in relation with her, he was prepared to twist the screw to its tightest, if by so twisting it he could aid in the development of his own plans.

Had Gilbert Lloyd no remnant of love for Gertrude, no lingering reminiscence of the time when, a trusting school-girl, she placed her future in his hands, gave up her whole life to him, and fled away from the only semblance of home which she had known at his suggestion ? Had he no thought of the time immediately succeeding that, when for those few happy weeks, ere the pleasant dream was dispelled, she lay nestling in his bosom, building O such castles in the air, such impossible pictures, prompted by girlish romantic fancies of the future ? Had Gilbert Lloyd any such reminiscences as these ? Truth to tell, not in the smallest degree. He had passed the wet sponge over the slate containing any records of his early life, and all trace of Gertrude had been effectually erased. When he heard of her now, when it became necessary for him to give a certain number of moments to thinking of her in connection with business matters, he treated the affair simply from a business point of view. To him she was as dead "as nail in door," as immaterial as the first woman he might brush against in the street; she might be turned to serve certain ends which he had in view; but he regarded her simply as one of the puppets in the little life-drama of which he acted as showman.

The pleasant gathering which Lord Ticehurst had looked forward to on the Cup-day at Ascot did not come off. Gilbert Lloyd had five minutes' interview with Lady Carabas on the subject; and two days afterwards Mr. Boulderson Munns announced the impossibility of his sparing Miss Grace Lambert's services for that evening. Not that Miss Lambert would have accepted Lord Ticehurst's hospitality if her services could have been spared, but it was best to put the refusal on a strictly professional footing. Mr. Lloyd did not in the least care about absenting himself from that pleasant gathering on the Heath, and it was of course impossible for him to be brought face to face with Lord Ticehurst's intended guest. So the recipients of his lordship's hospitality in the cottage at Windsor were Lady Carabas and Miss Macivor, a sprightly elderly spinster, who was as well known in society as the clock at St. James's Palace, and who was always ready to play what she imagined to be propriety in any fast party. The ladies enjoyed themselves immensely, they said; but their host's gratification was not so keen. He was bored and ruffled, and he did not care to disguise it.

And now a change came over Gilbert Lloyd, which was to him unaccountable, and against which he struggled with all the power of his strong will, but struggled in vain. This change came about, as frequently happens with such matters by which our whole future is influenced, in an unforeseen manner, and by the merest accident. The Ascot settling-day had not passed off very comfortably. Several heavy book-makers were absent; among them one who had lost a large sum of money to the Ticehurst party. This man was known to have won hugely on the Derby a fortnight before, and to have had a capital account at his banker's a few days previously. It seemed therefore clear to Gilbert Lloyd, with whom the management of the matter rested, that the money was still in the possession of the absconding book-maker, who would, in all probability, take an opportunity of leaving the country with the sum thus accumulated. Gilbert Lloyd put himself in communication with the police authorities, furnished a correct description of the defaulter, and caused a strict watch to be kept at the various principal ports. One morning he received a telegram from Liverpool, announcing that the offender had been seen there. It had been ascertained that he was about to leave by the Cunard boat for Boston the next morning; but that, as he had committed no criminal offence, it was impossible for the police to detain him. This news made Gilbert Lloyd furious; that he should have his prey under his hand, and yet be unable to close that hand upon him, was maddening. He thought some good might be effected by his hurrying to Liverpool by the afternoon express, finding the defaulter, and frightening him out of at least a portion of the money due. The more he turned this plan in his mind, the more feasible it seemed to him, and the more he was determined to carry it into effect. There were, however, certain affairs to be transacted that day upon which it was most necessary he should, before starting, communicate personally with Lord Ticehurst; and Gilbert, from recent experience, knew that he should have considerable difficulty in tracing that young nobleman's whereabouts. He made inquiries at all the various haunts, but without any success; at length, at the club some one said that Ticehurst had offered to drive him down to the Crystal Palace, for which place he had started a couple of hours ago. The Crystal Palace! What on earth could take him there? Gilbert Lloyd, who saw fewer " sights " than almost any man in London, had been there once, but brought away a dazed recollection of fountains and Egyptian idols, and statues and tropical trees, none of which he thought would have any interest for his pupil. But his wonderment was at an end when, taking up the newspaper and looking for the advertisement, he saw announced that a grand concert, by the principal singers of the Scandinavian Opera, would take place at the Crystal

Palace that afternoon, and that the chief attraction of the concert was to be Miss Grace Lambert.

A swift hansom bore him to Victoria, and a tedious train landed him at the Crystal Palace, just in time to hear the opening notes of Herr Boreas's solo on the ophicleide. A charming performance that of Herr Boreas, but one to which Mr. Lloyd gave no attention. He hurried through the crowd, looking eagerly right and left ; and at last his eyes fell upon a group, where they remained.

Lord Ticehurst, Mr. Munns, and two or three others were component parts of this little knot ; but Gilbert Lloyd saw but one person—Gertrude. How marvellously she had improved during the time that had elapsed since they parted ! She had been pretty as a girl ; she was lovely as a woman. How lovely she looked in her simple morning dress and coquettish little bonnet ! With what a perfect air of easy grace she listened to the men bending before her, and how quietly she received the homage which they were evidently paying ! An angry flush rose on Gilbert's pale cheeks, and his heart beat quickly as he witnessed this manifest adoration. What right had any one but he to approach her, to——It stung him like a cut from a whip, it flared like a train of gunpowder. He knew what it was in an instant : mad, raging, ungovernable jealousy— nothing else. He had thrown off all love for her—all thought of her ; and now, the first time they met, the passion which struck him when he first saw her, years before, looking out of the window of the Vale House, sprung up with renewed fury within him, and he raged and chafed as he recognized the obstacles which kept him from her, but which were no barriers to other men. She seemed utterly indifferent to them, though, he was glad to see—no ! her face lights up, she smiles and bends forward ; and when she looks up again there is a blush upon her cheek. Who has been speaking to her ?—the tall handsome man with the brown beard—Miles Challoner ! And Gilbert Lloyd swore a deep oath of revenge—revenge of which his wife and his brother should each bear their share.

CHAPTER III.

AT THE CRYSTAL PALACE.

TO Herr Boreas was allotted the pleasing duty of opening
the concert.   The jolly German gentleman, neatly and
seasonably dressed in black, with a large diamond-brooch in
his plaited shirt-front, and with stuffy-looking black-cloth
boots with shiny tips, opened his big chest, and puffed away
at his ophicleide, evoking now the loudest and now the
softest notes; while the crowds kept pouring in to the
railed-off space, and took their seats, laughing and chattering, and not paying the smallest attention to the performance.   It was a great day at the Palace, a day on which
great people thought it proper to be seen there.   The little
public-houses in the neighbourhood were filled with re-
splendent creatures in gorgeous liveries, whose employers
were making their way through nave and transept, looking
at nothing save the other people there, and looking at them
as though they were singular specimens of humanity
specially put out for show.   In the matter of staring, it
must be confessed that the other people returned the compliment.   The regular attendants at the Crystal Palace are,
for the most part, resident in the neighbourhood, and the
neighbouring residents are, for the most part, of or
belonging to the City.   The brokers of stocks, shares, and
sugar ; the owners of Manchester warehouses, the riggers of
markets, and the projectors of companies ; the directors of
banks, and the " floaters " of " concerns," have, many of
them, charming villas, magnificent mansions, or delicious
snuggeries at Blackheath, Eltham, or Sydenham ; and the
Palace is the great place of resort for their wives and
daughters, and for themselves when the cares of business are
laid aside.   How many successful matches, in which money
has been allied to money, have commenced in flirtations by
the side of the plashing fountains, or in the shade of the
stunted orange-trees !   What execution has not been done
by flashing eyes in the central promenade !   There, by the

Dying Gladiator, Lord Claude Votate proposed for Miss Meggifer, and secured the fortune which rescued the Calfington estates from his lordship's creditors; there, behind the Dancing Faun, Charles Partington, of Partington Nephews, kissed Minnie Black, daughter of Black Brothers—was seen to do it by Mrs. Black, consequently could not escape, and thus cemented an alliance between those hitherto rival houses, considered in Wood-street as the Horatii and Curiatii of the Berlin-wool trade. Pleasant place of decorous festivity and innocent diversion, whence instruction has been completely routed by amusement, and where the Assyrian gods and the Renaissance friezes are deserted for the dancing dogs and the Temple of Momus as constructed by Mr. Nelson Lee!

By the time that Herr Boreas had finished his solo— which was not until he had blown all the breath out of his body, and was apparently on the verge of apoplexy—the audience had taken possession of all the seats; and as the German gentleman bowed himself out of the orchestra, amidst a great deal of applause from people who, indeed, could not help having heard, but had not paid the least attention to him, there was a general reference to the programmes to see what was coming next, then a rustling, a whispering, and that curious settling stir which electrically runs through an audience just before the advent of a favourite artist. Gilbert Lloyd, not insensible to this, involuntarily looked round from behind the pillar by which he was standing to the spot where he had seen Gertrude, but she was no longer there. The next instant thunders of applause rang through the building as she advanced upon the platform. She bowed gracefully but coldly; then the conductor waved his baton, and dead silence fell upon the audience, leaning forward with out- stretched necks to catch the first notes of her voice. Soft and sweet, clear and trilling, comes the bird-like song, warbled without the smallest apparent effort, while thrilling the listeners to the heart—thrilling Gilbert Lloyd, who holds his breath, and looks on in rapture. He had heard her before, but in Italian opera; now she is singing an English ballad, of no great musical pretension indeed, but pretty and sympathetic. At the end of the first verse the applause burst out in peals on peals; and so carried away was Gilbert Lloyd, that he found himself joining in the general feeling—he who scarcely knew one note of music from another, and who had come to the place on a matter of important business. That must stand over now, though—he felt that. The absconding turfite might go to America, or to the deuce, for the matter of that; Gilbert Lloyd felt it an impossibility to leave the place where he then was, and tried to cheat himself by pretending that it was expedient for his own interest that he should keep a close watch upon Lord Ticehurst just at that time. That young nobleman certainly took no pains to conceal his warm admiration for Miss Lambert, and his intense delight at her performance. He applauded more loudly than any one else, and assumed an attitude of rapt attention, which would have been highly interesting if it had not also been slightly comic. When the song ceased, the cries for a repetition were loud and universal. Gertrude, who had retired, again advanced to the front of the orchestra. By an involuntary impulse, Gilbert Lloyd stepped from behind the pillar which had hitherto shielded him, and their eyes met—met for the first time since he left her at the Brighton hotel, on the day of Harvey Gore's death.

A deep flush overspread Gilbert Lloyd's usually pallid cheeks, but Gertrude's expression did not change in the slightest degree. Not a trace of the faintest emotion, even of curiosity, could be seen in her face. The conductor of the orchestra, just before he left her in front of the audience, addressed some remark to her; and as she replied, Gilbert noticed that her lips were curling with a slight sneer—an expression which he fancied he understood, when the band commenced to play an air which even he, all unmusical as he was, recognised as "Home, sweet home." But she never looked at him again during the song, which she sung even more sweetly than the first, and with a deep pathos that roused the audience to enthusiasm. Gilbert Lloyd kept his eyes fixed on her, never moving them for an instant; and as he marked the calm air with which she received the public applause, and the graceful ease of all her movements —as he saw how her face, always clear cut and classically moulded, had ripened in womanly beauty and intellectual expression—as he noticed the rounded elegance of her figure, the tasteful simplicity of her dress—and he noticed all these details down to the fit of her gloves and the colour of her bonnet-strings—he raged against himself for having been fool enough to relinquish the hold he once had on her. Could that hold be re-established? If he were again to have an opportunity—But while these thoughts were passing through his mind, Gertrude had finished her song and quitted the orchestra, and her glance had not fallen on him again.

Meantime Gilbert Lloyd saw he had been noticed by the group with whom Miss Lambert had been sitting previous to her performance, and as Miles Challoner was no longer with them he thought it better to join the party. His appearance amongst them was evidently a surprise to Lord Ticehurst, who expressed the greatest astonishment at his Mentor's finding any amusement in so slow a proceeding as a concert, and who grew very red and looked very conscious when Gilbert asked him what particular charm such an entertainment could possess for him. Lord Sandilands was, as usual in his behaviour to Mr. Lloyd, scrupulously polite, but not particularly cordial. He had nothing in common with Gilbert, detested the turf and all its associations, and looked on Lord Ticehurst's turf Mentor as very little better than Lord Ticehurst's stud-groom. Mr. Boulderson Munns still remained with them, and intended so to remain. It was part of Mr. Munns' business that he should be seen in close and confidential communication " with two nobs," as he elegantly phrased it, and he took advantage of the opportunity. Nothing pleased him so much as to notice when members of the promenading crowd would elbow each other, look towards him, and whisper together, or when he saw heads bent forward and opera-glasses pointed in his direction. It was his concert he thought: when Herr Boreas blew his ophicleide, or Miss Lambert sang her song, he felt inclined to place his thumbs in the arm-holes of his big white waistcoat, and go forward and acknowledge the applause. He had done so in former years in the transformation-scenes of pantomimes, when the people called for Scumble the scene-painter, and why not now? Boreas and the Lambert were quite as much his people as Scumble! Mr. Munns restrained himself, however, from motives of policy. It was pretty plain to him, as he afterwards explained to Mr. Duff, that this young swell, this Ticehurst, was dead spoons on the Lambert; and as he had no end of money, and was good for a box every night, and perhaps something more if the screw were properly put on, it would be best to make it all sugar for 'em. With this laudable intent he commenced talking loudly to Lord Ticehurst of Miss Lambert's attractions, and did not suffer himself to be interrupted for more than a minute by Lloyd's arrival.

"As I was telling you, my lord," he recommenced, "she's a wonder, this—this young lady—a wonder, and nothing but it! Not merely for the hit she's made, though it's a great go, and I don't mean to deny it; but I don't go by the public, I know too much of them. Why, Lord Sandilands here, he remembers when—Well, it's no good going into that; lots of them we've seen in our time, and then, after a season or two, all dickey! regular frost! But there's something very different from that with Miss Lambert—so quiet, and so quite the lady; none of your flaring up, and ballyragging the people about. Why Miss Murch, our wardrobe-woman, said to me only last night, that she only wished the other prima donnas were like her —won't wear this, and won't wear that—How d'ye do, Mr. Lloyd? I was talking to his lordship of Miss Lambert, who's just been singing, and saying what a stunner she was. Now, if you've got a filly to name—one that's likely to be something, and do something, you know—you should call her Grace Lambert——"

"No, I think not; not quite that, Mr. Munns!" interposed Lord Ticehurst; "that's scarcely the kind of compliment I should care to pay to Miss Lambert."

"You may depend upon it that it's one which, if Miss Lambert had the option, she would scarcely care to accept, my lord," said Lord Stanilands tartly; "however, there she is to answer for herself," and he pointed through the glass to the garden, where Gertrude was seen walking with Mrs. Bloxam. There was an evident intention on the part of all composing the group to join them, and seeing this Gilbert Lloyd would have withdrawn; but Lord Ticehurst took him by the arm, and saying, "I've long wanted to introduce you to Miss Lambert, old fellow, and now you can't possibly escape," led the way.

If he were ever again to have an opportunity! Had

that opportunity then come? Was his never-failing luck holding by him still, and giving him this chance of retrieving the blunder he had made in the Brighton hotel? He thought so. His breath came short and thick as he nerved himself for the meeting. He saw her as she and Mrs. Bloxam strolled before them up the garden-walk, noticed the swimming ease of her gait, the fall of her black lace cloak, as it hung from her shoulders, the graceful pose of her head. She turned, he heard the sound of her approaching feet, he felt her presence close opposite to him, he heard Lord Ticehurst's voice repeating the set formula of introduction, but he saw nothing until he looked up to catch the faintest inclination of Gertrude's head, and to see her face colder, more set, more rigid than ever. Neither spoke; and the silence was becoming awkward, when Lord Ticehurst said, " I imagine you must have heard me speak of my friend Lloyd, Miss Lambert? Good enough to manage my racing matters for me, and to manage them deuced well— with the greatest talent and skill, and all that kind of thing. Not in your line, I know, Miss Lambert; but still —still——" and his lordship's eloquence failed him, and he broke down.

Again neither of them spoke, but Gilbert Lloyd looked up from under his brow and saw the stony glance which Gertrude cast upon him for an instant, then turned to Mrs. Bloxam, and suggested that they should return to the concert-room, where she would speedily be wanted. Lord Sandilands was at her right hand, Lord Ticehurst on the other side of Mrs. Bloxam. Mr. Munns preceded them, and caused a great sensation, on which he had reckoned, when he flung open the door and ostentatiously ushered them into the building; but Gilbert Lloyd walked slowly behind, his hands plunged into his pockets, and his face—there was no one to heed him, no reason for him to don an unnatural expression —savage, set, and careworn.

So it had come at last, he thought. They had met after so long an estrangement; and that was to be the end of the meeting. No recognition—he had not expected that—no public recognition, no hint that they had ever been anything to each other. He recollected the words that he had addressed to her on their parting; they came surging up and ringing in his ears: " It is not very likely that we shall ever run across each other's path in the future, but if we do, we meet as entire strangers; and the fact of our having been anything to one another must never be brought forward to prejudice any scheme in which either of us may be engaged." Memory brought before him the dingy cold room of the second-rate hotel, with the dying sunlight streaking its discoloured walls, in which these words had been spoken; brought before him the slight figure and the deadly pallid face of the girl as she listened to them, and acquiesced in their verdict. In that verdict she acquiesced still, was acting up to its spirit—to its very letter. It was his proposition to leave her alone and unfettered "in any scheme in which she might be engaged." The fooling, the enslavement of this idiot Ticehurst, who was a mere tool in his hands, was the game which she was now playing, at which he was to look on helplessly, having himself spoken the words which rendered her independent of his control.

And she, how did she take it? Calmly enough; but not so calmly as Gilbert Lloyd supposed. She had never gone in for much feeling, and whatever she had was now completely at her command, far more completely even than when she last had parted from her husband. Moreover, while Gilbert had utterly given himself up to the business of his turf profession, resolutely refusing to think of his wife, or to acknowledge to himself that there was ever a possibility of their again being brought into contact, the chance of such a meeting had often occurred to Gertrude, and the manner in which she would demean herself, should the occasion arise, had been thought over by her and settled in her mind. And now that it had arisen, so far as her outward demeanour was concerned, she had behaved herself exactly as she had always proposed. And her facial control was such, that no one looking at her could have an inkling of what was passing in her mind, which was fortunate on this occasion, for she was considerably more disturbed than she had expected. The first sight of her husband was a complete shock to her, and it was only by the exercise of the greatest presence of mind that she prevented herself from betraying her perturbation. When the first shock was past—and she owed it to the strict discipline of professional training that she was enabled to get over it so quickly —her thoughts reverted to the subject, and she was able to discuss it calmly with herself. What brought Gilbert Lloyd to that place? She knew him well enough to feel sure that there must have been some strong inducement, and what could that be? Gilbert was *lié* with Lord Ticehurst; and that that full-flavoured young nobleman was considerably in love with her, Gertrude had never attempted to disguise from herself; but what could that matter to the man from whom she had been so long estranged, and who had never shown the smallest interest in her proceedings during that long estrangement? The possibility of a desire on Gilbert's part to negotiate for a renewal of intimacy crossed her mind for an instant, but was at once rejected; and not even for an instant did she imagine the desire for such a proceeding was based on anything but motives of policy. And, after all, what did it matter to her? To her Gilbert Lloyd was dead and buried, she had nothing to look for at his hands, nothing to fear from him—her lip curled as she recollected that; she would dismiss him entirely from her thoughts, she would—what could have brought him to that concert of all places in the world? It might be useful to know something of his mode of life. She would lead Lady Carabas to talk of him; the marchioness would be only too happy to dilate on such a subject.

By the time Miss Lambert was to sing again, she had quite made up her mind on this point, and the sight of Gilbert Lloyd, *planté là*, did not cause her the slightest emotion. He stood as one rapt, fascinated by her beauty, drinking in her voice, with one constant idea beating in his brain:—Was the past irrevocable? could not the mischief be undone? The power he had had in the old days remained to him still; he had but to exercise it, and all would be right again. True that just then she had rebuffed him; but that was her way, always had been; she had always piqued herself upon her pride, and after that had had its fling he should be able to do with her as he liked. Miss Lambert was in full song as these thoughts passed through Gilbert Lloyd's mind, when suddenly she changed colour, a transient flush overspread her face, dying away again almost instantaneously. At the same instant Gilbert Lloyd turned swiftly round in the direction in which he had noticed her glance fall, and saw Miles Challoner, who had recently entered and dropped into a chair just behind Lord Sandilands' seat.   No doubt of it, no doubt of it; her self-command was so shaken that her voice faltered for an instant, and he—look at his eyes fastened on her face with a look of perfect love and trust, and it was impossible to doubt the position.   Lloyd's heart sunk within him at the sight, and a bitter oath was rising to his lips, and would have found utterance, when he felt his arm pressed, and looking round, saw Tommy Toshington, of the clubs, standing behind him.   Mr. Toshington had on a new and curly wig, a light high muslin cravat, and looked bland and amiable.   He winked affably at Lloyd, and laying his finger lightly against his nose, said, "You're wrong, my dear boy;—it's all right!"   Mr. Gilbert Lloyd shortly bade his friend not to be an ass, but if he had anything to say, to out with it.   Nothing abashed at the strength of Gilbert's language, Tommy said—

"My dear fellow, I mean exactly what I say; you're under a mistake, while all the time it's all right for *you!*"

"What's all right for me?—with whom?—where?"

"There!" said Tommy Toshington, wagging his new wig and his curly-brimmed hat in the direction where Lord Ticehurst was sitting; "his lordship is *entêté* with a certain warbler, eh?   Fourth finger of the left hand—death do us part, and all that sort of thing, eh?   That wouldn't suit your book, I should think—have to give up your rooms; she persuade him to cut the turf, go to church, and that kind of thing.   Don't you be afraid, my boy; I know the world better than you, and that'll never come off!"

"You think not?" asked Gilbert.

"I'm sure not," replied Tommy.   "Look here; he'd like it fast enough.   Etchingham would marry her to-morrow if he got the chance; but she's full of pluck and spirit, and don't care a bit for him.   How do I know?   Because she cares for somebody else.   How do I know that?   My dear fellow, don't I know everything?   What used the old Dook to say.   'Ask Toshington, he'll know; he knows everything, Tommy does.'   And he didn't make many mistakes, the old Dook."

"Perhaps you know who is the 'somebody' else for whom the lady cares?" said Gilbert, an evil light dawning in his face, and his lips involuntarily tightening as he put the question.

"Of *course* I do!" said Tommy, with a crisp little laugh; "keep my eyes open, see everything; seen 'em together lots of times—Carabas House, Lady Lowndes', and lots of places. You know him, I should think; tall man from Gloucestershire—big beard—Chaldecott—some name like that!"

This time the oath broke from Lloyd's lips unchecked. He turned rapidly on his heel, and strode away.

"Dev'lish ill-bred young man that," said old Toshington, looking after him; "dammy, there's no manners left in the men of the present day!"

CHAPTER IV

PURSUIT.

THE clearance effected under the superintendence of the Office of Works, for the amalgamation under one roof of the various Courts of Law, has carried away a large portion of Clement's Inn, and has obliterated the pillared entrance to that dusky but genial home of the shady and impecunious. In the days of our story, however, Inn and entrance were still there; the former tenanted by human sheep of various degrees of blackness—roistering government-office clerks, with the Insolvent Court—which at the outset of their career had been but a light cloud as small as a man's hand, but which year by year had assumed larger and more definite proportions—ever lowering over them; third-rate attorneys, who combined law with discount, "doing" little bills for ten and twenty pounds with the afore-named government clerks, and carefully putting in an appearance at Somerset House on pay-days to receive their money, or the refresher which was to induce the withholding of the document—it is always "a document"—until another quarter had elapsed; agents for companies of all kinds of limited and unlimited liability; newspaper-writers obliged to have cheap chambers in the neighbourhood of their offices; foreigners representing continental firms, and wanting a cheap and quasi-respectable address; an actor or two, a score of needy men-about-town, and a few Jews. Round the pillars seethed and bubbled a scum of humanity of the nastiest kind—vendors of the fried fish and the pickled whelk, boot-blackers of abnormally horrid appearance; and emaciated children from the neighbouring Clare Market and the adjoining courts, thieves and impostors from their infancy, hung about the cab-rank, and added to the general filth and squalor. A pleasant Slough of Despond, that little spot, now standing bare and cleared, surrounded by the balmy Holywell, the virtuous Wych, with Drury Lane running from it at right-angles, and the dirtiest corner of the great legal cobweb of courts and alleys at its back.

It was a hot morning in July when a cab drew up at the pillars, and Gilbert Lloyd jumped out, paid the driver, and made his way into the Inn. The exhalations from the barrows of the fried-fish vendors were potent, and the change to the faint, sickly perfume of the West-Indian pine-apple, tastefully arranged in slices on an open barrow which blocked the immediate thoroughfare, was scarcely refreshing. Perhaps in July the second-hand garments, even the uniforms, which the Jewish gentlemen who deal in such trophies hang up at the entrances of their warehouses, are a thought stronger in flavour than in the winter; and a fifth-hand portmanteau, which has seen a great deal of service under various owners, is apt, under the influence of the sun, to suggest its presence. But Gilbert Lloyd paid no heed to anything of this kind; he had roughed it too long to care for what came between the wind and his nobility; not being a literary photographer on the look-out for "character," he paid no attention to any of the surroundings, but went straight on, making his way through the jostling crowd until he arrived at a door on the posts of which was painted "Gammidge's Private-Inquiry Office, ground-floor." A further reference to the right-hand door of the first-floor discovered a still more elaborate placard, announcing that "Nichs. Gammidge, many years in the detective police, undertook inquiries of a private and confidential nature; agents all over the Continent; strictest secrecy observed; divorce cases particularly attended to; ring right-hand bell; and no connection with foreign impostors trading on N. G.'s new invention."

Gilbert Lloyd with some difficulty—for in the dingy passage there was but little light even on that bright summer morning—read this description, and in obedience to its

suggestion pulled the right-hand bell. The sound of the
bell, vibrating loudly, apparently had the effect of putting
a sudden stop to a muttered conversation of a groaning
character, which had been dimly audible ; the door was
opened by a spring from the inside, and Gilbert entered. He
found himself in a low-ceilinged, dirty room, with no other
furniture than a couple of chairs and a very ricketty deal
table. The windows were covered more than half-way up
with blinds improvised out of old newspapers ; a clock with
one hand was on the wall ; an almanac, much ink-scored
and pin-marked, stood on the mantelshelf ; and a limp map
of Great Britain, evidently torn out of an ancient *Bradshaw*,
was pinned behind the door. At first, on entering, Gilbert
Lloyd thought himself the sole occupant of the room ; but
when his eyes had become accustomed to the partial darkness, he discovered some one rubbing himself against the
wall at the opposite end of the room, and apparently
trying to squeeze himself through into the next house. A
little hard looking at and careful study made him out a
very thin, small, white-faced young man, with hollow cheeks,
a sharp face, and a keen restless eye. As Gilbert's glance fell
on him, or rather, as he seemed to feel it fall on him, he
shook himself with an odd restless motion, as though to
endeavour to get rid of some spell of fascination, but evidently desired to keep as much as possible in the background.
The groaning, smothered conversation meanwhile had
recommenced in another quarter, and Gilbert, looking
round, noticed a door evidently leading into an inner
room.

"Is this Mr. Gammidge's office?" he asked abruptly of
the white-faced young man.

The white-faced young man gave a sudden start, as though
a pin had been run into him, but never spoke.

" Mr. Gammidge's office—is this Mr. Gammidge's office ?"
repeated Gilbert.

" I—I believe so," said the white-faced young man, taken
aback by the sharpness of the key in which the inquiry was
made. " I have no reason to think it's not."

" Where is Mr. Gammidge ?"

"Not in !" Wonderfully sharp and pert came this
reply ; constant lying in one groove oils the tongue so
splendidly.

"Not in?" echoed Gilbert half savagely.

"Not in! Sure to be in later in the day. Got most important business on just now for——"

"Stow it!" The words came not from the white-faced young man, nor from Gilbert, but yet they were perfectly audible.

On hearing them, the white-faced young man became silent at once, and Gilbert looked round in amazement. The muttered groans became fainter, a sound as of clinking money was heard, then as of the opening of a door, the farewell of a gruff voice, the departure of a thick pair of boots; then one door slammed, and the inner door, which Gilbert had noticed on his first entrance, opened, and a man stood in the doorway with a beckoning forefinger.

A short stout man in a brown wig, with a fat unintelligent face, with heavy pendulous cheeks and a great jowl, and a round stupid chin, but with an eye like a beryl—small, bright, and luminous; a man with just sufficient intelligence to know that he was considerably overrated, and that the best chance for him in keeping up the deception lay in affectation of deepest mystery, and in saying as little as possible. Mr. Gammidge had been made a hero in certain police cases during his professional career, by two or three "gentlemen of the press," who had described a few of his peculiarities—a peculiar roll of his head, a sonorous manner of taking snuff, a half-crow of triumph in his throat when he thought he saw his way out of a complication—in their various organs. Henceforth these peculiarities were his stock-in-trade, and he relied upon them for all his great personal effects.

When Gilbert Lloyd obeyed the influence of the beckoning forefinger, he passed through the door of communication between the inner and outer rooms, and found himself in an apartment smaller and not less dingy than that he had left. In the middle of it was a large desk, on which were a huge leaden inkstand, a few worn quill-pens, and a very inky blotting-pad. Sentinel on one flank stood a big swollen Post-office Directory, two years old; sentinel on the other, a stumpy manuscript volume in a loose binding, labelled "Cases." The walls blossomed with bills offering large sums as rewards for information to be given respecting persons who had absconded; and on a disused and paralytic

green-cloth screen, standing in a helpless attitude close by
the desk, was pinned a bill, setting forth the Sessions of the
Central Criminal Court for the year, with the dates on
which Mr. Gammidge was engaged in any of the trials
pending distinguished by a broad cross with a black-lead
pencil.

As soon as Gilbert Lloyd had entered the room, Mr.
Gammidge closed the door carefully behind him, and
placing himself in front of him, indulged him with the
peculiar roll of the head, while he took a sonorous pinch
of snuff, and said in a thick confidential voice, "Now,
captin ?"

"I'm no captain," said Lloyd shortly, "and you don't
recollect me ; though you're ready to swear you do, and
though I have employed you before this."

Lloyd paused here for a moment ; but as Mr. Gammidge
merely looked at him helplessly, and muttered under his
breath something about " such a many gents," he went on.

"My name is Gilbert Lloyd. I manage Lord Ticehurst's
racing matters for him ; and last year I employed you to
look after one of our boys, who we thought was going
wrong ; do you recollect now ?"

"Perfectly," said Mr. Gammidge, brightening. "Boy
had been laid hold of by a tout from a sporting-paper, who
was practisin' on him through his father, given to drink,
and his sister, on 'oom the tout was supposed to be
sweet."

"Exactly ; well, you found that out clearly enough,
and got us all the information required. Now I want
you again."

"More boys goin' wrong, sir ?" asked Mr. Gammidge.
" They're the out-and-outest young scamps ; they're that
precocious and knowin'——"

"It's not a boy that I want to know about this time,"
said Lloyd, checking the flow of his companion's eloquence ;
"it's a woman."

"That's more in my way ; three-fourths of my business is
connected with them. Did you 'appen to take any notice
of the young man in that room as you came through ? He's
the best 'nose' in London. Find out anything. Lor'
bless you, that young man have been in more divorce cases
than the Serjeant himself. He can hide behind a walking-

stick, and see through the pipe of a Chubb's latch-key. There's nothing like him in London."

"Put him on to my business at once, then. Look at this card." Mr. Gammidge produced a large pair of tortoiseshell-rimmed double eye-glasses, and proceeded to make an elaborate investigation. "You know the name? I thought so. Now, your man must keep account of every one who goes in here by day or night, so long as she's at home; and when she goes out he must follow her, and, so far as he can, find out who speaks to her, and where. There is a five-pound note to begin with. You understand?"

"You may look upon it as good as done, sir," said Mr. Gammidge, commencing to make a memorandum of the number and date of the bank-note in his pocket-book, "and to let you know at the old address?"

"No; when he has anything to tell, drop me a line, and I'll meet him here. Good-day."

The white-faced young man, entering fully into his new occupation, speedily deserved the encomiastic remarks which had been lavished upon him by his principal, and in a short time Mr. Lloyd was furnished with full information as to the personal appearance of the various visitors at the Bayswater villa, and of the friends whom Miss Lambert was in the habit of meeting away from her home. In both these categories Gilbert Lloyd found, as he had expected to find, a very accurate representation of Miles Challoner. The information, all expected as it was, irritated and chafed him; and he gave up a whole day to considering how he could best put a stop to the ripening intimacy between Miles and Gertrude, or, at all events, weaken it. Finally, he decided on paying a visit to Mrs. Bloxam, and seeing whether she could not be frightened with a suspicion perfectly undefined, of something horrible and mysterious which would take place if the intimacy were permitted to go on unchecked. Accordingly, upon a day when the white-faced young man had ascertained that Miss Lambert would be for some time absent from home, Mr. Lloyd presented himself at the Bayswater villa, and, without sending in his name, followed the servant into the room, where Mrs. Bloxam was seated. At first sight of the man who had dared in former days to invade the sanctity of her sheep-

fold and carry off one of her pet lambs, the old lady was
exceedingly indignant, and her first impulse was to order
the intruder to leave the house ; but a moment's reflection
convinced her that as he yet had the power of being exceedingly dangerous to Gertrude, or, at all events, of causing
her the greatest annoyance, it would be better to temporise.
She therefore listened to all Gilbert Lloyd's bland assurances
that, although there was an unfortunate estrangement
between his wife and himself, he took the greatest interest
in her career, and it was purely as a matter of friendship
that he had come to warn her, through her ablest and best
friend, of the danger she incurred in forming a certain acquaintance. So well did Mrs. Bloxam play her listening
part, and so earnest was she in her thanks to her informant,
that even the *rusé* turfite was taken in, and went away
convinced that he had made his *coup.*

A few days afterwards he called again, and this time
asked for Miss Lambert. The servant said that Miss
Lambert was out. For Mrs. Bloxam : Mrs. Bloxam was
out. Gilbert Lloyd then took out a card and handed it to
the servant, begging her to give it to her mistress ; but
the servant, just glancing at it, handed it back, saying she
had strict orders, in case the gentleman bearing that name
ever called again, to refuse him admittance, and to return
his card.

CHAPTER V

REBUFFED.

THE cool determination of Gertrude's conduct, the resolution which did not shrink from a proceeding calculated
to excite at least observation by her servants, took
Gilbert Lloyd completely by surprise. Concealing, by a
desperate effort, the passion of anger which flamed up in
him, he turned away from the door, and got into the hansom
awaiting him ; but when quite out of sight of the gilded-
bronze gates, and the miniature plantation of the Bayswater
villa, he stopped the cab, got out, and pulling his hat down

over his brow, walked on rapidly, in a mood strange indeed to his calculating and self-contained nature.

By what fatality had this woman once more turned up in his life—this woman of whom he was well rid, his marriage with whom had been a mistake—a failure—and his parting with whom had been the commencement of a new and decidedly fortunate era in his life? His thoughts were in a whirl, and for a time resisted his attempts to reduce them to order and sequence. The physical convulsion of rage claimed to have its way first, and had it. He had known that feeling many times in his life—the maddening anger which turns the face white and the lips livid, which makes the heart beat with suffocating throbs, and dims the sight. He knew all about that, and he had to bear it now, and to bear it in silence, without the relief of speech, with only the aid of solitude. He could not swear at Gertrude now, as he had done many a time when annoyance had come to him through her; he could not insult, threaten, strike her now; and much of the fury he felt was due to the power-lessness which drove him nearly mad, and which was his own doing. Ay, that was the worst of it, the least en-durable part of the wrath which raged within him. This woman, who had been in his power, and had been made to experience the full significance of her position; who had loved him once, and of whom he had wearied, as it was in his nature to weary of any desired object when attained,—this woman held him in supreme indifference and contempt, and set him at naught without fear or hesitation. In the force and irrationality of his anger, he forgot that she was acting quite within the letter and the spirit of the con-vention made between them; that he it was who had abandoned its spirit at almost the first sight of her, and had now received a humiliating check in endeavouring to violate its letter. For a long time his anger was blind, fierce, and unreasoning—directed almost as much against himself as against Gertrude—his wife! his wife! as he called her a hundred times over, in the vain assertion of a position which he had voluntarily abdicated, and which he knew, in the bottom of his angry heart—even while the anger seethed within it—he would not be prepared to re-sume, were the opportunity afforded him. But as he walked on and on, getting by degrees into outlying regions of the far west—almost as little known to him as California—the habit of calculation, of arranging his thoughts, of (metaphorically) laying his head on the exact process or combination which he required—a faculty and habit of which he felt the value every day—resumed its sway over him, and he no longer raged blindly about what had happened, but set himself to think it out. This, then, was a *parti pris* on the part of Gertrude; this, then, was a game in which he was her adversary—with a purpose to gain; she—his, with nothing in view but his defeat. Her cards were resolute ignoring of his existence; the absolute and inexorable adherence to the agreement made between them at Brighton. His cards were persistent following and watching of her, which the coincidences of his position and the facility with which he could make her circle of acquaintance his, added to the exigencies of her professional career, which she could not control, however unwelcome they might be, rendered easy of playing. The next question was, what end did he propose to himself in this sudden revulsion of feeling, this sudden irruption into his prosperous and pleasant life of an element which he had hoped, intended, and believed to be banished from it for ever? This question he could not answer clearly. The mists of anger and jealousy arose between him and the outline of his purpose. Was it to undo the past? Was it to woo and win once more this woman, whom he had driven away from him, and who had just made evident to him the weakness of his determination and the strength of her own? Was it to put himself entirely and unreservedly under the yoke of her power, from whose possible imposition he had been glad to escape by the final expedient to which he had resorted? Had he any such rash, insane notion as this in his thoughts? He did not know, he was not certain; he was not sure of anything but this—that Gertrude had refused to see him, and that he was resolved she should, come what might; she should not carry that point, she should not have the triumph at once of fidelity to their strange unnatural compact on her own part, and of having forced him to break it on his. He had dismissed her easily enough from his thoughts, but he could not dismiss her from them now; she kept possession of them now, in the pride of her beauty—how handsome she was! he had never supposed she would have grown into

such commanding, self-possessed beauty as hers was now—
and in the triumph of her talent—as she had never done
since the brief earliest days of their disastrous marriage.
Gilbert Lloyd was a man on whom success of any kind produced a strong impression. It counted for much in the
rekindling of his former passion for Gertrude that she was
now a successful artist, her supposed name in everyone's
mouth, holding her own before the world, a woman with a
position, an *entourage*, and an independent career. His
thoughts wandered away among scenes which he had long
forgotten, in which she was the central figure, and into
imaginary pictures of her present life; and he repeated
over and over again, with rage—waxing dull by this time
—"But she is my wife! she is my wife! no matter what
she chooses to do, no matter how she chooses to act towards
me, she is my wife! I have only to declare it if I choose."
And the consequences to which she, judging by her present
conduct, would probably be entirely indifferent—was he
prepared to face them? He could not answer this question
either; he was not yet cool-headed enough to estimate them
aright.

A devouring curiosity concerning Gertrude took possession of him—a craving eagerness to know what were her
movements, who were her associates, how she lived; even
the disposition of the rooms in her house, and her domestic
relations. The absolute ignorance of all these things in
which he remained, though his imperious will demanded to
be informed of them, exasperated him; and with his fruit-
less anger there was mingled a grim humour, as he thought
of the scenes through which they had passed together, as he
recalled Gertrude in the intimacy of their domestic life.
And now he was the one person in the world from whom
she concealed herself, the one person shut out from her by a
barrier erected by her inflexible will. Was he? Time
would tell. He had not been ignorant during the sometimes stormy, sometimes gay and careless, but always unsatisfactory, period which preceded their separation, that he
was by no means so indifferent to Gertrude as she was to
him. On the contrary, he had realized that clearly and
plainly, and it had sharpened his anger towards her and
hardened his heart in the hour of their parting; and he had
hated her then, and chafed under the knowledge that she

did not hate him, that she was only glad to be rid of him, had only ceased utterly to love him, and learned utterly to despise him. Justly esteeming himself to be a good hater, Gilbert Lloyd found it difficult to understand how it was that he had so soon ceased to hate Gertrude, had so easily yielded to the sense of relief in having done with all that portion of his life in which she had a share, and had never had any serious thought of her, or speculation about her future; for to such an extent had his cynicism gone now that this period of oblivion and ease had in its turn expired, and she had again crossed his path to trouble him. He could only account for this curious phase through which he had passed by what seemed to him an insufficient reason— the new interests in his life, the success which attended his speculation in that " rich brute Ticehurst's " affairs—for thus did the more fastidious and not less vicious man of the two characterize, in his meditations, the coarse animal he was devoting himself so successfully to *exploiter*. Such a chance, after so long a run of ill-luck, varied only by a *coup* on which he preferred not to dwell in remembrance—a chance, as he thought, with an ominous darkening of his evil face, which, if it had only been afforded him a little sooner, might have averted the necessity for such a *coup*, was calculated to occupy him entirely, and banish from his mind anything which might divert him from the pursuit of his object.

And now it seemed wonderful to him that he could have thus forgotten her—now, when he was under the renewed spell of her beauty and her scorn.

There was an extraordinary fascination for him, even in the midst of his anger, in the mingled strangeness and familiarity with which she presented herself to his mind. He had a good deal of imagination, though but little poetry, in his nature, and the extraordinarily exceptional position of this woman and himself—the strangeness of the knowledge that she had accepted the fact of there being nothing mutual or even relative in their position now or ever—appealed, in the midst of his passion, to his imagination.

That she should dare to treat him thus,—that she should know him so little as to dare to treat him thus. He thought this, he said this more than once through his shut teeth; but he was not a fool, even in his rage, and he knew he was talking folly to himself in the moment that he uttered the words. Why should she not dare? Indeed, there was no daring about it. He had made the position for himself, and he was for the first time brought face to face with all the details of it. What was that position externally in the world's sight, in the only point of view in which he had any practical right to consider it? Just this: Miss Lambert did not choose to admit him to her acquaintance. He was helpless; she was in her right. He might force her to meet him in the houses of other people—at the Marchioness of Carabas' house, for instance—simply because she could not afford, out of consideration for her own social position, to give up her patroness; and also (he began to understand Gertrude now sufficiently to know that this second argument was by far the stronger), because she would never suffer the consideration of meeting or not meeting him to influence her actions, to form a motive of her conduct in the smallest degree. He felt that with a smart twinge of pain, the keen pain of mortified self-love. He had simply ceased to exist for her—that was all; she had taken the full sense of their convention, and was acting on it *tout bonnement*. He might, therefore, calculate safely upon meeting her, without her consent, at other houses than her own; but, forcing or inducing her to admit him there, was, he felt, entirely beyond his power. He was wholly insensible to the extreme incongruity of such a possibility, had it existed; and no wonder, for in their position all was incongruous, and propriety or impropriety had lost their meaning.

In the conflict of feeling and passion in which Gilbert Lloyd was thus engaged, there was no element of fierce contention wanting. Love, or the debased feeling which he called and believed to be love, and which fluctuated between passion and hate, baffled design, undefined fear, and jealousy, in which not merely Gertrude was concerned, but another who had a place in his life of still darker and more fatal meaning, and a more bitterly resented influence over his fate. When he had fought out the skirmish with the newly reawakened love for the wife whom he had almost forgotten, and been beaten, and had been forced to surrender so much of the disputed ground to the enemy, fear marshalled its forces against him, and pressed him hard. But not to the point of victory. Gilbert Lloyd was a man with whom fear

had never had much chance; and if he had yielded somewhat to its influence in the separation from his wife, it was
because that influence had been largely supported by long-
smouldering discontent, *ennui*, a coincidence of convenience
and opportunity, and a deserved conviction that the full
potency of Gertrude's will was at work in the matter.
There was little likelihood that fear should master him now;
but it was there, and he had to stand, and repel its assaults.
If he attempted to molest, to control Gertrude in any way ;
if it even became her interest or her pleasure to get rid of
him in actual fact, in addition to their convenient theory,—
fear asked him, Can she not do so ? Is she not mistress of
the situation, of every point of it ? And he answered, Yes.
If she chose to carry out the divorce—which they had
mutually instituted without impertinent legal interference—
would he dare to intervene ? He remembered how he had
speculated upon the expediency of encouraging the " rich
brute's " *penchant* for the fashionable singer, when he had
no suspicion who the fashionable singer was ; and a rush of
fury surged all over him as he thought, if she had chosen to
encourage him, to marry him, for his rank, would he,
Gilbert Lloyd, her husband, have dared to interfere ? Fear
had the best of it there ; but he would not be beaten by
fear. This enemy was strong mainly because he could not
rightly calculate its strength. How much did Gertrude
know, or how little ? Was it knowledge, or suspicion only,
which had prompted her to the decision she had adopted,
and the prompt action she had taken upon it ? To these
questions it was impossible he could get any answer ; and
he would, or thought he would, just then—for he was an
unlikely man to stick to such a bargain, if he could have
made it—have given years of his life to know what had
passed that memorable day at Brighton, before he had
returned to the death-bed of his friend, and there encountered Gertrude. The dying whisper which had conveyed to the young woman the power she had used so
promptly was unknown by Lloyd ; on this point—the
great, the essential point of his musings—all was conjecture,
dark, terrifying, and undefined.

Had love and fear only possessed his dark soul between
them, the strife might soon have ended, in a division in
which the man's own safety would have been consulted.

Gilbert Lloyd would have made up his mind that, as his first fancy for Gertrude had passed away, so this eccentric renewal of it would also harmlessly decline. The whole difficulty might have resolved itself into his persuading Ticehurst to go abroad in his company, until the "rich brute" should have escaped all risk of an "entanglement," which Lloyd would have painted in the most alarming colours, and Lloyd himself have recovered from a passing fit of weak folly, which he might have been trusted to learn to despise, on a sober consideration of its bearing on his interests in the career in which he had contrived with so much difficulty to *lancer* himself.

But the look which he had seen in Gertrude's proud calm face—the smile which was so absolutely new to him, that it would have thrilled him through with jealousy to whomsoever addressed, because it revealed to him that she had never felt for him that which prompted its soft and trusting sweetness—the smile which had fired all the evil passions in his exceptionally evil nature—had shown Gilbert a far more terrible truth : she had never given him such a smile. *Soit.* He had had such as he had cared for, and he was tired of them, and done with them, and as bright and beautiful were to be had for love or money, particularly for money. Thus he might have thought, half in consoling earnest, half in mortification, and acted on the reassuring argument. But the smile, the unknown smile, which had not lighted her face upon their bridal day, which had never adorned the happiest hour—and they had had some happy hours—of their marriage, had beamed upon the man whom of all men living Gilbert Lloyd hated most bitterly—and that man was his brother. His brother, Miles Challoner, their dead father's darling son—(and when Lloyd thought of his father his face was horrible to see, and his heart was foul with curses and unnatural hate, for he hated his dead father more than his living brother),—the heir who had been his rival always, his master in their nursery, the object of his bitterest envy and enmity when he was so young that it was a mystery of the devil how such passions could have a place in his childish heart. In the name of the devil,—in whom Gilbert Lloyd was almost tempted to believe as he watched that smile, and felt the tempest rise in his heart, like the waves under the moonbeams,—how had *this* complication

come about! This he could readily ascertain, but what
would it avail him to know it? If she loved this hated
brother of his, what could he do? Enjoy the hideous revenge of keeping quiet, and letting their mutual love grow
into the blessing and hope of their existence perhaps, and
then come forward and expose all the truth, and crush the
two at once? And then? His own share in this, what
would it be? Utter ruin; and for his brother the sympathy
of the world! To be sure it would be deep disgrace for the
woman who, secretly a wife, encouraged a man to love, and
to hope to win her; but she could deny her love and the
encouragement, and nobody could prove either, and she was
entirely ignorant of the relation subsisting between Miles
Challoner and him. Of this Gilbert Lloyd did not feel a
moment's doubt. Miles would not divulge a fact in which
a terrible family secret was involved, to anyone; he had
taken his line towards Gilbert on their first accidental
meeting far too decidedly for the existence of any doubt on
that point. If, on the other hand, Gilbert Lloyd were to
yield to the promptings of passion and revenge, and betray
the relationship, ruin of a double kind would inevitably
overtake him; vague indeed as to its source or manner, but
not admitting of any doubt. He knew that such would be
the case, thus: One communication only had been addressed
to the man who is here called Gilbert Lloyd, by his father,
after his sudden departure from Rowley Court. It was
brief, and contained in the following words:

*" I have placed in the hands of a friend in whom I have
entire confidence, the narrative of the events which have
ended with your banishment from my house, and your erasure
from our family annals for ever. This friend is not acquainted with your personal appearance, and cannot therefore
recognize you, should your future conduct enable you to
present yourself in any place where he may be found; but he
will be in close and constant intercourse with my son; and
should you venture, either directly or remotely, to injure my
son, in person, reputation, estate, or by any means whatever, this friend being warned by me to investigate any
such injury done to my son, on the presumption that it
comes from you, will be enabled to identify you; and is, in
such case, bound to me by a solemn promise to expose the
whole of the facts, and the proofs in his possession, in such*

manner as he may judge best for bringing you most certainly and expeditiously to that punishment which human weakness has prevented my being the means of inflicting upon you. I give you this information and warning, in the interest of my son, and also because I desire to turn you, by the only motive available for my purpose, from the commission of a crime whose penalty no one's weakness will enable you to evade."

Gilbert Lloyd had never been able during all the vicissitudes of his career—in all its levities, its successes, its failures, its schemes—to forget the warning, or even the phrasing, of this terrible letter. He had burned it in a fury which would have hardly been assuaged by the blood of the writer, and had tried to persuade himself afterwards that he scoffed at the suspicions and the threat and the precaution alike. But the effort failed : he did not scoff—he believed and feared, and remembered ; and in this strange and ominous complication, which had brought his brother across his path under circumstances which any man might have feared, he felt the futility of his pretended indifference to an extent which resembled terror.

He wondered at himself now, when he remembered that whenever he had thought about his wife at all in the early days after their separation, in the few and scattered speculations which had arisen in his mind about her, the idea of her ever loving another man had found no place. So intense was his egotism, that, though he did not indulge in the mere vanity of believing that she still loved *him,* and would repent the step she had taken, he did not in the least realise her matter-of-fact emancipation from the ties which they loosed by mutual consent. He had sometimes wondered whether she got on well with her liberty and her hundred pounds ; whether she had gone back to the drudgery of school-life, in the intensified form that drudgery assumes to a teacher ; whether she had any friends, and how she accounted to them for her isolation ; with other vague and placid vaticinations. But that this young and handsome woman, who had found out the unworthiness of her first love, had been rudely awakened from her woman's dream of happiness, and had exchanged all the sentiment with which she had regarded him for horror and contempt, and a steadily maintained purpose of utter separation—that she

should have a second love, should dream again, never occurred to him. As little had he thought about the probability of his meeting her in the widely divergent course
which his own life had taken from any within the previous
experience of either. But he had met her ; and one of the
unexpected results of that undesirable event was to awaken
him, with a shock, to the strongest suspicion that she did
love and dream again, and that the object of the love and
the dream was the man he most hated—was his brother.
How Gilbert Lloyd would have regarded this circumstance,
had he carried out his acceptation of the situation with
such good faith and such complete indifference as Gertrude
evinced, had he been able to see her again perfectly unmoved
and without the slightest wish to alter anything in their
position, he did not stop seriously to consider. This might
have been ; and for a minute or two his mind glanced at
certain cynical possibilities in such a case, which might have
enabled him to gratify his spite towards both his wife and
his brother, in comparative security. But it was not ; and
that which was, absorbed him wholly.

Alternately raging against the feelings which possessed
him, and arranging the facts of the case in order, and
forcing himself to ponder them with his accustomed coolness, Gilbert Lloyd walked on for many miles without
taking note of distance. When at length he bethought
him of the time, and consulted his watch, he found he must
hasten back to town, to be ready to dine with the " rich
brute," who was to entertain a party of choice spirits devoted to the turf that day. The occasion was an important,
and Gilbert Lloyd intended that it should be a profitable,
one. In the midst of the anger and perturbation of his
spirit, he was quite capable of attending to his own and his
patron's interests—when they were identical ; and there was
no mental process, involving no matter what amount of
passion or scheming or danger, which Gilbert Lloyd could
not lay aside—ranged in its due place in his memory—to
await its fitting time ; a valuable faculty, and not a little
dangerous in the possession of a man at war, more or less
openly, with society.

The next day, as Gilbert Lloyd, as usual admirably
mounted, turned into the Park, and made for the then
almost deserted Lady's Mile, a carriage swept rapidly by.

Two ladies occupied the back-seat, and on the front Lloyd beheld the unusual apparition of Lord Sandilands. The ladies were the Marchioness of Carabas and Miss Lambert. They saw him; and Lady Carabas gave him a bow at once graciously graceful and deliciously familiar; but Miss Lambert looked straight before her with such exquisitely perfect unconsciousness, that it never occurred to either of her companions that she had recognised Gilbert Lloyd.

Then savage anger took possession of him once more, and scattered all the process of thought he had been going through to the winds, and he swore that, come what might, he would meet her where it would be impossible for her to avoid him.

CHAPTER VI.

GERTRUDE SPEAKS.

LORD TICEHURST'S attachment to the turf was by no means of a lukewarm or of a perfunctory character. He was not one of the young men of the present day, who keep a racing-stud as they keep anything else, merely for their amusement; who exult indecently when they are successful, who are even more indecently depressed when they are unfortunate. Having such a man as Gilbert Lloyd for his "confederate," manager, and agent, the young nobleman did not require to look into the details of his stud and his stable as he otherwise would have done; but nothing was ever done without his knowledge and approval, and his heart was as much bound up in turf-matters as it had been when, under the initiation of Plater Dobbs, he first made his entrance into the Ring. Perhaps if this attachment to racing-matters and racing-men had been less strong, Lord Ticehurst would have noticed a certain change in Lloyd's manner towards him which would have displeased him much. For, notwithstanding that he struggled hard against the display of any such feeling, there arose in Gilbert's breast a sullen animosity, a dogged dislike to his friend and patron, which very often would not be kept down, but came surging up into his face, and showed itself in knit

brows and tightened lips, and hard cold insolence of bearing.
This was very different from the deep and bitter hatred with
which Gilbert Lloyd regarded Miles Challoner, though it
sprang from the same cause, the admiration which each of
them felt for Gertrude. In the present state of his feelings
for her, it enraged Gilbert to think that any one should dare
to pay attention to one who had been, who by the law still
was, his property; but the depth and measure of his
hatred was very much acted upon by the knowledge that
Lord Ticehurst was merely regarded by Gertrude as one of
a hundred hangers-on, while Miles Challoner stood in a very
different position. But though this angry feeling from time
to time got the better of Gilbert Lloyd's usually placid and
equable temperament, and led to exhibitions of temper
which he was afterwards frightened at and ashamed of, they
were never noticed by the kindly-hearted, thick-headed
young man whom he had in training, or, if they were, were
ascribed to some of those "tighteners" and "botherations"
which were supposed to fall naturally to "old Gilbert's" lot
in transacting his business of the turf. "There's bad news
up from the Pastures, I suppose," Lord Ticehurst would say
to some of his friends, after the occurrence of some little
episode of the kind; "old Gil's uncommon cranky this
mornin', and no two ways about it. It's always best to
leave him to come round by himself when he is in this way,
so lets you and me go down to Rummer's and get some luncheon." But throughout all his annoyances, and the renovated passion for his wife,—passion of the strongest, wildest,
most enslaving kind, was now always present in his heart,—
Gilbert Lloyd held carefully to his business career, losing no
opportunity of showing himself of service to his pupil,
and taking every care that his pupil was made aware of the
fact.

"I say, Etchingham," said Gilbert one morning, glancing
up from his accounts at his lordship, who was moodily
looking out of window, smoking, and wondering whether he
should propose to Miss Lambert before the season finally
broke up, or leave it until next spring,—"I say, Etchingham, I'm pretty near sick of town."

"Same here!" replied his lordship; "fusty and beastly,
ain't it? Well, we're close upon cutting it; it's Goodwood
the week after next, and then there's Brighton——"

"O, curse Brighton!" broke in Lloyd.

"All right," said Lord Ticehurst, lazily dropping into a chair. "Curse Brighton by all means. But what a rum fellow you are! You wouldn't go to the Brighton Meeting last year; and I recollect that there was a talk about it at Rummer's; and Jack Manby—the Bustard, you know—said you'd never go there again, since in Gaslight's year, I think he said, the sea-air spoiled your complexion."

"Manby's a chattering idiot," said Lloyd, savagely; "and next time you hear men talking of why I don't go to the Brighton Meeting, you may say I don't go because it isn't a meeting at all, a third-rate concern with a pack of platers to run, and a crowd of cockneys to look at them. You may say that."

"Much obliged," said Lord Ticehurst; "you may say it yourself, if you want to. I don't hold with mixin' myself up in other fellows' shines;" and he sucked solemnly at his cigar, and did his best to look dignified.

"My dear old Etchingham, don't be angry. I was vexed at hearing you repeat the gabble of those infernal fellows at that filthy tavern—it isn't anything better—because it's not only about me they talk. However, that's neither here nor there. I suppose you'll have the wind-up dinner at Richmond as usual."

"All right, Gil, my boy!" said his good-tempered lordship; "there's no bones broke, and it's all squared. Of course we'll have the dinner. Let's see," looking at his memorandum-book; "Friday-week, how will that suit? Mrs. Stapleton Burge's party. O, ah, that's nothing!" he added quickly, growing very red.

"Very well," said Gilbert quietly. "Friday-week, since you've only got Mrs. Stapleton Burge's party; and that's nothing, you say. Friday-week will do. I'm to ask the usual lot, I suppose?"

"Yes, usual lot, and one or two more, don't you think? It was deuced slow last time, I remember. Only old Toshington to talk, and everybody's tired of his old gab. Ask some one to froth it up a bit, one of those writing-fellows one sees at some houses, or an actor who can mimic fellows, and that kind of thing, don't you know?"

"I know," said Gilbert, by no means jumping at the suggestion; "but I generally find that your clever fellows who write are miserable unless they have all the talk to themselves ; and the actors are insulted if you ask them to do any of their hanky-panky, as though, by Jove, they'd be invited for anything else. However, I'll look up some of them, and do my best. Anybody else ? "

" No, I think not. Unless, by the way, you were to ask that man that my aunt's taken up lately—Challoner."

The name brought the blood into Gilbert's face, and he paused a moment before he said : ".I don't think I'd have that fellow, Etchingham, if I were you."

" What's the matter with him ? Ain't he on the square ? Bad egg, and that kind of thing ? "

" I know very little about him," said Gilbert, fixing his eyes on Lord Ticehurst's face ; " nothing, indeed, for the matter of that ; and he's never crossed me, and never will have the opportunity. I said, ' if I were you.' "

" Yes, well—I know. Drop the riddle business and speak out. What do you mean ? "

" Plainly, then, I've noticed—and I can't imagine how it has failed to escape you—that this man Challoner is making a strong running for a lady for whom I have heard you profess the greatest admiration—Miss Lambert."

" O, ah, yes—thanks ; all right," said Lord Ticehurst, looking more foolish than usual—in itself a stupendous feat ; " well, I ain't spooney particularly on Challoner, so you needn't ask him."

Peers of the realm, and persons known as " public characters," command more civility and attention in England than any one else. With tradesmen, hotel-waiters, and railway-porters this feeling is so strongly developed that they will leave any customer to serve a great lord or a popular comedian. Lord Ticehurst's name stood very high at the Crown and Sceptre at Richmond, not merely because he was an earl—they see plenty of them during the season at the Crown and Sceptre—but because he was freespoken, lavish with his money, and " had no cussed pride about him." Consequently, whenever he dined there the dinner was always good, which is by no means always the case at the C. and S. ; and the present occasion was no exception. There were about twenty guests, all men, and nearly all men of one set, who, though they were mostly well-born, and, in the main, tolerably educated, apparently never sought for and certainly never attained any other society. The outside world was familiar with their names, through seeing them printed in the newspapers as attending the various great race-meetings ; and with their personal appearance, through seeing them at Tattersall's and in the Park, especially on Sundays in the season. Some had chambers in the Albany, some in smaller and cheaper sets ; many of them lived humbly enough in one bedroom in the lodging-house-swarming streets round St. James's ; all of them haunted Rummer's in Conduit-street ; and most of them belonged to some semi-turf, semi-military, whole card-and-billiard-playing club. Some of them were believed to be married, but their wives were never seen with them by any chance ; for they never went into society, to the opera, or the theatres ; and they were always put into the bachelor quarters at country-houses, and into the topmost rooms at the hotels, where they treated the female domestics in a pleasant and genial way, a compound of the manners of the groom and the commercial bagman.

They gathered in full force at the Crown and Sceptre that lovely July afternoon ; for they knew that they would have a good dinner and wine without stint. Captain Dafter was there—a little wiry man with sandy scraps of whisker and a mean little white face, but who was the best amateur steeplechase rider in England, with limbs of steel and dauntless pluck. Next to him sat a fat, heavy-headed, large-jowled man, with a face the shape and colour of an ill-baked quartern loaf ; a silent stupid-looking man, who ate and drank enormously, and said, and apparently understood, nothing ; but who was no less a personage than the "Great Northern," as he was called, from having been born at Carlisle ; the enormous bookmaker and King of the Ring, who began life as a plumber with eighteenpence, and was then worth hundreds of thousands. There, too, with his neatly-rolled whiskers and his neatly-tied blue bird's-eye scarf, with its plain solid gold horse-shoe pin, was Dolly Clarke, the turf-lawyer. Years ago Dolly would have thought himself lucky if he ever made six hundred a-year. Six thousand is now nearer Dolly's annual income, all brought about by his own talent, and " not standing on any repairs," as he put it, a quality which is to be found in the dictionary under the word " unscrupulousness ; " for when

old Mr. Snoxell, inventor of the Pilgrim's-Progress Leather
for tender feet, died, and left all his money to his son Sam,
who had been bred to the law, Sam took Dolly Clarke into
partnership, and by combining shrewdness with bill-dis-
counting, and a military connection with a knowledge of
turf-matters, they did a splendid business.   You would
almost mistake Dolly Clarke for a gentleman now, and
Samuel Snoxell calls all the army by their Christian names.
Next to Dolly Clarke was Mr. Bagwax, Q.C., always
retained in cases connected with the turf, and rather preferring to be on the shaky and shady side, which affords opportunities for making great fun out of would-be-honest
witnesses, and making jokes which, of all the persons in
court, are not least understood by Mr. Justice Martingale,
who knows a horse from a wigblock, and is understood to
have at one time heard the chimes at midnight.   The re-
doubtable Jack Manby, called " the Bustard," because in his
thickness of utterance he was in the habit of declaring that
he " didn't care about bustard so long as he got beef," was
there ; and old Sam Roller, the trainer, looking something
like a bishop, and something more like Mr. Soapey Sponge's
friend, Jack Spraggon ; and a tall thin gentlemanly man,
who looked like a barrister, and who was " Haruspex," the
sporting prophet of the *Statesman.*   Nor had Gilbert Lloyd
forgotten his patron's hint about the enlivening of the company by the representatives of literature and the drama.
Mr. Wisbottle, the graphic writer, the charming essayist,
the sparkling dramatist ; Wisbottle, who was always
turning up in print when you least expected him ; Wisbottle, of whom his brilliant friend and toady M'Boswell had
remarked that he had never tetigited anything which he
hadn't ornavited ;—Wisbottle represented literature, and
represented it in a very thirsty and talkative, not to say
flippant, manner.   As the drama's representative, behold
Mr. Maurice Mendip, a charming young fellow of fifty-five,
who, in the old days of patent theatres and great tra-
gedians, would have alternated Marcellus with Bernardo,
playing Horatio for his benefit, when his landlady, friends,
and family from Bermondsey came in with tickets sold for
his particular behoof, but who, in virtue of loud lungs and
some faint reminiscence of what he had seen done by his
betters, played all the "leading business" in London when

he could get the chance, and was the idolized hero of Californian gold-diggers and Australian aborigines. He was, perhaps, a little out of place at such a party, being heavy, grave, and taciturn ; but most people knew his name, and when told who he was, said, " O, indeed ! " and looked at him with that mixture of curiosity and impertinence with which " public characters " are generally regarded. The other guests were men more or less intimately connected with the turf, who talked to each other in a low grumbling monotone, and whose whole desire was to get the better of each other in every possible way.

The dinner, which had called forth loud encomiums, was over ; the cigars were lighted, and the conversation had been proceeding briskly, when in a momentary lull Dolly Clarke, who had the reputation for being not quite too fond of Gilbert Lloyd, said in a loud voice : " Well, my lord, and after Goodwood comes Brighton, and of course you hope to be as lucky there."

" We've got nothing at Brighton," replied Lord Ticehurst, looking uneasily towards where Gilbert was occupying the vice-chair.

" Nothing at Brighton ! " echoed Dolly Clarke, very loud indeed ; " why, how's that ? "

" Because we don't choose, Mr. Clarke," said Gilbert, from the other end of the table—he had been drinking more than his wont, and there was a strained, flushed look round his eyes quite unusual to him—" because we don't choose ; I suppose that's reason enough."

" O, quite," said Dolly Clarke, with a short laugh. " I spoke to Lord Ticehurst, by the way ; but in your case I suppose it's not an ' untradesmanlike falsehood ' if you represent yourself as ' the same concern.' However, you used to go to Brighton, Lloyd."

" Yes," replied Gilbert quickly, " and so used you, when you were Wiggins and Proctor's outdoor clerk at eighteen shillings a-week—by the excursion-train ! Times have changed with both of us."

" Lloyd had him there, Jack," whispered Bagwax, Q.C., to his neighbour the Bustard. " Impudent customer, Master Clarke ! I recollect well when he used to carry a bag and serve writs, and all that ; and now——"

" Hold on a binnit," said the Bustard ; " he's an awkward

customer is Clarke, and he'll show Gilbert no bercy." And, indeed, there was a look in Mr. Dolly Clarke's ordinarily smiling, self-satisfied face, and a decision in the manner in which his hand had, apparently involuntarily, closed upon the neck of the claret-jug standing in front of him, that augured ill for the peace of the party in general, or the personal comfort of Gilbert Lloyd in particular. But old Sam Roller's great spectacles had happened to be turned towards the turf-lawyer at the moment ; and the old fellow, seeing how matters stood, had telegraphed to Lord Ticehurst, while Mr. Wisbottle touched Clarke's knee with one hand under the table, and removed the claret-jug from his grasp with the other, whispering, " Drop it, dear old boy ! What's the good ? You kill him, and have to keep out of the way, and lose all the business in Davies-street. He kills you, and what becomes of the policies for the little woman at Roehampton ? Listen to the words of Wisbottle, the preacher, my chick, and drop it." And it having by this time dawned upon Lord Ticehurst that there was something wrong, that young nobleman cut into the conversation in a very energetic and happy manner, principally dilating upon the necessity of his guests drinking as much and as fast as they possibly could. The first part of the proposition seemed highly popular, but certain of the company objected to being hurried with their liquor, and demanded to know the reason of their being thus pressed. Then Lord Ticehurst explained that he was under the necessity of putting in an appearance that night at the house of a very particular friend, where an evening party was being held ; that it was an engagement of long-standing, and one which it was impossible for him to get off. This, he added, need be no reason for breaking up their meeting ; he should only be too delighted if they would stop as long as they pleased ; and he was quite sure that his worthy vice would come up to that end of the table, and fill his place much more worthily than it had hitherto been filled.

But to this proposition there was a great deal of demur. Several of the guests, keen men of business, with the remembrance of the morrow's engagements and work before them, and having had quite sufficient wine, were eager to be off. Others, who would have remained drinking so long as any drink was brought, scarcely relished their cups under the presidency of Gilbert Lloyd, who was regarded by them as anything but a convivalist; while others, again, had engagements in town which they were anxious to fulfil. Moreover, the plan proposed by his patron was anything but acceptable to Gilbert Lloyd himself. Ordinarily almost abstemious, he had on this occasion taken a great deal of wine, and, though he was by no means intoxicated, his pulses throbbed and his blood was heated in a manner very unusual with him. From the first moment of Ticehurst's mentioning that he was going on this evening to a party at Mrs. Stapleton Burge's house, Gilbert felt convinced, by his friend's manner, that he must have some special attraction there, and that that attraction must be the presence of Gertrude. This thought—the feeling that she would be there, surrounded by courtiers and flatterers—worried and irritated him, and every glass of wine which he swallowed increased his desire to see her that night. What matter if he had been rebuffed! That was simply because he had not had the chance of speaking to her. Give him that opportunity, and she would tell a very different tale. He should have that opportunity if he met her face to face in society; it would be impossible for her, without committing a palpable rudeness—and Gilbert Lloyd knew well that she would never do that—to avoid speaking to him. *Château qui parle est pret de se rendre.* A true proverb that; and he made up his mind to tell Lord Ticehurst to take him to Mrs. Stapleton Burge's gathering, and to run his chance with Gertrude.

So that when he heard his patron propound that he should remain behind, to fan into a flame the expiring embers of an orgie which, even at its brightest, had afforded him no amusement, his disgust was extreme, and uncomplimentary as they were to himself, he fostered and repeated the excuses which he heard on all sides. Nor did he content himself with passive resistance, but went straight to Lord Ticehurst, and taking him aside, told him that this was, after all, only a "duty dinner;" that all that was necessary had been done, and that it was better they should break up then and there. " Moreover," said he, " I've a fancy to go with you to-night. You're always telling me I don't mix enough in what you call society; and as this is the end of the season, and we're not likely to be—well, I was going to say bothered with women's parties for a long time, I don't mind going with you; in fact, I should rather like it. These fellows have done very well, and we can now leave them to shift for themselves." Lord Ticehurst's astonishment at this suggestion from his Mentor was extreme. "What a queer chap you are, Gil!" he said; "when I've asked you to go to all sorts of houses, first-class, where everything is done in great form and quite correct, you've stood out and fought shy, and all that kind of thing. And now you want to go to old Mother Burge's,—old cat who stuffs her rooms with a lot of people raked up here and there! 'Pon my soul there's no knowing where to have you, and that's about the size of it!" But in this matter, as in almost every other, the young man gave way to his friend, and the party broke up at once; and Lord Ticehurst and Gilbert Lloyd drove home to Hill-street, dressed themselves, and proceeded to Mrs. Stapleton Burge's reception.

Mrs. Stapleton Burge lived in a very big house in Great Swaffham-street, close out of Park-lane, and though a very little black-faced woman herself, did everything on a very large scale. Her footmen were enormous creatures, prize-fed, big-whiskered, ambrosial; her chariot was like a family ark; the old English characters in which her name and address were inscribed surged all over her big cards. She had a big husband, a fat, fair man with a protuberant chest, and receding forehead, and little eyes, who was a major in some Essex yeomanry, and who was generally mistaken by his guests for the butler. Everybody went to Mrs. Stapleton Burge's; and she, sometimes accompanied by the major, but more frequently without him, went everywhere. Nobody could give a reason for either proceeding. When the Stapleton Burges went out of town at the end of the season, nobody knew where they went to. Some people said to the family place in Essex, but Tommy Toshington said that was all humbug; he'd looked up the county history, and there wasn't any such place as Fenners; and he, Tommy, thought they either retired to the back of the house in Great Swaffham-street, or took lodgings at Ramsgate. But the next season they appeared again, as blooming and as big as ever. Lord Ticehurst, in his description of Mrs. Burge's parties, scarcely did that worthy woman justice. People said, and truly, that those gatherings were "a little mixed;" but Lady Tintagel took care that some of the very best people in London were seen at them. If Mrs. Burge would have her own friends, that, Lady Tintagel said, was no affair of hers. Mrs. Burge swore by Lady Tintagel, and the major swore at her. "If it wasn't for that confounded woman," he used to say, "we shouldn't be going through all this tomfoolery, but should be living quietly at——" He was never known to complete the sentence. Lady Tintagel was Mrs. Burge's sponsor in the world of fashion, and the major lent money to Lord Tintagel, who was an impecunious and elderly nobleman. When Lady Tintagel presided over a stall at an aristocratic fancy-fair for the benefit of a charity, Mrs. Burge furnished the said stall, and took Lady Tintagel's place thereat during the dull portion of the day. Lady Tintagel's celebrated *tableaux vivants* were held in Mrs. Burge's big rooms in Great Swaffham-street, the Tintagel establishment being carried on in a two-roomed house in Mayfair. Mrs. Burge "takes" Lady Tintagel to various places of an evening, when the Tintagel jobbed horses are knocked up, and never has "her ladyship" out of her mouth.

When Lord Ticehurst and Gilbert Lloyd arrived at the hospitable mansion, they found the rooms crowded. It was a great but trying occasion for Mrs. Burge—trying, because it was plainly the farewell *fête* of the season; and all the guests were talking to one another of where they were going to, while she, poor woman, had a dreary waste of seven months before her, to be passed away from the delights of fashionable life. To how many people did she promise a speedy meeting at Spa, at Baden, in the Highlands, in Midland country-houses? and all her interlocutors placed their tongues in their cheeks, and knew that until the next summons of Parliament drew the town together, and simultaneously produced a card of invitation from Mrs. Burge, they should not meet the hostess of the night. Meantime, the success of the present gathering was unimpeachable. Everybody who was left in London had rallied round Great Swaffham-street; and there was no doubt but that the *Morning Post* of the coming day would convey to the ends of the civilized world a list of fashionables which would redound in the most complete manner to the *éclat* of Mrs. Stapleton Burge.

The necessary form of introduction had been gone through —scarcely necessary, by the way, in Great Swaffham-street; for the men always averred that Mrs. Burge never knew half the people at her own parties—and Lord Ticehurst, having done his duty in landing Gilbert, had strolled away among the other *convives*, with what object Gilbert well enough knew. He, Gilbert Lloyd, had rather a habit ot trusting to chance in matters of this kind ; and, on the present occasion, he found that chance befriended him. For while his patron, eager and anxious-eyed, went roaming round the room in hot search for the object of his thoughts, Gilbert, no less anxious, no less determined, remained quietly near the entrance-door, and narrowly watched each passing face. He knew most of them. A London man ct half a dozen seasons can scarcely find a fresh face in any evening party on which he may chance to stumble. We go on in our different sets, speaking to every other person we meet, and familiar with the appearance of all the rest— what freshness and variety ! Some of the passers-by raised their eyebrows in surprise at seeing Lloyd in such a place ; others nodded and smiled, and would have stopped to speak but for the plain *noli-me-tangere* expression which he wore. He returned the nods and grins in a half-preoccupied, half-sullen manner, and it was not until he heard Miles Challoner's voice close by him that he seemed thoroughly roused. Then he drew back from the door-post, against which he had been leaning, and ensconcing himself behind the broad back of a stout old gentleman, his neighbour, saw Gertrude enter the room, on Miles Challoner's arm. They had been dancing ; she was flushed and animated, and looked splendidly handsome, as evidently thought her companion. Her face was upturned to his, and in her eyes was a frank honest look of love and trust, such a look as Gilbert Lloyd recollected to have seen there when he first knew her years ago, but which had soon died out, and had never reappeared until that moment. And it was for Miles Challoner that her spirits had returned, her love and beauty had been re-newed ; for Miles Challoner, whom he hated with a deadly hate, who had been his rock ahead throughout his life, and who was now robbing him of what indeed he had once thrown aside as valueless, but what he would now give worlds to repossess. Gilbert Lloyd's face, all the features of

which were so well trained and kept in such constant sub-
jection, for once betrayed him, and the evil passion gnawing
at his heart showed itself in his fiery eyes, surrounded by a
strained hot flush, and in his rigidly set mouth. Tommy
Toshington, tacking about the room to avoid the pressure of
the crowd, and coming suddenly round Lloyd's stout
neighbour, was horrified by the expression in Gilbert's
face.

"Why, what's the matter, Lloyd, my boy?" asked the
old gentleman ; "you look quite ghastly, by Jove ! Ellis's
claret not disagreed with you, has it ?"

"Not a bit of it, Tommy ; I'm all right," said Gilbert
with an effort ; "room's a little hot—perhaps that's made
me look a little white."

"Look a little white ! Dammy, you looked a little black
when I first caught sight of you. You were scowling away
at somebody ; I couldn't make out who."

"Not I," said Gilbert, with an attempt at a laugh ; "I
was only thinking of something."

"O, shouldn't do that," said Mr. Toshington ; "devilish
stupid thing thinking ; never comes to any good, and makes
a fellow look deuced old. Lots of people here to-night ;"
then looking round and sinking his voice, "and rather a
mixture, eh ? I can't think where some of the people come
from ; one never sees them anywhere else." And the old
gentleman, whose father had been a dissenting hatter at
Islington, propped his double gold-eyeglass on his nose,
and surveyed the company with a look of excessive *hauteur*.

"See !" he said presently, nudging Gilbert with his
elbow ; " you reck'lect what I told you, down at the Crystal
Palace that day, about Etchingham and Miss What-do-you-
call-'em, the singer !—that it wasn't any go for my lord,
because there was another fellow cutting in in that quarter
—you reck'lect ? Well, look here, here they are,—What's-
his-name, Chaldecott or something, and the girl."

"I see them," said Lloyd, drawing back.

"All right," said Toshington ; "you needn't hide yourself ; don't you be afraid, they're much too much taken up
with each other to be looking at us. Gad, she's a devilish
pretty girl, that, ain't she, Lloyd ? There's a sort of a something about her which—such a deuced good style too, and
way of carryin' herself ! Gad, as to most of the women now

—set of dumpy little brutes!—might be kitchen-maids, begad!"

"Just look, Toshington, will you? I can't see, for this old fool's shoulder's in the way. Has Challoner left Miss Lambert?"

"Yes, he's stepped aside to speak to Lady Carabas; Miss Lambert is standing by the mantelpiece, and——"

"All right, back in half-a-second!" and made straight for the place where Gertrude was standing.

"Now, that's a funny thing!" said old Toshington to himself, as he looked after him. "What does that mean? Is Lloyd making the running for his master, or is that a little commission on his own account? No go either way, I should say; the man in the beard means winning there, and no one else has a chance."

As Gilbert Lloyd crossed the room, Gertrude looked up, and their eyes met. The next instant she looked round for Miles Challoner, but he was still busily engaged in talking to Lady Carabas. Then she saw some other ladies of her acquaintance, seated within a little distance, and she determined on crossing the room to them. But she had scarcely moved a few steps when Gilbert Lloyd was by her side. Gertrude's heart beat rapidly; she scarcely heard the first words of salutation which Gilbert uttered; she looked quickly round and saw that, though Miles was still standing by Lady Carabas's chair, his eyes were fixed on her and Lloyd. What could she do? What is that her husband says?

"Too much of this fooling! You *must* hear me now?"

With an attempt at a smile, Gertrude turned to her persecutor and said, "Once for all, leave me!"

"I will not," said he, in a low voice, but also with a smile on his face. "You cannot get away from me without exciting the suspicion, or the wonder at least, of the room. How long do you imagine I am going to let this pretty little play proceed? How long am I to look on and see the puppets dallying?"

Gertrude flushed scarlet as he said these words, but she did not speak.

"You're carrying this business with too high a hand," said he, emboldened by her silence. "You seem to forget that I have a word or two to say in the matter."

"See, Gilbert Lloyd," said Gertrude, still smiling and playing with her fan, "you sought me; not I you. Go now, and——"

"Go!" said Gilbert, who saw Miles Challoner looking hard at them,—"go, that he may come! Go! You give your orders freely! What hold have you on me that I am to obey them?"

"Would you wish me to tell you?"

"Tell away!" said Lloyd, defiantly. "I don't mind."

"Here, then," said Gertrude, beckoning him a little closer with her fan, then whispering behind it. But one short sentence, a very few words, but, hearing them, Gilbert Lloyd turned death-white, and felt the room reel round before him. In an instant he recovered sufficiently to make a bow, and to leave the room and the house. When he got out into the street, the fresh air revived him; he leaned for a moment against some railings to collect his thoughts; and as he moved off, he said aloud, "He *did* suspect it, then; and he told her!"

———

CHAPTER VII.

HALF-REVEALED.

OF all the places on which the autumnal moon, approaching her full like a comely matron, looks down, there are many far less picturesque and less enjoyable than that bit of Robertson-terrace, St. Leonards, which adjoins the narrow strip of beach communicating with the old town of Hastings proper. On this beach the moonbeams play

> "Among the waste and lumber of the shore,
> Hard coils of cordage, swarthy fishing nets,
> Anchors of rusty fluke, and boats updrawn,"

casting grim and fantastic shadows, and bringing oddest objects into unwonted and undue prominence. Robertson-terrace—as hideous, architecturally considered, as are the majority of such marine asylums for the temporary reception of Londoners—stands back from the road, and has its stuccoed proportions somewhat softened by the trees and shrubs in the " Enclosure," as the denizens love to call it, a small oblong strip of something which ought to be green turf, but what, under the influence of promenading and croquet-playing, has become brown mud. In the moonlight on this lovely night in early autumn, some of the denizens yet linger in the Enclosure. Young people mostly, of both sexes, who walk in pairs, and speak in very low tones, and look at each other with very long immovable glances ; young people who cannot imagine why people ever grow old, who cannot conceive that there can be any pleasure except in that one pastime in which they themselves are then employed—who cannot conceive, for instance, what enjoyment that old gentleman, who has been so long seated in the drawing-room balcony of No. 17, can find in life.

That old gentleman is Lord Sandilands, who, the London season over, has come down to St. Leonards for a little sea-air, and quiet and change. One reason for his selection of St. Leonards is that Miss Grace Lambert and Mrs. Bloxam are staying within a few miles' distance, at Hardriggs, Sir Giles Belwether's pretty place. Lord Sandilands had been invited to Hardriggs, also, but he disliked staying anywhere except with very intimate friends ; and, moreover, he had come to that time of life when rest was absolutely essential to him, and he knew that under Sir Giles Belwether's ponderous hospitality he would simply be moving the *venue* of his London life without altering any of its details. Moreover, the old gentleman, by coming to St. Leonards, was carrying out a kindly scheme long since laid, of giving Miles Challoner occasional opportunities of seeing Miss Lambert.

Miles was not invited to stay at Hardriggs ; he did not even know Sir Giles Belwether ; but he became Lord Sandilands' guest in the lodgings in Robertson-terrace, and, as such, he was taken over by his friend to Hardriggs, introduced to the host, and recceived with the greatest hos-pitality. Lord Sandilands has this advantage over the youthful promenaders in the " Enclosure," that while they cannot imagine what he is thinking of, he perfectly well divines the subject of their thoughts, and is allowing his own ideas to run in another vein of that special subject. He has just made Miles confess his love for Grace Lambert, and all the drawbacks and disadvantages of the position are opening rapidly before him.

"I might have expected it," said the old gentleman half-aloud; "I knew it was coming. I saw it growing day by day, and yet I never had the pluck to look the affair straight in the face—to make up my mind whether I'd tell him anything about Gertrude's parentage; and I don't know what to do now. Ah, here he is !—Well, Miles, had your smoke ? Lovely night, eh ? "

"A lovely night, indeed ! No end of people out by the sea."

"You wouldn't mind a turn in that lime-walk at Hard-riggs just now, Miles eh ? with—Kate Belwether, or some one else ? "

"Rather the some one else, dear old friend. And so you weren't a bit astonished at what I told you to-day ? "

"Astonished, my boy ! I astonished ? Why, where do you think my eyes have been ? I declare you young fellows think that to you alone has been confided the appreciation of beauty and the art of love ! "

"Any one who imagines that must have ears, and hear not, so far as your lordship is concerned," said Miles, laughing. "Now, of John Borlase, commonly known as Baron Sandilands, the ladies whom he courted and the conquests which he made, are they not written in the *Chronique Scandaleuse* of the period ? "

"Well, I don't know that. I'm of an old-fashioned school, which holds that no gentleman should so carry on his *amourettes* that the world should talk about them. But the idea of your thinking that I should be astonished when you told me that you were head over ears in love with—with Miss Lambert ! *Nourri dans le sérail j'en connais les détours*, Master Miles."

"And if not astonished, you were also not annoyed ? "

"Annoyed ! Not the least bit in the world. I don't mean to say that the matter looks to me entirely one of plain-sailing, my dear boy ; there are certain difficulties which will naturally arise."

"Do you think that Grace's friends will make any obstacle ? By the way, my dear lord, do you know anything of Miss Lambert's relations ? I have never heard of or seen any connection but Mrs. Bloxam ; but you who are so intimate with the young lady will probably know all about them."

A half-comic look of embarrassment overshadowed Lord Sandilands' face as he heard this inquiry, and he waited for a moment before he replied, "Not I, indeed, my dear Miles ; Miss Lambert has never spoken to me of her relations— indeed, I understood from her that she was an orphan, left to Mrs. Bloxam's charge. I shouldn't think you need look for any objection to your marriage being made by the lady's friends."

" That is one point happily settled ; then the world ? "

" The what ? "

" The opinion of the world."

" Ah, that's a very different matter ! You're afraid of what people will say about your marrying a singer ? "

" To you, dear old friend, I will confess candidly that I am. Not that I have any position, God knows, on the strength of which to give myself airs."

" My dear boy, that's where you mistake. If you *had* a position, you might marry not merely a charming and amiable and lovely girl like this, against whom no word ought to be uttered, but even a person without the smallest rag of reputation ; and the world would say very little about it, and would speedily be silenced. Look at—no need, however, to quote examples. What I have said is the fact, and you know it."

" I am forced to acknowledge the truth of your remark, but while acknowledging it, I shall not permit the fact to turn me from my purpose. If Miss Lambert will accept me for a husband, I will gladly risk all the tattle of all the old cats in Belgravia."

" Your sentiments do you credit, my dear boy," said the old nobleman with a smile, " though the juxtaposition of 'tattle' and 'cats' is scarcely happy. I've noticed that when people are in love, the arrangement of their sentences is seldom harmonious. I suppose you feel tolerably certain of Miss Lambert's answer to your intended proposal. You are too much a man of the present day to anticipate any doubt in the matter."

" I should not be worth Miss Lambert's acceptance if I had any such vanity ; and I know you're only joking in ascribing it to me."

"I was only joking; but now seriously, do you fear no rivals?   You see how very much the young lady is sought after.   Are you certain that her preference is given to you?"

"As certain as a man can be who has not 'put it to the touch to win or lose it all,' by ascertaining positively."

"And there is no one you are absolutely jealous of?"

"No one.   Well,—no, not jealous of,—there is one man whom I regard with excessive distrust."

"You don't mean Lord Ticehurst?"

"O, no!   Lord Ticehurst's manners are rough and odd; but he is a gentleman, and, I'm sure, would 'behave as such,' in every possible way, to Miss Lambert.   Indeed, no duchess of his acquaintance can be treated with greater respect than she is by him.   I would not say as much of the other man."

"Who is he?"

Miles hesitated a moment before he said, "Lord Tice-hurst's great friend, Mr. Gilbert Lloyd."

"Mr. Gilbert Lloyd!" repeated Lord Sandilands, with a low whistle—"that's a very different matter.   I don't mind telling you, my dear Miles, that I have had an uncomfortable impression about that young man ever since the first night we met him at Carabas House.   It's singular too; for I know no real harm of the man.   His tastes and pursuits are not such as interest or occupy me; though, of course, that is the case with scores of persons with whom I am acquainted, and towards whom I feel no such dislike.   Very odd, isn't it?"

Miles looked hard at his friend to see whether there were any latent meaning in the question; but seeing that Lord Sandilands was apparently speaking without any strong motive, he said:

"It is odd.   Perhaps," he added, "it is to be accounted for by the feeling that this—Mr. Gilbert Lloyd is not a gentleman?"

"N—no, not that.   Though the man, amongst his own set, has an air of turfy, horsey life which is hideously repellent, yet with other people he shows that he knows at least the *convenances* of society, and is not without traces of breeding and education.   I fancy that in this case I am suffering myself to be influenced by my belief in physiognomy. The man has a decidedly bad face; deceit, treachery, and cruelty are written in the shifty expression of his sunken eyes, in his thin tightened lips."

"And you really believe this?" said Miles, earnestly.

"I do; most earnestly. Depend upon it, Nature never makes a mistake. We may fail to read her properly sometimes, but she never errs. And in this case her handwriting is too plain to admit of any doubt."

Miles shuddered. The old gentleman noticed it, and laid his hand kindly on his friend's knee; then he said:

"But, after all, there's no reason for us to fear him. You say that he has been somewhat marked in his attention to Grace?"

"More than marked. Did you not notice the other night at the house of that odd woman, Mrs. Burge—O, no, I forgot, you were not there; but it was just before we left town, and Miss Lambert had been dancing with me, and I had only left her for a minute when Lloyd went up and spoke to her."

"Well?"

"Of course I don't know what he said, but they both seemed to speak very earnestly, and after a very few moments he left her abruptly and hurried away."

"Well, I don't think that proceeding ought to cause you much disquietude, Master Miles. In all probability, from what you say, Miss Lambert was giving Mr. Lloyd his *congé*, or, at all events, saying something not very pleasant to him. Have you ever spoken to her about Lloyd?"

"Once or twice only."

"And what has she said about him?"

"She seems to have taken your view of the question, my dear old friend, for she spoke of him with cold contempt and irrepressible dislike, and begged me never to mention his name to her again."

"Really, then it seems to me that you have nothing to fear in that quarter. That this Mr. Lloyd is a dangerous man I am convinced; that he would be desperate in any matter in which he was deeply interested, I don't doubt; but he may be as desperate as he pleases if Grace dislikes him, and loves you. By the way, as that question is still a moot point, Master Miles," added the old gentleman with a sly look, "the sooner you get it settled the better. We shall be driving over to Hardriggs to-morrow, and I should think you *might* find an opportunity of speaking to the lady in private. I know I would at your time of life, and under the circumstances. And if you want an elderly gooseberry-picker, you may command me."

But seeing that Miles Challoner's face wore a stern and gloomy expression, Lord Sandilands dropped the tone of *badinage* in which he had been speaking, and said with great earnestness and softness :

"There is something strangely wrong with you to-night, Miles ; something which keeps crossing your mind and influencing your thoughts ; something which I am convinced is apart from, and yet somehow connected with, the subject we have been discussing. I have no wish to pry into your secrets, my dear boy ; no right and no desire to ask for any confidence which you may not feel disposed to give. But as, since the death of my dear old friend, I have always regarded myself as your second father, and as I have loved you as I would have loved a son, I cannot bear to see you in obvious grief and trouble without longing to share it, and to advise and help you."

There was a pathos in the old man's tone, no less than in his words, which touched Miles deeply. He took his friend's hand and pressed it, and his eyes were filled with tears, and his voice trembled as he said :

"God knows, my dearest friend, how willingly I acknowledge the truth of all that you have just said, and how recognisant I am of all your affection and kindness. I *am* troubled and disturbed, but there is nothing in my trouble that need be hid from you ; nothing, indeed, which your sympathy and counsel will not lighten and tend to disperse."

"That's right," said the old nobleman, brightening up again. "Come, what is this trouble ? You're not worried for money, Miles ?"

"No. I had an odd letter from my lawyers yesterday about some mortgage that Sir Thomas Walbrook is interested in, but I haven't gone into the matter yet. No, not money,—I wish it were only that !"

"What then ? You've not gone and mixed yourself up with any—any connection—you know what I mean—that you feel it necessary to break off before you propose to Miss Lambert ?"

"Not I, dear old friend; nothing of the sort. Though my trouble is caused by what I think the necessity of giving a full explanation on a very difficult and delicate matter, before I ask Grace to become my wife."

"In the name of fortune, what is it, then?" asked Lord Sandilands.

"Simply this," said Miles, his face resuming its grave expression; "you know that my father's life was overshadowed and his own mental peace destroyed, at a period when he might reasonably have looked forward to much future enjoyment, by the conduct of my younger brother, Geoffrey?"

"Ah! now I begin to comprehend——"

"Wait, and hear me out. That conduct, the nature of which I never could learn, and do not know at this moment, blighted my father's life, and changed him from an openhearted, frank, genial man, into a silent and reserved valetudinarian. For years and years Geoffrey's name was never mentioned in our house. I was brought up under strict orders never to inquire about him, directly or indirectly; and those orders I obeyed to the letter. Only when my father was on his deathbed—you recollect my being telegraphed for from your house, where I was staying? I spoke of Geoffrey. I asked why he had been sent away, what he had done——"

"Your father did not tell you?" interrupted Lord Sandilands, eagerly.

"He did not, he would not. It was just before he expired; his physical prostration was great; all he could say was that Geoffrey was, and for ever must be, dead to me. He implored me, he commanded me with his dying breath, if ever I met my brother to shun him, to fly from him, to let nothing earthly induce me to know him or acknowledge him."

"Your poor father was right," said Lord Sandilands; "he could have said nothing else."

"Do you justify my father's severity?" cried Miles in astonishment. "Do you hold that he was right in dying in anger with one of his own children, and in bequeathing his anger to me, the brother of the man whom in his wrath he thus harmed?"

"I do; I do indeed."

"Do you tell me that any crime not punishable by law

could justify such a sentence ?—a sentence of excommunication from his home, from family love, from——"

"Stay, stay, Miles. Tell me, how has this subject cropped up just now ? What has brought it into your thoughts ?"

" Because, as a man of honour, I feel that I ought to tell Miss Lambert something at least—as much as I know—of the story before I ask her to be my wife. Because I would fain have told her that my father was harsh and severe to a degree in his conduct to Geoffrey."

" That is impossible; that you can never say. Listen, Miles ; I know more of this matter than you suspect. I know every detail of it. Your father made me his confidant, and I know the crime which your brother attempted."

" You do ?—the crime !"

" The crime. The base, dastardly, hideous crime, which rendered it impossible for your father to do otherwise than renounce his son, and bid you renounce your brother for ever."

" Ah, my God !" groaned Miles, burying his head in his hands.

" There is no reason to be so excited, my poor boy," said Lord Sandilands, laying his hand gently on him. " You need tell Grace nothing of this ; and be sure that this wretched Geoffrey will never trouble you again. He is most probably dead."

" Dead !" shrieked Miles, raising his livid face and staring wildly at his friend. " He lives—here amongst us ! I have seen him constantly ; he has recognized me, I know. This man of whom we were just speaking,—this man whom you call Gilbert Lloyd,—is my younger brother, Geoffrey Challoner !"

CHAPTER VIII.

L'HOMME PROPOSE.

WHEN a man of Lord Ticehurst's character and disposition makes up his mind to achieve a certain result —in the turf slang of the day, "goes in for a big thing"—

he is not easily thwarted, or, at all events, he does not give
up his idea without having tried to carry it through. The
indiscreet, illiterate, but by no means bad-hearted, young
nobleman aforenamed had given himself up, heart and soul,
to a passion for the opera-singer known to him as Miss Grace
Lambert, and had gone through a psychological examination
of his feelings, so far as his brain-power permitted, with the
view of seeing how the matter lay, and what would be his best
means for securing his ends. The notion of succeeding dis-
honourably had never entered his head, or at least had not
remained there for a moment. In that knowledge of the
world which comes, no one knows how, to persons who are
ignorant of everything else—that *savoir faire* which is learned
unconsciously, and which can never be systematically
acquired—Lord Ticehurst was a proficient. He was not, as
times go, an immoral man, certainly not a wicked one ; but
he lived in a loose set, and it did not arise from conscientious scruples that he had not "tried it on" that Grace
Lambert should become his mistress. Such a result would
have given him considerable *éclat* amongst his friends, and
his religious notions were not sufficiently developed to make
him shrink from taking such a step. He did *not* take it
because he knew it would be useless ; because he knew that
any such offer would be ignominiously rejected ; that he
would be spurned from the door, and never permitted again
to be in the society of the girl whom he really loved. There
was only one way out of it—to offer her marriage. And
then the question came, Did he really love her sufficiently
for that, and was he prepared to stand the consequences ?

Did he really love her ? He thought he could put in
an answer to that, by Jove ! Did he really love her ? You
should ask old Gil about that ! Old Gil knew more of him
than any one else ; and he could tell you—not that he knew
what it was, what was the reason of it, don't you know ?—
that for the whole of last season he had been an altered man.
He knew that himself—he confessed it ; he felt that he had
not taken any proper interest in the stable, and that kind
of thing ; indeed, if he had not had old Gil to look after it,
the whole thing would have gone to the deuce. He knew
that well enough, but he could not help it. He had been
regular spoons on this girl, and he was, and he should be to
the end of the chapter, amen. That was all he had got to

say about it.   His life had been quite a different thing since he had known her.   He had left off swearing, and all that cussed low language that he used to delight in once upon a time ; and he'd got up early, because he thought there was a chance of meeting her walking in the Park (he had met her once, and solemnly walked between her and Mrs. Bloxam for an hour without saying a word) ; and he had cut the *ballet* and its professors, with whom formerly he had very liberal relations.   The *coryphées* and the little *rats* whom he had been in the habit of calling by their Christian names, who knew him by the endearing abbreviation of "Ticey," and to whom formerly he was delighted to stand and talk by the hour, received the coldest of bows from their quondam friend, as he stood amongst the wings of the opera-scenery on the chance of a word of salutation from the *prima donna* as she hurried from her dressing-room on to the stage.   But that word and the glance at her were enough.   "It's no good," he used to say ; " it won't do after that.   If I go away to supper at old Chalkstone's, and find Bella Marshall and Kate Herbert and half a dozen of the T. R. D. L. *ballet* there, 'pon my soul it don't amuse me when they put the lobster-claws at the end of their noses ; and I think Bagwax and Clownington and old Spiff—well, damme, they're old enough to know better, and they might think about—well, I don't want to preach about what we're all coming to, and what must be precious near for them."

A man of this kind thus hit suffers very severely.   The novelty of the passion adds considerably to his pangs.   The fact that he cannot speak out his hopes and wishes irritates and worries him.   To throw the handkerchief is easy enough at the first start—becomes easier through frequent practice ; but to win the prize is a very different matter. With a lady of his own rank it would have been much easier wooing ; but with Grace, Lord Ticehurst felt himself placed at a double disadvantage.   He had to assuage the rage of his friends at the honour he was doing her, and he had to prove to her that he was doing her no honour at all.   The former, though a difficult, was the easier task. Lord Ticehurst knew his aunt, Lady Carabas, quite well enough to be aware that, though she was the first *grande dame* who had introduced Miss Lambert into society, and that though up to that minute she had been the young lady's most steadfast friend, she would be the very first to rail against the *mésalliance*, and do all she could to cry down that reputation which she had so earnestly vaunted. Others would follow suit at once, and he and his wife would have to run the gauntlet. His wife! Ah, that was just the point; he would not care a rap if she were his wife, if he had her brains and her beauty to help in winning the game for him. But Lord Ticehurst's knowledge of the world was too great to permit him to flatter himself thus far; he knew that he had never received any substantial acknowledgment from Miss Lambert; and he recollected, with a very unpleasant twinge, what Gilbert Lloyd had said about Miles Challoner's attentions in that quarter— attentions received almost as favourably as they were earnestly proffered, as Lord Ticehurst had had an opportunity of witnessing at Mrs. Stapleton Burge's reception.

Young noblemen of large fortunes are not in the habit of fighting with their inclinations and wishes. Lord Ticehurst felt that he must do his best to make this girl marry him—whether she would or not, he felt was doubtful, and acknowledged the feeling to himself with an honest frankness which was one of his best characteristics. He bore away with him his dull, wearying heartache, his "restless, unsatisfied longing," to Goodwood, where it cankered the ducal hospitality, and made him think but little of the racing-prizes which he carried off. He bore it away with him to the hotel at Eastbourne, where, pending the Doncaster week, he and his friends had set up their Lares and Penates, and were doing their best to gain health and strength from the sea-breezes and quiet, and make up for the ravages of the London season.

Except in the desultory manner already narrated, Lord Ticehurst had not revealed to his confederate the state of his feelings towards Miss Lambert. He had said nothing positive to him regarding what was now his fixed intention, of proposing for that young lady's hand, and it is probable he would have been consistently reticent had not chance brought the confession about in this way.

It was a splendid August morning, and the two gentlemen were seated in the largest sitting-room of the pretty hotel, with its bay window overlooking the pleasant promenading crowd of sea-side loungers, bathable children, bathed young ladies with their limp hair hanging down their backs, old gentlemen walking up and down with mouths and nostrils wide open to inhale as much ozone as possible during their stay, and the other usual common objects of the sea-shore. Breakfast was just over, and cigars had already been lighted. The blue vapour came curling round the sides of the sporting-print in which Gilbert Lloyd's head and shoulders were enveloped, and mixed with another blue vapour which stole over the more massive folds of the *Times*, with which Lord Ticehurst was engaged.

A shout of "Hallo!" betraying intense astonishment, roused Gilbert from his perusal of the vaticinations of "Calchas." "What makes you hallo out like that? What is it?" he asked.

"What is it! O, nothing particular," replied Lord Ticehurst; adding immediately, "By Jove, though!"

"No, but I say, Etchingham, something must have roused you to make you give tongue. What was it, old boy? No more scratchings for the Leger?"

"No, something quite different to that. Well, look here, if you must know;" and his lordship lazily handed the paper to his friend, and pointed to a particular paragraph.

"Advertisement!" said Lloyd as he took it. "Now what the deuce can you find to interest you among the advertisements?" But the expression of his face changed as he saw, in large letters, the name of Miss Grace Lambert; and on further perusal he found that Mr. Boulderson Munns, whose noble style he immediately recognised, informed the British public that he had made arrangements with this distinguished *prima donna* for a tour during the winter months, in the course of which she would visit the principal cities in England, Ireland, and Scotland, accompanied by a *troupe* of distinguished talent, superintended by Mr. Munns himself, who would lend all the resources of the justly-celebrated band and *répertoire* of the Grand Scandinavian Opera-house to the success of the design.

Gilbert Lloyd, who had felt his colour ebb when he first saw his wife's name, read through the advertisement carefully, but said nothing as he laid the paper down.

"Have you read it?" asked Lord Ticehurst.

"I have."

"And what do you think of it?"

"Think of it! What should I think of it, except that it will probably be a profitable speculation for—for Miss Lambert, and certainly a profitable one for Munns?"

"Well but, I say, look here! It mustn't come off."

"What mustn't?"

"Why, this what's-its-name—tour!"

"Then it will be a bad thing for Munns. But, seriously, Etchingham, what on earth do you mean? What are you talking about?"

"Well, I mean that—that young lady, Miss Lambert, mustn't go flitting about the country."

"Why not? What have you to do with it?"

"Why, haven't I told you—don't you recollect before Ascot and all that?—only you're so deuced dull, and think of nothing but—well, never mind. Don't you recollect my saying I intended to ask Miss Lambert to be my wife?" And Lord Ticehurst, whom the avowal and the unusual flux of words rendered a bright peony colour, glared at his Mentor in nervous trepidation.

Gilbert looked at him very calmly. The corners of his mouth twitched for an instant as he began to speak, but he was otherwise perfectly composed as he said, "I had forgotten; you must forgive me; the stable takes up so much of my time that I have scarcely leisure to look after your other amusements. O, you intend to propose for this young lady! Do you think she will accept you?"

"That's a devilish nice question to ask a fellow, that is. 'Pon my soul, I don't think there's another fellow in the world that would have had the—well, the kindness—to ask that. I suppose it will be all right; if I didn't, I shouldn't——"

"Shouldn't ask, eh? Well, I suppose not, and it was indiscreet in me to suggest anything different. What do you propose to do now?"

"Well, what do you think? Perhaps I'd better go up to town—deuced odd town will look at this time of year, won't it?—and see Miss Lambert, and make it all straight with her; and then go off and see old Munns, and tell him he'll have to give up his notion of the what's-its-name—the tour. He'll want to be squared, of course, and we must do it for him; but I shall leave you to arrange that with him."

"Of course; that will not be a difficult matter." Gilbert Lloyd waited a minute before he added, "But there is no necessity for you to go to London on this portentous matter. Miss Lambert is much nearer to you than you imagine."

"Much nearer! What the deuce do you mean?" asked Lord Ticehurst, looking round as if he expected to see Gertrude entering the room.

"Exactly what I say. I had a letter this morning from Hanbury; he's staying at Hardriggs, old Sir Giles Belwether's place, not a dozen miles from here; and he mentioned that Miss Lambert was a guest there too. Wait a minute; I'll read you what he says. No, never mind, it's only some nonsense about Lady Belwether's insisting on old Bel having a Dean to stay in the house at the same time to counteract the effect of the stage, and——"

"D—d impertinence!" muttered Lord Ticehurst. I always did hate that Hanbury—sneering beast! O, about twelve miles from here, eh? Might drive over to luncheon? What do you say, Gil? Do us good, eh?"

"Do *you* good, very likely, Etchingham! At all events, if you have made up your mind to this course, it's the best and the most honourable way to bring it to an issue at once. And I'm not sure that this is not an excellent opportunity. You will find the lady unfettered by business, free from the lot of fribbles who are always butterflying about her in town, and have only to make your running. I can't go; I've got letters to write, and things to do, and must stop here."

Within half an hour Lord Ticehurst's phaeton came spinning round to the door of the hotel, and Gilbert, tepping out on to the balcony, saw him—got up to the ghest pitch of sporting *négligé*—drive off amid the unsuppressed admiration of the bystanders. Then Lloyd walked back into the room and flung himself on a sofa, and lit a fresh cigar, and as he puffed at it soliloquised, "What was that I saw on a seal the other day? *Quo Fata ducunt.* What a wonderful thing that they should have led to this; that they should have led me to being the most intimate friend of a man who is now gone off to propose to my wife!

My wife! I wonder when I shall make up my mind as to
what my real feelings are towards her. After years of
indifference, of absolute forgetfulness, I see her, and fall
madly in love with her again—so madly that I pursue her,
plainly seeing it is against her will, and, like an idiot,
give her the chance of saying that to me which makes me
hate her worse than ever—worse even than when we parted,
and I *did* hate her then. But I've a feeling now which I
had not during all that long interval of our separation.
Then I did not care where she was or what she did. Now,
by the Lord, if I were to think that she cared for any man
—or not that, I know she does, curse him! I know she does
care for that man—I mean, if she were to give any man the
position that was mine—that was?—that *is*, when I choose
to claim it—he and I would have to settle accounts. That
poor fool has no chance. Gertrude has no ambition—that's
a fault I always found in her; if she had had, we might
have risen together; but she was nothing when she was not
sentimentally spoony; and she would throw over my lord,
who really loves her in a way that I never thought him
capable of, the title, money, and position, for the *beaux yeux*
and the soft speeches of my sweet brother. What will be
the end of that, I wonder? By heavens, if I saw *that*
culminating—if I thought that she was going to claim the
freedom we agreed upon for the sake of bestowing herself on
him, I'd stand the whole racket, run the whole risk, declare
myself and my position openly, and let her do her worst!"
He rose from the sofa and walked to the window, where he
stood looking out for a few moments, then returned to his
old position. "The worst, eh? How I hate that cursed
sea, and the glare of the sun on the cliffs! It always
reminds me of that infernal time. Do her worst! She's
the most determined woman I ever saw. I shall never
forget the look of her face that night, nor the tone of her
voice as she whispered behind her fan. Well, sufficient for
the day, &c. That's to be met when it comes. It hasn't
come yet. I may be perfectly certain what reply will be
given to my dear young friend Etchingham, who has just
started on his precious fool's-errand; and as for the other
man—well, he's not staying at Hardriggs, or Hanbury
would have mentioned him. There will be this country
tour to fill up the winter; and by the time next season

arrives, he may be off it, or she may be off it, or a thousand things may have happened, which are now not worth speculating about, but which will serve my turn as they come." And Gilbert Lloyd turned to his writing-desk, and plunged into calculations and accounts with perfectly clear brains, in the working of which the thoughts of the previous half-hour had not the smallest share.

Meanwhile, Lord Ticehurst sat upright in his mail-phaeton, driving the pair of roans which were the cynosure of the Park during the season, and the envy of all horsey men always, through some of the loveliest scenery in Sussex. Not that scenery, except Grieve's or Beverley's, made much impression on his lordship. Constant variety of hill and dale merely brought out the special qualities and paces of the roans ; wooded uplands suggested good cover-shooting ; broad expanse of heath looked very like rabbits. To such a thorough sportsman thoughts like these occurred involuntarily, but he had plenty beside to fix what he called his mind. Though he had made as light as possible to his hench-man of the expedition on which he was engaged, and given himself the airs of a conquering hero, he was by no means so well satisfied of his chances of success, or of his chances of happiness, were success finally achieved. His chances of success occupied him first. Well, he did not know—you could never tell about women, at least he couldn't, whether they meant it or whether they didn't. He didn't know ; she was always very friendly, and that kind of thing ; but with women that went for nothing. They'd draw you on, until you thought nothing could be more straight ; and then throw you over and leave you nowhere. N-no ; he couldn't recollect anything particular that Miss Lambert had ever said to induce him to hope : she'd admired the roans as the groom moved them up and down in front of her windows ; and she'd said more than once that she was glad some song of hers had pleased him, and that was all. Not much, indeed ; but then he was an earl ; and the grand undying spirit of British flunkeydom had led him to believe, as indeed it leads every person of his degree to believe, that " all thoughts, all passions, all delights, whatever stirs this mortal frame," are at the command of any one named in *Debrett*, or eulogised by Sir Bernard Burke : " Ticehurst, Earl of, Viscount Etchingham, b. 1831, succeeded his father the 3rd Earl in," &c. &c. What was the use of that, if people were not to bow down in the dust before him, and he were not to have everything he wished? Heaps of fellows had been floating round her all the season, but no such large fish as he had risen at the bait; and though she had not particularly distinguished him, still he had only to go in and win the prize. What was it that Gilbert Lloyd had let drop about some rival in the field? O, that man Challoner! Yes, he had himself noticed that there had been a good deal of attention paid in that quarter, and by no means unwillingly received. Queer customer that old Gil! sees everything, by Jove! fancy his spotting that! Good-looking chap, Challoner, and quite enough to say for himself; but, Lord, when it came to the choice between him and the Earl of Ticehurst!

Lord Ticehurst smiled quite pleasantly to himself as this alternative rose in his mind, and flicked his whip in the air over the heads of the roans, causing that spirited pair to plunge in a manner which made the groom (a middle-aged, sober man, with a regard for his neck, and a horror of his master's wild driving) look over the head of the phaeton in fear and trembling. As the horses quieted down and settled into their paces, Lord Ticehurst's spirits sunk simultaneously. Suppose it were all right with the lady, what about the rest of the people? Not his following—not Bardolph, Nym, and Pistol, and the rest of the crew. Lord Ticehurst might not be a clever man, but he had sufficiently "reckoned up" his *clientèel*, and he knew, whatever they might think, none of their tongues would wag. But the outsiders—the "society" people—what would they say to his bringing a lady from the boards of the opera to sit at the head of his table at home, and demand all the respect due to her rank abroad? They wouldn't like it; he knew that fast enough. O yes, of course they'd say that he was not the first who'd done it, and it had always been a great success hitherto and so on; but still he had to look to his own position and hers, and—by Jove, Lady Carabas! she'd make it pleasant for them, and no mistake! Her ladyship liked her *protégée*, liked to flaunt her in the eyes of rival lion-hunters, gloried in the success she achieved, and the excitement she created; but her nephew knew well enough what her feelings would be if she had to acknowledge the brilliant *prima donna* of the opera-house as a relation; if she had to endure the congratulations of her female friends on the distinguished addition to the family circle which her kindness and tact had brought about.

What the deuce did it matter to him! The roans were then pulling well and steadily together, and the phaeton bowled merrily along the level turnpike-road. What the deuce did it matter to him! Was not he the Earl of Ticehurst, and was he not to be his own master? and was not he old enough, and rich enough, and big swell enough to do what he pleased, and to take a sight at the world's odd looks, and pooh-pooh the world's odd remarks? He was, and he intended to prove it; and after all, he would like to see one of them to compare with his pretty Grace. Why, who had they made a fuss about last season? Alice Farquhar, an insipid-looking, boiled-veal kind of girl, with her pale freckled face and her red hair; and Constance Brand, with her big black eyebrows, and her flashing eyes, and her hook nose—talk about tragedy queens, well, there was Constance Brand cut out for that to a T! Everybody said what a charming thing it was when Alice Farquhar married old Haremarch, and how ever since he had been clothed and in his right mind; and as for Constance Brand—well, every one knew she had saved the family credit by marrying young Klootz, who now called himself Cloote, and who only suffered himself to be reminded by his income that he was lineally descended from old Jacob Klootz, the banker and money-lender of Frankfurt-am-Main. Neither of these girls was to be compared to Miss Lambert, and he was determined that—Lord Ticehurst's spirits sunk again just at this juncture, as the gates of the Hardriggs avenue came within sight.

The Belwethers were very pleasant old-fashioned people, who lived the same life year after year without ever getting tired of it. They were at Hardriggs, their very pleasant ancestral seat, from August until the end of March, and at their very pleasant town-house in Brook Street from April till the end of July. When in the country, old Sir Giles shot, fished, and attended the Quarter-sessions, the Conservative demonstrations, and the Volunteer reviews of his county. When in town, he slept a good deal at the Carlton, and rode a clever cob about the Park between twelve and two, distinguished for the bottle-green cutaway coat with velvet collar, and the high muslin checked cravat of sixty years ago. Lady Belwether's character was well summed up in the phrase "kind old goose," which a particular friend applied to her. A madness for music was the only marked feature of her disposition; at home she visited all the old women, and helped the curate, and gave largely to the Flannel Club, and looked after the schools and worried the doctor, and played the harmonium in the village church on Sunday; and in town, what with the opera three nights a, week, and the Monday Popular Concerts, and the *matinées* and *soirées musicales* of distinguished creatures, with a dash of Exeter Hall oratorio, and a *soupçon* of Philharmonic, the old lady's life was one whirl of delight. Lady Belwether had fallen in love with Gertrude at first sight. She was by no means a gushing old lady, nor, though so devoted to music, had she ever made the acquaintance of any professional. Hitherto she had always stood on her dignity when such a proposition had been made to her. She had no doubt, she used to say, that the artists in question were pleasant people in their way, but that was not her way. However, the first glance at Miss Lambert made the old lady wild to know her : there never was such a sweet face —so interesting, so classical—yes, the old lady might say, so holy; "and her voice, my dear, it gives me the notion of an angel singing." So, worthy old Lady Belwether having ascertained that Miss Lambert was perfectly "correct" and ladylike, procured an introduction to her, and commenced heaping upon her a series of kindnesses which culminated in the invitation to Hardriggs. This invitation was accepted principally by the advice of Lord Sandilands, who had known the Belwethers all his life, and who felt that Gertrude could not enjoy the quiet and fresh air requisite after her London season with more thoroughly respectable people.

It was after the invitation had been given and accepted that Lady Belwether began to feel a little nervous and uncomfortable about what she had done. For in the pride of her heart and the warmth of her admiration for Gertrude, she told everybody that dear Miss Lambert was coming to them at Hardriggs in the autumn. Among others she mentioned the fact to Miss Belwether, Sir Giles's sister, a dreadful old woman, who lived in a boarding-house at Brighton, in order to be in the closest proximity to her "pastor," the Reverend Mr. Tophet, and who uttered a yelp of horror at the announcement. "I have said nothing, Maria," said this horrible old person, "to your gaddings-about and the frivolous style of your existence, but I must lift up my voice when you tell me you are about to receive a stage-player as your guest." "Stage-player" is an awkward word to be thrown at the head of a leader of county society, and it hit home, and rather staggered dear old Lady Belwether; not that the gallant old lady for an instant entertained the notion of giving up her intended guest, or suffered herself to appear the least abashed in the eyes of her antagonist. "It's a mere matter of taste, my dear Martha," she replied; "for my own part, I would sooner associate with a lady who, though a singer, is undoubtedly a lady, than with a man who calls himself a minister, who was a shoemaker, and who always must be a vulgar boor." Having fired which raking shot at the Reverend Tophet, the old lady sailed away and closed the conversation.

But she felt that it would be a great advantage if she could have some one staying in the house at the same time with Miss Lambert, whose presence would prove an effectual check on the ridiculous gossip likely to be prevalent in the county. The lay element would be excellently represented in the respectably dull and decorous people who were coming; but there was wanting an infusion of the clerical element, which could best be met by inviting Sir Giles's old friend the Dean of Burwash. Henry Asprey, Dean of Burwash, had been known as "Felix" Asprey at school and college, from his uninterrupted run of luck. The son of a poor solicitor, a good-looking idle lad, of capital manners and address, but with very little real talent, he had won an exhibition from his school, a scholarship, a fellowship, and a double-second at the University, no one knew how. He had taken orders, and travelled as tutor to the then Premier's son through Egypt and the Holy Land; on his return had published a little book of very weak poems, under the title *Palm-leaves and Dates*, which, with his usual luck, happened to hit the very bad taste of the day and went through several editions. His friend the Premier gave him a good living, and he had scarcely been inducted into it when he won the heart of a very rich widow, whom he married, and whom with his usual luck, within the course of four years he buried, inheriting her fortune of three thousand a-year. It was to console him in his deep affliction that his friend the Premier, just then quitting office for the third and last time, bestowed upon him the Deanery of Burwash. He was now some fifty years old, tall, thin, and eminently aristocratic-looking ; had a long transparent hand, which was generally clasping his chin, and a soft persuasive voice. He liked music and poetry, and good dinners ; was found at private views of picture-exhibitions ; belonged to the Athenæum Club ; and liked to be seen there conversing with professional literary men. People said he would be a Bishop some day, and he thought so himself—he did not see why not ; he would have looked well in his robes, spoken well in the House of Lords, and never committed himself by the utterance of any extreme opinion. That was a thing he had avoided all his life, and to it much of the secret of his success might be ascribed. His sermons were eloquent—his friends said "sound," his enemies "empty" ; he deplored the division in the Church with sympathetic face and elegant gesture ; but he never gave adhesion to either side, and showed more skill in parrying home-questions than in any other action of his life.

Such was Dean Asprey, to whom Lady Belwether wrote an invitation to Hardriggs, telling him frankly that Miss Grace Lambert would be one of the guests, and asking if he had any objection to meet her. The Dean's reply, written in the neatest hand on the thickest cream-laid note-paper, arrived by return of post. He accepted the invitation as heartily as it was given ("Genial creature !" said dear old Lady Belwether) ; he fully appreciated dear Lady Belwether's frankness about her guest, for he was aware—how could he fail to be ?—of the censoriousness of the world towards persons of his calling. He had, however, made it his rule through life, and he intended to pursue the same course until the end, to shape his conduct according to the dictates of that still small voice of his conscience rather than at the bidding of the world. ("The dear !" said Lady Belwether.) He should therefore have the greatest pleasure in making the acquaintance of Miss Grace Lambert, of whom he had already heard the most favourable accounts, not merely as regarded her great genius, but her exemplary conduct. And he was, with kindest regards to Giles, his dear Lady Bel-wether's most sincere friend, Henry Asprey. "A Christian gentleman," said the old lady, with tears of delight standing in her eyes as she finished the letter; "and Martha to talk of her stage-players and Tophets indeed, when a man like that does not mind!"

The Belwethers were rather astonished when, just after the party had sat down to luncheon, they heard Lord Tice-hurst announced. For though there was a certain similarity of sporting tastes between him and Sir Giles, the disparity of age caused them to move in widely different sets; while Lady Belwether knew his lordship as the nephew and one of the principal attendants on, and abettors of, Lady Carabas, whom the old lady held in great aversion. "One of the new style of ladies, my dear," she used to say, with a sniff of disdain; "finds women's society too dull for her, must live amongst men, talks slang, and I dare say smokes, if one only knew." However, they both received the young noble-man with considerable *empressement;* and Lord Ticehurst, on taking his seat at the luncheon-table, found that he knew most of the assembled party. The Dean was almost the only one with whom he had not a previous acquaintance; and Lord Ticehurst had scarcely whispered to Lady Belwether a request to know who was the clerical party on his left, when the Dean turned round and introduced himself as an old friend of the late Lord Ticehurst's. "I used to meet your father at Lady Walsingham's receptions when Lord Walsingham was Premier, and he allowed me to call him my very good friend. We had certain tastes in common which bound us together—geology and mineralogy, for in-stance. You are not a geologist, I believe, my lord?"

"Well, no," said Lord Ticehurst, frankly; "that ain't my line."

"N-no," said the Dean. "Well, we all have our different tastes—*tot homines, quot sententiæ.* Your father was a man who was passionately fond of science; indeed, I often used to wonder how a man absorbed as he was in what generally proves to others the all-engrossing study of politics could find time for the discussion of scientific propositions, and for the attendance at the lectures of the Royal Institution.

But your father was a man of no ordinary calibre; he
was——"

"O yes, he was a great gun at science and electricity, and
all that kind of thing; at least so I've been told. Excuse
me for half a minute; I want to get some of that ham I see
on the sideboard." And Lord Ticehurst rose from the seat,
to which he did not return after he had helped himself,
preferring a vacant place at the other end of the table, by
the side of Sir Giles Belwether, whose conversation about
hunting and racing proved far more entertaining to his
lordship. Moreover, from his new position he could keep a
better view of Miss Lambert, who did not, he was pleased
to observe, seem particularly gratified or amused at the
rapid fire of conversation kept up by the young men on
either side of her.

When luncheon was over, and the party rose and dispersed, Lord Ticehurst was seized upon by Sir Giles, who
took him to the stables, expatiating lengthily and wearily
on the merits of his cattle; and it was not until late in the
afternoon that the visitor could make his escape from his
host. He thought that he would have had his journey for
nothing, seeing no chance of getting a private interview
with Miss Lambert, when on his return to the house to see
if he could find Lady Belwether, to whom he intended
making his adieux, he heard the sound of a piano, and
recognized the prelude of a favourite ballad of Gertrude's.
Before the song could begin, Lord Ticehurst had entered
the room, and found Miss Lambert, as he expected, alone at
the piano. Gertrude looked round at the opening of the
door, and when she saw who it was, half rose from her seat.

"Pray don't move, Miss Lambert," said Lord Ticehurst,
approaching her; "pray don't let me disturb you."

"You don't disturb me in the least, Lord Ticehurst," said
Gertrude, sitting down again. "I was merely amusing
myself. I had not even the business excuse of being 'at
practice.'"

"Don't let me interfere, then. Amuse yourself and me
at the same time. Do now, it will be a charity; 'pon my
word it will."

"No, no, no; I'm not so cruel as that. I know the
terrible infliction music is to you in London. I've watched
too often the martyr-like manner in which you've suffered

under long classical pieces, and the self-denying way in which you have applauded at the end of them, without deliberately exposing you to more torture in the country."

"Assure you you're wrong, Miss Lambert; but I'm too happy to think you've done me the honour to watch me at all, to go into the question. No, please don't go. If you won't sing to me, may I speak to you?"

Gertrude, who had again half-risen, turned round to him with a look of wonder in her eyes. "May you speak to me, Lord Ticehurst? Why, of course!"

The answer was so manifestly simple and genuine, that it quite took Lord Ticehurst aback, and there was a moment's pause before he said, "Thanks, yes—you're very good. I wanted to speak to you—wanted to say something rather particular to you, in point of fact."

The hesitation in his manner, an odd conscious look in his face, had revealed the object of his visit. Gertrude knew what he was about to say, but she remained perfectly calm and unembarrassed, merely saying,

"Pray speak, Lord Ticehurst; I am quite at your service."

"Thanks very much—kind of you to say so, I'm sure. Fact of the matter is, Miss Lambert, ever since I've had the pleasure of knowing you I've been completely stumped, don't you know?—bowled over, and that kind of thing. I suppose you've noticed it; fellows at the club chaff most awfully, you know, and I can't stand it any longer; and, in short, I've come to ask you if—if you'll marry me, and that kind of thing."

"You do me great honour, Lord Ticehurst," commenced Gertrude; "very great honour——"

"O," interrupted his lordship, "don't you think about that; that's what they said at White's, but I said that was all d——d stuff—I beg your pardon, Miss Lambert; all nonsense I mean—about honour, and all that. Why," he went on to say, having worked himself up into a state of excitement, "of course I know I'm an earl, and that kind of thing. I can't help knowing about my—my station in life, and you'd think me a great ass if I pretended I didn't; but when you're my wife, you'll be—I mean to say you'll grace it and adorn it—and—and there's not one in the whole list fit to be named along with you, or to hold a candle to you."

" I cannot thank you sufficiently for this expression of kind feeling towards me, Lord Ticehurst," said Gertrude. " No, hear me for one minute ; " as he endeavoured again to interrupt her. " Ever since you have known me you have treated me with the utmost courtesy and kindness, and you have now done me the greatest possible honour. You may judge, then, how painful it is to me"—Lord Ticehurst's jaw and hat here dropped simultaneously— " how painful it is to me to be compelled to decline that honour."

" To—to decline it ? "

" To decline it."

" To say no ! "

" To say no."

" Then you refuse me ! Case of chalks, by Jove ! Miss Lambert, I—I'm sorry I've troubled you," said Lord Ticehurst, picking up his hat and making for the door. " I hope you won't think anything of it, I—good-morning !— Damme if I know whether I'm on my head or on my heels," he added when he got outside, and was alone.

Lord Ticehurst was so completely *bouleversé* that he scarcely knew how he got to his phaeton, or how he tooled the roans, who were additionally frisky after the Belwether oats, down the avenue. He knew nothing until he got to the gate, on the other side of which was an open fly. He looked vacantly at its occupants, but started as he recognized Lord Sandilands and Miles Challoner.

" O, that's it, is it ? " said his lordship to himself. " Damme, old Gil was right again ! "

<hr>

CHAPTER IX.

DIEU DISPOSE.

THE effect of Miles Challoner's startling communication upon Lord Sandilands was very great ; but the long-cultivated habit of self-command enabled him to conceal its extent and somewhat of its nature from his younger friend. It was fortunate that Miles was just then so much engrossed with his love, so full of the hope of the success of his suit, so relieved and encouraged by discovering that Lord Sandilands did not attempt to dissuade him from a project in which he had felt very doubtful whether he should have the support of a man of the world—and though nothing would have induced him to abandon that project, Lord Sandilands' acquiescence made a wonderful difference to him in the present, and would, he felt, be of weighty importance in the future,—that he was not keenly observant of the old nobleman. As soon as it was possible, Lord Sandilands got rid of Miles, but not until he had received from the young man a grateful acknowledgment of his kindness, and until they had finally agreed on the expedition to Hardriggs for the following day.

When he was quite alone, the familiar friend of Miles Challoner's father gave way to the feelings with which this revelation had filled him. This, then, was the explanation of the instinctive aversion he had felt towards Gilbert Lloyd —fate had brought him in contact with the man whose story he alone of living men knew, and under circumstances which might have terrible import. The one hope of his dead friend—that the brothers might never meet—had been defeated ; the fear which had troubled him in his later days had been fulfilled. If Miles Challoner's impression concerning this man should be correct—if indeed he was or intended to become a suitor to Gertrude, a fresh complication of an extremely dangerous nature—knowing what he knew, he could well appreciate that danger might arise. The skeleton was wearing flesh again, and stalking very close by the old man now. Hitherto only the strong sympathy which had united him with Miles Challoner and his father —his friendship for the latter had been one of the strongest and deepest feelings of a life which had, on the whole, been superficial—made the fate of the outcast son and brother a subject of any interest to Lord Sandilands. He might have turned up at any time, and this unfortunate meeting and recognition between the brothers have taken place, and beyond the unpleasantness of the occurrence, and the necessity he should have recognized for impressing upon Miles as stringently as possible the importance of observing his father's prohibition, he would not have felt himself personally concerned. But Gertrude ! the girl whom he had come to love with such true fatherly feeling and solicitude—the girl who had brought into his superficial life such mingled feelings of pain and pleasure—what if she were about to be involved in this family mystery and misery ? Very seldom in the course of his existence had Lord Sandilands experienced such acute pain, such a sensation of helpless terror, as this supposition inspired. Supposing that Miles Challoner was right in the dread which Gilbert Lloyd's manner with regard to Gertrude had awakened in him,—and the eyes of a lover not sure of his own position, and anxiously on the look-out for possible rivals, were likely to be more acute and more accurate than those of an old gentleman much out of practice in the subtleties of the tender passion, and without the spur to his perceptions of suspicion,—supposing he was really in love with Gertrude, and that by any horrible chance Gertrude should prefer him to Miles ! Very unpleasant physical symptoms of disturbance manifested themselves after Lord Sandilands had fully taken this terrible hypothesis into consideration, and for a time the old gentleman felt that whether it was gout or apoplexy which was about to claim him for its own was a mere question of detail. He had lived so long without requiring to test the strength of his nerves, without having any very strong or urgent demand made upon him for the exercise of his feelings, that anything of the kind now decidedly disagreed with him, and he went to bed in a rueful state of mind, and a shaky condition of body. The night brought him calmness and counsel, and the symptoms of illness passed off sufficiently for him to resolve on keeping the engagement he had made with Miles for the following day. " The sooner his mind is at ease, the sooner will mine be, on his account and my own." Thus ran Lord Sandilands' thoughts as he lay awake, listening against his will to the splash of the sea, and inclined to blame its monotonous murmur for the nervousness which had him in its grip. " I suppose it's not the right thing for me to help Miles to marry Gertrude—my old friend would not have liked the notion of his son and heir's marrying my natural daughter ; but what can I do ? The young fellow is not like other men of his age and position ; in fact, he isn't, strictly speaking, I suppose, a 'young' fellow at all.   If he were, and resembled the young men of the day a little more, I fancy he never would have thought of marrying her.   And then there's an awful blot upon the Challoners, too—and she is such a charming girl, no tongue has ever dared to wag against her. Suppose I did not encourage it, that I set myself against it, what could I do?   I have literally no right in Miles's case, and none that I can acknowledge in Gertrude's, and I should only make them both dislike me, without preventing the marriage in the least.   I wish—because of what poor old Mark would have thought—that they had never met; but I can't go beyond that—no, I can't.   But if she cares for that wretch, good heavens! what shall I do?"   The old man put his shrunken hands up to his bald temples, and twisted his head about on his pillow, and groaned in his solitude and perplexity.   "Must I threaten him with exposure, and so drive him out of the country? or must I tell her the truth about herself, and ask her to believe, on the faith of my unexplained assertion, that the man is one whom she must never think of marrying?"

The position was one of indisputable difficulty; the "pleasant vice"—that long-ago story of a dead woman, deceived indeed, but with no extraordinary cruelty, a story which had not troubled Lord Sandilands' conscience very much—had manufactured itself finally into a whip of stout dimensions and stinging quality, and he was getting a very sufficient taste of it just now.

Miles must try his luck.   That was the only conclusion which could be immediately reached.   If he could sleep a little, he might feel all right in the morning, and be able to accompany him to Hardriggs.   If he were not well enough, Miles must go all the same.   If the young man should feel surprise and curiosity at finding his old friend so impatient, it could not be helped; it must pass as a vagary of an old man's.   But Miles would not remark anything; the vagary was sufficiently cognate to his own humour and his own purposes to pass unnoticed.

When Lord Sandilands and Miles Challoner arrived at Hardriggs on the following day, a close observer would have discerned that they were both under a strong impression of some kind.   Lord Sandilands was not feeling well by any means, but he had assured Miles the drive would do him

good, and he had found his indisposition so far useful, that
it explained and excused his being very silent on the way.
Neither was Miles much inclined to talk. He was of an
earnest nature, never at any time voluble, and when under
the influence of strong feeling silence was congenial to him.
He well understood that the revelation he had made to
Lord Sandilands on the preceding day had produced a
startling and disagreeable effect; and having perceived
plainly, beyond the possibility of doubt, that the secret
which he so earnestly desired to know was in Lord Sandilands' possession, and was of a darker and direr nature
than he had ever guessed at, but was, at the same time,
quite as securely beyond his reach as ever, he made up his
mind to let the subject drop. Unless this man had cut him
out, or was likely to cut him out with Grace Lambert, he
had no power to harm him. The truth was, Miles Challoner
was very sincerely and heartily in love, and he had as little
power as inclination to occupy his thoughts for long at a
time with anyone but Grace, with any speculation but his
chance of success with her. Luckily, Sir Giles and Lady
Belwether were the least observant of human beings. Sir
Giles was stupid to an extent which is not to be realised
except by those who understand the bucolic gentry of our
favoured land, and Lady Belwether was—though superior,
as we have seen, to her baronet in intelligence, and distinguished by a taste for music—very short-sighted. Close
observers were therefore not "on hand," when Lord Sandilands and Miles arrived at Hardriggs. Sir Giles was con-
templating the turnips at a distant point of his "pretty
little place;" Miss Lambert had gone out into the garden,
or the lime-walk, the servants said, some time before;
and Lady Belwether and Mrs. Bloxam were in the morning-
room.

Lord Sandilands did not lose much time in arranging the
situation as he wished it to be arranged, so far as Miles was
concerned—his consummate ease of manner, which Miles
admired to the point of envy, rendered any little disposition of affairs of that kind a very simple proceeding to
him. Miles was despatched in search of Sir Giles, Mrs.
Bloxam was begged on no account to interfere with Miss
Lambert's saunter in the garden—they might join her
presently, perhaps—and Lady Belwether was engaged in a

discussion upon the comparative merits of "our" native composers, within a space of time whose brevity would have been surprising to any one unacquainted with the rapid action of a fixed purpose combined with good manners. Mrs. Bloxam had directed one searching glance at Lord Sandilands on his entrance, and, as she withdrew her eyes, she said to herself, "Something has happened. He wants to speak to me ; but I had rather he did not, so he sha'n't." And strange to say, though he made a protracted visit to Hardriggs that day, Lord Sandilands did not succeed in getting an opportunity of speaking a word to Mrs. Bloxam. This annoyed him a good deal. "Confound the woman!" he said to himself; "either Mrs. Bloxam is too stupid to see that I want to speak to her, or Lady Belwether is too clever to leave off talking!" In his capacity of gooseberry-picker, Lord Sandilands was led on this occasion into anything but pleasant pastures.

The shortest way to the turnips, just then occupying the mind and demanding the presence of Sir Giles Belwether, fortunately lay through the garden, otherwise Miles Challoner might not have profited so readily and unsuspected by the strategy of his clever old friend. Through a side-gate of the garden the lime-walk was to be gained, and as Miles closed that gate behind him he caught sight of Grace Lambert. She was walking slowly along in the shadow of the trees, her head bent down in a thoughtful attitude. Miles went quickly towards her, and she looked up and recognised him with a slight start and a vivid blush ; in fact, with the kind of recognition which takes place when the person who intrudes upon a reverie happens to be its subject. Gertrude had been thinking of Miles —she thought of him very often now ; and the interview which had taken place between herself and Lord Ticehurst had made her think of him more seriously than ever. She loved him. She did not deny the truth, or palter with it, or fail to recognise its consequences. She had mistaken pleased and excited fancy and flattered vanity for love once, but this was nothing of the kind. She knew this was true love, because she thought of *him*, not of herself; because she did not hope, but feared he loved her. How would she have listened to such an avowal from Miles's lips as that which, made by Lord Ticehurst, had produced mere contempt, and a desire to get rid of it and him as quickly as possible ? Gertrude had accepted her position in such perfect good faith, that its difficulties never presented themselves in a practical form at all ; and she pondered this matter now in her heart, as if she were really the free unmarried girl she seemed to the world. If he should come to her and tell her a love-tale, what should she say to him ? She had asked herself the question many times and had not found the answer, when, raising her eyes at the sound of steps, she met those of Miles Challoner, and saw in them what he had come to say.

There was manifest embarrassment on both sides, and each was distinctly conscious of its cause. Why could they not meet to-day as they had met so often before ? Why were the ordinary commonplaces so hard to think of and so incoherently said ? Gertrude was the first to recover her composure. She asked Miles if Lord Sandilands had come with him ; and on his saying he had, and was then in the house, she turned in that direction, and said something about going in to see him. But Miles checked her steps by standing still.

" Don't go into the house," he said ; " he does not expect you. Let us walk this way ; let me speak to you." She glanced at him, and silently complied. She knew it all now, and she began to feel what it was that she must say, and what it would cost her to say it. She felt his eyes upon her, and the delicate colour faded away from her face.

Neither she nor Miles Challoner could have told afterwards, or even exactly recalled in their thoughts, the words then spoken between them. He told her how he had loved her from the first—he who had never loved before—and how fear and hope had alternated in his heart until now, when hope was the stronger, and he had determined to tell her how all his happiness, all his life, was in her hands. He spoke with the frank manliness of his nature, and Gertrude's heart thrilled as she listened to him with intense pain, with keen delight. At least he loved her well and worthily ; nothing could deprive her of that exquisite knowledge. She would, she must, put away the wine of life offered to her parched lips, but she knew its sweetness, had seen the splendour and the sparkle of it.

A thousand thoughts, innumerable emotions, crowded upon her, as she listened to the words of Miles ; but when he prayed her to speak and let him know his fate, prayed her with eagerness and passion, but with hope that was almost confidence, then she put them all down with her strong will, and addressed herself to her task. She drew the hand which he had taken away from his hold, and told him in one short sentence that she could not give him the answer he desired.

"You cannot, Grace ? You refuse me !" he said hoarsely. "You tell me, then, that I have deceived myself ? "

"No," she said, "I do not. Let us sit here awhile "— she seated herself on a bench under a lime-tree as she spoke—"and let me speak frankly and freely to you, as you deserve."

Miles obeyed her with bewilderment. What was she going to say ? She would not marry him, and yet he had *not* deceived himself ! She was deadly pale, and he might have heard the beating of her heart ; but she was quite firm, and she turned her steady eyes upon him unfalteringly.

"There is only one thing you can say to me," he said, "if you persevere in forbidding me to hope—that is, to send me out of your sight for ever."

"Perhaps," was her reply ; "but listen. I have said you don't deceive yourself, and I mean it. I know you love me ; I know what perfect sincerity there is in you—hush ! let me speak—and I—I do love you—you not have mistaken me, I have not misled you."

"Then what does anything else matter ?" said Miles, and he caught her hands and kissed them, unresisted, unrebuked. "With that assurance, Grace, surely you will not refuse me ? "

"I must," she answered. "Have patience with me ; I will tell you why. It is for your own sake."

"My own sake !" he exclaimed passionately ; "you deprive me of all hope and happiness for my own sake ! I shall need patience indeed to understand that."

"It is true, nevertheless. I could not marry you, Miles Challoner, without doing you a great injury ; and I love you too well, much more and better than myself, to do that. Take that assurance, and believe that nothing can shake my determination. My fate is decided, my way of life is quite fixed. I shall never be your wife—never, never, never ! " —his face was hidden in his hands, he did not see the suffering which broke all control and showed itself plainly in her every feature—"but I shall never love you less, or any one but you." The low distinct tones of her voice thrilled him with a horrid sense of hopelessness. She spoke as one who had taken an irrevocable resolution.

"What do you mean ? " he said. " You must tell me more than this. What do you mean by doing me an injury ? I protest I have not the faintest notion of your meaning. It cannot be——" He hesitated, and she took up his words.

" Because you are a gentleman of old name and a responsible position in society, and I am a singer, an actress, a woman with no name and no station, you would say. Yes, it is precisely for this cause, which you think impossible. I know you don't regard any of these things, but the world does; and the man I love shall never be censured by the world for me."

How well it was, she thought, how fortunate, that such a real genuine difficulty did exist ; that she could give some explanation which he might be induced to receive.

" Then you would make me wretched for the sake of the world, even if what you say of my position and your own were true ? And it is not. Is your genius nothing ? Is your fame nothing ? I speak now as reasonably as yourself ; not as a man who holds you peerless, far removed above all the world, but as one discussing a question open to argument. What am I in comparison to the men who would be proud to offer you rank and wealth ? What have I to give you that others could not give a thousandfold ? "

" You give me all I value, all I care for," she said ; " but I must not take it. You must not, you shall not, deceive yourself. My genius, as you call it, my fame, are real things in their way and in their sphere, but they are not of any account in yours. Ask your friend Lord Sandilands ; he is a kind friend to me also, and a man who knows the world thoroughly ; and he will tell you I am right."

" No, he won't ! " said Miles triumphantly. " No, he won't ! He will tell *you*, on the contrary, that *you* are quite wrong ; he will tell you that he knows I love you, and have dared to hope, to believe that you love me. He will tell you that I have told him what is my dearest hope, and that he shares it; and more, Grace, more than that, he will tell you that he came here with me to-day on purpose that I might learn my fate, and be no longer in suspense; and that he is on duty at this moment, keeping the old ladies in talk, just to give me this precious opportunity. Now, where are all your arguments? where are my wise friends? where is this terrible world to whom we are to be sacrificed? You have nothing more to say, Grace; your 'never, never, never!' cannot hurt me any more."

For one brief moment he triumphed. For one moment his arm was around her, and his lips were pressed to hers. But the next she had started from his embrace, and stood pale and breathless before him.

"Is this really true?" she said; "does Lord Sandilands approve?" She asked him only to gain a moment's time for thought; she was terribly disconcerted by this complication, it increased her difficulties immensely. But Miles saw in the question only a symptom of yielding, only a proof of his victory.

"Yes, yes," he said eagerly, "it is true; it is indeed! He is the only real friend I have in the world, the only man whose opinion I care for, and he is on my side. Now, Grace, you must yield; you cannot refuse me."

She stood for a moment motionless and silent. Then her nerves, generally so strong, so completely under control, gave way. The violence of the struggle, the intensity of the pain she was suffering, that overwhelming remembrance of the past, the agonizing sense of what might have been, but was now quite impossible, the feebleness of the only weapon which she could venture to use in this battle in which her own heart was her adversary,—all these overcame her, and she sunk upon the bench in a helpless agony of tears.

Terrified by her distress, Miles Challoner knelt before her, and implored her to explain the cause of this sudden grief. But all his prayers were vain. She wept convulsively for many minutes, and was literally unable to speak. When at last she conquered the passion of tears, she felt and looked so very ill that he became alarmed on a fresh score.

"You are ill," he said, "shall I go for Mrs. Bloxam? Shall I take you to the house?"

She made a sign with her hand that he should not speak, then leaned her head against the bench, and closed her eyes. He stood by, awkward and silent, watching her. After a little while she sat up, and said faintly:

"Will you leave me? Go away from me for the present —I am ill; but it is only from agitation. Let me be alone for a while; you shall see me again when I am able."

"Of course I will leave you, if you wish it," said Miles, with all the timidity and embarrassment of a man in the presence of feminine weakness and suffering; "but I am afraid you are not fit to be left alone."

"I am indeed," she urged, and her face grew whiter as she spoke; "I shall recover myself, if I am left alone. Don't fear for me. Go to the house, and do not say you have seen me. Go by the lime-walk into the avenue; I will go by the garden. No one will see me; and if I can get to my room and lie down for a little, I shall be quite well. Pray, pray go."

She put her hands before her face, and Miles saw a quick shudder pass over her from head to foot. He was afraid to go, afraid to stay; at length he obeyed her, and took the way towards the house which she had indicated, feeling bewildered and alarmed.

When Miles Challoner reëntered the drawing-room at Hardriggs he found Lord Sandilands still there, held in durance by Lady Belwether and Mrs. Bloxam. Lord Sandilands had found his hostess immovable, and no other afternoon callers had had the kindness to come and partially release him. Mrs. Bloxam kept her eyes and her fingers steadily and unremittingly engaged with her fancy-work, and Lady Belwether persisted in discoursing on music and religion. With his accustomed philosophy Lord Sandilands accepted the situation, consoling himself by the reflection that a day or two could not make any difference in what he had to say to Mrs. Bloxam, and that the chief object of his present exertions had at least been secured, for he entertained a satisfactory conviction that Miles and Gertrude had met "somewhere about." Miles returned too soon, in one sense, for the old gentleman's wishes; he would rather have found him utterly oblivious of time; in that case, and if no consideration of anybody's convenience had occurred to Miles, Lord Sandilands would have felt confidence in the prospering of the suit.   But Miles came in looking as little like a successful and happy lover as he could look, and Lord Sandilands perceived in an instant that things had gone wrong.   He did not give Miles time to speak before he rose, and saying, "You have clear ideas of time, Miles; we ought to be back before now.—Business, Lady Belwether, business —you don't understand its claims, happily for you.—Goodbye, Mrs. Bloxam; tell Miss Lambert I'm sorry not to have seen her;" he got himself and his melancholy, and indeed frightened-looking, companion out of the room and out of the house.

"Now tell me all about it," said Lord Sandilands to Miles when they were in the carriage; "what has happened? You have seen her, of course?"

"Yes," said Miles ruefully, and then with much embarrassment he told Lord Sandilands what had occurred.

The narrative perplexed and distressed the listener.   He understood Gertrude's feelings up to a certain point, but no farther; he could not understand why Miles's representations of his advocacy of his suit had had no effect in moderating her apprehensions of the world's view of such a marriage.   He could say little or nothing to console Miles, but he told him he did not regard Miss Lambert's decision as final, or the nervous attack which had so alarmed him as of any import.

"I will see her, and have it out with her," said Lord Sandilands to himself; "and if it is necessary for her happiness's sake and that of Miles, I will tell her the truth."

Book the Third.

—

CHAPTER I.

ÆGROTAT ANIMO.

MISS GRACE LAMBERT had made herself so popular at Hardriggs, had so ingratiated herself with all staying in that hospitable mansion, that the news, duly conveyed to the breakfast-table by Mrs. Bloxam on the morning after Miles Challoner's visit, that she was too unwell to leave her room, threw a considerable damp over the company assembled. Old Sir Giles, who had been very much impressed by Gertrude's quiet manner and cheerful spirits since she had been staying in the house—who had been perfectly astonished at the discovery that, though an opera-singer and a great public favourite, she had, as he phrased it, "no d——d nonsense about her"—was the first to break out into loudly-expressed lamentation, mingled with suggestions of sending off at once to Hastings for medical advice, or telegraphing to London with the same object. Lady Belwether was distressed beyond measure; the idea of any one so charming, any one capable of yielding such exquisite delight, suffering from pain or sickness seemed to be something quite beyond the old lady's ken. She was at Gertrude's bedside within five minutes after she had heard of her young friend's indisposition, and was shocked at the swollen eyelids and pallid drawn face of her idol. The Dean, too, received the news with great regret: he had experienced much pleasure in Miss Lambert's society. The very fact of her position had had its secret charm; there was something specially pleasant in being brought into daily communion with one whose status in life was considered equivocal, but whose conduct was unexceptionable, and, if occasion required, would bear any amount of scrutiny. All great men have their enemies ; the Dean was not without his. The *odium theologicum*, than which there is nothing stronger, had made him its butt on various occasions, and many of his clerical brethren had poured out the vials of their wrath, through the medium of the Church journals to which they contributed, on his devoted head. The Dean had hitherto never replied to any of these attacks ; but he had thought more than once, as he sat nursing his knee and looking out through the bay-window of the library at Hardriggs, that he should be by no means sorry if the contemporaneous visit of Miss Lambert and himself were made the subject of attack ; and he had planned out a very brilliant and taking letter in reply—a letter abounding in charity and in quotations from the Fathers, Pollok's *Course of Time*, and the *Christian Year*. The Dean expressed to Lady Belwether that, charming as her guests were in the aggregate, Miss Lambert's secession would leave among them a blank, a *hiatus*, which was not merely *valde deflendus*, but which, in point of fact, it would be impossible to fill up ; and the old lady, though she did not understand Latin, comprehended the general nature of the remark, and found in it new cause for self-gratulation, and fresh weapons of defence against the insidious attacks of Martha and the Reverend Tophet. There were, it is true, certain people staying at Hardriggs who seemed to take it as a grievance that any "person in Miss Lambert's position," as they were good enough to call it, should be taken ill at all ; but they were in a decided minority, and most of them were very much ashamed of the opinion they had held when they found the Dean of Burwash taking the young lady's indisposition so much to heart.

Had any one of them the slightest suspicion of the real cause of Gertrude's ailment ? Not one. Would any one of them have given credence for a moment, if they had been told, that on the previous day the girl had refused the proffered hands of two men, one of them an earl, the other a wealthy commoner ? Not one. "Such things are all very well in books, my dear," Lady Belwether would have told you, adding from memory a list of ennobled actresses who had all done honour to the position in life to which they had been raised ; but the chances came but seldom, and were always taken advantage of by those to whom they were offered. What would have been the effect on the host and hostess, and on the rest of their company, if it had become known that Lord Ticehurst had made Miss Lambert an offer, it would be impossible to say. They would have wondered at him, they would have wondered much more at her, and they would have professed to pity, and probably have cordially hated them both. However, that was a secret which of all in that house was known but to Gertrude alone, and she was not one who would wittingly let it pass her lips.

She was ill; she had a perfect right to say so, and was not uttering the slightest falsehood in the assertion. That dreadful sinking of the heart, that utter prostration, that deep, dead blankness of spirits, that hopelessness, that refusal to be comforted—if this did not constitute illness, what did? He *did* love her, then? She had known it long, but what bliss it was to hear him avow it! Should she ever lose the remembrance of him as he stood before her—the light in his eye, the *pose* of his head, the tone of his voice? True? She would stake her life on that man's truth. What a difference between his diffident earnestness and the theatrical swagger with which Gilbert Lloyd asked her the same question—ah, how many years ago! Lord Ticehurst, too,—she had almost forgotten his visit and its purport, so overshadowed was it by the importance of the affair which immediately succeeded it,—Lord Ticehurst— he was, in his way, considerate and kindly—meant to be all courteous and all honest; she hoped her manner to him had not been brusque or abrupt. Countess of Ticehurst, eh?—rank, wealth, station. For an instant a hard, cold, proud look, which had been a stranger to her face of late, flitted across her features, and then faded away. No! Those might have had their allurements when she first learned Gilbert Lloyd's worthlessness, and re-commenced her life, scorning to yield, and merely looking on all human weaknesses as stepping-stones for her advancement. She had learned better things than that now. Miles! Could it be possible that but a comparatively short time ago he had been supremely indifferent to her? that she had looked on and seen the love for her growing in his heart, without a dream of ever reciprocating it? And now—Refused him! she could have done nothing else. And for his own sake—

as she had told him, but as he seemed unable to comprehend,—for his own sake. For the love of such a man as Miles Challoner she would have risked everything, in the first appreciation of such a sentiment, so fresh and novel to her in all her experience of life—and that experience had been singular and not small ; to be the recipient of such a passion as that man proffered and laid at her feet, she would have let her dead past bury its dead ; forgotten, buried, stamped down out of all chance of resurrection the events of her early life—her marriage, her separation from her husband. The compact made between her and Gilbert Lloyd should have been more than ever religiously fulfilled. That she held that husband at her mercy she knew perfectly well : only once had he ventured to question her power that evening at Mrs. Burge's reception, and his conduct then had given her ample proof of the impossibility of his resistance to her will. She had nothing to fear from him ; and she knew him well enough to be certain that he had kept that secret at least locked in his own breast. But Miles ? No ! she had done rightly ; even if her appreciation of Miles Challoner's warm admiration and generous regard had not grown and deepened into a feeling, the strength of which forbade her striving against it, and which she knew and confessed to herself to be love, she would have rebelled against any attempt to hoodwink or deceive that loyal-hearted gentleman. But now the attempt had been treachery of the basest kind. She loved him—loved him wildly, passionately, and yet with an intermingled reverence and respect such as her girlish fancy had never dreamed of ; and she had refused him, had told him—not indeed calmly or quietly, for once her self-control had failed her, but with earnestness and decision—that her fate was decided, her way of life quite fixed, and that she could never be his wife ! Ah, if they could have known all, those good people downstairs, they would scarcely have wondered at Miss Lambert's indisposition. They ascribed her illness to over-exertion, over-excitement, the reaction after the feverish professional life of the past few months. A little rest, they said to each other, would " bring her round." A little rest ! Something more than a little rest is required, as they would have allowed, could they have seen what no one, not even Mrs. Bloxam, saw,—the favourite of the public with dishevelled hair and streaming eyes stretched prone upon her pillow, and sobbing as though her heart would break !

Miss Grace Lambert's illness or indisposition, thus evoking the compassion of the company staying at Hardriggs, was, whatever the company might have thought about it, known to herself to spring purely from mental distress. The same *teterrima causa* acted on Lord Sandilands, but brought about a different physical result. On the morning after Miles had communicated the result of his interview with Gertrude the old nobleman awoke with a return of the symptoms which had previously alarmed him so much increased that he felt it necessary to send for a local practitioner, by whose report he would be guided as to the expediency of summoning his own ordinary physician from London.

Hastings is so essentially a resort of invalids, that the faculty is to be found there in every variety. Allopathy seated far back in its brougham, looks sedately and snugly at the saunterers on the promenade ; while Homœopathy thinking to assume a virtue even if it have it not, and to wear the livery of medicine though scorned by regular practitioners, whirls by, black-clothed and white-chokered, in its open four-wheeler. Nor are there wanting the followers of even less generally received science. On that charming slope, midway between Hastings and St. Leonard's, where a scrap of green struggles to put in an arid appearance amidst the vast masses of rock and sand, Herr Douss, the favourite pupil of Priessnitz (what a large-hearted fellow he must have been, to judge by the number of his favourite pupils !), opened a water-cure establishment, to which, for financial reasons, he has recently added the attractions of a Turkish bath, and invariably has a houseful of damp hypochondriacs. And in the immediate neighbourhood is there not the sanatorium of the celebrated Mr. Crax ? a gentleman who has discovered the secret that no mortal ailment can withstand being rubbed in a peculiar manner, and who shampoos you, and rubs you, and pulls your joints, and pommels you all over until you become a miracle of youth and freshness, to which the renovated Æson could not be compared.

It is not for an instant to be supposed that any of this unlicensed band were allowed to work their will on the person of Lord Sandilands. The old gentleman was far too careful of his health to quit the immediate precincts of his private physician without being relegated to some one to whom that physician had knowledge, and in whom he had trust. Sir Charles Dumfunk, of Harley Street, habitually attended Lord Sandilands, and was liked by his lordship as a friend as well as esteemed as a physician. A very courtly old gentleman was Sir Charles, one who for years had been honorary physician to the Grand Scandinavian Opera, and had written more medical certificates for sulky singers and dancers than any other member of his craft. In his capacity of fashionable physician—the lungs and throat were supposed to be his speciality—Sir Charles Dumfunk had the power of bidding many of his patients to quit their usual pursuits, and devote themselves to the restoration of their health in a softer climate. The ultra-fashionables were generally sent to Nice, Cannes, or Mentone ; " it little matters," the old gentleman used to remark ; " they will carry Belgrave Square and its manners and customs with them wherever they go." *Nouveaux riches* were despatched to Madeira, energetic patients to Algiers, while mild cases were permitted to pass their winter at Hastings. At each one of these places the leading physician was Sir Charles Dumfunk's friend. Little Dr. Bede of St. Leonard's swore by the great London Galen, who invariably sent him a score of patients during the winter, and was as good to him as a couple of hundred a-year. Lord Sandilands had come down armed with a letter of introduction to Dr. Bede, and had sent it on by his servant, accompanied by a brace of partridges from the Belwether estate, very soon after his arrival. Dr. Bede had acknowledged the receipt of letter and birds in a very neat little note, had looked-up Lord Sandilands in the *Peerage*—the only lay book in his medical library—and had left his card at his lordship's lodgings. Consequently, when, the morning after Miles's *fiasco* at Hardriggs, Dr. Bede was summoned to come to Lord Sandilands at once, physcian and patient knew as much about each other as, failing a personal interview, was possible.

Symptoms detailed, examination made, Dr. Bede—a very precise and methodical little gentleman, with a singularly neatly-tied black neckerchief, towards which the eye of every patient was infallibly attracted, and a curiously stony and expressionless blue eye of his own, out of which nothing could ever be gleaned,—Dr. Bede, tightly buttoned to the throat in his little black surtout, gives it as his decided opinion that it is gout, "and not a doubt about it." Lord Sandilands, really half-gratified that he is literally laid by the heels by an aristocratic and gentlemanly complaint, combats the notion—no hereditary predisposition, no previous symptoms. Dr. Bede is firm, and Lord Sandilands is convinced. An affair of time, of course; an affair very much at the patient's own will; entire abstinence from this and that and the other, and very little of anything else: perfect quiet and rest of mind and body—of mind quite as much as body—repeats the little doctor, with a would-be sharp glance at the patient, whose mental worry shows itself in a thousand little ways, all of which are patent to the sharp-eyed practitioner. Lord Sandilands promises obedience with a half laugh; he is very much obliged to Dr. Bede, he has thorough confidence in his comprehension and treatment of the case; there is no need to send to town for Dumfunk? Dr. Bede, with confidence dashed with humility, thinks not—of course it is for his lordship to decide; but he, Dr. Bede, has not the smallest fear, provided his instructions are strictly obeyed; and he is quite aware of the value of the charge Sir Charles Dumfunk has confided to him. So far all is arranged. The doctor will look in every day, and his lordship promises strict compliance with his instructions.

So far all is arranged; but when the doctor is fairly gone, and the door is shut, and Lord Sandilands has heard the sound of the wheels of the professional brougham, low on the sand and loud on the stones, echo away, the old gentleman is fain to admit—first to himself, secondly to Miles, whom he summons immediately—that it is impossible for him to keep his word so far as being mentally quiet is concerned.

"If I'm to be clapped down on this particularly slippery chintz sofa, my dear boy," said he, "I must accept the fiat. It might be better, but it might be much worse. I can hear the pleasant plashing of the sea, which, though a little melancholy, is deuced musical; and I can see the boats floating away in the distance; and I have every opportunity of making myself acquainted with the hideousness of the prevailing fashion in female dress ; and if I am feeling too happy, there's safe to arrive a German band, and murder some of my favourite *morceaux* in a manner which reminds me that, like that king Thingummy, I am mortal, begad ! But it's no use for that little medico—polite, pleasant little person in his way, too—no use for that little medico to tell me to keep my mind perfectly quiet, and not to excite myself about anything. What a ridiculous thing for a man to prescribe ! as though we hadn't all of us always something to worry ourselves about !"

Miles Challoner was, as times go, a wonderful specimen of a selfless man. He had temporarily laid aside his own trouble on finding that his old friend was really ill, and it was in genuine good faith that he said—

"Why, what in the world have you to worry you now, old friend ? What should prevent your keeping rigidly to that mental repose which Dr. Bede says is so essential to your well-doing ? "

"What have I got to worry me ? What is likely to prove antipathic to my being quiet ? " asked Lord Sandilands in petulant querulous tones. " 'Gad, when a man's old it's imagined that he has no care, no interest but in himself ! You ought to know me better, Miles ; 'pon my soul you ought ! "

" I do know all your goodness, and——"

" No, no ! Goodness and stuff ! Do you or do you not know the interest I take in you ? You do ? Good ! Then is it likely I could allow affairs to remain as they are between you and Miss Lambert without worrying myself about them ? without trying my poor *possible* to bring them right ? '

" My dear old friend——"

" Yes, yes ! your dear old friend ; that's all very well ; you treat me like a child, Miles. I know you mean it kindly ; but I've been accustomed to act and think for myself for so long that I can't throw off the habit even now, when that dapper little fellow tells me I ought ; and I must at once go into this business of Grace Lambert's. I have my own ideas on that matter, and I won't at all regard her decision as final, notwithstanding your solemn face and manner. Now, look here, my dear boy, it's of no use lifting up that warning finger ; if you cross my wishes I shall become infinitely worse, and less bearable. I've always heard that gout is a disease in which, above all others, the patient must be humoured. I must see—— There! you're jumping up at once—and quite enough to give me a sharp attack—simply because you thought I was going to name your divinity. Wasn't it so? I thought as much. Nothing of the sort; I was about to say that I must see Mrs. Bloxam at once. I have some very special business to talk over with her, and I should be much obliged if you, Miles, would take a fly and go over at once to Hardriggs and bring Mrs. Bloxam back with you."

"I?—go over to Hardriggs after——"

"Go over to Hardriggs! And why not? I'm sure you could not complain of your reception by Sir Giles and Lady Belwether; they have been most cordially polite to you on every occasion of your visiting them, and *they* are the host and hostess at Hardriggs, I believe. Besides, I ask you to do me a special favour, in doing which you need expose yourself to no disagreeables, even to seeing any one whom you would rather not see."

"You are quite right, and I will be off at once."

"That's spoken like my dear good fellow! Good-bye, Miles, good-bye!—If he does come across her in the house or the grounds?" said the old gentlemen, as the door closed behind his *protégé*. "Well, you never can tell; it might have been whim, a mere passing caprice, in which case she might be perfectly ready to revoke to-day; and no harm could be done by his meeting her again. Or it might be something more serious—is something more serious probably, for Gertrude is a girl with plenty of resolution and firm will. At any rate, I'm right in having Mrs. Bloxam here to talk it over, and I think I shall hold to the programme which I have already arranged in my mind."

The Hastings fly, drawn by the flea-bitten gray horse, which conveyed Miles Challoner to Hardriggs, went anything but gaily over the dusty, hilly road. The driver, a sullen young man, with dreary views of life, saw at a glance that his fare was in an abstracted frame of mind, and looked anything but likely to pay for extra speed. So he sat on his box, driving the usual half-crown-an-hour rate, giving the flea-bitten gray an occasional chuck with the reins, producing a corresponding "job" from the bit, and occupying himself now by fitting a new end to his whip-lash, now by humming dolorous ditties in the hardest Sussex twang, with a particularly painful and constantly recurring development of the letter " r." Miles sat leaning back in the carriage, his hat thrust over his eyes, his hands plunged deep in his pockets. He was buried in thought of no pleasant kind, and neither heard nor heeded the chaff of the passers-by, which was loud and frequent. The first portion of the way to Hardriggs lies along the Fairlight-road, and numerous parties of cheerful Cockneys, in vehicles and on foot, on their way to the romantic Lover's Seat, and the waterfall where there is no water, and the pretty glen, passed the carriage containing the moody young man, and commented openly on its occupant. "He don't look like a pleasurer, he don't ! " was a remark that gained immediate sympathy ; while a more comic suggestion that "he looked as if he'd lost a fourpenny-piece," was received with tumultuous applause. Neither style of comment had the least effect on Miles Challoner, who remained chewing the cud of his own reflections until the stopping of the fly at the outer gate of Hardriggs Park reminded him of having seen Lord Ticehurst driving through that gate on the occasion of his visit on the previous day. Suddenly it flashed across him that the young nobleman's manner had been specially odd and remarkable. Could it have been that—and yet the expression of Lord Ticehurst's face was chapfallen and disconsolate, anything but that of a successful suitor. All the world had said, during the past season, that his lordship had been very strongly *épris* of Miss Lambert, he had paid her constant attention, and—— That could have had no influence on her decision of yesterday ; she could never have listened to Lord Ticehurst's protestations, even if he had made any such, or he would not have gone away in so melancholy and depressed a state. Besides, had not Grace told him that she loved him, Miles—that he was not mistaken in her—that she had not misled him ? And yet she would not marry him ? Ah, there must be some mistake, something which could be explained away ? Lord Sandilands had evidently felt that when he had asked him to come over with this message to Mrs. Bloxam. He would see Miss Lambert—not asking for her directly, that would be too marked, but taking an opportunity of chancing on her and—well, after all, the dearest object of his life might be obtained.

They were pleased to see the good-looking young man at Hardriggs, as he descended from the fly and joined the pre-luncheon croquet-party on the lawn. He had been there very recently, it is true; but good-looking young men are always welcome in country-houses, where indeed a fresh face, a fresh voice, a few fresh ideas, are priceless. Miles threw a hurried glance over the croquet-players. Miss Lambert was not amongst them. They were all young people, who, after the first greeting, returned to their game and its necessary accompaniment of flirtation. But Dean Asprey was seated under "a wide-spreading beech-tree," reading the *Times*, and he rose as he saw Miles approach, dropped the paper, and went to meet him. As the Dean approached, Miles could not help noticing his aristocratic appearance; could scarcely help smiling at the wonderful way in which the tailor had combined the fashionable and clerical element in his dress.

"How do you do, my dear Mr. Challoner?" said Dean Asprey, in those bland mellifluous tones which had won so many hearts. "So delighted to see you here again! With only one fear tempering my pleasure, and that is that—believing you to be alone? yes, that is so?—the fear that my dear old friend Lord Sandilands is indisposed? Say I'm wrong, and set my fears at rest!"

"I would gladly, Mr. Dean; but I cannot. Lord Sandilands has a sharp attack of the gout."

"Of the gout? Well, well, I can recollect John Borlase these—ah, no matter how many years; too many to trouble to recollect—and the gout was the last complaint one would have ascribed to him."

"Well, he has it now, without a doubt. Dr. Bede of St. Leonards has seen him, and pronounced definitely in the matter. I have come over to ask Mrs. Bloxam, who is a very old friend of his, to go and see him."

"Ay, ay, indeed! Mrs. Bloxam—a very charming and estimable person, by the way, and apparently well versed in many questions which, for females at least, would be con-sidered abstruse—Mrs. Bloxam is in great request just now. Her young charge Miss Lambert is also ill, and——"

"Miss Lambert ill!" cried Miles; "what is the matter?"

"O, nothing of any consequence, I believe," replied the Dean. ("Charmingly ingenuous the youth of the present day," he said to himself: "he has at once revealed the reason of his coming over here again so soon, without having the smallest idea that he has done so.") "Nothing of any consequence; a trifling indisposition, a *migraine*, a *nichts*, which in any one else would be thought nothing of, but which in Miss Lambert is naturally regarded with special interest. You know her, of course. I mean know how to appreciate her, rather than know in the mere ordinary sense of acquaintance?"

"I—I—yes, O yes! I've had the pleasure of seeing Miss Lambert frequently in town, and think her—of course, most charming—You're sure there's nothing serious the matter with her, because Lord Sandilands, don't you know, is such an old friend of hers, and takes such interest, that——"

"I know that perfectly, and would not dream of deceiving you for an instant. Some of us, I know, are suspected of doing evil that good may come," said the Dean, with a specially sweet smile; "but it is a very dangerous doctrine, which I have always held in abhorrence. I see a servant passing the end of the lawn, and I suppose I may be considered sufficiently at home here to venture to give an order. —James, would you be good enough to let Mrs. Bloxam know that Mr. Challoner is here, and would gladly speak with her? Thank you, very much.—And now, my dear Mr. Challoner, to return to our very interesting conversation. What were we talking about?"

"You were mentioning that Miss Lambert was ill, and——"

"Ay, to be sure, Miss Lambert! What a charming girl! what grace and beauty! what amiability! what unaffected—— And you have known her for some time! I can well understand her creating a great sensation in London. Such a mixture of beauty and talent is very rare, and naturally very impressive. What says Dryden?—

'Old as I am, for ladies' love unfit,
The power of beauty I remember yet.'

What a charming couplet, is it not? And so, as you were saying, Miss Lambert is a great success in London society?"

"Rather as you were saying, Mr. Dean," said Miles, with a feeble attempt at a smile,—he knew he should not see Gertrude, and the conversation was beginning to bore him,—"though I can cordially indorse the remark. Miss Lambert made a complete conquest of every one she met, including Lady Belwether, who is hastening towards us.—How do you do, Lady Belwether? I'm sorry to learn I have left one sick friend to come to another."

"Our dear Grace is certainly better, my dear Mr. Challoner.—Dean, you will be glad to hear that.—Fancy my position, Mr. Challoner; the responsibility of having any one like that in one's care, on whom so much might be said to hang, you know. Sir Giles was for telegraphing off at once to London for advice, but Grace would not have it. And she has proved to be right, as she always is, dear creature! She is much better, and she heard the message you brought, Mr. Challoner, about Mrs. Bloxam, and has not raised the least objection to her going. Indeed, so like her, sweet thing! she seems to have forgotten herself in anxiety about Lord Sandilands."

"I suppose, Lady Belwether, that there is not much chance of my seeing Miss Lambert?"

"Seeing her? To-day? My dear sir, not the remotest chance in the world. I strictly forbade her thinking of leaving her room to-day; and when Mrs. Bloxam has gone away with you, I shall take her place at Grace's side.— You think I'm right, Dean? The importance of such a case as this is—Exactly, I knew you'd agree with me. What do you think Lady Hawksley said when she heard the darling was ill?"

"Knowing Lady Hawksley," said the Dean, again with his pleasant smile, "the field of speculation is too vast for me to attempt to enter on it. What did her ladyship remark?"

"She said it must be a horrid bore for me; and what would Miss Lambert have done if she had been taken ill in the season, when she was singing? Did you ever hear such horrible things? But I told her that if Miss Lambert had been taken ill in town she would have had everybody's sympathy, from the Queen downwards ; which is more than can be said of some people, I could not help adding."

As the old lady finished speaking, Mrs. Bloxam appeared, and very shortly afterwards she and Miles took their leave, and started off for Hastings in the fly. Miles had rather looked forward to this drive in Mrs. Bloxam's company. The thought of it had afforded him some little consolation when he found that there was no chance of his seeing Grace. In default of the presence of the adored one it is the lover's greatest delight to find some one who will either talk about her, or will listen to his outspoken raptures. Miles thought that in Mrs. Bloxam he might possibly find both these virtues combined ; and accordingly they had scarcely cleared the gates of the Hardriggs avenue before he began to ply his companion with a series of questions concerning Miss Lambert. These questions were artfully framed, and a less worldly-wise woman than Mrs. Bloxam might have been deceived as to their purport. But that worthy lady was not merely always perfectly cute and observant, but on this particular occasion she was, if possible, more than ever on her guard. Although during the previous day her fingers had been unremittingly engaged on her "fancy-work" during the entire period of Lord Sandilands' visit her eyes had strayed now and then to the large looking-glass close by her, which reflected a window and a part of the garden beyond, leading to the lime-walk. In that looking-glass Mrs. Bloxam had seen her charge and Miles Challoner walking together, talking earnestly, and through the same medium Mrs. Bloxam had seen each of them return separately and ill at ease. The ex-schoolmistress had all her life been in the habit of putting two and two together, and arriving at the result with commendable quickness and accuracy, and her perspicacity did not fail her now. She felt certain that Miles had proposed, and that Gertrude had refused him, though she loved him ; equally certain that Lord Sandilands was aware of a portion—she couldn't tell how much—of the real state of affairs, and that he had sent for her with the intention of discussing them with her : and Mrs. Bloxam very much deprecated the idea of any such discussion. She did not know where it might end, or what it might lead to ; and there were passages in the life of her quondam pupil which Mrs. Bloxam had not thought

it necessary to dilate upon, or indeed to introduce to Lord
Sandilands' notice ; and circumstances might render the
further suppression of those passages impossible.

So Mrs. Bloxam sat back in the fly and answered all
Miles Challoner's questions in monosyllables, and was glad
when, finding it impossible to extract anything from his
companion, the young man lapsed into silence and left her
to her own reflections, occupying himself with his. Neither
were roseate-hued. The hope which had sprung up in
Miles's breast as he journeyed to Hardriggs seemed suddenly to have paled and faded out—why he knew not.
Grace was ill, to be sure, but the fact of her illness did not
account for the sudden change in the aspect of his fortunes
—did not account for that sinking of the heart, that depression, that *avertissement* of coming trouble which we
have all of us experienced many times in our lives, and
which just then was settling down in thick black clouds
over Miles Challoner. And Mrs. Bloxam's reflections were
sombre and unpleasant. What Mr. Browning calls " the
conscience-prick and the memory-smart " were beginning
to tell upon her ; she had lost the power of self-possession,
and the faculty of lying—at least of lying in that superior
manner which she had once possessed—had deserted her.

So they drove along in silence, and the holiday excursionists to Fairlight had more fun out of them and much
openly-expressed chaff, opining how that "his mother had
found him out courtin' the gal, and had fetched him away ; "
how that " he'd married the old woman for her money, and
found out his mistake." But when they arrived at Robert-
son's-terrace, they found that Lord Sandilands had experienced a renewal of his attack, and that Dr. Bede had
expressed a strong desire that his patient should be left
perfectly quiet and undisturbed. To this, however, Lord
Sandilands would not agree, and, pursuant to his orders,
Mrs. Bloxam was shown to his room immediately after her
arrival.

She found the old nobleman faint and weak, just recovering from a sharp bout of pain. The sight of her seemed
to rouse and please him. He asked her a few unimportant
questions about the people at Hardriggs, seemed difficult
to convince that Gertrude's indisposition was only of a
temporary character, spoke in a manner that was anything

but cheerful or reassuring about his own health, and remained so long flying round the real matter at his heart, that Mrs. Bloxam began to think he would never settle on it. At length, when the landlady of the lodgings had left the room and they were alone, Lord Sandilands said—

"Our acquaintance dates so far back, Mrs. Bloxam, and has been of such a character, that there need be no reticene on either side."

Mrs. Bloxam winced at his words, and moved uneasily on the chair which she had taken by the sick man's bedside. But she was sufficient mistress of herself to bow and utter a few polite commonplaces.

"I could not get an opportunity of speaking to you yesterday," continued his lordship ; "but I know how generally observant you are, and I am sure you cannot have failed to remark that my visit to Hardriggs with my young *protégé*—for so I must regard Mr. Challoner—was not a mere ceremonious call. There is no need in disguising from you—if indeed you do not know it already—that he is desperately in love with Gertrude. It will further tend to place us in our proper position if I tell you plainly, and without reserve, that Mr. Challoner yesterday proposed to Gertrude, and—was rejected."

If Mrs. Bloxam had seen all plain sailing before her it is probable that she would have professed the liveliest astonishment, the greatest stupefaction, at this statement. But as she knew that she should have to wind her course through very doubtful channels, and would require all her skill to avoid shoals and contest storms, she thought it better to rely upon Lord Burleigh's plan, and content herself with a nod.

This nod Lord Sandilands took to mean acquiescence. "You did comprehend all that ? " he asked. " I was only doing justice to the acuteness which I have always ascribed to you when I imagined such was the case. Now we come to the more serious part of the question. Why did Gertrude refuse that young man's offer ? Not that she did not, does not, love him ? I'm an old fellow now, but I'm not old enough to have forgotten entirely that pleasant mute language; and if woman's looks and woman's ways are the same as they were thirty years since, Gertrude is decidedly

in love with Miles Challoner. You have not had many opportunities of seeing them together, and therefore cannot judge
so well. But I *know* it. Why did she reject him then ?
Why, ma'am, because, thank God, she inherits a certain
proper pride ; and she felt that she, an unknown woman
—unknown so far as family and friends are concerned, and
with a precarious income dependent on her health and
strength—was not going to permit a member of an old
county family to enter into what might be thought a
mésalliance for her."

"Very proper," murmured Mrs. Bloxam, having nothing
else to say.

"Exactly ; very proper, under circumstances. But those
circumstances must be changed ; they must no longer be
permitted to exist. It must be my care, Mrs. Bloxam,"
continued Lord Sandilands, with additional gravity, "as it
is my duty—yes, my bounden duty—to endow that young
lady with such means that she can freely and frankly give
herself to the man she loves, without any obligation on
either side."

"But to do that, my lord, you must acknowledge your
relationship to Gertrude ? "

"I have made up my mind to that already, Mrs. Bloxam,"
said the old gentleman ; "I have a sort of idea that I
shan't get over this attack, and that is a reparation which
must be made before I die. O, not that I'm going to die
just now," he added, as he saw her face change ; "but
still——"

"Dont' you think you should have a nurse, my lord,—
some one more accustomed to illness, and more able to
devote herself entirely to your service, than the landlady
here ? If I could be of any use——"

"A thousand thanks, Mrs. Bloxam. But I have telegraphed to town for my housekeeper—ah, I forgot you have
not seen her ; she has only recently come to me, but seems a
clear-headed, sensible woman—and she will come down and
nurse me. I am a little faint just now, Mrs. Bloxam, and must
ask you to leave me for the present. I will speak again to
you on that subject before you and Gertrude leave Hardriggs."

Mrs. Bloxam left the room with sentiments of a very
unpleasant kind. Lord Sandilands thought it was the want

of fortune that induced Gertrude to refuse Miles Challoner. But what about her relations with Mr. Gilbert Lloyd, of which his lordship was totally unaware?

CHAPTER II.

RECOGNITION.

THE meditations of Mrs. Bloxam as she returned to Hardriggs were not agreeable. She was exceedingly puzzled as to what her best line of action would be, in consideration of her own interests, and, indeed, to do her justice, those of Gertrude. Justice is the more easily done in this respect, as the two were identical, and not to be separated by any of the ingenuity which Mrs. Bloxam would no doubt have found for the occasion, had there been any profit in its employment. The position was a difficult one, and she was glad of the solitary drive, which enabled her to lay it all out, like a map, before her mind, and study it at comparative leisure. The temporary illness of Gertrude was, she felt, in the present conjuncture of affairs, a point in her favour. She could not go to Lord Sandilands, and, during the continuance of his attack of gout, Lord Sandilands could not go to her. That they should not meet until a decisive line of action had been arranged—first by Mrs. Bloxam in her own mind, and then imparted to and acceded to by Gertrude—was of the last importance; and that was safe. The revelation of her parentage to Gertrude by Lord Sandilands would so immediately and radically alter the relations between her and her noble friend, that it could hardly be practicable to keep the fact of her marriage concealed from Lord Sandilands. That revealed, the sequel to the marriage must also be made known; and what view would the old nobleman be likely to take of the remarkably original arrangement into which Gilbert Lloyd and Gertrude had entered? Would he be excessively shocked, and insist at once on its reversal? or would he regard it as on the whole the best and most sensible proceeding for two persons, who had discovered their marriage to be an immeasurable mistake and an incalculable evil, to have given themselves such redress and relief as the law would have afforded them only at the cost of much expense and publicity? Mrs. Bloxam entertained a conviction that the latter view was much the more probable one to be taken by Lord Sandilands; but, in any case, how should she stand with him? Not only should she be convicted of having deceived him, and of gross negligence and breach of trust as regarded the young girl placed under her care, but she should be proved guilty of having received money for Gertrude's maintenance and education for two years after they had ceased to be any concern of hers—after the girl's husband had undertaken the one, and the world had become the vehicle of the other. There was a double awkwardness and difficulty in this part of Mrs. Bloxam's puzzle. It was almost as unpleasant to admit the fact to Gertrude as to have it stated to herself by Lord Sandilands. Under no circumstances would it do for her to quarrel with Gertrude, that was clear. If she ran the risk of contracting another marriage, the secret of the first would remain in Mrs. Bloxam's possession, and she would always be in Mrs. Bloxam's power. It must not be supposed that the woman was altogether heartless and cold-blooded in making these calculations: she had real affection for Gertrude at the bottom of them all; but she was of a cool temperament and business-like habits, and she thoroughly understood the useful art of classifying her sentiments, and not permitting one order of them to interfere with another out of time and place. The position was a difficult one; and it was the business aspect of it she had to consider just now. A comfortable home for the remainder of her life, a reasonable amount of the kind of pleasure and society which she liked, and a necessity for only the most trifling inroads upon her savings; such were the blessings to the attainment of which Mrs. Bloxam looked forward as the legitimate value of her lien upon Gertrude. In the event of her declining to run the risk of marriage, and remaining on the stage, Mrs. Bloxam's material interests would be almost as secure; so that she could afford to consider the matter with tolerable impartiality. She did not like to face the discussion which must take place between her and Gertrude, because of the money-transaction involved in it. Could she avoid acknowedging it, she thought, and trust to Lord Sandilands, though he must find it out, being too careless and indifferent to think about it? *That* would be very nice, only she had no reason to suppose that Lord Sandilands was by any means careless or indifferent in money-matters. It was very unpleasant; but it must be left to right itself somehow; and as for the other and greater breach of trust? After all, the girl eloped from the Vale House; she did not assist or connive at the affair; and she might excuse herself to Lord Sandilands on the plea of the readiness and kindness with which she acceded to Gertrude's request when she proposed to return to her house. What would Gertrude think, how would she act, when the revelation and the offer should be made to her? Mrs. Bloxam had not answered any of these questions to her satisfaction, or dispelled any of these anxieties, when she reached Hardriggs.

Miss Lambert was better, Lady Belwether was happy to say; she had had some refreshing sleep, and would no doubt get on nicely now. Mrs. Bloxam went to the invalid's room, and found Grace awake and looking very much better. Her face bore traces of mental strife and suffering, but they had passed over, and she was now quite composed. Mrs. Bloxam was a judicious woman in everything, and she took care not to agitate Gertrude.

"Lord Sandilands is very ill," she said, "but not dangerously so; and he is comfortable enough there, and not badly looked after. But he has sent for his own housekeeper, which is a good move. It is nothing but gout; but he is not strong, and he will probably be laid up for some time."

Gertrude asked some general questions, and Mrs. Bloxam answered them; and then, settling herself in a comfortable attitude, and keeping Gertrude's face well in view, she told her that, in requesting her to visit him, Lord Sandilands had a particular object in view. The colour deepened a little on Gertrude's cheek as she inquired its nature.

"I mean to tell you all about it, my dear," said Mrs. Bloxam; "but if I am to do so, I must break through the reserve which I have always maintained—as I think it was best for both of us I should—and refer not only to your marriage"—Gertrude started—"but to later circumstances, which render your position difficult. I suppose I have your permission to speak plainly?"

"Certainly," replied Gertrude. "I am sure you would not, unnecessarily or without due consideration, say anything to wound my feelings; and I am prepared to listen to anything you think it right to say."

This was not a cordial speech, but Mrs. Bloxam did not mind that. She wanted permission to speak, and she had gotten it; the manner of it was of no consequence. Things had changed since Gertrude had written the letter which procured her readmittance to the Vale House, but the natures of the two women had not undergone much alteration, and they felt only as much more warmly towards each other as prosperity and success predispose towards general kindliness and complacency.

" You are right," said Mrs. Bloxam; "I would not. You have not told me any particulars concerning your quarrel with your husband, and I don't wish to know—I really do not. I am not more free from curiosity, no doubt, than other people; but I would rather not gratify it in this instance. There is only one thing that I must know, if you will tell it to me." She paused, and Gertrude said, looking steadily at her,—

"What is it? I may use my discretion about answering your question at all when I hear it; but if I decide on answering it, be quite sure that I will tell you the exact truth."

"No, you won't, my dear," said Mrs. Bloxam; "I don't require it. I want only the vague truth; tell me that. Is the secret of your quarrel with your husband one which puts him in your power—which secures your liberty, your right of action, to you under all circumstances—which makes the carrying out of this daring scheme of yours, this self-divorce, a matter distinctly of your choice, in which he cannot thwart or foil you?"

Gertrude's gaze at the speaker did not relax, her eyelids did not droop, but she took a little time before she answered.

"I will tell you what you ask. The secret of my quarrel with Gilbert Lloyd is one which puts him in my power. He *must* do as I choose in every matter in which I am concerned. I am perfectly free ; he is hopelessly bound. But the agreement between us is mutual. I have no right over him, as he has none over me. I shall never recognize his existence in any way."

" That you have the power of carrying out that resolution is the only thing I need to know," said Mrs. Bloxam. " It makes me clear about the advice I am going to give you. Having this perfect guarantee for his not venturing to interfere with you, you consider yourself of course entitled to act as if no such person as your husband were in existence. Have you any objection to tell me whether you are disposed to push this right of action to the extent of marrying again —of marrying Miles Challoner, for instance ? "

Mrs. Bloxam shifted her position as she asked this question, laid her head well back against the cushion of her chair, and did not look at Gertrude, who took longer to reply than before. When she spoke, the words came with difficulty.

" You must have some very strong reason for asking me such a question."

" I have, my dear. Mere curiosity, or even anything short of the necessity which exists for our understanding each other to a certain extent, would never have induced me to ask it. Will you answer me ? "

" Yes," said Gertrude, " I will. I acknowledge no limits to the extent to which I am disposed to push my right of action. I should marry without hesitation from motives of ambition ; I should marry without hesitation if the man were any but what he is—*if he were any one but Miles Challoner.*"

Mrs. Bloxam sat bolt upright, and gazed at Gertrude in irrepressible, unmixed amazement. " What do you say ? " she asked. " Can it be possible that we are all mistaken ? Lord Sandilands and I, and Miles Challoner himself—for he thinks you love him. I am as certain as I ever was of any human being's sentiments. Have you been blind to his love, his devotion to you ? What *do* you mean ? "

" I mean this," said Gertrude : " I know that Miles Challoner loves me ; he has told me so ; but I knew it before ; I have not been blind to his devotion ; and I love him." She paused. The listener's attitude and expression of uncomprehending astonishment remained unchanged. " I love him ; I know the difference now, and I know that what I once took for love did not deserve the name. I would not deceive *him;* I would not dishonour *him;* I would not involve *him* in the degradation of my life—for the degradation of the past is still upon me—for any joy the world could give me, not even for that of being his wife."

The passion and earnestness of her speech almost transformed Gertrude. She surprised Mrs. Bloxam so much, that all her previously-arranged line of argument escaped her memory, and she could say nothing but—

"Gertrude, Gertrude, you *do* astonish me !"

"Not more than I astonish myself, I assure you ; not so much. Before I knew him I don't think I could even have imagined what it was like to care more for the peace and happiness of another than for my own. I have learned what it is like now, and the lesson, in one word, means love. Go on with what you have to say to me, Mrs. Bloxam ; remembering in it all that I love Miles Challoner, and will never involve him in any way in my life."

"But this completely upsets what I was going to say to you," said Mrs. Bloxam ; "it changes the whole state of things, but it renders it no less necessary that you should make up your mind how you will explain matters to Lord Sandilands."

"To Lord Sandilands ?" said Gertrude, inquiringly. "What have I to explain to him, and why ?"

"Because he is Miles Challoner's friend and yours ; and because he knows that Miles wants to marry you, and most earnestly desires that the marriage should take place."

"*He* desires it ! How can that be ? How can a man of Lord Sandilands' rank wish his friend to make so unequal a marriage—a marriage which the world he lives in would so utterly condemn ?"

"Probably because he has lived long enough in that world to know that its opinion is of no great value, and to think that Miles Challoner had better consult his own happiness than its prejudices. He is a great friend and admirer of yours also ; and, in short, I may as well tell you plainly and abruptly, he sent for me to consult me on the best means of overcoming what he considers misplaced pride and overstrained delicacy on your part, and inducing you to consent to his arranging the preliminaries to the marriage ; I mean"—here Mrs. Bloxam hesitated a little—"settling everything as your mutual friend."

"It is well for him it cannot be," said Gertrude, bitterly, "or the world would hardly praise his conduct in helping Miles Challoner to a marriage with me. The interest Lord Sandilands takes in me deserves all my gratitude and as much of my confidence as I can give, and he shall have them. He may be displeased that his kind projects are not to be carried out, but he will understand that it is impossible."

"I don't see that he will understand it," said Mrs. Bloxam, "unless you tell him about your marriage ; and how are you to do that ?" She forgot for the moment that she spoke with the knowledge of Gertrude's parentage in her mind, but that Gertrude was quite ignorant of it.

"Tell Lord Sandilands of my marriage ! " said Gertrude ; "what can you be thinking of ? That must never be known *to any one;* he is a kind friend indeed, but nothing would induce me to tell him *that.*"

"I beg your pardon ; of course not," said Mrs. Bloxam, recovering herself, and remembering that the communication Lord Sandilands intended to make must not be forestalled. "Your resolution surprised me so much, I grew confused. But how will you account for refusing Mr. Challoner ? "

"I shall account for it," said Gertrude, "on the best grounds—grounds which would be adequate in my own judgment had I never made the fatal mistake of my miserable marriage. If I were nothing more than the world knows or believes me to be, I should still hold myself an unsuitable wife for *him,* and should still refuse him for his own sake."

"And this is what you will tell Lord Sandilands ? " said Mrs. Bloxam. "Gertrude, are you sure you can stand firm to your decision against the pleading of your lover and the support and arguments of your friend ? "

"I am quite sure," said Gertrude, "for I shall stand firm for their own sakes. To yield would be to injure, to hesitate would be to torment them : I will neither yield nor hesitate."

"Lord Sandilands wishes to see you as soon as you can come with me to see him," said Mrs. Bloxam. "I know he intends to urge Mr. Challoner's cause with all the argument and all the authority in his power."

"No argument and no authority can avail," said Gertrude.

"And you are determined to go on in this stage-life ?"

"Yes ; it is delightful to me in some respects, and it is independent and free. I don't say I have not had a struggle in reaching the determination I have arrived at, but I have reached it, and there is nothing more to be said or done. Whenever you choose, after a day or two, I will see Lord Sandilands ; he will help me to impress on Miles Challoner the uselessness, indeed the cruelty, of pressing a suit which can only pain me and avail him nothing. I shall convince *him* easily ; he knows the world too well to be difficult of persuasion of the justice of all that I shall say to him."

"It appears to me," thought Mrs. Bloxam, "that I shall get out of this business safely whatever happens, if she only perseveres in hiding her marriage ; and I don't think there's much danger of her not doing so."

"I am rather tired, dear," said Gertrude, after a pause, during which they had both kept silence, and turning towards Mrs. Bloxam with perhaps the sweetest smile and the friendliest gesture she had ever bestowed upon that lady ; "and I think we will not talk any more just now. Tell Lady Belwether I shall try to come down for a little this evening. I am far from suspecting the kind old lady of wishing me to tumble for the company ; but I should like to oblige her and the Dean, if possible."

Mrs. Bloxam took the hint. Gertrude was left alone, to endure all the agony caused her by the resolution she had taken ; but yet to feel that she derived strength from having taken it, and that to get her decision finally and authoritatively communicated to Miles Challoner by Lord Sandilands, with the addition of an earnest request that he would not remain in England at present, and subject her and himself to the pain of meeting, was a very sensible relief. The bitterness of the suffering through which she passed at this time never quite died out of Gertrude's memory. There was something in it which wrung her soul with a far keener and deadlier anguish than all the coarser, more actual miseries which had beset her miserable married life. By the measure of the increased strength and refine-ment of her feelings, of the growth of her intellect, and the development of her tastes, the power and the obligation to suffer in this instance were increased. Of the man whom she had once fancied she loved, Gertrude never thought with any distinctness either of abhorrence, fear, or regret. The few words she had spoken to him in the midst of the fashionable crowd where they had last met. had, she felt, effectually freed her from his pursuit henceforth; and in her present frame of mind, with her whole nature softened by her love for Miles, she was accustomed to look back rather on her own errors of judgment and perception as the fatal folly of her own girlhood, as the origin of her misfortunes, and to allow the sinister figure of her husband to slink in the backgrounds of her memory, something to be shunned and left in obscurity. In the wildest and deepest of her misery, and when her resolution was highest and sternest, there was one steadfast feeling in Gertrude's heart, by which she clung in all the tempest of emotion, while the clamour was loudest in her storm-tossed heart. It was the indestructible happiness of knowing herself beloved. Nothing could take that from her, whatever befell; life might have many more trials, many more deprivations in store for her, but it could not deprive her of that—not even change on his own part : and she did not think he would change. Very early in their acquaintance she had recognized, with the pleasure of a kindred disposition, the tranquil stability of Miles Challoner's character; but not even change could alter that truth, could efface that blessedness, could deprive her of that priceless treasure. She even asked herself, in the mood of mournful exultation in which she was, whether she could have felt this secret, subtle joy so keenly if she had not learned to distinguish the false from the true by such a terrible experience? If this had been a first love, could it have been so awfully dear and precious, a consolation so priceless, as to be hugged and hidden in her utmost heart; a talisman against misery, a talisman sufficiently powerful to subdue the anguish of its own ineffectualness, its own hopelessness? Could any girl unversed in the world's way, unskilled in the world's delusions, innocent and ignorant, knowing no ill of herself or others, have loved Miles Challoner as she loved him—this woman who had been brought in such close contact with crime, meanness, degradation, who had passed from girlhood to womanhood, on the border of respectability, with a tolerably uninterrupted look-out, very little space intervening over the debateable land of scheming, shifts, and general Bohemianism—this woman, whose dearest hope was to keep the knowledge of the truth about her—her life—her very name—from the man she loved ?

The task of speaking with Lord Sandilands, of destroying the hopes the kind old man cherished for his friend and for her, of defending the position she had to take up, for the destruction of all the prospect of happiness which life had to offer her, was not one to be contemplated with anything but intense reluctance. But Gertrude forced herself to the contemplation of it, and made up her mind to get the interview over as soon as possible. She had not forgotten that she had promised Miles to see him again, to speak with him again, on the subject of the suit he had urged. She knew well how impatient he would be ; but while her illness and seclusion continued, he would know the fulfilment of her promise was not possible. What if she made an effort to go down to the drawing-room to-night, and found him there —was forced to meet him in the presence of strangers ? She could not endure that ; she felt that her nerves, in such a trial, would refuse to obey her will. She would write a line to him, asking him to remain away from Hardriggs until he should hear from her again. There could be no harm in that ; but suppose he should be intending to come there that evening, the intimation of her wish would reach him too late. She rang the bell, and sent her maid for Mrs. Bloxam, to whom she propounded the difficulty.

"I know he will be here," Mrs. Bloxam said ; "Lady Belwether has just said so."

"Then I must write," said Gertrude, "and you must give him the note."

Mrs. Bloxam conveyed the few lines, in which Gertrude begged Miles to abstain from appearing in the drawing-room after dinner, to the hands of that anxious and almost-despairing lover, and he instantly obeyed the behest which it contained. Lord Sandilands' illness and need of his society furnished an excuse which was not only valid, but did him credit with his hostess and Mr. Dean, who was pleased to remark that his attention to his noble friend was a very gratifying spectacle, very gratifying indeed. When Miles rejoined his noble friend he told him most ruefully of the fresh rebuff he had received, and presented a doleful aspect anything but exhilarating to an invalid in want of cheerful companionship. Lord Sandilands did not seem to notice the depressed state of his spirits, but listened to him with an air rather of satisfaction than otherwise.

"Never mind, Miles," he said; "it's a good sign that she did not choose to meet you in the presence of a lot of strangers. Have patience, my dear boy, and I promise you, on the faith of your old friend, which never failed you yet, all will be well."

Miss Lambert made her appearance that evening in the drawing-room at Hardriggs for a short time. She was warmly congratulated on her recovery, and had many pretty things said to her about her temporary eclipse. She even ventured to sing—just one song; a simple but beautiful one, which went to the hearts of the company in general, and apparently to the nose of Mr. Dean in particular, as that dignitary used his handkerchief with prolonged solemnity while the concluding cadence was yet lingering in the air. It was agreed on all hands that never had Miss Lambert been more completely charming.

On the day but one after,—a bright, balmy day, when the earth looked its best, and the sky its bluest,—one of the Hardriggs equipages conveyed Mrs. Bloxam and Miss Lambert to Lord Sandilands' seaside abode. The visit had been duly notified by a message from Mrs. Bloxam, and the ladies had the satisfaction of learning that his lordship was much better, and quite able to receive them. They were ushered upstairs, and into a sitting-room on the first-floor. The room was empty, and the folding-doors which communicated with another room were closed. In a few moments they opened, and gave admittance to a middle-aged woman, plainly dressed, very respectable; the exact model of all a housekeeper ought to be. On her steady arm Lord Sandilands leaned, and, as he limped slowly towards his visitors with extended hand, expressing his pleasure at seeing them, Gertrude recognized in the housekeeper Mrs. Bush, and Mrs. Bush recognized in the lady whom she had heard announced as Miss Lambert the wife of her *ci-devant* lodger, Gilbert Lloyd.

———

CHAPTER III.

A MINE IS LAID.

REFUSED! rejected! Lord Ticehurst could scarcely believe it. "Declined the honour," she said; that was the way she put it. Declined the honour! "Whish!" went the whip over the heads of the roans, who became marvellously unsteady at the sound, and reared, and plunged, and pulled, and caused the middle-aged groom once again to peer over the head of the phaeton more nervously and uncomfortably than ever.

Lord Ticehurst could not understand the experience of the morning. The more he thought over it the more preposterous it appeared to him. Throughout the whole course of his life he had never had one wish thwarted. At Eton his fag did his exercises, and at Oxford the dons toadied him as dons only can toady; and in later life he had had henchmen innumerable, who had received his every word as law. As for this affair with Miss Lambert, he,—well, he didn't know; he had not been so cocksure about it at first, when he first began to be spooney on her. She was a deuced nice girl, there was no denying that,—clever, and all that kind of thing; sort of person that any fellow might be proud of to see sitting at the head of his table, and look deuced well at the Opera, and all that. Was not half so cocksure when he first began to be spooney; that was perhaps because he was spooney; fellows always thought they were not good enough for the woman they were spooney on; and—not good enough? that's a great notion! the idea of the Earl of Ticehurst not being good enough for —no, he couldn't say anything against her; she was an opera-singer, every one knew, but she was a perfect lady. O d—, what a nuisance it was! Since he had made up his mind to it he had begun to look upon it as quite certain, as a result about which there could not be the smallest doubt; and now he saw that all his conjectures had been false and his plans foundationless. What could be her motive? No

question of hoping to hook a larger fish ?   That was absurd.
Lord Ticehurst reflected with a certain amount of consolation
that there were very few larger fish than he in the waters
preserved for matrimonial angling, and of those few none
were likely to make Miss Lambert an offer.   Not any question
of personal objection ?   Even if such a thing were probable
to a person in his position, Miss Lambert's manner to him
had always been courteous, and occasionally cordial.   No one
could have been making mischief about him ?   No, he
thought not ; he did not go in to be straitlaced, and all that
kind of thing, any more than any other fellow of his age ;
but there was nothing that any one could lay hold of and
make a fuss about ; his name was not mentioned in con-
junction with any woman's, or anything of that kind that a
woman might find objectionable in the man who wanted to
marry her.   What, then, could it be ?   Could it be shyness,
modesty, and all that ?   Jove ! he'd never thought of that,
never looked at it in that light.   Could it be possible that
Miss Lambert had refused him because she did not feel herself up to the mark—didn't think herself equal to the
position he had proposed to her to occupy ?   The notion
was a very pleasant one to Lord Ticehurst ; it gratified his
vanity, and it gave him hope.   It might come off after all !
He had not had much experience of women—not of that
sort, at least—and it was impossible to make them out ;
there was never any knowing what to do with them.   After
all, perhaps, she only wanted a little more pressing ; he
certainly had nipped off rather sharp, without asking her to
explain, or anything of that kind.   He supposed that was
what fellows usually did,—asked the women " Why," and
all that sort of thing.   " Declined the honour," she said ;
perhaps if he had given her the chance she would not have
declined it a second time.   He would give her the chance ;
he would go over again to what's-a-name, old Belwether's
place, and tell Miss Lambert that he really meant it, and
that——

As the thought of "what's-a-name, old Belwether's place,"
passed through Lord Ticehurst's mind, simultaneously arose
therein the very uncomfortable recollection of having seen
Miles Challoner at the gate.   The young nobleman's spirits,
which had risen rapidly under the roseate influence of his
hopes, sunk at once to zero when he remembered that

Gilbert Lloyd had told him of the manner in which this man Challoner was making " strong running " for Miss Lambert, and bade him beware of him as a dangerous rival. Jove! that might account for her declining the honour, and all that. Of course it was a ridiculous thing to imagine any woman taking a fellow like Chaldecott—Challoner, or whatever they called him—before a man in his position; but one never knew, it was impossible to say; and—he did not know what the deuce to do one way or the other.

" Princes and women must not be contradicted," says the proverb. Young noblemen, or old noblemen for the matter of that, with health and wealth, are pretty much in the same category. For the first time in his life Lord Ticehurst found himself debarred from the fulfilment of a special wish, and he raged inwardly and chafed against his destiny. He could have cried from sheer spite and vexation; he stamped his foot in his rage, and once more startled the roans out of all propriety. He felt that he was morally " cornered ;" he did not like to give up all idea of this girl, for whom he had a certain liking and a certain passion, and in the possession of whom he would have had the justification of that pride which was perhaps the most thoroughly developed of all the various component parts of his character. On the other hand, he dared not run the chance of a second rejection, as the news of it might get wind, and he might be made to appear ridiculous; and, like most of his order, Lord Ticehurst was more afraid of ridicule than of anything else. To be laughed at had always been looked on by him as the greatest possible infliction, for he knew that neither his position nor his wealth rendered him invulnerable to " chaff ;" and he was sufficiently man of the world to feel that these advantages in themselves would tempt the aim and barb the arrows of the sharpshooters. He could not face it out, by Jove he couldn't! The mere thought of being bantered on the subject of his rejection by Miss Lambert gave an apoplectic hue to his lordship's cheeks, and brought large beads of perspiration on to his forehead.

" I couldn't stand it," he said half aloud, and forgetting the proximity of the serious groom. " 'Gad! I think I should go mad, and that kind of thing. Don't think I'll give old Gil the chance of having a crow over me just yet. He's sure to ask me how I got on, and all that, and I'd better hold it over for an hour or two. He's rather spiky in his chaff, I've noticed lately, Master Gil is; I don't know what's come to him!"

So, on further reflection, Lord Ticehurst struck off the road leading to Eastbourne, and turned back, tooling the roans along the St. Leonards parade, to the immense delight of the promenaders there assembled, and finally pulling up at the door of the principal hotel in Hastings. Here he alighted, and bidding his groom to bring the phaeton round at eight in the evening, entered the hotel, ordered an early dinner, and strolled out on to the parade.

A person in Lord Ticehurst's position and of Lord Ticehurst's habits is almost certain to find a number of acquaintances in every place of anything like pretension to fashion which he may visit; and his lordship had not lounged up the promenade for more than a dozen paces ere his arrival was known to as many persons. Old Lady Spills, who was always seated at the bow-window of her lodgings with a powerful opera-glass, marked the young nobleman's arrival at the hotel, and immediately called to her granddaughter, then resident with her, to get her hat and accompany her on the parade as quickly as possible. "Not that it's of any use," the old lady remarked to herself; "for Julia is as stupid as an owl, and not likely to be attractive even to the most innocent of youths, much less to a young man like this, who is, no doubt, perfectly able to take care of himself." The Duke of Doncaster, a melancholy old man, in a crumpled wig and dyed whiskers, wearing the bell-hat, large-checked neckerchief, and cutaway green coat of the past generation, was driving his team up and down the parade, solemnly and methodically as was his usual afternoon practice, and he recognized Lord Ticehurst's presence by jerking his whip-elbow into the air in true coachman-like fashion. The sisters Lavrock, of the Scandinavian Opera and the nobility's concerts—brave little women, who in the off-season went round to the different watering-places, and made a good deal of money by giving a little musical entertainment—blushed and giggled in great delight as his good-natured lordship stopped them on the promenade, and inquired with unaffected interest after their well-doing. That eminent landscape-painter Scumble, R.A., who had often met Lord Ticehurst at Carabas House, over

which mansion he seemed to have the right of free warren,
happened to be staying at Hastings, partly for the sake of
studying marine effects, partly for the purpose of pacifying
Mrs. Scumble, who had but a dull time of it in London;
and he tore off his wideawake as he met Lord Ticehurst's
eye, and pretended to have nothing to do with Mrs.
Scumble, who at that moment was a little way off, placidly
bargaining for a shell pincushion.　Lastly, Bobby Maitland
—who had come ashore for two days from Mr. Stackborough's yacht, with the view of meeting his solicitor, and
settling pecuniary matters during his absence—Bobby
Maitland, looking over the blind of the coffee-room of the
Marine Hotel, along which blind he had been thoughtfully
rubbing his nose, spied his lordship, and announced his discovery to his friend Stackborough in these flattering terms :
"By Jove, Haystacks, old man, here's that ass Ticehurst!"

"Haystacks" and "old man" were both terms of en-
dearment and familiarity.　Mr. Stackborough was about
three-and-twenty, very rich, very foolish, and with an irrepressible yearning for what he called "high society."　He
had chambers in the Albany, splendid horses, a capital
yacht, and more clothes than any other man in London.
He was always extensively got-up, and never looked like a
gentleman.　Bobby Maitland, who lived with him and on
him, could influence him on everything except his wardrobe
—in that matter he always would have his own way.　On
the present occasion he was elaborately appareled in
maritime fashion, dark-blue jacket with gilt buttons, very
open white waistcoat, flap shirt-collar, trousers tight to the
knee, then loose and flapping, black oilskin-hat with blue
ribbon.　Mr. Stackborough generally suited his language
as far as possible to his style of costume.　When that was
horsey he talked turf, now he talked sea; consequently he
said—

"Ticehurst, eh ?　Where does he hail from ? "

"How the deuce should I know! " replied Bobby.
"He's only just come in sight."

"T'other craft in company, of course ? " suggested Mr.
Stackbrother.　"He's always under convoy, Ticehurst is !
T'other craft's close by, I suppose, or at all events in the
offing."　And Mr. Stackborough peered from under his
hand at his friend as though scanning the horizon.

"Look here, Haystacks, old man!" said Bobby Maitland thoughtfully; "you must moderate your transports, you must indeed. There's too much of this bold-smuggler business about you—a deal too much. I daresay it's a kind of gaff that takes with some people, but it don't with me, and so you may as well drop it. It isn't good style either; so drop it, old flick, and tell me in the Queen's English what you mean."

Mr. Stackborough wriggled uneasily in the maritime suit and blushed. "All right," he said, after a minute's pause, "I'll take care. Thank you for telling me, Bobby. What I meant to say was, wasn't Lloyd there? He's always with Ticehurst, you know."

"O, I understand now; No; Ticehurst seems to be by himself for a wonder. No doubt Lloyd's close at hand, though; he never lets my lord go far without him."

"Shall we 'bout ship and—I mean, shall we go out and speak to him?" asked Mr. Stackborough. It *was* so difficult to resist the influence of the maritime garments.

"Well, yes; there's no harm," said Bobby, knowing his young friend was dying to speak to and be seen speaking to a recognized "swell."

So Mr. Stackborough put on the glazed hat with the blue ribbon, and they strolled into the street. Now, though Lord Ticehurst did not much affect Bobby Maitland, and had a great contempt for Mr. Stackborough, he had such a horror of being alone and being thrown on his own resources for amusement, that, as soon as he saw these gentlemen approaching, he brightened up, and received them with a warmth which completely captivated Mr. Stackborough. Bobby Maitland was older and less enthusiastic. He disliked Ticehurst; and as he knew there was nothing to be got out of his lordship, he always spoke to him with charming frankness.

"We could scarcely believe it was you, Etchingham," said he, after the ordinary salutations had been exchanged.

"O, ah!" replied his lordship, "didn't expect to find me in this place, eh?"

"Well, no, perhaps one wouldn't have thought of finding you here. Nothing going on that you can understand—horses, I mean, and that kind of thing. But that was not what I meant."

" What did you mean, then ?" asked his lordship, somewhat crossly, for he understood and appreciated the sneer.

" Well, we didn't think you were ever let out without your dry-nurse—Lloyd, don't you know ? Don't be angry old fellow, it's only my chaff ! "

" It's a deuced bad style of chaff," said Lord Ticehurst, who had grown very white, and whose lips trembled as he spoke,—" a deuced bad style of chaff ; and I'll trouble you not to try it on me, Mr. Maitland ! "

" ' Mr.' Maitland ! Come, that be hanged !" said Bobby, who saw that he had gone a little too far. " I'm very sorry if I've offended you, Etchingham, and I apologize. I can't say more."

The good-natured young man accepted the apology at once, and the three walked on together. Lord Ticehurst, then explaining that he was only in the town for a few hours, and that he had ordered a solitary dinner at the Queen's Hotel, was easily persuaded to let Mr. Stackborough (who was too delighted to fetch and carry for a lord) go and countermand it, while his lordship agreed to dine with his new-found acquaintances at the Marine. So, to the intense delight of Mr. Stackborough, they strolled up and down the parade, listening to the band, looking after the pretty women, and criticising the horses. " Haystacks' " conversation became almost unintelligible during this walk ; for Lord Ticehurst being eminently horsey, and the talk running on the breeding and look of horses, Mr. Stackborough would, under ordinary circumstances, have turned on the turf tap, and drawn his idioms from the stable ; but the maritime clothes still from time to time asserted their influence, and the result was that the unfortunate youth got into a series of linguistic knots which he could not untie, and with which no one could assist him.

The dinner at the Marine was a success. Boffham, who keeps the hotel, had been *chef* to Count Krammetsvogel, of the Hanoverian embassy, in former days, and had turned out many excellent official dinners, of which Lord Ticehurst's father had partaken. When he heard that the young lord was to be a guest of one of his guests, Boffham went himself to the kitchen, and showed that neither Time nor the gout had robbed his hand of its cunning. The wines too—notably some Chateau Yquem and some Stein-berger Cabinet, which had been bought by Boffham out of the Krammetsvogel cellar when the count was recalled— were delicious; so delicious, that many bottles were drunk, and the hearts of the drinkers were warmed, and their tongues loosened. Something which Bobby Maitland had said to him when they first met that day had stuck in Lord Ticehurst's throat. He had tried to swallow it, but the attempt had been unsuccessful. Under the influence of the wine he felt he must mention it—he could see no reason why he should not.

"Bobby!" he said, as they were sipping their claret, "my horses will be round in a minute; but I want to say two words to you before I go.—Don't you move, Mr. Stacks,"—Stackborough made a kind of blundering attempt to rise,—"don't you move, there's nothing secret or private," —here Lord Ticehurst looked long and earnestly at the wick of the candle close by him, then proceeded—"or at least, if there is, you're far too good a fellow, Stacks, to—to—you know what I mean.—So do you, Bobby."

"All right, Etchingham, old boy, I know," said Mr. Maitland. "What do you want to say?" Mr. Maitland had to repeat his question, Lord Ticehurst having again become absorbed in the contemplation of the candle. "What do you want to say?"

"What do I want to say?" said his lordship, after a pause—"ah, that's just it! I wonder—O, I know! Don't you know when you folks first met me to-day, you said something, Bobby—something about Lloyd?"

"Yes, I recollect—what then?"

"You asked me where my nurse was, or something of that sort, didn't you?"

"I think I did."

"Ah! just tell me, like a good fellow—is that the way men talk about me and Lloyd?"

"What way?"

"Do they say that he—that I—that he's like what you said—my nurse?"

"They say you daren't call your soul your own without his leave. That you never move hand or foot without him; some say he washes you and parts your hair; but that's

their way of putting it. What they mean is, that he's your
master, and you're his most obedient."

"And do you think Lloyd knows they say this?"

"Knows they say it!" repeated Bobby Maitland, with a
loud vinous laugh; "knows they say it! why, he says it
himself; boasts of it!"

"The deuce he does!" said Lord Ticehurst, rising with
an unsteady gait. "That must be stopped! There are
some things that a man can stand; and there are some
things he——My carriage. Thank you!—Good-night, Mr.
Stacks; very glad to have looked you up.—Good-night,
Bobby; see you at Doncaster, I suppose? No! well, then
—never mind.—Right, Martin!" and his lordship dashed
off at a tremendous pace, while the serious groom, who had
seen his master reel on the phaeton-step, looked more
serious than ever as he jumped up behind.

When the other two gentlemen returned to their room,
Mr. Stackborough said, "He didn't half like what you
said about Lloyd just now. Shouldn't wonder if there was
a row when he gets home."

"Serve Master Gil deuced well right," said Maitland;
"I've owed him one for a long time, and now I think I've
paid him. Teach him to give himself airs over me next
time we meet in the ring."

"Devilish pleasant, gentlemanly fellow is Etchinghurst,"
said Mr. Stackborough, steadying himself by holding on to
the table.

Bobby Maitland regarded him with a smile. "His name
is Etchingham, not Etchinghurst; but you're not sufficiently
intimate with him to call him anything but Lord Ticehurst.
Haystacks, dear old boy, you've had too much wine; have
a tumbler of soda, plain, and go to bed."

There was no reason for the serious groom's apprehensions,
so far as the safety of his person was concerned. It is a
received axiom that the effects of intoxication are increased
when gentlemen labouring under them are exposed to the
influence of the air; and the groom's perturbation was
probably based upon this theory. He had not, however,
probably made allowance for the fact—which possibly had
never come within his ken—that when the mind is actively

at work it becomes an admirable counter-irritant to the influence of the wine. That feeble nonsense of the hiccupping toper of the past generation relative to the drowning of dull Care in bowls was as void of reason as of rhythm. That men in good spirits will have those spirits made livelier by good drink in good company is intelligible enough ; but dull Care—whatever he may have suffered in the three-bottle days—declines to be drowned or in any way got rid of by such a quantity of liquor as is at the present time drank in society. The confirmation of his suspicions about Gilbert Lloyd, which Bobby Maitland had communicated with so much charming frankness to Lord Ticehurst, had had a singularly sobering influence on the young nobleman. The anger arising in his heart seemed to have chased away the fumes which had been obscuring his brain ; and after he had been five minutes on the road he was in as good condition as he ever was—which, perhaps, is not saying much—to think the matter calmly through. It was a lovely night ; the roans, knowing they were on their homeward journey, stepped out splendidly and refrained from indulging in any of the capers and antics which had characterized their morning's performance ; and Lord Ticehurst, getting them well in hand, settled himself down to think over all he had heard, and to endeavour to arrive at some definite conclusion before the end of his drive.

Was it what we have no adequate expression for, but what the French call the *vin triste*, that was exercising its malign influence over the young man ? Had his "potations pottle deep" but resulted in stirring up dull Care instead of drowning him ? Had Boffham's Chateau Yquem and Steinberger Cabinet an effect exactly opposite to that of the waters of Lethe ? Certain it is, that as Lord Ticehurst rolled rapidly homewards his memory, which very seldom troubled him, was actively at work, and his reflections were of anything but a pleasant character.

So they said that he was a mere child in Gilbert Lloyd's hands, did they ?—that he dare not call his soul his own ; that he had no will, no opinion,—chaffed, and said Lloyd was his dry-nurse, did they ? Pleasant that, by Jove !—to have things like that said about you by fellows to whom you had always been civil and polite, and all that kind of thing —more than that, hospitable, and letting them stand in with good things, and putting them on to everything you knew. And they went about and said this—not before your face, of course ; they would not do that ; but thought it before your face, and went about and said it as soon as your back was turned. Made you their laughing-stock and their butt ; poked their fun at you all the time they were eating your dinners, and made game of you while they borrowed your money. It was d——d unfriendly and blackguard conduct ; that's what it was. And Bobby Maitland was as bad as any of them—worse, for he would never have heard of it but for him. They all thought he was a fool, and Bobby must have thought so too, sneering about him and Gilbert Lloyd, and pretending to think he would not notice it. He would let them see pretty sharp he was not such a fool as they took him for ; let them see he knew how they laughed at and chaffed him. Next time any of them wanted a fifty for a fortnight, that would be the time. They should laugh the wrong side of their mouths then, he would take care. Called himself a gentleman too, did Bobby Maitland, and gave himself airs because he was a peer's son. Why, damme, that other chap, that poor fellow, Haystacks, or whatever his name was, with all his ridiculous nonsense about his get-up and all that, he was more of a gentleman than Bobby Maitland. He looked quite queer and uncomfortable, Haystacks did, when Maitland was going on all that chaff about the nurse.

About the nurse ? That riled him more than anything else. "How was it he was let out without his nurse ?" That's what Maitland had said. As he thought of that speech Lord Ticehurst kicked out against the splashboard in front of him, startled the roans into a gallop, and woke the groom from an elysian dream of eating boiled beans and bacon in the back-parlour of a public-house which was his own. And when he had asked if Gilbert knew about the chaff that was going on, Maitland said he did, and, more than that, had started it and laughed at it himself. Could that be true ? He could scarcely think that ; he had been so doosid kind to old Gil, and doosid fond of him, and done all sorts of things for him one way or the other, and he did not believe old Gil would go against him in that way. Fellows are always talking about ingratitude and that kind of thing, but he did not think any one would be such a thorough-paced duffer as to go in against a fellow who had shown him nothing but kindness ever since he had known him. Ever since he had known him? Well, that was not so long ago, when he came to think about it, but it seemed like his whole life. He thought with an odd kind of incredulous wonder on that portion of his life anterior to his acquaintance with Gilbert Lloyd. The Plater-Dobbs *régime* seemed like a dream. He was a vulgar old cad, the Plater, but he would not have played double, he would not have allowed any of the fellows to chaff. No fellows had ever been allowed to chaff him, even at Eton—Eton, hey presto! At that reminiscence the clouds rolled away, and scenes of bygone time and the actors in them, unthought of for years, rose before the young man's mind. Some of those fellows who had been with him at Eton, and were now doing so well and making such stir in the world—Brackenbury, who had made such a hit in the House, and who, everybody said, would be A1 some of these days; and Graves, who had written a devilish clever book about something; and Hammond, who was under-secretary in one of those office-places down at Whitehall, and who the newspapers said was a rising man, and all that. Lord! he recollected when he first went to Eton, his old governor took him, and—— What a crowd there was when they buried his governor in the family-vault at Etchingham! He recollected Lord Tantallon the Premier standing at the foot of the grave after the service, and looking in, with the tears running down his face. No end of official swells came down to see the last of their old colleague. He recollected seeing the great black marble top of the tomb, which had been taken off, lying on its side among the weeds; and he remembered the smell of the newly-turned earth, and the trodden turf, and he could see just as plainly as on the day itself the men from the London newspapers bending over to read the inscription on the coffin. Poor old governor! he was a clever fellow, and was awfully respectable and respected. He would not think much of the life his son was leading, mixed up with horses and betting-people and jockeys, and all that kind of thing. Whew! it could not be helped, he supposed. It was too late to change it. Steady there! Arrived!

When Lord Ticehurst entered the rooms in the hotel

which he occupied conjointly with Gilbert Lloyd, he found
that gentleman asleep on the sofa, with a decanter of brandy
on a small table by his side.   The decanter was half-empty;
and when Gilbert, awaking at the noise made by his friend's
arrival, turned round, his face, especially round the eyes,
had a strained, flushed look, and his voice, when he began
to speak, was rather thick and husky.

"Hallo!" he said, raising himself on his elbow, and shad-
ing his eyes with his other hand, "you've got back!"

"Yes," replied his lordship; "here I am!"

"Perhaps the next time you are going to stop out to
dinner you will have the goodness to say so."

"Don't be cross, old man; you knew I was going, fast
enough."

"I knew you were going out to luncheon, but there
was nothing said about dinner, I believe; and as to being
cross, it's enough to make a fellow savage, having had to
cool his heels about here for an hour and a half, waiting
dinner for a man who never came; and then to sit down
to a lot of stuff cooked to rags, half cold, and quite un-
eatable."

"Sorry for that, Gil," said Lord Ticehurst with unim-
paired good-humour; "very sorry, but you should not have
waited."

"Oh, I like that!" said Lloyd; "and suppose your lordship had not had your dinner, and had come in when I
had half-finished mine, you would have been pleased, wouldn't
you!"

"I don't suppose 'my lordship,' as you call me, would
have cared one straw about it.   What a rum fellow you
are, Gil!   What's the matter with you to-night, that you
are going on in this way?"

"Going on in what way?   I merely suggested that it
would have been pleasanter if you had said you would
not be back to dinner, and——"

"But I didn't know that I should not.   I had no intention of stopping when I went away.   Can't you understand!"

"O yes, I understand!   *Chapeau bas, chapeau bas!*
However, that's no matter now.   I ought to have known
that the young lady would suggest your stopping there—
that the old Belwethers would be delighted to receive a
person of your lordship's quality, and that——"

"There, you may drop that silliness as soon as you like. It's very funny, I daresay; but it's all thrown away, because I didn't stop at Hardriggs after all."

"The deuce you didn't! Why, where did you dine, then?"

"At the hotel at Hastings, with Bobby Maitland and that young fellow he's always about with now—Haystacks."

"I know," growled Gilbert. He hated Maitland, and half-despised him, as men do their unsuccessful rivals. "What on earth made you dine with them?"

"Well, I don't know," said the earl, blushing a little, in spite of vigorous attempts to prevent it and look unconcerned. "I—I had stopped later there than I intended at Hardriggs, and I thought you would have dined, and so I put up at Hastings, and those fellows saw me and asked me to dinner."

"And you went, deuced Samaritan-like and benevolent, and all that, I declare! That fellow Stackborough will be set up for life; there will be no holding him, now that he has once dined in company with a real live earl."

"Well, I don't know; Mr. Stackborough seemed to me to behave like a gentleman."

"O yes; but you like a fellow who bows down before you, Etchingham, we all know that; and it's natural enough. However, that's neither here nor there. What about the object of your visit to Hardriggs? You saw the young lady?"

"Yes, I saw her."

"And you carried out your intention?"

"What intention?" asked Lord Ticehurst, summoning up courage, and looking his friend full in the face. And then Gilbert knew for certain, what he had decidedly anticipated, that Lord Ticehurst had been rejected by Gertrude.

"What intention?" he replied, with a sneer already dawning on his face; "why, the intention of proposing to Miss —what does she call herself?—Miss Lambert."

"Yes," said Lord Ticehurst quietly, "I carried out that intention."

"Well, and we are to ring the joy-bells, and to roast the whole ox, and set the barrels of ale flowing, and order the bishop to be in readiness at St. George's, and select the new carriages, and have Etchingham new furnished. And when are we to do all this?"

"Not just now, at all events," said Lord Ticehurst. "First catch your hare, don't you know?" and his lordship tried to look knowing—a process in which he failed sublimely.

"Why, you don't mean to say that——"

"I mean to say that I proposed to Miss Lambert—you know her name fast enough—and she refused me."

"Refused you!" screamed Gilbert with admirably-assumed astonishment; "refused you,—the opera-singer, the tragedy-queen, the Princess Do Re has refused my lord with his thousands and his tens of thousands! The world is coming to an end! People will next question the value of an hereditary legislature. You astound me!"

"I'll tell you what, Lloyd," said Lord Ticehurst sulkily, "I wish you to drop that style of chaff; I don't see the fun of it."

"You never saw the fun of anything, Etchingham ; it is not your *métier ;* Providence has ordained otherwise. It's for us poor devils to see the fun that you big swells make for us."

Rage swelled within Lord Ticehurst's heart as he listened to these words, which were so eminently corroborative of what Bobby Maitland had said to him, and of what he had thought to himself on his homeward drive. But he controlled himself, and said :

"Well, what I see or what I don't see don't matter much just now. Perhaps I see more than some people think I do ; more than I give tongue about, that's certain. However, I don't care about being chaffed on that subject, and so please drop it."

"Poor old boy !" said Lloyd, with an elaborate affectation of compassion ; "of course he's very sore, that's natural enough : and of course it comes much harder to a fellow in his position, who thinks that he has only to lie under the wall and the ripe cherries will tumble into his mouth, to find that they sometimes hang on the stalk and *won't* tumble. It puts me in mind of the little stories in one syllable that we used to learn at school. 'There was once a small boy, and he cried for the moon, and when——' "

"D—n it, sir, will you stop?" cried Lord Ticehurst, angered beyond all patience. "Look here, Lloyd, you and I have been friends for a long time ; but if you go on in this way I shall——"

"What?" interrupted Gilbert, turning quickly on him.

"Cut the whole concern, stock, lock, and barrel," said his lordship, "and part from you for ever."

The two men stood confronting each other ; Lord Ticehurst flushed and heated, Lloyd wonderfully pale and calm, and only betraying agitation in the twitchings of the muscles of his mouth. He was the first to speak.

"Part from me for ever, eh?" he said in slow deliberate tones, each word clipping out from between his thin tight lips. "O no, you wouldn't do that! You are not very wise, Lord Ticehurst, but you would not be such a fool as to quarrel with or part from the man who has made you what you are. Ah, you may stare and pretend to be astonished, but I repeat, who has made you what you are. And you need not come down upon me, as you are going to—I see it! —with the whole long story of your birth and position and status, and all the rest of it. I know all that from *Debrett ;* and still I stick to my text,—that I made you what you are! The time has come—you have brought it about, not I ; I could have gone on for ever as we were—but the time has come for plain speaking ; and I say that whatever you are, and whatever you may be thought of in the world, you owe to me, to me ; without whom you would have remained the unformed cub you were when I found you in the hands of that old duffer, Plater Dobbs!"

The prospect of a row with his pupil—not a separation, of course, but a brisk breeze to freshen up the tamely-flowing current of their ordinary life—had often occurred to Gilbert Lloyd. He had thought over calmly what should be his conduct under such circumstances, and he had determined upon using the strongest possible "bounce," and acting in the most offensive and most truculent manner. His remembrance of Lord Ticehurst's behaviour in the quarrel with the Frenchman, M. de Prailles, at Baden, prompted him to this line of action, and he found it was the correct one. Lord Ticehurst did not knock him down, or fling a chair at him, or take any other prompt and decisive step. His cheek flushed angrily, certainly, but he only said :

"Major Dobbs might have been a duffer, as you say he
was, but at all events he did not pitch into people who were
kind to him, didn't blackguard them before their faces, as
some people do, or what's worse, make game of them behind
their backs."

He laid such stress on this last sentence that Gilbert
Lloyd looked hard at him, and said, "Make game of you
behind your back! What do you mean by that?"

"What I say," said Lord Ticehurst; "chaffin' about my
not being able to do anything without asking you, and you
being my dry-nurse, and all that kind of thing!"

"Ah, ha!" said Gilbert Lloyd; "you haven't dined with
our friend Bobby Maitland for nothing! That's his stab,
I'll swear. Now look here, Ticehurst, you've talked about
our parting, and I never let a man threaten me twice. So
part we will. We must wait over Doncaster, because there
are some things coming off there in which we are mutually
interested; but after that I'll square up all the accounts and
hand over everything to you."

He looked hard at his pupil as he said these words,
expecting that the announcement would evoke a burst of
protestations and disavowals. But Lord Ticehurst merely
said "Very well; all right;" and took up his candle and
left the room.

CHAPTER IV

PERPLEXITY.

L ORD SANDILANDS was looking and feeling ill and
feeble, and was mainly occupied, as he hobbled across
the not-magnificently-proportioned drawing-room of that
most desirable lodging-house, with an unrivalled view of the
Esplanade, in so putting down and moving his feet as to
cause himself the least possible pain, when he came, leaning
on the arm of his housekeeper, to meet Mrs. Bloxam and
Miss Lambert. But he was a man of too quick perception
at all times, and his mind had been dwelling of late with so
much anxiety upon Gertrude and her interests, that he was
additionally keen in remarking every incident in which she

was concerned. As he put out his disengaged hand and took Gertrude's, he glanced from her face to that of the housekeeper, and back to hers again, and saw that each recognized the other.

"You know Mrs. Bush?" he asked, still holding Gertrude's hand in one of his, still leaning with the other on Mrs. Bush's arm.

"Mrs. Bush and I have met before," Gertrude answered calmly ; " but she does not know my stage name. I am a singer, Mrs. Bush," she added ; "and my stage name is Lambert."

"O, indeed, ma'am!" said Mrs. Bush, in a singularly unsympathetic voice, and with an expression which said pretty plainly that she did not think it signified much what the speaker called herself.—"Shall I put your lordship in the chair near the window?"

"Yes, yes," said Lord Sandilands testily ; and then he added, with the perversity of age and illness, "and where did you know Miss Keith, Mrs. Bush?" He seated himself as he spoke, drew the skirts of his gray dressing-gown over his knees, and again looked from one to the other. Mrs. Bloxam, to whom the scene had absolutely no meaning, stood by in silence. Gertrude was very calm, very pale, and her eyes shone with a disdainful, defiant light, as they had shone on the fatal day of which this meeting so vividly reminded her. Mrs. Bush smiled, a dubious kind of smile, and rubbed her hands together very slowly and deliberately, as she answered :

"If you please, my lord, I didn't never know a Miss Keith. It were when the young lady was Mrs. Lloyd as she come to my house at Brighton."

"When the young lady was Mrs. Lloyd!" repeated Lord Sandilands in astonishment, and now including Mrs. Bloxam, who looked extremely embarrassed and uncomfortable in the searching gaze he directed towards the housekeeper and Gertrude. "What does this mean?"

"I will explain it to you," said Gertrude firmly but very gently, and bending over him as she spoke ; "but there is no occasion to detain Mrs. Bush." The tone and manner of her words were tantamount to a dismissal, and so Mrs. Bush received them. She immediately retreated to the door, with an assumption of not feeling the smallest curiosity concerning the lady with whom she was thus unexpectedly brought into contact, and left the room, murmuring an assurance that she should be within call when his lordship might want her. A few moments' pause followed her departure. The astonishment and vague uneasiness with which Lord Sandilands had heard what Mrs. Bush had said kept him silent, while Gertrude was agitated and puzzled— the first by the imminent danger of discovery of her carefully-kept secret, and the second by hearing Lord Sandilands allude to her as " Miss Keith." When she thought over this strange and critical incident in her life afterwards, it seemed to her that something like a perception of the truth about to be imparted to her came into her mind as Lord Sandilands spoke. Mrs. Bloxam experienced a sensation unpleasantly akin to threatened fainting. What was coming? Must all indeed be told? Must her conduct be put in its true light before both Gertrude and Lord Sandilands? Could she not escape either of the extremes which, in her mental map of the straits in which she found herself, she had laid down? But she was a strong woman by nature, and a quiet, self-repressed woman by habit, and in the few moments' interval of silence she did not faint, but sat down a little behind Lord Sandilands, and with her face turned away from the light. As for the old nobleman himself, the mere shock of the dim suspicion, the vague possibility which suggested itself, shook his composure severely, through all the restraint which his natural manliness and the acquired impassiveness of good breeding imposed. Gertrude was the first to speak. She stood in her former attitude, slightly leaning over him, and he sat, his head back against the chair, and his keen, gray, anxious eyes raised to her handsome, haughty face.

" You sent for me, my dear lord, my good friend," she said,—and there was a tone in the rich, sweet voice which the old man had never heard in it before, and in which his ear caught and carried to his heart the echo of one long silent and almost forgotten,—" and I have come ; in the first place to see you, to know how you are, and to satisfy myself that this illness has had nothing alarming in it. In the second place, that I may hear all you mean to say to me ; I know about what,"—her eyes dropped and her colour rose—" Mrs. Bloxam has told me ; she has fully explained all your kindness, all your goodness and generosity to me. Will you tell me all you intended to say to me, and let me say what I meant to say to you, just as if Mrs. Bush had never called me by that strange name in your hearing, and then I will explain all." The lustrous earnestness of her face rendered it far more beautiful than Lord Sandilands had ever before seen it. Her mother had never looked at him with that purposeful expression, with that look which told of sorrow and knowledge, and the will and resolution to live them down.

"I will do anything you wish, my dear," said the old nobleman ; and it was remarkable that he discarded in that moment all the measured courtesy of manner which he had hitherto sedulously preserved, and adopted in its stead the deep and warm interest, the partial judgment, the protecting tone of his true relationship to her. "Sit here beside me, and listen. I have some painful things to say, but they will soon be said ; and I hope—I hope happy days are in store for you ; " but his face was clouded, and doubt, even dread, expressed itself in his voice. Gertrude did not exactly obey him. Instead of taking a seat, she placed herself on her knees beside his chair ; and in this attitude she listened to his words.

"I know how it is with you and Miles Challoner, my dear, and Miles is dearer to me than any person in the world except one,—and that one is you."

"I !" said Gertrude, amazed. "I dearer to you than Miles Challoner, your old friend's child ! "

"Yes," he said, with a faint smile, "for you are my own child, Gertrude ; that is what I sent for you to tell you, and I want to make you happy if I can." So saying, the old man took her bent head between his hands, and kissed her. Gertrude did not evince any violent emotion—she turned extremely pale, and her eyes filled with tears ; but she did not say anything for a little while, and she afterwards wondered at the quietness with which the revelation was made and received. She was not even certain that she had been very much surprised. Mrs. Bloxam rose, opened the window, stepped out upon the balcony, and carefully closed the window behind her. During a considerable time she might have been observed by the numerous promenaders on the Esplanade, leaning over the railing, which was more ornamental than solid, in an attitude of profound abstraction. By those within the room her very existence was forgotten until, in the course of their mutual interrogation, her name came to be mentioned. Still kneeling beside him, but now with her head resting against his breast, and one long thin white hand laid tenderly upon the bright masses of her chestnut hair, Gertrude heard from her father the story of her mother's brief happy life and early death ;—and the sternest might have forgiven the old man the unintentional deception which was self-delusion, which made him tell his daughter how only that early death had prevented his making Gertrude Gauthier his wife. For the first time he realized now in the keenness of his longing, in the misery of his dreaded powerlessness to secure the happiness of his child, the full extent of the injury inflicted upon her by her illegitimate birth.

"I know," he said, "that Miles loves you, and I think you love him, and I know you would be happy. I have lived long enough in the world, and seen enough of it, to know how rarely one can say that with common sense and justice of any two human beings. Tell me, Gertrude, why it is that you have refused Miles,—why it is that you seem determined not to let me smooth away all obstacles to your marrying him ? "

The conversation had lasted long, and had embraced many subjects, before it reached this point. Gertrude had undergone much and varying emotion, but she had not lost her calmness, partly because of her exceptional strength of mind and body, and partly because she never suffered herself to forget the danger of over-excitement to Lord Sandilands. She had listened quietly to the story of her mother (the idea of actually learning about her own parentage, and being able to realize it, was quite new to her—and abstract sentiment was not in Gertrude's way), and had rendered to it the tribute of silent tears. She had heard her father tell how he had first recognised her at Lady Carabas' concert, and how he had felt the strong instinctive interest in which he had never believed, and which he had never practically experimented in, arise at the sight of her ; how he had found first with misgiving, and afterwards with increasing pleasure, ratified and approved by his conscience because of his knowledge of Miles Challoner's tastes and character that his young friend and companion was attached to her. She had heard him tell how he had watched the ill-success of Lord Ticehurst's suit with pleasure, and how he had won Miles to confide to him his hopes and plans, and encouraged him to hope for success, and then had been induced by her refusal of Miles and his belief that that refusal was dictated by disinterested regard for Challoner's worldly interests, and in no degree by her own feelings, to take the resolution of telling her all the truth—upon which resolution he was now acting.

So far Gertrude had been wonderfully composed. Her father had said to her all he had urged with himself, when he had been first assailed by misgivings that his old friend would have resented his endeavouring to bring about a marriage between Miles and a woman to whom the disadvantage of illegitimate birth attached ; and she had assented, adding that while she only knew herself utterly obscure, she had felt and acted upon the sense of her own inferiority. The conversation had strayed away from Gertrude's early life—the father met his acknowledged daughter for the first time as a woman, and they made haste to speak of present great interests. Mrs. Bloxam might have been quite easy in her mind about the amount of notice her share in any of the transactions of the past would be likely to excite. But now, when Lord Sandilands pleaded earnestly the cause of Miles Challoner, and in arguing it argued in favour of the weakness of Gertrude's own heart, her fortitude gave way, and a full and overwhelming knowledge of the bitterness of her fate rushed in upon her soul. The veil fell from her eyes ; she knew herself for the living lie she was ; she realized that the unjustifiable compact she had made with her husband was a criminal, an accursed convention, bearing more and more fruit of bitterness and shame and punishment, as her father unfolded the scheme of a bright and happy future which he had formed for her.

"If he had been any other than Miles Challoner," she had said to Mrs. Bloxam, she would have married him, would have incurred the risk for rank and money—or she had thought so, had really believed it of herself. What had possessed her with such an idea ? What had made her contemplate in herself a creature so lost, so utterly, coldly wicked ? It was so long since she had permitted herself to think of her real position; she had deliberately blinded, voluntarily stultified her mind for so long, that she had ceased to feel that she was playing a part as fictitious off, as any she performed on, the stage. But now, as her father's voice went on, speaking lovingly, hopefully, telling her how conventionalities should be disregarded and wealth supplied in her interests; telling her she need have no fear in the case of such a man as Miles—had he not known him all his life ?—of any late regret or after reproach ; now the tide of anguish rushed over her, and with choking sobs she implored him to desist.

"Don't, don't!" she said. "You don't know—O my God!—you don't know—and how shall I ever tell you? There is another reason, ten thousand times stronger ; all the others I gave were only pretences, anything to keep him from suspecting, from finding out the truth ; there is a reason which makes it altogether impossible."

"Another reason ! What is it ? Tell me at once—tell me," said Lord Sandilands; and he raised himself in his chair, and held her by the shoulders at arms' length from him. Dread, suspicion, pain were in his face ; and under the influence of strong emotion, which reflected itself in her features, the father and daughter, with all the difference of colouring and of form, were wonderfully like each other.

"I will tell you," she said ; but she shut her eyes, and then hid them with her hand while she spoke, shrinking from his gaze. "I will tell you. I am not free to be Miles Challoner's wife. I am married to another man."

"Married ! You married ?"

"Yes," she said, "I am married. Your housekeeper knows me as a married woman. The name she called me by is my real name. You know the man who is my husband, unhappy wretch that I am !"

"Who is he ?" said Lord Sandilands, hoarsely, his nerveless hands falling from her shoulders as he spoke. She looked at him, was alarmed at the paleness of his face, and rose hurriedly from her knees.

"You are ill," she said. "I will go——" But he caught her dress, and held it.

"Tell me who he is."

"Gilbert Lloyd !"

Gertrude was horrified at the effect which the communication she had made to her father had upon him. He had set his heart strongly indeed upon her marriage with Miles Challoner, she thought, when the frustration of the project had the power to plunge him into a state of prostration and misery. As for herself, the alarm she experienced, and the great excitement she had undergone in the revelation made to her by her father, the agony of mind she had suffered in the desperate necessity for avowing the truth, were quickly succeeded by such physical exhaustion as she had never before felt. This effect of mental excitement was largely assisted by the weakness still remaining after her illness, and was so complete and irresistible, that when she had seen the doctor hurriedly summoned to Lord Sandilands by Mrs. Bloxam's orders—that lady's meditations on the balcony had been terminated by Gertrude's cry for help—and learned that the patient was not in danger, but must be kept absolutely quiet, she yielded to it at once.

Not a word was said by Mrs. Bloxam to Gertrude concerning the disclosure made by Lord Sandilands. In the confusion and distress which ensued on the sudden attack of violent pain with which her father was seized, Gertrude lost sight of time and place, and thought of nothing but him so long as she was able to think of anything. Little more than an hour had elapsed since Lord Sandilands had told her the secret of his life, and she was speaking of him freely to Mrs. Bloxam as her father, and the word hardly sounded strange. She could not return to Hardriggs; she was not able, even if she would have left Lord Sandilands. There was no danger of her seeing Miles if she remained at St. Leonards. Lord Sandilands had told her early in their interview that he had sent Miles up to town, and procured his absence until he should summon him back by promising to plead his cause in his absence. She and Mrs. Bloxam must remain—not in the house, indeed, but at the nearest hotel. She would send a message to that effect to Lady Belwether, and inform Mrs. Bush of her intention.

Mrs. Bush had not relaxed her suspicious reserve during all the bustle and confusion which had ensued on the sudden illness of Lord Sandilands. She had been brought into contact with Gertrude frequently as they went from room to room in search of remedies, and ultimately met by the old nobleman's bedside after the doctor's visit. Mrs. Bush did not indeed call Gertrude "Mrs. Lloyd" again, but she scrupulously addressed her as "Madam;" and there was an unpleasant, though not distinctly offensive, significance about her manner which convinced Gertrude that not an incident of the terrible time at Brighton had been forgotten by the *ci-devant* lodging-house keeper, whose changed position had set her free from the necessity of obsequiousness.

Gertrude had taken a resolution on the subject of Mrs. Bush, on which she acted with characteristic decision, when at length her father was sleeping under the influence of opiates, and she and Mrs. Bloxam had agreed that their remaining at St. Leonards was inevitable. She asked Mrs. Bush to accompany her to the drawing-room, and then said to her at once :

"You are surprised to see me here, Mrs. Bush, no doubt; and as I understand from Lord Sandilands that he has great confidence in you, and values your services highly, I think it right to explain to you what may seem strange in the matter."

Mrs. Bush looked at the young lady a little more kindly than before, and muttered something about being much obliged, and hoping she should merit his lordship's good opinion. Gertrude continued :

"It will displease Lord Sandilands, to whom I am closely related, if the fact of my being married is talked about. I am separated from Mr. Lloyd, and it is customary for singers to retain their own names. Mine is Grace Lambert. If you desire to please his lordship, you may do so by keeping silence on this subject, by not telling any one that you ever saw me at Brighton under another name."

With the shrewdness which most women of her class and calling possess by nature, and which the necessities of her struggling career as a lodging-house keeper had developed, Mrs. Bush instantly perceived her own interest in this affair, and replied very civilly that she was sure she should never mention anything his lordship would wish concealed; and that she was not given to gossip, thank goodness! never had been when she had a house herself, and which her opinion had always been as lodgers' business was their own and not hers. Consequent, she had never said a word about the poor dear gentleman what had died so sudden, —at this point of her discourse Gertrude's jaded nerves thrilled again with pain,—although it had injured her house serious. With a last effort of self-command, Gertrude listened to her apparently unmoved, and dismissed her, with an intimation that she should return in the morning to take her place by Lord Sandilands. Mrs. Bush had both a talent and a taste for nursing invalids, and she established herself in the darkened room, there to watch the troubled sleeper, with cheerful alacrity. Her thoughts were busy with Gertrude, however, and with what she had said to her. "So she's his near relation, is she?" thus ran Mrs. Bush's cogitations. "*What* relation now, I wonder? Lambert is not a family name on any side, and he called her Miss Keith too—and I'll be hanged if *he* knew she was married! I'm sure he didn't. There's something queer in all this; but it's not my affair. However, if his lordship asks me any questions, I'm not going to hold my tongue to him. Separated from Mr. Lloyd! I wonder was she ever really married to him? She looked like it, and spoke like it, though; a more respectable young woman in her ways never came to my place, for the little time she was in it. I wonder what she has left him for?—though in my belief it's a good job for her, and he's a bad lot."

The hours of the night passed over the heads of the father and the daughter unconsciously. With the morning came the renewed sense of something important and painful having taken place. On the preceding evening, Gertrude had entreated Mrs. Bloxam to refrain from questioning her. "I am too tired," she had said. "I cannot talk about it; let me rest now, and I will tell you everything in the morning." To this Mrs. Bloxam had gladly assented; she was naturally very anxious, and not a little curious; but anxiety and curiosity were both held in abeyance by the satisfaction she experienced in perceiving that the revelations which had been made had not seriously injured her position with Lord Sandilands or with Gertrude. The mutual recognition between Gertrude and Mrs. Bush had been unintelligible to her. That it had produced important results she could not doubt; but on the whole, she did not regret them. The acknowledgment of Gertrude's marriage might prevent future mischief, in which she (Mrs. Bloxam) might possibly be unpleasantly involved, and at present it was evident that, in the overwhelming agitation and surprise of the discovery, her conduct had been entirely forgotten or overlooked. That she might continue to occupy a position of such safe obscurity was, for herself, Mrs. Bloxam's dearest wish; and Mrs. Bloxam's wishes seldom extended, at all events with any animation, beyond herself.

Lord Sandilands awoke free from pain, but so weak and confused that it was some time before he could bring up the occurrences of yesterday, in their due order and weight of import, before his mind. He had received a shock from which his physical system could hardly be expected to recover; but the extent of the mental effect—the fear, the horror, the awakening of remorse, not yet to be softened into abiding and availing repentance—none but he could ever estimate. The past, the present, and the future alike menaced, alike tortured him: the dead friend, the sole sharer of whose confidence he was; the dead man's son, whom he loved almost as well as if he were of his own flesh and blood; the dead woman, whom he had deceived and betrayed (in the wholesome bitterness of his awakened feelings Lord Sandilands was hard upon himself, and ready to ignore the ignorance which had made her a facile victim); the dreadful combination of fate which had made the daughter whom he had neglected and disowned the wife of a man whose tremendous guilt her father alone of living creatures knew, and had thrown her in the path of that same guilty man's brother, to love him and be beloved by him. In so dire a distress was he; and this girl whom he loved with an anxious intensity which surprised himself, imprisoned in the hopeless meshes of the net in which his feet were involved. No wonder he found it hard, with all his natural courage, and all the acquired calmness of his caste, to marshal these facts in their proper order, and make head against the dismay they caused him. But this was no time for dismay. He had to act in a terrible emergency of his daughter's life, and to act, if indeed it were possible for any ingenuity or prudence to enable him to do so, so that the real truth of the emergency, the full extent of its terrible nature, should be known to himself alone, never suspecteb by her. The housekeeper came softly to the old nobleman's bedside while his mind was working busily at this prodlem, the most difficult which life had ever set him for solution; and seeing his eyes closed and his face quiet, believed him to be still sleeping, and withdrew gently.

By degrees, the facts and the necessities of the case arranged themselves somewhat in this order. Gertrude had told her father of her marriage, of the misery which had speedily resulted from it, and of the strange bargain made between her husband and herself. She knew Lloyd's worthlessness then, though she had spoken but vaguely of him as a gambler and a reckless, unprincipled man, not giving Lord Sandilands any reason to think she could regard him as capable of actual crime. The shock of the disclosure Gertrude had imputed simply to his horror of the clandestine nature of her marriage, and the moral blindness and deadness which had made the bargain between her and Lloyd present itself as possible to their minds (the light of a true and pure love had shone on Gertrude now, and shown her the full turpitude of the transaction); his sudden seizure had prevented his hearing more than a brief, bare outline of the dreadful episode of his daughter's marriage. She knew nothing of the real, appalling truth; she was ignorant that the man she had married was a criminal of the deepest dye, the secret of his crime in her father's hands, his own brother the object of her affections, and the only possible issue out of all this complication and misery one involving utter and eternal separation between her and Miles Challoner. If he and Gertrude ever met again, she must learn the truth; she must learn that Gilbert Lloyd was Geoffrey Challoner, and an additional weight of horror and anguish be added to the load of sorrow her unfortunate marriage—in which Lord Sandilands humbly and remorsefully recognized the consequence, the direct result, of his own sin—had laid upon her. If she could be prevented from ever knowing the worst? If he, invested with the authority and with the affection of a parent, could induce her to consent to an immediate separation from Miles Challoner, to a prompt removal from the possibility of seeing him, by strengthening her own views of the insuperable nature of the barrier between them? She would not, however, yield to Miles's prayer for their marriage; but that would not be sufficient for her safety: she must never see him more; she must be kept from the misery of learning

the truth. How was this to be done? For some time
Lord Sandilands found no answer to that question; but at
last it suggested itself. Miles—yes, he would make an
appeal to him; he would tell him all the truth—to him who
knew that Lord Sandilands also possessed that other secret,
which, to judge by its consequences, must be indeed a
terrible one; and Miles would be merciful to this woman,
who, though she had sinned by the false pretence under
which she lived, was so much more sinned against; and,
appearing to accept her decision, Miles would not ask to see
her again. Yes, that would do; he was sure that would
succeed. And then he would acknowledge Gertrude as his
daughter to all who had any claim to an explanation of any
proceedings of his—the number was satisfactorily small—
and he would leave England for ever, with Gertrude. It
was wonderful with how strong and irresistible a voice
Nature was now speaking to the old man's heart; how all
the habits and conventionalities of his life seemed to be
dropping suddenly away from him, and something new, but
far more powerful, establishing itself in their stead as a law
of his being. The tremendous truth and extent of his
responsibility as regarded Gertrude presented themselves to
him now in vivid reality, and the strongest desire of his
heart was for strength, skill, and patience, to carry out the
plan which presented itself for her benefit. He felt no
anger towards her for what she had done. Poor motherless,
fatherless, unprotected girl, how was she to understand the
moral aspect of such a deed? He pitied the folly, but he
did not seriously regard the guilt, while he deplored the consequences. Gertrude's professional career, he saw at once,
must come to an immediate and abrupt close. There was
no safety for her in the terrible unexplained attitude of the
brothers Challoner, and her total unconsciousness of it and
its bearing upon her own fate, but absence from the scene
of the secret drama. With the grief of her hopeless,
impossible love at her heart, and with the help and safety of
her new-discovered relationship to him, security for her
future and escape from the present, Gertrude would not
hesitate about abandoning her career as a singer. It had
never had for her the intoxicating delight and excitement
with which such a success is invested for the fortunate few
who attain it; and as for the world, the lapse of the

brilliant star from the operatic firmament would be a nine-days' wonder, and no more, like such other of the episodes of her story and his as the world might come to learn. That part of the business hardly deserved, and certainly did not receive, more than the most passing consideration from Lord Sandilands. It was all dreadfully painful, and full of complications which involved infinite distress; but Lord Sandilands began to see light in his difficult way. It was not until he had thought long and anxiously of Gertrude and of Miles that his mind turned in the direction of Gilbert Lloyd; and then it was with inexpressible pain that he contemplated the fact that this man, whom of all men he most abhorred, was the husband of his daughter; had had the power to make her girlhood miserable, to blight her life in its bloom, and to continue to blight it to the end. How great a villain Gilbert Lloyd was, he alone knew; but no doubt Gertrude had had considerable experience of his character. On this point he would find out all the truth by degrees. His thoughts glanced for a moment at the probable effect it would have on Lloyd when he should discover that the one man in the world in whose power he was, was the father of his wife, and had constituted himself her protector. At least there was one bright spot in all this mass of misery : knowing this, Lloyd would never dare to molest Gertrude, would never venture to seek her or trouble her, in any straits, however severe, to which his un-principled life might drive him. In this perfectly reasonable calculation there was but one item astray : Lord Sandilands had no suspicion of the state of feeling in which Gilbert Lloyd now was with respect to his wife. If he had known the fierce revival of passion for her, and the rage which filled his baffled and desperate heart, Lord Sandilands would not have looked with so much confidence upon the prospect of suffering no molestation from Lloyd. Whether his tigerish nature could ever be wholly controlled by fear, was a question to which no answer could yet be given. But Lord Sandilands did not ask it, and his thoughts had again reverted to Miles, and were dwelling sadly on the caprice of fate which had brought his brother once more so fatally across his track, and had erected so strange a link between the calamity which had overshadowed his dead friend's life and that which must now be the abiding sorrow of his own when the arrival of the doctor interrupted his musings, and obliged him to confess to being awake.

When the visit was concluded, with a favourable report but many cautions on the part of the medical attendant, Lord Sandilands inquired of Mrs. Bush when the arrival of the two ladies might be looked for. They had already sent to ask how his lordship was, and would be there at eleven. Lord Sandilands then bethought him that the recognition of the preceding day, which had no doubt led to his receiving his daughter's confidence, and being preserved from blindly pursuing a course of persuasion and advocacy of Miles Challoner's suit, which might have led to most disastrous consequences, could now be made still more useful, as affording him an opportunity of learning more about his daughter's married life than she had had time or probably inclination to tell him.

The old man looked very weak and curiously older all of a sudden, and Mrs. Bush, a kind-hearted woman in her narrow little way, was sorry to see the change. The sympathy in her manner and voice inspired Lord Sandilands with a resolution somewhat similar to that one which Gertrude had noted on the previous day. He asked Mrs. Bush to take a seat, requested her best attention to what he was going to say, and then told her without any circumlocution that the lady called Grace Lambert, whom she had known as Mrs. Lloyd, was his daughter, whom he intended to acknowledge and to take abroad with him. The housekeeper showed very plainly the astonishment which this communication occasioned her, and her embarrassment was extreme when Lord Sandilands continued : " And now, Mrs. Bush, I wish you to tell me all you know about my daughter, and all that occurred while Mr. Lloyd, from whom she separated immediately afterwards, lodged at your house at Brighton."

" Of course, my lord," replied Mrs. Bush, in a nervous and hesitating manner, " I cannot refuse to do as your lordship wishes, nor do I wish so to do ; but Mrs. Lloyd did not lodge at my house at all in a manner ; she only came there unexpected, and went away at night, after the poor gentleman died, as were took so sudden—dear, dear, how sudden he were took, to be sure ! "

" What gentleman ? I don't understand you. Pray tell

me the whole story, Mrs. Bush ; don't omit any particulars you can remember ; it is of great importance to me."

Mrs. Bush possessed no ordinary share of that very common gift of persons of her class—circumlocution, and she told her story with a delightful sense of revelling in the fullest details.   Her hearer, not under ordinary circumstances distinguished for patience, neither hurried nor interrupted her, but, on the contrary, when he asked her any questions at all, put to her such as induced her to lengthen and amplify the narrative.   When the housekeeper took her seat beside his bed, Lord Sandilands had been lying with his face towards her.   As she progressed in her account of the sojourn of Gilbert Lloyd and Harvey Gore at her house, he turned away, and lay towards the wall against which his bed was placed, so that at the conclusion of the story she did not see his face.   Ashy pale that face was, and it bore a fixed look of horror ; for, bringing his own secret knowledge of Gilbert Lloyd to bear upon the story told by the housekeeper, Lord Sandilands readily divined what was that swift, unaccountable illness of which Lloyd's friend had died, what the irresistible power his wife had wielded in insisting upon the separation which had taken place.   "The wretched girl !   What must she not have suffered !" the father thought.   "Alone, in the power of such a man, in possession of such a secret, whether by positive knowledge or only strong suspicion, no matter. Good God, what must she not have suffered !   What has she not yet before her to suffer ! "

Here, as he afterwards thought, in reflecting upon the unconscious disclosure which Mrs. Bush had made to him— here was another barrier against any possible molestation of Gertrude by her husband, a horrible truth to grasp at with something like ghastly satisfaction.   But horrible truths were all around them in this miserable complication, on every side.

"Thank you," said Lord Sandilands, when Mrs. Bush had concluded her narrative.   "I am much indebted to you for telling me all these particulars.   You will oblige me very materially by not mentioning the subject in any way to any one."

Mrs. Bush was aware that Lord Sandilands not only

possessed the means but the inclination to make it very well worth any one's while to oblige him, so she immediately resolved upon maintaining undeviating fidelity to the obligation he imposed upon her ; and she afterwards kept her resolution, which she found profitable.

When Gertrude arrived, Mrs. Bush met her with a request that she would go to his lordship at once, which implied that Mrs. Bloxam was to remain in the drawing-room. This she did, composedly occupying herself with needlework, and feeling her hopes that she should be entirely overlooked in the crisis of affairs growing stronger and stronger. It may as well be said here, once for all, that these hopes were justified. Mrs. Bloxam was never called to account by Lord Sandilands for his money, or her own conduct.

"I take it upon myself, my dear," said Lord Sandilands to his daughter, when many hours passed in close and mournful consultation between them had gone by ; " as soon as I am able to move—and, you see, I am greatly better already—the arrangements shall all be made."

From the bed where he lay, the old man's eyes were turned anxiously, sadly, towards the figure of his daughter. Gertrude was seated in a deep chintz-covered chair, in the bay of the window, which overlooked a small garden of the sterile and sandy order, familiar to the memory of occasional dwellers in seaside lodging-houses. She was leaning forward, her head resting on her hands, her arms supported by a little three-legged table, her attitude full of grace and dejection. The afternoon sun tinged her pale cheek and her clustering hair, but for the moment the brilliance that was so characteristic of her appearance was gone. But she touched the old man's heart all the more keenly for the lack of brilliancy, for she was more like her mother without it,— the dead mother whom she had never seen, and whose name had as yet been barely mentioned between them.

"Yes," she said, absently, drearily, "I must leave it all to you. How strange it is to me to know that I have you to help me, to leave it all to!"

"You will not pine for the excitement and applause to which you are so accustomed, Gertrude?"

"No; they have been very wearisome to me of late, since I have known how much might have been mine that never can be now."

"No indeed, my dear," said her father earnestly, "it never, never can be now; and your true courage, your true good sense is in acknowledging this at once, and consenting to turn your back upon it all promptly. You shall have none of the misery of severing these ties; I will write to Munns, and tell him I am ready to indemnify his real or imaginary losses."

"It will cost you a great deal of money," she said, still absently, still drearily.

"It is almost time that I began to spend it on *you*," said her father, with a very unsuccessful attempt at a smile.

The past, the present, and the future had been discussed during the hours they had passed together, and emotion had worn itself out. Steadily keeping in mind the concealment he desired to practise, and the effect he designed to produce, the old nobleman had received the confidences which his daughter—who more and more strongly felt the tie between them hour by hour, and softened under its influence—imparted to him with the utmost tenderness and indulgence, but with as little effusion as possible. He had induced her to tell him the whole truth concerning her separation from her husband; and had received the terrible revelation with calmness which would have perhaps shocked Gertrude had she not been too much absorbed in the newer, sacred sorrow of her hopeless love to perceive as keenly as was her wont, had she not also been much exhausted physically, and thus mercifully less sensible to impressions. She had also told him of Gilbert Lloyd's late pursuit of her; and at that portion of her narrative Lord Sandilands ground his still strong white teeth with furious anger, and a thrill of exultation mingled with the rage and misery of the circumstances, as he thought how utterly this villain was in his power, how soon he would set his foot upon his neck and see him writhe in impotent anguish and humiliation. But this was one of the feelings which he had to conceal from Gertrude, and he did effectually conceal it.

The plan decided upon was that Gertrude and Mrs. Bloxam should return on that evening to Hardriggs, and

terminate their stay there as soon as possible ; and then go
to London and occupy the interval which must elapse before
Lord Sandilands could travel, in making preparations for
departure. The pretty villa was to be given up ; the
household gods which Gertrude had gathered around her
were to be dispersed, and her life was " to begin over again."
Is there any drearier phrase than that ? can words represent
any harder fact, any more painful idea ? Then Lord Sandilands and his daughter would go abroad, and leave the
English world behind them, to think and say just what it
might please. The place of their abode was not even discussed. All foreign countries were alike new to Gertrude,
and old to Lord Sandilands. One little point of detail had
been mentioned between them. If Gertrude wished it, her
father would take Mrs. Bloxam with them. He inclined to
the belief that it would be better not ; better to be away
from every one connected with the past, from which it was
their wish, their object to escape. And his daughter agreed
with him, as did Mrs. Bloxam, when the matter was
mentioned to her. She hated foreign countries—her trip to
Italy was a standing grievance—and she was very glad to
retire from her post of *chaperone* to Miss Lambert, with such
a handsome present in money from Lord Sandilands—an ill-
deserved acknowledgment of her services—as, added to the
savings she had accumulated at the Vale House, rendered her
free from the presence or the apprehension of poverty. When
the time of parting came, this lady, on the whole a not
unfortunate member of society as human affairs are constituted, took leave of Lord Sandilands and his daughter with
the utmost propriety ; and it is more than probable that by
this time she has ceased to remember their existence.

Gertrude took leave of her father, when the appointed
time came for her return to Hardriggs, with little visible
emotion. She was dazed and exhausted ; and it was not
until the events of the last few days were weeks old, and she
passed them in review under a foreign sky, in a distant land,
far away from the man she loved and the man she hated,
that she began to realize them in detail, and to feel that she
had, indeed, " begun life over again."

When Lord Sandilands contemplated the prospect of the
interview he was about to have with Miles Challoner, he
shrunk from it with dread. But he had to go through with

it; and perhaps the most painful moment of the many painful hours he and his friends passed together was that in which the young man advanced to him with beaming looks with outstretched hand, with agitated voice, and said, " You have sent for me? you have good news for me?"

The task was done—the task in which the old man felt the hand of retribution striking him heavily through the suffering of those he loved—the pain was borne, and the day after that which witnessed the arrival of Gertrude and Mrs. Bloxam in London saw Miles Challoner leaving the great city for Rowley Court, where he shut himself up in such gloomy seclusion that the people about began to talk oddly of it. Somehow the Court seemed an unlucky place, they said. First, the mysterious disgrace and banishment of the younger son; then the lonely, moping, moody life of the Squire; and now here was the young Squire going the same gait. There was surely something in it which was not lucky, that there was, and time would tell.

The world did talk, as they had anticipated, of the departure of Lord Sandilands and Miss Lambert for foreign parts; and as it was some little time before it got hold of anything like a correct version of the story, it started some very pretty and ingenious theories to account for that " unaccountable " proceeding. Managers were savage, *débutantes* delighted, and Lady Carabas, who knew nothing whatever of the matter, was charmingly mysterious, and assured every one that her dear Grace had been guided in everything by her advice, and that that dear Lord Sandilands was the most perfect of creatures, and had behaved like an angel. And then, in even a shorter time than Lord Sandilands and Gertrude had calculated upon, the world, including Lady Carabas, forgot them.

CHAPTER V.

AN EXPLOSION.

WHEN Gilbert Lloyd awoke the next morning after an excellent night's rest, his first impression was that something disagreeable had happened on the previous evening, but it was some time before he could exactly recollect all the circumstances and pass them calmly in review before him. Even when he had done so he felt by no means certain how far matters had gone. He had taken too much of that infernal brandy, he remembered with disgust—taken it because he had been brooding over that business at Brighton which happened years ago, it is true, but which some confounded fate seemed to have set people talking about lately. He had not thought about it, it had never troubled him, and now he found his mind continually running on that one subject. It must have been the constant references made by those about him to—to his wife that must have turned his thoughts in that direction. Curses on that Sunday regulation of shutting the telegraph-offices! If he had only been able to send that telegram as he had originally intended early in the morning, it would have stopped her coming down, and prevented her having that fatal hold over him, of which she is well aware, and which she is determined to exercise if necessary. It was thinking last night of all these things combined that had sent him to the brandy-bottle, a dangerous habit, which seemed to be growing upon him, he thought, and which he must at once break himself of, as ruinous and destructive of all chances of keeping that clearness of brain which was to him a vital necessity. He was muddled the previous night ; he felt it then ; he only saw through a glass darkly what had happened, and the retrospect was by no means agreeable. Etchingham had annoyed him, he recollected that ; and he had replied without measuring his language, and the result had been that they had agreed to part. O yes, now he remembered what Bobby Maitland had told Etchingham about him. What an idiot he had been to make a row about such a thing as that ! He knew well enough that Bobby Maitland had been trying all he knew for years to supplant him in Etchingham's confidence, that he was awfully jealous of him, and would say or do anything to get a rise out of him. He must have taken an amount of brandy to have made such an ass of himself. It was a comfort to know that Etchingham was sure to be all right in the morning, and to be in a great fright at what had occurred. He knew his pupil well enough to be certain of that. No doubt his lordship had also dined, and had taken quite enough of Mr. Stackborough's wine. They were both of them excited, no doubt, but he must take care and stand on his dignity, and then Etchingham would come round at once.

So, thinking over these things, Gilbert Lloyd took his cold sea-water bath, which got rid of most of the ill effects of the previous night, and having leisurely dressed himself, descended to the room where breakfast was laid. He was the first; Lord Ticehurst had not yet appeared. So Gilbert took up the newspaper, and after glancing at the state of the odds and the sporting intelligence generally, remained expectant. He had not to wait very long. In a few minutes Lord Ticehurst, looking very white and seedy, and with his small eyes more tightly screwed up and sunk more deeply into his head than usual, entered the room. Gilbert bade him "good morning," which his lordship, walking round the table and flinging himself into an easy-chair, only answered by a short nod. He then rang the bell, and on the waiter's appearing, ordered brandy and soda-water. This, Lloyd argued to himself, was merely the effect of the "morning after," the result of too much indulgence in Stackborough's wines. His lordship's digestion was impaired and consequently his temper suffered: both would improve simultaneously. But after his brandy and soda-water, Lord Ticehurst pulled his chair to the table, and commenced and proceeded with a very excellent breakfast, during the discussion of which he said never a word to his anxiously-expectant confederate, while, at its finish, he lit a big cigar, and, still mute, armed himself with a telescope, flung open the window, and stepped into the balcony to inspect the exhibition of the naiads bathing in the foreground.

For once in his life Gilbert Lloyd was nonplused. He had made perfectly certain that Etchingham would have cried peccavi, would have come to him begging to have their relations replaced on the old footing; and here was the recalcitrant apparently quite at ease, not taking the least notice of him, and obviously rather enjoying himself than otherwise. Had he been blind, or had Etchingham's character suddenly changed? One thing was quite certain, that all was going wrong, and that he must take prompt measures to set himself right. Gilbert Lloyd was not an adept at leek-swallowing. He had played his cards so well during the latter portion at least of his life that he had seldom been required to perform that humiliating feat, but he saw that he must do it now. Lord Ticehurst was, like most good-natured men, intensely obstinate and sulky when affronted, and though Lloyd had had no experience of this state of his pupil's mood so far as he was regarded, he had seen it evidenced against others. It was perfectly plain that one of these fits, and a very strong one, was on Lord Ticehurst at present, and Lloyd was compelled to acknowledge to himself that if he wanted to retain his position in the future he must knuckle under unreservedly and at once.

He laid down the newspaper which he had made a pretence of reading, and looked towards the window. There, in the balcony, sat his lordship, the light-blue smoke from his cigar curling round his head, and his eye fixed at the telescope which he held in his hand. Gilbert rose and went behind him, but Lord Ticehurst, although he must have heard the footstep, never moved. Then Gilbert laid his hand on his pupil's shoulder, and said, "Etchingham!"

His lordship moved his eye from the telescope, and looked quietly at Lloyd. "Well?" said he, in a sufficiently sulky manner.

"I have come to ask your pardon. I——"

"O, there, that's all right," said his lordship, preparing to recommence his performance with the telescope.

"No, it's not all right. You and I have been intimate allies for a very long time. Until last night there has never been a word of difference between us. Nor would there have been then but for the infernal meddling of people who——"

"O, just look here! I didn't name any names, remember. It was you who said you knew Bobby Maitland had been making mischief."

"It was I; I acknowledge it. You are quite right. You are far too good a fellow to say a word against even such a bad lot as that. I lost my temper, and I spoke out. But why? Because I was in a tremendous rage at the impudence of that fellow Maitland daring to put his own words, and his own sentiments into my mouth, and to pretend that I had said them. His own words and sentiments, I say, and no on else's."

"What! Do you mean to say that you never said—all that confounded stuff about the 'nurse,' and all that?"

"I pledge you my word of honour I never said anything of the kind."

Lord Ticehurst looked straight at him as he said these words, but Gilbert Lloyd met the look firmly, without the smallest increase of colour, without the movement of a muscle in his face.

"Well," said his lordship, after a momentary pause, "of course after that I cannot say any more. I was most infernally riled when I heard you'd been chaffing about me, I'll allow; because, after all, don't you know, when you and a fellow have lived together, and been regular pals, and that kind of thing——"

"And you thought I could have been such a scoundrel as to do that? No, Etchingham, I don't pretend to be straitlaced, and I don't go in to be demonstrative and gushing in my affection for you, like those duffers who are always hanging about you in town, and whose game you see through perfectly, I know. My regard for you I endeavour to show in another way, in devoting myself heart and soul to the management of your affairs; and if you look into them I think you'll find that I am faithful and true to you."

Into his voice, as he uttered these last words, Gilbert Lloyd threw a little tremulous touch of sentiment, which gave evidence of a hitherto undeveloped histrionic ability, and which was really excellent of its kind. It was so close an imitation of the genuine article that most people would have been taken in by it, and Lloyd looked to see a responsive twinkle in his pupil's eyes; but, clever and telling as it was, it failed to touch Lord Ticehurst. He said, "All right, Gilbert, old fellow; of course I know that. Here, there's an end of it!" and he stretched out his hand; but there was no heartiness, no enthusiasm in his tone, no warmth in the grasp he gave, and Gilbert Lloyd recognized all this, and began to feel a dim prescience that his hold on his lordship was beginning to wax faint, and that his position as chief manager of Lord Ticehurst's affairs was manifestly insecure.

Was Gilbert Lloyd's luck really beginning to fail him?

Had the devil, who had stood his friend so long, and aided him in his advancement so wonderfully, grown tired of and forsaken him? It seemed like it, he was forced to confess to himself. By nature cool, crafty, and clear-headed, and from long practice in matters in which the exercise of those qualities is constantly required, Lloyd was by no means a man to suffer himself to remain blind to any danger which might threaten him. There are men amongst us passing for sane, nay, even reputed to be clever, who obstinately shut their eyes against the sight of the chasm towards which they are pressing forward, who are obstinately deaf to the roar of the avalanche which in a few seconds must overwhelm them, when by merely striking out into a new path—not so pleasant indeed, and that is mostly what they look at—they might avoid their fate. These are the men who, Micawber-like, are always expecting something to turn up, who refuse to see the plainest portents, to listen to the most obvious warnings, who think that bills disregarded are payments indefinitely deferred, and who put away unpleasant-looking letters unopened with the idea that the bad news they bring will thereby be staved off, who go on *quo Fata ducunt*, and who are astonished when they find themselves involved in misery and ruin. Gilbert Lloyd was very different from this. Let a cloud, even though it were " no bigger than a man's hand," appear above the horizon, and he took note of it instantly. He was specially observant of the slightest change in the character or demeanour of those with whom he was brought in contact, even of persons of inferior grade. In fact, although for a long time past his life had been one of comparative ease and undoubted luxury, he had never forgotten the habits acquired in the early days of poverty and shifting and scheming, when his hand was against every man and every man's hand against him, and he was prepared to go to the end of the world, or out of it altogether for the matter of that, if he saw plainly the necessity of absconding, or felt that his Fate had arrived.

Was his luck going? Was his game nearly played out? There had been a great change lately, without a doubt ; he must not shut his eyes to that. Etchingham was certainly changed. Very civil and acquiescent in all that was suggested to him, never referring to their dispute on that unlucky night, but still without a particle of the heartiness which formerly characterised him, and which was the salt of his otherwise unpleasant disposition. There had been a turn of luck, too, in turf matters. Some of his own private speculations (for Gilbert had a book of his own in addition to the "operations" in which he had a joint interest with Lord Ticehurst, and was said also to do a great deal by anonymous commission) had been very unfortunate during the past season, and so far as he could see he was not likely to recoup himself by any success at Doncaster, where one of Lord Ticehurst's cracks had been disgracefully beaten for the Cup, while another, which had been one of the leading favourites for the Leger, had run down the scale in the most alarming manner, and was now, on the eve of the race, scarcely mentioned in the betting.

Was his luck going? Was his game nearly played out? *Venit summa dies et ineluctabile fatum!* Where had he heard that, Gilbert Lloyd wondered as he sat on the edge of his bed at the Angel Inn at Doncaster, turning all these things in his mind. *Ineluctabile fatum.* He gave a half-shudder as he repeated the words, and he gulped down half the tumbler of brandy standing on the table by his side. He felt a *frisson* run through him—that kind of creeping feeling which silly old women ascribe to the fact of some one " walking over your grave" —on which the brandy had no effect, and he stamped his foot in rage at his weakness. He was all wrong somehow ; out of health, perhaps? But his clear sense refused to be deluded by that excuse. *Ineluctabile fatum!* that was it, the *summa dies* for him was at hand ; he felt it, he knew it, and found it in vain to struggle, impossible to make head against it. The roar of the crowd in the street came through the open window of the room in which he sat, that hideous roar which fills the streets of every country town at race-time, and which he knew so well, with its component parts of ribaldry, blasphemy, bestiality, and idiotcy. The day was bright and hot and clear—what did the noise outside and the bright day remind him of? Something unpleasant, he felt, but he could not exactly fix it in his memory. He rose, and his eyes fell on the big, heavy, old-fashioned four-post bedstead on which he had been seated, and on the table with the glass and bottles standing by it. And then in an instant what had been dimly haunting his memory flashed all bright across his brain : Brighton, the crowd of racing-men on the cliff in the hot, bright weather, and the lodging, with Harvey Gore dying on the bed ! Gilbert Lloyd swallowed the remainder of the brandy, and hurried downstairs into the street. Immediately opposite the inn-door, and surrounded by a little crowd, a preacher—as is often to be seen on such occasions—was holding forth. The crowd mocked and jeered, but the preacher, secure in the stentorian powers of his lungs, never stopped in his attacks on the wickedness going on around him ; and the first words which Lloyd heard as he issued from the inn were, " Prepare to meet thy God."

The gentlemen who had "operated" against Lord Ticehurst's horse in the betting-ring were, on the succeeding day, proved to be perfectly correct in their prognostications ; that eminent animal being as far behind the winner of the Leger as his stable-companion had been in the race for the Cup. This result did not affect Lord Ticehurst much, so far as his betting losses were concerned ; he had so much money that it mattered little to him whether he won or lost ; but he did not like losing the *prestige* which had attached to his stable ever since Lloyd had succeeded poor old Dobbs and taken the stud in hand. And he particularly disliked the half-pitying, half-chaffing way in which several men condoled with him about it.

" What's come to you, dear old Etchingham ? " said Bobby Maitland, who had been unable to withstand the fascinations of the Doncaster Meeting, and had accordingly persuaded Mr. Stackborough to leave the yacht at anchor off Dover while they came north ; " what's come to you, old man ? The white jacket and cherry spots seem now always to be where the little boat was—all behind ! "

" We have not been very lucky lately, have we ? " replied his lordship, with an attempt at a grin—he writhed under Bobby's compassionate familiarity ; " but we did very well early in the year ; and you can't have it always, don't you know."

" An yes, to be sure, you had some little things, I recollect," said Bobby Maitland more furtively than ever.

" Don't know what you call 'little things,' Maitland," said Lord Ticehurst, twitted out of his usual reticence ;

"the One Thousand, and the Ascot Cup, with two of the best things at Stockbridge. That seems pretty good to me; but I suppose it's nothing to you. You never even won a donkey-race that I heard of."

"O yes, he did," said Gilbert Lloyd, who had come up to them unseen, and overheard the last remark ; "O yes ; Bobby won a donkey-race once, and he was so proud of it, he always takes the animal about with him. He's somewhere in the neighbourhood now, I'll swear !"

There was a shout of laughter at this remark from all the men standing round, which was increased to a roar as Mr. Stackborough, dressed most elaborately, was seen approaching the group. It was always said that Bobby Maitland had never been seen to lose his temper. At that instant he was within an ace of it ; but he controlled himself with an effort, and said, "That's not bad, Lloyd ; not at all bad, for you. When you order Lloyd's man's new livery, Etchingham, you must have a cap and bells added to it. 'Gad, you're like one of those great swells in the olden time, who used to keep a fool to amuse their friends !"

"Haw, haw ! Maitland had him there !" shouted "Barrel" Moss, a fat, handsome Israelite, ex-gambling-house-keeper, now racehorse-proprietor and betting-man, admitted into the society of the highest patrons of the turf.

"What are you grinning at, Barrel ?" retorted Gilbert. "You may thank your stars you did not live in the days of those 'great swells of the olden time.' Why, when Jews wouldn't pay, they used to pull their teeth out ; and what would have become of you when you were posted in Teddington's year? Why you wouldn't have had a single grinder left !"

Once more the laugh was on Lloyd's side, and taking advantage of his triumph he pushed through the knot gathered round him, and, taking Lord Ticehurst by the arm, moved off towards the hotel. The colloquy between the two, as they walked along, was brief. His lordship was more than a little "out of sorts." His rejection by Miss Lambert yet rankled in his mind ; his recent want of success on the turf upset and annoyed him. He was fidgety and fretful, and when Gilbert asked him what they should do, and where they should go to next, he confessed as much, and said that he did not care so long as he was " out of the whole d——d thing ! " Such a state of mind rather coinciding with Gilbert Lloyd's own feelings at the time, that astute counsellor, instead of opposing his patron's unmistakable though oddly-expressed views, fell in with them at once ; declared that everything from British Dan to British Beersheba was barren, and suggested that they should go abroad for a month or two, lie fallow, and pick up health. Lord Ticehurst fully agreed with the idea of going abroad, but "would not have any of your touring ; " he had had enough of Switzerland, thank you ; and as for any of those dead-alive old cribs where fellows poked about among pictures and those kind of things, well, he would as soon cut his throat off hand ! He did not mind going to Hombourg or Baden, or one of those places where there was something to be done, and plenty of people to be seen.

It was Gilbert's policy just at that time to keep his pupil in good humour if possible, so that even if the notion of a visit to Baden had not happened to be agreeable to him he would doubtless have suppressed his own feelings and assented with a good grace. But situated as he was, wanting a thorough change, and yet so ill at ease as to fear being left alone to his own resources in a dull place, the gaiety of a foreign watering-place was exactly what he would have chosen. So, two days after, the *Morning Post* recorded that " the Earl of Ticehurst and Mr. Gilbert Lloyd passed through town yesterday *en route* for Baden."

Men of middle age, who recollect Baden before the fatal facility of travel, or the invention of Mr. Cook and his excursionists, must look back with deep regret upon the pleasant days when comparatively few English people found their way along the newly-opened railway that crept along the bank of the Oos. The place was known, of course ; but the difference between the visitors then and nowadays was as great as between the visitors to the gardens of Hampton Court on any ordinary fine day in early spring or on Easter Monday. The style of the company, despite the importing of many of the great British aristocracy who in former years never visited the place, but now find it much cheaper and more amusing than " entertaining " for partridge-shooting at home, has gradually been decaying ; but since the establishment of the races it has received a large proportion of that

very worst ingredient, the sporting-cad. When Lord Ticehurst and Lloyd arrived, the races were just about to take
place, and there was a strong muster of the " professionals "
of high and middle grade, the worst being kept away by the
difficulty of obtaining means of transport from England,
which is a mercy of which the Germans are not sufficiently
aware to be properly thankful for. The lowest order of
sporting-man is the lowest order of anything. If any one
wishes to be impressed with the depth of degradation to
which the human species can be successfully reduced, he has
only to go into the Strand on a day when some great
" event " is coming off, and observe the persons gathered
round the office of the great sporting-newspaper about four
in the afternoon. He will see a crowd of men of all ages—
wizened old creatures, big burly roughs, shambling knock-
kneed hobbledehoys, in battered hats, in greasy, close-fitting
caps, most of them shirt-collarless, but with belcher hand-
kerchiefs twisted round their thick throats ; many of them
have the long, flat thieves' curl on the side of the face ;
nearly all have the hair cut close round the nape of the
neck : costermongers, butchers, the scum and refuse of the
population ; dirty, half-starved, in clothes whose looped and
windowed raggedness would be dear at half-a-crown for the
whole lot. These be the gallant sporting-men, without the
slightest knowledge of or care for sport, who, in order to
enable them to bet their half-crowns on a race, empty
tradesmen's tills, burst into our houses, and " put the hug "
on us in the open street.

Of course this class was unrepresented in the great
gathering at Baden ; but there was a large influx of people
who had never been seen there before. They filled the
hotels and lodging-houses ; they swaggered over the pro-
menades ; they lounged about the Kursaal, outraging the
dignity of the officials by talking and laughing loudly ; and
they played at the tables, slapping their coins down with a
ring, or motioning and calling to the grave croupiers " just
to hook 'em that louy they'd left behind." They were a
cause of great offence to Tommy Toshington, on whom
Gilbert lighted on the morning after his arrival at the springs,
where the old gentleman was holding a tumbler of very
nasty water with a very shaky hand, and, in default of
having any one to talk to, was vainly endeavouring for the

five-hundredth time to find out the meaning of some very tremendous frescoes in front of him.

"I've been in the habit of comin' to this place for an immense number of years, and thought I could go on till I died. Devilish comfortable quarters I've got at the Roossy, and nice amusin' place I've always found it ; but I must give it up, by George ! I can't stand the set of racin'-fellows that come here now, 'pon my soul I can't ! God knows who they are, my good fellow. You, who go about to all these what-do-you-call-'em meetings, you may know some of 'em ; but I, who only toddle down to the Derby and Ascot on Sumphington's drag, and get over to Goodwood when the Dook's good enough to ask me—I've never set eyes on any of 'em before."

"Well, but how do they annoy you, Toshington ? " asked Gilbert, who was rather amused at this outbreak on the old gentleman's part.

"They don't actually annoy me, except by bein' such a dam low-bred lot, yahooin' all over the place. And to think of 'em comin' just now, when we were so pleasant. It's rather late in the season, to be sure ; but there's a very nice set of people here. My Lady Carabas is here, but that *you* knew, of course ; and the Dook and Duchess of Winchester, and the Dashwoods, and the Grevilles, and the Alsagers, and Tom Gregory and half the First. It's monstrous pleasant, you can't think ! "

"It must be," said Gilbert quietly. "So new and fresh and charming. Such a change, too, for you all, not to see anybody you are accustomed to meet in London,—it must be delightful. Good-bye, Toshington ; I'm going in for rusticity, and intend to have a turn before breakfast."

Although Mr. Toshington's sense of humour was very slight, and although he took most things *au pied de la lettre*, he detected some sarcasm in Gilbert's remarks, and looked after him from under scowling brows. "That's another of 'em," he muttered ; "another of your horse-racin' customers, though he is in society, and all that. Damme if I know how they let 'em in ; I don't, by George ! They'd as soon have thought of lettin' a fiddler, or a painter, or a fellow of that sort into society when I was a young man. But it's best to keep in with this one ; he has the orderin' of everything at Etchingham's, and might leave me out of many a good thing if he chose to be disagreeable." So saying, the old worldling finished his second glass of Brunnenwasser, paid his kreutzers, audibly cursed the coinage of the country in a select mixture of the English and German languages prepared expressly by him for his own use, and departed.

Mr. Toshington was perfectly right in stating that the Marchioness of Carabas was enthroned in great state at Baden, but wrong in imagining that Gilbert Lloyd was aware of that fact. Truth to tell, there had been a slight misunderstanding, what is vulgarly but intelligibly called a "tiff," between her ladyship and Lloyd, and for a few weeks past he had not been enlightened as to her movements. The fact was, that when Lloyd had sufficiently used the *grande dame* as a means to various business ends, as a stepping-stone to certain objects which without her aid he would have been unable to reach, he began to find his position rather a wearying one. It was pleasant to be the custodian and hierophant of the Soul while it served his purpose, but it was dreary work when that purpose was achieved, and his interest in the Soul's owner was consequently gone. He attended at the shrine as regularly as ever for reasons of policy, but his policy was not sufficiently strong to keep him from occasionally gaping and betraying other signs of weariness. Lady Carabas was too observant a woman not to mark this immediately on its first occurrence, but she thought it might be accidental, and determined to wait a repetition of it before speaking. The repetition very shortly afterwards took place, and even then her ladyship did not speak. After a little reflection she determined on adopting another plan. She resolved upon taking to herself some one else who should be admitted into the mysteries of the Soul. This, she thought, would capitally answer a double purpose; it would tend to her amusement—and she was beginning to feel the want of a little novelty, she confessed to herself—and would probably have the effect of rendering Gilbert Lloyd jealous. A little time showed the result. In the turf-idiom which she had learned of Lloyd, and which she sometimes used in self-communion, she acknowledged that "while the first event had come off all right, the second had gone to grief;" which, being interpreted, meant that while she (Lady Carabas) was thoroughly amused, and indeed at the height

of one of her Platonic flirtations with the new possessor of
the Soul (a young man in the Foreign Office, with lovely
hair parted in the middle, charming whiskers, and brilliant
teeth), he (Gilbert Lloyd) had not shown the smallest
symptom of jealousy. On the contrary, Gilbert Lloyd was
unfeignedly glad to find that his place had been satisfactorily filled up, and that he would no longer be constantly required to be on escort-duty. And when Lady
Carabas found that this was the case—and she discovered it
very quickly, being a woman of great worldly penetration
and tact—she made up her mind that the best thing for her
to do was to accept the position at once, and give Lloyd his
liberty. This accordingly she did ; and when they met at
Baden,

> "They seemed to those who saw them meet,
> Mere casual friends of every day ; "

as Lord Houghton says in a very charming little poem,
though there was an echo of bygone tenderness, of the voice
of the Soul, in fact, pervading her ladyship's tones for many
a day after. Meantime she was the queen of a very
pleasant little coterie. Half the frequenters of Carabas
House did a little passing homage at her ladyship's temporary court at Baden on their way to and from the other
watering-places. The promenade contained types of all the
people usually seen seated on the Hyde-Park chairs, with a
large sprinkling of others never seen in that aristocratic
locality. For though H.R.H. the Duke of Brentford, the
captains and commanders and mighty men of valour, the
senators, the clerks in the Government offices, and the
nothing-doers have plenty of time to lounge about in
London, the working-bees—the judges and barristers, the
doctors, the civil-engineers, the cunning workers in ink and
pigment, all of whom grind their brains to make their
bread—have no such opportunity when in town, and are
only seen idling in daylight during their brief autumn
holiday. "Society"—except that Carabas House set,
which knew them very well—stared very much at most of
these people, and called Jack Hawkes of the F. O. to its
aid to explain who they were ; and Jack Hawkes, who was
only too delighted to act as cicerone to society when it had

a handle to its name, explained, "Tall man, with the round high shoulders and the long grey hair, is great lady's doctor, don't you know? uses up three pair of horses a-day whippin' about town; that's his wife and daughter with him—think her pretty, the daughter? nice-lookin', they call her. The man with the red face, not him in the white hat—that's Kollum the portrait-painter; that one in the wideawake is Sir Blewson Bagge, one of the judges—say he knows more law than any other three men in England. The fat man with the cigar is Protheroe, and the man talkin' to him dressed all in black is Tuberville; they're great engineers—one laid out the John o' Groat's and Land's End Extension Line, and the other designed the Channel Islands Submarine Railway. Wonderful how they stick together, those railway fellows; if one knows a good thing, he tells the other of it, and they hunt in couples to keep other fellows off the game. Tuberville's son has married Protheroe's daughter; and the money that's there passes all count. There are two writin' chaps comin' this way; they belong to the *Kreese*, that blackguard paper that attacks everybody, don't you know? Don't look bad fellows, do they? and they're always laughin' and keepin' it up at the Badischer. Who's the little round fat fellow they've stopped and are talkin' to?—that's Bellows of the Old Bailey Bar; first-rate in his business, and such good company; and the man with him of course you know? No! Why that's Finchington, the light comedian of the Minerva. Yes, he does look different in the daylight, as you say. These? No; these are people who have come over for the races, and I don't know anything about them. We must get Lloyd to give us that information.—Here, Lloyd, come and tell her grace who are these odd people who are coming this way; they're turf-people, I suppose, so you'll know all about them."

But Gilbert Lloyd, objecting very much to be patronised either by Mr. Hawkes or the great people to whom that social barnacle had temporarily attached himself, declared his inability to perform the duties assigned to him, and took himself off with a bow. It was the night before the first race-day, and all the Baden world was enjoying itself on the promenade in front of the Kursaal. There had been a grand excursion-party that day to the Favourite, a party of which Lady Carabas had been the reigning star, and after a delightful outing they had returned, and were now formed into a large group, laughing and talking loudly. Gilbert Lloyd carefully avoided these people, and steered equally clear of another group in the midst of which the Duchess of Winchester was enthroned. These two great ladies had never much liked each other, and when they met at Baden their antagonism was patent, and their rivalry openly declared. Each had her circle of admirers, and whatever one did the other tried to outdo. The Winchester faction having heard that the Carabas people were going that day to the Favourite, had themselves had a pic-nic at Eberstein Schloss, and both were now planning their next day's diversion at the races.

Gilbert Lloyd was in no humour to join either of these parties at that moment, though each would have been glad to have secured him as an adherent. He was in a bad temper, having just had some sharp words with Lord Ticehurst on a question on which that young nobleman a few weeks since would not have dared to offer an opinion. Just before they left town for Doncaster, Lloyd had dismissed a groom; the man appealed to Lord Ticehurst in a letter. This letter Lloyd opened, read, and contemptuously threw into the fire. The man heard of this, and made a fresh appeal to his lordship, setting forth the treatment his former letter had received, and defying Lloyd to deny it. This letter was forwarded to Lord Ticehurst at Baden, and made him exceedingly angry. He went at once to Lloyd, and spoke very plainly, said that he would not be treated like a child, that all letters addressed to him—no matter on what subject—should be brought to him, and even hinted that on their return to England Lloyd's position and responsibility must be more exactly defined.

"It was that infernal Maitland's hint that he can't swallow," said Lloyd, as he seated himself at an empty table on the verge of the crowd and ordered, some brandy. "He referred to it just now when he said he wouldn't be treated like a child. O, my dear Bobby, if ever I have the chance to come down heavily on you, just see how I'll do it! I never saw Etchingham in such a rage, and he's never spoken to me like that since we've been together.—Here!" to the waiter who brought the brandy, "*encore ;* another of these *carafons.*   What's the good of a drop like that to a man !—He's never been the same since that night he dined with those fellows, after he had been over to that place to—Lord ! I forgot—to propose to *her !*   Of course *she* must be mixed up in everything that's unlucky for me !   How I wish I'd never set eyes on her ! how I wish—What the devil does this fellow want ! "

" This fellow " was a short, square-built man of about fifty years of age, with sunken eyes, a sharp-pointed nose, and a close-cut beard, the original red colour of which was fast fading into gray.   His seedy clothes were of a foreign and fantastic cut, and round his neck he wore a long, dirty-white cravat, folded quite flat, and wonderfully neatly tied, and fastened in front with a flashy mock pin.   " This fellow " had been hanging round the table for some time, dodging in and out so as to get a better view of its occupant in the dim light.   At length, when Gilbert Lloyd raised his head and looked up at the strange figure, " this fellow " seemed to be satisfied, and shambling up to the table, placed his hands upon it, leaned over, and said in a thick, husky voice,

" Gilbert Lloyd ! "

Lloyd looked at him steadily, and then said, " That's my name ; who are you ?"

" I thought you would not know me," said the stranger with a laugh, "none of my old pals do ; at least, most don't, and some won't, so it don't make much——"

" Stay," interrupted Lloyd ; " I know you now ; knew you directly you threw your head back and I saw your cravat.   There's only one man in the world can tie a neckerchief like that, or get its folds to lie as flat.   You're Foxey Walker."

" I am that same," said the stranger ; " at least, I was when I was alive, for I'm nothing but a blessed old ghost now, I verily believe.—Here, you fellow, bring some brandy ; Cognac, you know !—I ain't of much 'count now, Lloyd, and that's a fact."   He was shabby and bloated and shaky, altogether very different from the tight, trim little Foxey who was found leaning over the rails on Brighton Esplanade at the commencement of this story.

" Ah, I remember," said Lloyd ; " you came to grief the Derby before last, in the Prior's year ?"

"I did so. Went a regular mucker. That was a bad business, sir ; a regular bad business. I could show you my book now. There were men that I dropped my money to over that Epsom Meetin' that had owed me hundreds—ay, hundreds, on other events. I'd always given them time, much as they wanted, I had ; but when I asked 'em for it then—for I had a rattlin' good book for Ascot, and some good things later on in the season—O no, not a bit of it ! 'Pay up,' they says, 'pay up !' All devilish fine ; I couldn't pay up—so I bolted."

"Ah, recollect perfectly your being proclaimed a defaulter," said Lloyd, pleasantly. "It made rather a talk at the time, you were so well known. What have you been doing since ?"

"Well, I've been cadgin' about on the Continent, doin' what I could to keep body and soul together.—You're goin' to pay for this brandy, you know ? I suppose you don't mind standin' another go ? all right.—But there's little enough to be done. I ain't much good at cards ; and, besides, there's nothing to be done with them unless you get among the swells in the clubs and that, and that's not likely ; and there's not much to be picked up off the foreigners at billiards, let alone their not playing our game. I've won a little on the red and black here and there, and I've come across an old friend now and again who's helped me with a fiver or so."

"You don't speak in riddles, Foxey," said Lloyd with a half-laugh. "You make your meaning tolerably clear. I must not be worse than the others, I suppose ; so here, catch hold ;" and he took a couple of bank-notes from his pocket-book and handed them to his companion.

"Thank'ee, Lloyd," said Foxey, pocketing the money. "I ain't proud, and hadn't need to be. Besides, you've become a tremendous swell since you got hold of young Ticehurst, eh ? I see your name regular in *Bell* amongst the nobs. Rather different from what we reck'lect in the old days : 'Ten to one, bar one !'—don't you remember ?" and Foxey put his hand to the side of his mouth and shouted loudly in imitation of the worthies of the outer ring.

"Ye-es," said Lloyd, who did not at all relish being told that he had "got hold of" anybody, and who was much disgusted by Foxey's recollections and performance. "Yes," said he, rising from his chair as he spoke; "I think I must go now."

"Must you?" said Foxey, who had become very much flushed and invigorated by the brandy; "must you? That's a bore, that is, for I had somethin' very particular to say to you; somethin' that concerns you much more than it does me; somethin'," added Foxey, looking hazily at his companion, "that would be d——d awkward for you if it got blown. Don't you fear for me! I'm as close as wax, I am; only—however, I'll see you about it to-morrow or next day. Good-night, old fellow; compliments to my lord."

"Something that concerns me more than it does him? That would be awkward for me if it got blown? What the devil does he mean?" said Lloyd to himself, as he walked down the *allée*. "Awkward for me?—the old brute was drunk, and did not know what he said. Probably a plant to get more money out of me. He *could* know nothing that would have the slightest bearing on me or my affairs. I dare say he'll try it on again when I see him next; but he'll find it difficult to draw me of any more money, more especially if he attempts to bounce me out of it."

The next day was bright and cheerful, and the little race-course, though much sneered at by the "talent," served its purpose very well, and was thronged with a merry, animated crowd. The natives, to be sure, did not understand very much what it was all about. The women cried, "Ach, Herr, Je!" at the sight of the tight little English jocks stripping off their outer coats and appearing in all the glory of flashing silk; and the men took their pipes from their mouths and swore "Donnerwetter!" as the horses went thundering by. The Winchester and Carabas faction had each one side of the little stand, the leaders exchanged sweet hand-kissings, the followers bowed and grinned and nodded with all the warmth and sincerity which form the basis of our social relations. Lady Carabas, as usual, wore pink; the Duchess of Winchester, who was very fair and *petite*, wore blue; and the retainers followed suit. Mr. Toshington was as much divided in his allegiance and as much perplexed to know which colour to sport as a London cabman on the morning of the University boat-race. He had enjoyed the hospitality of both houses, and indeed had earned many a good dinner by carrying tattle from one to the other; but up to this time he had never been called upon to make his election, to say "under which queen;" and those who were in the secret, in which category was included every one present, were greatly amused to see the difficulty which the old gentleman had in trimming his sails and steering his course in safety. There were some who, unlike Tommy Toshington, were independent, who sided with neither party, but were friendly and familiar with both. Among those were Lord Ticehurst—who, though bound by family ties to Lady Carabas, never allowed his clanship to "mix him up in any of her ladyship's rum starts," as he phrased it—and Gilbert Lloyd, whose worn and haggard appearance was the cause of much solicitude and anxious inquiry from Lady Carabas. Lloyd appeared rather annoyed at the *prononcé* manner which her ladyship adopted towards him, and at which some of the most daring followers smiled, more especially when the reigning favourite, the gentleman in the Foreign Office, looked very much displeased. He seemed very much happier when, at a later period in the day, he found himself seated by the Duchess of Winchester, who rallied him with much piquancy on his defection.

"I am astonished at you, Mr. Lloyd, quite astonished," she said, laughingly. "Do you know we used to call you the Undying One!"

"Well, you could not call Toshington that, could you, Duchess?" said Gilbert; "look how very purple his whiskers are in the sunlight."

"No, no, of course I don't mean that; how can you be so absurd? You know our dear friend opposite is like somebody in old time I read of once, who used to kill her admirers regularly at the end of a certain time. It's a notorious fact that—over there—no flirtation lasts longer than twelve months, and we call you the Undying One because you have held undisputed sway over that Soul for— O, it must be years! And now, after all this, you have the baseness to shut your ears to the voice of the charmer—we saw the spell tried on an hour ago—and to come over here!"

"I don't think there's much harm done, Duchess, even if all were as you say, which I am very far from admitting.

Calypso is the only instance on record of a woman who '*ne pouvait se consoler après le départ*' of any one she liked. I am certain that no lady of modern days would be so weak."

"Ah, I know what you mean ; you mean Mr. Pennington. Well, he's very good-looking, certainly, in his own red-and-white way, but he's insufferably stupid ; and a stupid man, however handsome he may be, always bores me to death. I——Who is this dreadful man down here ? Is it to you or to me he's making those horrible grimaces ?"

Lloyd looked over in the direction in which the Duchess pointed, and to his horror saw Mr. Foxey Walker, who apparently had had a great deal too much to drink, whose fantastic clothes looked infinitely shabbier and seedier in the daylight than they had on the previous evening, and who was throwing up his arms, endeavouring to attract the attention of some one in the stand. Foxey no sooner saw that Gilbert Lloyd had recognized him than he approached the stand, and called out, "Hi, Lloyd ! hollo there, Lloyd ! Just come and pass me up there, will you ? I want to speak to you."

"It's to you he's calling, Mr. Lloyd !" said the Duchess, arching her pretty eyebrows and making a little *moue* of astonishment. "What a strange-looking creature ! who in the world is he ?"

"He's a poor half-witted fellow, an old friend of mine, Duchess," said Lloyd, with the utmost calmness. "He is a man of family, and once had a large fortune ; but he lost every sixpence on the turf, and that quite turned his brain. He's eccentric, as you see, but perfectly harmless ; a few of us make him a little allowance, on which he lives, and he thinks this gives him a claim upon us, poor fellow ! I—— Yes, yes ; I'm coming !" he called to Mr. Foxey, for that gentleman had recommenced bellowing, "Hi, Lloyd !" with redoubled vehemence ; "I'm coming !—I think I had better go down and calm him, Duchess, if you will excuse me." And with a bow Gilbert Lloyd leisurely retreated from the stand.

He smiled so pleasantly—he knew he was still under observation—at Mr. Foxey, who was waiting for him in front, that that worthy, who had been somewhat doubtful of the wisdom of the course he had pursued, felt perfectly reassured, and said, "Hallo, Gil, my boy ! sorry to call you away from such stunnin' company ; but I want a word with you." It was not until they had walked a few paces and were well out of sight of the people in the stand that Lloyd caught his companion tightly by the arm, and said, " You infernal drunken old idiot, how dare you come and annoy me when you saw me with my friends ? "

" Come, I say, drop that," said Foxey ; " you're pullin my arm off; don't you hear ? "

" You scoundrel, I'll have your head off if you don't take care ! What fool's game is up now ? What do you want with me ? Have you anything really to say, or is it only to repeat the rubbish of last night ? "

" What rubbish ? what did I say last night ? I didn't— no, of course I didn't ; I recollect now. I know what I'm doin' fast enough, and what I can do."

" And I know what I can do, and what I will do too, if you interrupt me again when I'm talking with friends, and that is, have you moved off the course by the gend'armes as a drunken nuisance."

" O, that's it, is it ? " said Foxey, glowering at him, and speaking in a dull thick voice. " Moved off the course ! a drunken nuisance, eh ? You'll sing a very different toon to this, Master Lloyd, before I've done with you. O, you can't come the high jeff over me," he continued, raising his tone ; " for all your standin' in with big swells now ; we know what you were once ; we know——"

" Will you be quiet, you old fool, and say what you want ? " said Gilbert, turning fiercely upon him.

" What I want ? Ah, that's more like it ! What I want ? Well, that's easily told, and that's more than most people can say. What I want is money."

" I gave you money last night—more than you can have spent, or ought to have spent."

" Ah, that's more like it : what I *can* spend—Well, no matter. However, that's not the way I mean in which I want money. Look here, Gilbert Lloyd ; I'm tired of this cadging life ; I'm sick of hikin' up and down from one gamblin'-place to another ; I'm disgusted with the Continent, and the foreigners, all the lot of 'em."

" O, you are, eh ? " said Lloyd with a sneer ; " I should scarcely have thought it."

" Yes," replied Foxey, in perfect good faith, " I am

thoroughly. What I long for is to get back to England, to see my old pals, to lead my old life."

"Indeed," sneered Gilbert again; "but from what I understand from you there would be some difficulty in carrying out that pleasant little arrangement."

"None that you couldn't help me to settle at once. They all think their money's clean gone; but if I'm to come on the turf again, it would never do for me to come out as a welsher, so I must pay 'em something; but ever so little would square it. Then, if I just had a little trifle in hand to start with, and you gave me the office when you knew of a good thing—and you must hear lots, havin' the management of that young swell's stable—well, I should do as right as ninepence."

There was a minute's pause, and then Lloyd said:

"You are a great creature, Mr. Walker, a very great creature, and your power of sketching out a happy future is something wonderful. But to my great astonishment I find that I play a part in this notable scheme of your life, and that its being carried out successfully wholly depends upon me. Now, we may as well understand each other clearly, and at once. From me you'll never get another sixpence."

Foxey started, looked hard at his companion, and said, "You mean that?"

"No," said Lloyd, "I don't mean it literally; I'll give you another ten pounds on the day I leave this place."

It was Foxey's turn to sneer now. "That's generous of you," he said, "regular generous; but you always were a free-handed fellow with your money, Lloyd. I reck'lect we used to say in the old days how pleased you always were to have to part. Now look here," he cried, changing his tone; "I will have all I've asked from you: the money to square it with those fellows, the sum to start fresh with, the straight tips from young Ticehurst's stable; I'll have this, or else——"

"Or what else?" asked Gilbert Lloyd, without any alteration in his usual calm manner.

"Or else I'll ruin you, root and branch; horse and foot; stock, lock, and barrel! You laugh and sneer; you think I can't do it? I tell you I can."

"You tell me a pack of lies and blather. You begun

last night, and you've done nothing else for the last half-hour. How can you do it ?"

"By blowing the gaff on you ; by telling something I know which would make all these swells cut you and hunt you out of society ; which would——"

"There, there's enough of this !" cried Lloyd, interrupting him ; "my time's too valuable to waste over such trash. It's the old game of hush-money for a secret, after all. I should have thought you would have known some better dodge than that, Master Foxey, after all the life you've seen. If you were going in for the extortion-of-money business in your old age, you might have learnt something fresher than that very stale device. Now, be off, and give me a wider berth for the future, if you're wise. Your drunken stupidity—for I suppose you would not have acted thus if you had not taken to drink—has lost you ten pounds. Take care it does not get you a horsewhipping." As he said these words he turned shortly on his heel and strode away.

Foxey looked after him, his face lit up with rage and disappointment. "All right, my fine fellow," he muttered, shaking his fist at the fast-receding figure ; "all right ; you will have it, and you shall. It will be quite enough to cook your goose as it is ; but if I'd only had time to learn a little more, I think I could have hanged you."

There was a little extra excitement in the rooms that night. Count Nicolaeff, a Russian nobleman, who had on two previous occasions broken the bank, had returned to Baden, and was playing with a boldness and success which augured the repetition of the feat. A crowd was gathered round him as he sat, calm and composed, quietly gathering the *rouleaux* which the croupiers pushed across to him. In this crowd was Lloyd ; the qualities which the Russian was displaying were just those to excite his admiration, and he was watching every movement and trying to account for each calculation of the gambler, when he felt a tap on his shoulder. He looked round and saw Dolly Clarke, the sporting lawyer, who beckoned him away.

Gilbert was annoyed at the interruption. "Not just now," he said impatiently ; "I'll come to you later."

"Come this instant," said Dolly Clarke; and there was something in his tone that made Gilbert Lloyd leave the table and follow him into the open space outside. By the lamplight Lloyd saw that Clarke was very pale; noticed also that he stood back as if avoiding contact with him.

"What is it?" asked Lloyd. "It should be something special by your tone and manner, Clarke?"

"It is something special," replied Clarke; "it is a matter of life or death for you. Do you know a man called Foxey Walker?"

"Pshaw! is that all?" said Lloyd, whose heart had failed him at the solemnity of his companion's manner, and whose courage now as suddenly revived. "Is that all? Yes, I know him; a defaulting ring-man, a mere common 'welsher.' I saw him on the course to-day, and he threatened me that if I did not give him money he would expose something in my past life—some trick or dodge I practised, I suppose, when I was in the ring, and had to be a sharp practitioner to hold my own with my fellows. That's all, eh?"

"No," said Clarke earnestly, "nothing of the sort; the man has made a revelation, but not of the kind you imagine —a thousand times more serious. There's never been much love lost between you and me, Lloyd, and you may wonder why I'm here to counsel and help you; so understand at once, it's for Ticehurst's sake; you're so mixed up with him that any public *exposé* would be the deuce and all for him."

"What do you mean by public *exposé*, Mr. Clarke? what do you——"

"Stop; don't bounce—it won't do. Do you remember when we dined at Richmond six weeks ago, you answered me very sharply because I asked why you never went to Brighton now? I've always had my own opinion on that matter; but I don't chatter, and I kept it to myself. This man Walker stopped Ticehurst and me as we were coming from the course, and begged so earnestly for an interview that Ticehurst listened to him. I need not go into all he said; it appears he had his suspicions too, and determined to trade on them; went the next year to your old lodgings, pumped the landlady; saw the doctor who attended Harvey Gore; has been working it since he left England through friends ; and has made up a case which, if not positive, is at all events infernally suspicious."

" What—what did Etchingham say about it ?" asked Lloyd.

" I never saw a fellow so completely knocked over in all my life. You know he is not strong-minded, and he—well, he funks death, and that kind of thing, and——"

" Does he believe it ? what does he say about me ?"

" He does believe it fully, and he says he will never set eyes on you again. I see—your eyes are blazing—you see there's nothing proved, and your place is too good a one to give up on mere suspicion ? You'll say you'll have the matter sifted, and all that. Don't; take my advice—given as a lawyer who sees queer things in his practice—drop it, clear out of this at once, get over to England, make up Ticehurst's accounts, and then get away to Australia, America—anywhere !"

" Thank you ; and leave my ' place,' as you call it, to you, eh ? " It was the last remaining touch of bravado in his voice, bravado belied by the ashy paleness of his face, and he set rigidity of his mouth.

" To me ! I'm a lawyer, not a turfite. Pshaw ! don't try to humbug any longer—you're too clever a man. You can post over to Carlsruhe to-night, and get straight through to-morrow. I'll come with you to the hotel ; I promised Ticehurst I'd see you off. Come."

Gilbert Lloyd saw that there was no use in fighting the question any longer. He felt as though his career was at its close, as though he should drop as rapidly as he had risen. He turned on his heel and walked towards the hotel, Dolly Clarke walking by his side. It was all over, then ? The position he had gained for himself amid the envy and hatred of all his compeers was shattered at its base, and——

No ! Before he reached the hall-door, he had carefully searched his hand, and found in it one last trump-card, which he determined on playing directly he arrived in England.

CHAPTER VI.

THE LAST CHANCE.

MR. LLOYD gone! They could scarcely believe it at Baden. Lady Carabas was in despair, and the Duchess of Winchester was vexed, for she was fond of flirtation, and she had found Mr. Lloyd "very nice." The led captains and the other male retainers of both factions looked on Gilbert as a dangerous rival, and were rather glad than otherwise that he was out of the way. Gone to England, eh? Yes. Summoned by a telegram on most important business, so Dolly Clarke said; he happened to be with him at the time the telegram arrived, and so of course knew all about it. On Lord Ticehurst's business, of course? Well, Dolly Clarke supposed so; in fact, he might go so far as to say "yes," and rather unpleasant business too. Lord Ticehurst was rather annoyed about it, and so perhaps you would be so good as not to mention it to him? Needless to say there were some people who did not believe this statement, even when vouched for on such excellent authority as Mr. Dolly Clarke's. There are some people who will not believe anything. Mr. Toshington is one of them. He thinks it a "deuced odd story," and sets about to investigate it. He sees the landlord, porter, waiters, *hausknecht* of the hotel, every individual separately, and puts them through the strictest investigation in the most extraordinary *mélange* of languages; finally, he goes to the telegraph-office and ascertains triumphantly that for the Herr Lloyd, Englander, no telegraphic despatch received was. Tommy opines that Gilbert's absence has reference to some infernal chicanery connected with the turf, and sets that down as the reason why Ticehurst is so shy about speaking about it. Queer business for peers of the rel-lum to be mixin' up in such matters, Tommy thinks, and any-thin' but a good sign in these infernal levellin' times. Lady Carabas is really very sorry. She had a sort of idea that Gilbert was "coming round;" but his having gone away in this sudden manner, and gone away without a hint of his going, or word of adieu to her, was a death-blow to that hope. And Mr. Pennington, the gentlemanly creature in the F. O., though charming to look at and pleasant so far as his conversation lasted, was soon exhausted, and was not to be compared with Gilbert Lloyd as a bright and amusing companion. "He might have thought of me before he went away," Lady Carabas thought to herself. She had no idea that Gilbert Lloyd had thought about her, and with considerable earnestness too, as he was walking away from the Kursaal in company with Mr. Dolly Clarke, immediately previous to his quitting Baden. He had carefully weighed in his mind whether there was any use in getting her to appeal to Lord Ticehurst in his behalf, founding his appeal on a tremendous story of his innocence and of his being the victim of circumstances, which story he could arrange during the night. But he finally rejected the notion ; there was something decisive and pitiless about Mr. Clarke's manner, which told Lloyd it would be useless for him to indulge himself with any hopeful view of the case. As he travelled through the night, and turned all the events of the past days, of the past years, over and over in his mind, during his weary journey, he felt convinced that he had acted wisely in this matter. Only one thing annoyed him ; if the worst came to the worst, and he was obliged, as Clarke had hinted, to go away to Australia or America, he should want all the money he could lay his hands on, and he might have "bled" her ladyship for a good round sum. He had letters of hers in his possession, written in all innocence it is true, but quite sufficiently compromising if read from the legal point of view, which ought to have effected that.

When Lloyd arrived in London, he did not go to Lord Ticehurst's house in Hill Street, where were all his goods and chattels ; he would go there later, he thought, and see what could be done after a careful examination of the books and papers. He drove to a house in Duke Street, St. James's, where he had lodged years before ; and the landlady of which, looking scarcely a day older, came out to the door, told him his old rooms were vacant, and welcomed him heartily. Gilbert Lloyd always was popular with his inferiors ; it was part of his policy in life to be so, and he took every opportunity of saying polite things to them, and doing them cheap civilities. Even now, as he jumped out of the cab, he told Mrs. Jobson how well she was looking, and how he felt quite pleased at the notion of coming back to the old rooms ; and then he bade her take his luggage in, and ran upstairs.

The old rooms ! He looked round them, and found them scarcely changed. The furniture was a little shabbier, perhaps, and looking through the window the opposite side of the street seemed, if possible, a little closer than before. The same slippery chintz on the sofa, the same regulation number of chairs, the same portrait of the Princess Charlotte, at which Gertrude had screamed with laughter, and called it a " hideous old thing," the first day he brought her there. Gertrude ? Yes ; that was their first lodging after their marriage. He brought her there, and at that instant he seemed to see her as she was when she first entered the little room ; how she looked round in surprise, and then ran to the window and knelt and looked up for the sky. The chain of his reflection was broken by the entrance of Mrs. Jobson, who expressed her delight at seeing him again.

" But, do you know, I did not reckernize you at first, Mr. Lloyd—I did not, indeed. Seeing you alone, I suppose it was. I hope you're not alone in the world, Mr. Lloyd ?— that you've not lost that dear sweet lamb ? "

" O no, Mrs. Jobson, thank you ; Mrs. Lloyd is alive and very well."

" That's good hearing, I'm sure ; and grown into a fine woman, I've no doubt. Those slight slips of girls with plenty of bone, when they fill out, improve wonderful ; " and then Mrs. Jobson changed the subject, and launched into questions of domestic economy into which it is not necessary to follow her.

And the next day Gilbert Lloyd prepared to play the last trump-card which he found in his hand when he so carefully examined it on the night he left Baden. He had given deep consideration to his plan since, had gone through every detail, had turned and twisted the intended mode of working his scheme, and had definitely resolved upon the manner in which he would carry it out.

And this was his resolution—to claim his wife. He had calculated exactly all the risk that was contained in that one sentence, and he had determined to brave it, or at all events to pretend to be prepared to brave it. From those few words which Gertrude had whispered to him, when in his rashness he had braved her at Mrs. Stapleton Burge's party, he knew that she was mistress of the secret of Harvey Gore's death. But the question then arose, would she dare to avail herself of the knowledge she possessed? Yes, he thought she would, sooner than be forced to return to him. Except during the first few months of girlish idolatry, she had never cared for him, and now she had many reasons for positively hating him. The manner in which he had treated her would have been quite enough to a girl of her spirit, without the suspicion of his crime, the position which she had subsequently gained for herself in the world, and—her love for another man. Even in the strait in which he found himself, that last thought was sufficient to tempt him to run almost any risk to prevent her being anything to any other man, but to that man above all others in the world.

Another question then arose; how much did she know about what had transpired in those accursed Brighton lodgings? Foxey Walker, with all his knowingness, with all the means which he had employed, with all the tremendous inducement he had to endeavour to find out everything, to drag its deepest depths, and expose all he could rake therefrom in the light of day, had only been able to patch up a case of suspicion. So Dolly Clarke had said. To be sure he, Gilbert Lloyd, had taken fright at the bogey thus raised, and had run away; but he was taken aback, the charge was brought forward so suddenly, and it was impossible to face the *charivari* which would have risen round him, or to silence the accusation off-hand on the spur of the moment. Impossible, and not particularly worth his while. He had always thought that the connection between him and Lord Ticehurst must be brought to an end some day, and had often imagined, more especially during the last few weeks that it would terminate in a row. Well, that could not be helped. He had had wonderfully good pickings for a very long time; and though he had lost all that he had put by in his recent unfortunate speculations, the mine was not yet exhausted, the milch-cow was not yet dry. In the message which Clarke had conveyed to him from Lord Ticehurst, he was directed to go to Hill Street, and make up the books and balance the accounts between them; and it was odd if he could not show a considerable balance due in his favour; ay, and claim it too, so long as a portion of his lordship's banking-account was responsive to checks bearing Gilbert Lloyd's signature. The question remained then, how much did Gertrude know? He could not guess from the few words she had whispered to him that night, for on that occasion also he had taken fright and rushed off without probing the matter. But if Foxey Walker could bring forward nothing positive, nothing actually damnatory, the odds were very strongly against Gertrude's being able to do so. And it was a great stake he was going in for now. She could always earn a huge income by her voice; but this was not all. This old Lord Sandilands, who had almost adopted Gertrude as his daughter — so, at least, Lady Carabas had told him, and she ought to know—had the reputation of being immensely rich. He lived so quietly and unostentatiously, that the world insisted he had been putting by two-thirds of his income for years; and he had no relatives to whom to bequeath it. It would, therefore, probably all be Gertrude's, or of course, his identity once established, Gertrude's husband's. Now, what course, would they adopt? Would they accept him; let him live with her during the old man's lifetime, and inherit with her at the old man's death? Even if all the capital were tied down, the interest would afford a splendid income. Or would they offer to buy him off with a sum down and a yearly income? Either would do, though the first would be best, for—yes, by Jove! much best, for the second would leave Gertrude open to the attentions of his brother Miles. However, he was in a strait, and could not afford to be particular, unless they fought him, and then—well, he would risk that, and play his last trump-card.

So Gilbert Lloyd, on the morning after his arrival in London from Baden, sat down and wrote a long and elaborate letter to his wife. He told her that from the first he had never ceased to grieve over that unfortunate step which they had taken under the influence of temper and youthful folly. He did not repine; indeed, he had no doubt that the separation had had a properly chastening effect

—had given them time and opportunity to see the mistake of indulging in headstrong passion, and had probably rendered them both—he certainly could speak for himself—worthier members of society ; but the time, he thought, had arrived when it would be not merely advisable, but proper, to place themselves right with each other and before the world. There existed between them a tie which was far more solemnly obligatory on them than any human-made law,—although he need scarcely point out to his wife that their marriage had never been legally dissolved,—and while both the spiritual and moral contracts were in force it was impossible to shirk their influence. He owned that he had been profoundly touched, on the several occasions on which he had met her recently in society, by the fact that he, her legitimate protector, who should have been at her side, whose proper position was at her right hand, should have had to stand aloof and look on, while others pressed round her, owing to the foolish step they had taken. She would agree with him, he felt sure, that this was a false position, and one which should be at once set right ; and the only way in which that could be done would be by their at once coming together and assuming their proper relations before the world. He, on his part, would not object, if it was thought necessary or advisable, for an entirely fresh marriage between them ; that detail could be arranged afterwards. He was writing this in his old lodgings in Duke Street, which she would recollect, to which he had first taken her after their marriage. She was a *grande dame* now, but he did not think he wronged her, or flattered himself, in stating his belief that she had never known more real happiness than when inhabiting those little rooms. Might the omen prove propitious!—Ever hers, G. L.

"And for a sort of thing that's not the least in my line I don't think that's bad," said Gilbert Lloyd, as he read it over. "It seems to me to combine the practical with the romantic, a very difficult thing to hit off, and one likely to please both phases of Gertrude's character." Then he sealed it, and addressed it to Miss Lambert, to Sir Giles Belwether's care, despatched it, and waited the result.

There must be a clear day at least before he could receive a reply, and that day he found it very difficult to get through. He could not go to Hill Street, though there was

plenty of work awaiting him there, because on the tone of
Gertrude's reply to his letter would greatly depend the tone
of his conduct towards Lord Ticehurst. If his wife, no
matter from whatever motives of policy, thought it better
to yield to his views, he would then be in a position to
resent his sudden dismissal, and to speak his plain and unadorned sentiments to his lordship in equally plain and
unadorned language. If, on the contrary, Gertrude tem-
porised or refused point-blank, and he saw there was no
chance of carrying out his wishes, then all he had left him
was to go to Hill Street to see the very best arrangement
he could make for himself, by which he meant to ascertain
the largest amount he could draw on the fund for which
his signature was good at Lord Ticehurst's banker's—other
available funds he had none—and making the best of his
way to Australia or America under a feigned name, begin
life again *de novo*. So he mooned about during the dreary
day—it was dreary enough ; none of his friends were in
London, and the aspect of the town was deserted and
wretched in the extreme—and was not sorry when it was
time to go home and to bed. The next morning before he
was yet up Mrs. Jobson knocked at his door, and pushed in
a letter which had just arrived by the post. Lloyd sprang
up, and seized it at once. It was a large folded letter, addressed not in Gertude's hand, but in writing which had
once been bold and was still large, but a little shaky and
tremulous, and was sealed with a coronet and a cipher.
Gilbert broke it open hurriedly, and read as follows :

"Hastings, Sept. 26, 186—.

" GEOFFREY CHALLONER,—for it would be absurd in me
to address you by any other name,—the lady who has the
inexpressible misfortune of being your wife has placed in
my hands the letter which you have addressed to her, and
has begged me to reply to it. The reply to such a letter
could not be confided to fitter hands than those of the lady's
father, in which position I stand. The young lady whose
professional name is Miss Grace Lambert is my natural
daughter ; the fact has been duly acknowledged by me, and
the first act after the avowal is to champion my daughter's
cause against a villain. For you are a villain, Geoffrey
Challoner ; though God knows it is with the deepest pain

that I write such words of any man bearing your paternal name ; for in applying this term to you I am not actuated by a remembrance of the wrongs you have done to Gertrude, I am not even thinking of the fearful crime which you committed, and which was revealed to her by your victim with his dying breath on the occasion of your final separation. I am looking back across a gulf of years to the time when the dearest friend I had in the world was your father. Now, Geoffrey Challoner, do you begin to understand ? To me your father confided the narrative of the events which ended with your banishment from home, and your erasure from the family annals for ever. That narrative I have by me now. Your career has been hitherto so successful, you have gone so long unpunished, that you will be sceptical on this point, but I will prove it to you. That narrative, written in your father's own hand, sets forth your boyish disobedience, your tendency to dissipation, the impossibility to make you think or act rightly ; and finally, your awful crime. When you have read thus far you will still cling to the hope that the knowledge of the nature of that crime may have passed into the grave with him whose heart it broke, who never held up his head after its discovery. If any such hope arises in you, it is my duty to stamp it out. Geoffrey Challoner, in my possession, complete in every detail from its commencement to its frustration, is the story of your attempted fratricide. There can be read, couched in your father's homely, serious, truth-begetting phrases, the record of how you, finding it impossible to undermine your father's confidence in your elder brother by lies and slanders of the most malignant nature, at length determined to step into that brother's position by taking away his life by poison. Do you admit the force of my position now, or would you wish the details brought out one by one into the light of day, before the public eye ?

"This letter is written in self-defence, or, what is the same thing, in defence of my child. The letter she has received from you, however pleasantly and skilfully worded, was a threat, an order to her to receive you as her husband, a threat as to what she might expect if she refused. Now beware. Had you been content to leave Gertrude unmolested, had you shown the slightest remorse for the horrible crimes, one of which you contemplated, the other which, as I verily believe, you committed, I would have tempered justice with mercy, and left you to the never-failing retribution which your conscience would sooner or later have claimed of you. That is now impossible. By your own act you have prevented my using any such discretion in the matter. You have thrown down the gauntlet, however covertly, and must take the consequences. I have telegraphed to your brother and to my solicitor to come to me at once. I shall place before them your father's narrative, and shall tell them what Gertrude has told me. Do not flatter yourself with the notion that a wife cannot be a witness against her husband. There is plenty of other evidence, some of which I find has been already worked up ; and we shall take such steps as may seem to us advisable.

" SANDILANDS."

" I've knocked twice with Mr. Lloyd's breakfast, and I can't make him hear," said Mrs. Jobson to her servant that morning ; " and he such a light sleeper too, in general. I'll try once more, and if he don't answer, I'll peep in."

The landlady knocked again, but with no effect ; and when she " peeped in " she found Gilbert Lloyd fallen prone on his face on the floor, with a letter grasped in his stiffened hand.

———

CHAPTER VII.

INELUCTABILE FATUM.

IT was fortunate that Mrs. Jobson was a practical woman of resources and presence of mind, for the first thing she did was to fling the contents of the water-jug over Lloyd's head (he was a favourite with her, or she would scarcely have risked damaging the carpet by such a proceeding) ; the second was to open he window ; and the third was to loosen his collar, and raise him into a half-sitting position. She then called out to the servant to run for the doctor ; but Lloyd, who had by this time opened his eyes and come to his senses, vehemently opposed this suggestion, declaring himself to be quite recovered, and leading Mrs. Jobson to believe that these were attacks to which he was by no means unaccustomed—which, though unpleasant to the lookers-on, were not dangerous to the sufferer, and that he knew how to treat himself, to prevent the recurrence of the seizure for some time to come. Mrs. Jobson was much pleased to hear this, for, with all her practicality, she had that vague fear of sudden death, and its necessitated coroner's inquest, which is so often found among people of her class. After her fashion, too, she really liked her lodger, for Gilbert Lloyd had always been civil and agreeable—had given little trouble, and paid his way with consistent punctuality; so she was glad to find him looking something like himself, and lightly treating what she had at first imagined would be a very serious matter.

But when he was left to himself, and the reaction after the cold water, and the mental spurt which he had put on to talk to the landlady, set in, Gilbert Lloyd felt that the blow which for the last few days he had been certain was impending, had fallen at last. The depression under which he had been recently labouring was then accounted for; that attempted crime, which had brought upon him the sentence of banishment from his father's house, the loss of his ancestral name and family position, which had sent him forth into the wilderness of the world, there to stand or fall entirely by his own arts or luck,—this crime was to be visited on him again, just at the very time when everything else was going wrong with him!

Lord Sandilands, then, was the friend to whom his father had confided that horrible secret. He had often wondered to whom his father's letter had alluded, but had never thought of identifying the bland, pleasant old nobleman with the man who held the history of his dishonour in his keeping. His father's letter had said, "This friend is not acquainted with your personal appearance, and cannot therefore recognize you, should your future conduct enable you to present yourself in any place where he may be found." Even in the desperate circumstances in which he was placed, Gilbert Lloyd almost laughed as he recalled these words, and thought how frequently his conduct had "enabled him to present himself" in places where old Sandilands was to be found; how, indeed, he had been a leader and prime favourite in the very society which the old nobleman most affected. "Not acquainted with his personal appearance:" of course not, or Lord Sandilands would never have consented to meet him on the terms on which they had met, and which, though not intimate, were sufficiently familiar; would never have suffered him to be the second-self of Lord Ticehurst—his lordship could endure Gilbert Lloyd the turfite, but Geoffrey Challoner——How had he learned about Geoffrey Challoner, then?—whence had come this secret information? Not from Gertrude: that little fact was yet to be broken to her, he thought with bitter delight. Who had been Lord Sandilands' informant? Miles, of course!—he had forgotten him, his dear, charming brother Miles! O, that boyish hatred had not been misplaced; there was something in it beyond the mere desire to get rid of one who stood between him and the estate. If Miles had been nothing to him, he should have hated him. Miles, of course! His father's letter had told him that this friend would be "always in close and constant intercourse with my son." Close and constant intercourse!—that was true enough; and now this precious pair had put their heads together for the purpose of his humiliation. Why just at that time? It could only have been recently that Miles had told the old gentleman, though he had known it so long ago. Why had he only just told Lord Sandilands, when he had known it ever since Gertrude's first appearance at Carabas House? Gertrude—and Miles! was that the clue? Miles was desperately in love with Gertrude—he had seen that with his own eyes; and, besides, Toshington—everybody—had told him so. In their confidence on this point, can Miles have revealed this fact to his old friend? Gilbert did not see what end could have been gained by that, more especially as the greatest secret of all—the existence of the marriage between him and Gertrude—was evidently not yet known to Miles.

And Gertrude was Lord Sandilands' daughter? That was a surprise to Gilbert. That the old nobleman would have adopted her, and made her his heiress, Lloyd had expected; but the thought that she was his natural daughter had never suggested itself to him. Ah, what an infernal fool he had been! All these years he had been congratulating himself on his good fortune, and now he found he had been merely running after the shadow and neglecting the substance. What a dolt he had been to allow Gertrude to leave him at all! He might have lived on her in a princely manner—first on the money which she made by her profession, and secondly by properly working this secret of her relationship to Lord Sandilands. And now he had lost all!

His time was come, he thought. *Venit summa dies et ineluctabile fatum!* That line remained haunting his brain. He felt that matters were closing round him very rapidly. What was that he had read in Lord Sandilands' letter about that cursed Brighton business with Harvey Gore? He could not distinctly recollect; he would read the letter again. He turned round to look for it; it was nowhere to be found.

He hunted for it high and low; searched every portion of the room again and again; examined, as people will do in the desperation of such circumstances, the most impossible places. He did not like to ask Mrs. Jobson about it. If she had seen it her curiosity might have been aroused; she might have read it, and then—— At length he rang his bell, and Mrs. Jobson appeared; and Gilbert saw in an instant by her face that whatever might have happened she had not read the letter.

"When you were good enough to come to my assistance just now, Mrs. Jobson, when I had that little attack, did you happen to see an open letter lying about?" said Gilbert.

"A letter, sir?" said Mrs. Jobson dubiously; "there were no letter that I saw, 'cept the one in your hand."

"In my hand?"

"Clinched tight up, as was both your fists, so that I could hardly uncrook your fingers; and in one of 'em there *was* a letter all squeezed up."

"That must have been it. What did you do with it?"

"Put it on to the table by the window, just as it might be there," said Mrs. Jobson, taking an exact aim, and marking a particular spot on the table with her finger.

"It's no good looking there," said Gilbert testily—for Mrs. Jobson still kept peering on the table as though she expected to see the letter swim up to the surface through the wood—"it's not there. What can have become of it?"

"Well, now I recollect," said Mrs. Jobson slowly, "that I thought you would be all the better for a puff of fresh air, so I opened the window, and the paper might have blowed out."

"Good God, woman, what have you done!" cried Gilbert, starting up and rushing towards the street, pushing past Mrs. Jobson, who this time began to be seriously alarmed, thinking her lodger was going out of his mind.

The street was tolerably empty when Gilbert Lloyd reached it. There is not much doing in Duke Street, St. James's, in the month of September—a slack season, when even the livery-stable-keepers' helpers are probably out of town, and there were but few people about to express surprise at seeing a gentleman fly out of a house, and begin searching the pavement and the kennel with intense anxiety and perseverance. In the season, a dozen young gutter-bloods, street-boys, would have been round him in a moment, all aiding in the search for an unknown something, the probable finding of which, if seen, would bring them a few coppers, the possible stealing of which, unseen, might fill their pockets. But on this calm September morning a Jew clothesman going his rounds, the servant of a lodging-house opposite, and an elderly-gentleman lodger, who never went out of town, and who in the winter never got out of bed, and who at the then moment was calmly looking on at Lloyd's proceedings as at a show, were all the spectators of the hunt for the missing paper, in which none of them evinced anything but the most cursory interest.

Not so the seeker. He hunted up and down, poked in wind-swept corners, peered down rusty gratings, seemed to have at one time a vague idea of following the chase up the livery-stableman's yard, and glared at the barrel swinging in mid-air from the crane outside the oilman's warehouse-door, as though it might have sucked up the precious document. He must have it, Gilbert Lloyd kept repeating to himself; he must have it. But he could not find it, and at the end of an hour's search he returned to the house, worn out with fatigue, and in a state of feverish anxiety.

If it had blown out of the window, as the woman had suggested, into the street—and the probabilities were that it had done so—somebody must have picked it up. There was

no wet or mud to discolour the paper or efface the writing;
it was a peculiar and striking-looking letter, and any one
finding it would doubtless read it through. If such had
been the case it was lost—irretrievably, for ever. Great
beads of perspiration stood upon his pallid forehead as this
notion flashed across him. His name headed the letter, the
name of his accuser was signed at its foot, and its contents
plainly set forth one attempted crime and hinted at the
knowledge of another, which had been more than attempted,
which had been carried into effect. Any one reading this
would see the whole state of affairs at a glance, would feel
it incumbent on them to give information to the police, and
—he was a dead man! What was that Lord Sandilands
had said about further inquiries relative to Harvey Gore?
Foxey had been doing his best to find out something
definite in that quarter, and had failed; but then Lord
Sandilands was a man of influence, with plenty of money,
which he would not scruple to spend freely in any matter
such as this. That made all the difference; they might
succeed in tampering with that wretched doctor fellow, who
plainly had had his suspicions—Gilbert had often recalled
his expression about the *rigor mortis*—and there would be
an end of it. Pshaw! what a fool he was! He passed his
hand across his damp brow, sprang from the chair on which
he had been sitting, and commenced pacing the room. An
end of it? No, not yet. He had always had his own
notion of how that end should be brought about, if the
pressure upon him became unbearable. Most men leading
such precarious shifty lives have thus thought occasionally,
and made odd resolves in regard to them. But there was
hope yet. He was seedy, weak, and unhinged; a glass of
brandy would set him all right, and then he would go off to
Hill Street, look through the accounts, draw on the bankers
to the uttermost farthing, and start for America. It was
hard lines to leave town, where he had played the game so
long and so successfully. However, that was all over, he
should never play it any more, and so he might as well—
better, much better—begin his new life in a fresh place.

He dressed himself, got into a cab, and drove to Hill
Street. The house had been left in charge of some of those
wonderful people who occupy houses during the temporary
absence of their legitimate owners; but when Gilbert rang

the bell the door was opened, to his intense surprise, by Martin, Lord Ticehurst's valet, whom he had left behind with his lordship at Baden.

"You here, Martin!" said Lloyd, with an astonishment mingled with an uncomfortable sensation which he could not conceal. "Why, when did you arrive, and what has brought you?"

"Arrived last night, sir," said Martin, with a jaunty air, very different from his usual respectful bearing. "Came by his lordship's orders."

"By his lordship's orders?" echoed Lloyd. "That was rather sudden, wasn't it?"

"Yes, sir; very sudden, sir; done all in a hurry, sir; after a long talk with Mr. Clarke the lawyer, sir."

"With Mr. Clarke, eh?" again echoed Lloyd, feeling more and more uncomfortable. "Well, no matter; it's all right, I suppose. Just come up to my room and tell me all about it;" and he was passing on into the house.

"Beg pardon, sir," said Martin, placing himself before him and barring the way; "beg pardon, sir, but you're not to come in; his lordship's orders, sir."

"Not to come in!" cried Lloyd, white with passion; "what the devil do you mean?"

"Just what I say, sir," replied Martin, with perfect coolness; "his lordship's orders, sir; last words he said to me. Got a note here for you, sir. Lordship said if you was here I was to give it you at once; if you wasn't, I wasn't to trouble about finding you until you came here."

"Give it here!" said Lloyd, savagely; and Martin dived in his pocket, fetched out the note, and handed it to him with a polite bow. It was in Ticehurst's unformed, round, schoolboy hand, which Gilbert knew so well; was very short, but very much to the purpose. It said that Lord Ticehurst had given orders that Mr. Lloyd should be denied access to the house in Hill Street; the question of accounts between them could be gone into on Lord Ticehurst's return from the Continent, which would be in the course of the ensuing week. Lord Ticehurst would remain a couple of days in London on his way to his place in Sussex, and would devote those days to settling all matters with Mr. Lloyd. It would be advisable, in the mean time, that Mr. Lloyd should draw no cheques on the account hitherto

open to his signature at Lord Ticehurst's bankers, as Lord
Ticehurst had given instructions to his bankers to close that
account so far as Mr. Lloyd was concerned.

"That's that infernal Clarke's doing," said Gilbert to
himself; "Etchingham's writing, certainly, but Clarke's
suggestion and dictation; Etchingham would not have
thought of the idea, and could not have expressed it half so
succinctly. There's a chance yet. That order to the bankers
could not have been sent by telegram. They would not
have risked that. Perhaps I'm in time.—Martin, did you
bring any other letters to England?"

"Yes, sir; one from his lordship to Messrs. Tilley and
Shoveller. Delivered it at the bank at nine this morning,
sir."

"Thanks; I'll write to his lordship. Good day, Martin."
He saw the man bow ironically and stick his tongue in his
cheek, but he took no notice. He turned round, but had to
make an effort to gather all his strength together and walk
away without staggering. The pavement surged up in front
of him; the houses on either side threatened to topple over
him. When he got out of sight of the valet still lingering
at the door, he stopped, and leaned against some railings to
recover himself.

It was all over, then! The last chance had been tried,
and failed. A day sooner, and he could have carried out his
notion of drawing on the bankers and escaping to America.
That accursed couple—his wife and his brother—had been
against him in that, as well as in all his other misfortunes
lately. If he had not waited for that answer from Gertrude,
—that answer which, when it came, filled him with so much
anxiety,—he would have gone to Hill Street on the previous
day, before Martin had arrived, have drawn his cheques,
and made all square. Curses on them both! That letter
from Gertrude—from Lord Sandilands rather—this last
business in Hill Street had driven from his mind; but the
thought of it now returned in tenfold agony. It was lost,
with all its terrible accusations! Had been found and read,
and was probably now in the hands of the police. And he
had no means for providing for flight. The few pounds in
his purse were all he possessed in the world. He should be
taken, and have to die on the scaffold! No, not that: he
knew a better trick than that yet.

Once again he had to stop. His legs failed him; his head was burning; he felt his heart beating with loud thick throbs. A dizziness came over him, and it needed all his strength to prevent himself from falling. After a minute or two he felt a little relieved. He called a cab, and was driven to his club. The porter was away from his post, and his deputy, one of the page-boys, failed to recognize the dashing Mr. Lloyd in the pallid man who passed him with unsteady gait, and asked him for his name. He went into the deserted coffee-room, swallowed a glass of brandy, which revived him; then made his way to the writing-room, and wrote a note. It was to a sporting acquaintance of his, who happened at the time to be house-surgeon to one of our largest hospitals, and ran as follows :—

"(Private.)"

"DEAR PATTLE,—A nag that has carried my lord (and master) for ten years has become past work, and is dangerous to ride. But his l'ship won't give him up, and some day he'll get his neck broken for his pains. To prevent this I want to put the poor beast *quiet y* out of the way, and I can't trust our vet., who is a blab. Nor do I want to buy any 'stuff' at a chemist's, as, if anything came of it, and it got wind, chemist might peach. Can you manage to send me a small bottle of strychnine by bearer? Do so; and the next good thing that comes off, you shall stand in with the profit. *Keep it dark.*

"Yours,
"GILBERT LLOYD."

"That's vague enough," said Lloyd, as he read the letter before placing it in an envelope. "But Pattle's a great ass; he'll be flattered to think he is helping my Lord Ticehurst's 'confederate,' and he'll have a dim idea that there's a chance of making some money—quite enough to make him do it." And Gilbert was right. He stopped the cab outside the hospital, and sent in the note. Within five minutes the porter appeared at the door with a parcel, which he handed in "With Mr. Pattle's compliments," and with which Lloyd drove off to his lodgings.

His haggard looks on alighting alarmed Mrs. Jobson, who expressed a hope that he had been to see a doctor. This gave him the opportunity for making an explanation which he had been seeking to bring about as he came along in the cab. He told the worthy landlady that he had consulted his physician, who told him that the attacks, one of which she had been a witness to, were highly dangerous, and that every means should be taken to check them. With this view the doctor had recommended him, if he felt one coming on, as was not unlikely, judging from the present deranged state of his health, to take a slight quantity of the medicine which he prescribed for him, and which would give him instant relief. Upon which Mrs. Jobson remarked that of course the doctors knew best. She did not herself "hold with" sedatives, confessing at the same time that her experience as regarded their application was confined to certain interesting cases, in which she looked upon the taking of them as flying in the face of Providence, which would not have sent pain if it was not meant to be endured.

Gilbert Lloyd retired to his room, and did not see his landlady again until about nine o'clock that evening, when he sent for her to tell her that he felt a renewal of the symptoms of his attack, that he should at once get to bed, and that he begged he might not be disturbed. This Mrs. Jobson promised, and took her leave. When she was gone, Gilbert opened his despatch-box, and commenced the following letter : —

"MY DEAR LORD,—You tell me you hear that my relations with Lord Ticehurst are at an end, and you ask me if I will undertake the management of your stud, and personally supervise your affairs. I need scarcely say that I am highly flattered by the proposal, thus repeated, I believe, for the third time. At present, however, I must, in all respect, decline to entertain it. I have been so far lucky that my circumstances are such as to prevent any necessity for my doing any more work for the remainder of my life, while my state of health, especially during the last few weeks, peremptorily forbids my doing anything but nurse myself for some time to——"

Here he finished abruptly, leaving the sheet on the blotting-pad, by the side of the open despatch-box.

"They'll not be able to get over that," he said, with a

shudder; "and the woman's testimony will be concurrent. It's an odd thing that a man who can do it should care about what people say of him after it's done."

He shuddered again as from his dressing-case he took a small phial of medicine, which he had purchased at a chemist's for the purpose, and, from the drawer in which he had locked it, the strychnine-bottle, and placed them side by side on the table. He then leisurely undressed himself, turned the bedclothes back, and rumpled the bed to give it the appearance of having been slept in; then he extinguished the light, took the phial of strychnine in his hand, lifted it to his mouth, drained it, and with one convulsive spring managed to throw himself on the bed.

"And he's quite gone, sir?" inquired weeping Mrs. Jobson the next morning of the doctor who had been hastily summoned.

"Gone, madam!" said the doctor, who was a snuffy Scotchman of the old school—"he's as dad as Jullius Cæsar. And this is another case o' the meschief of unauthorized parsons doctorin' themsalves and takkin' medicines in the dark."

CHAPTER VIII.

A LAST MESSAGE.

WORDSWORTH has written of one of those beautiful scenes which he loved so intensely, and with whose loveliness he was so familiar—

> "The spot was made by Nature for herself;
> The travellers know it not.   *   *   *
>   *   *   *   But it is beautiful,
> And if a man should plant his cottage near,
> Should sleep beneath the shelter of its trees,
> And blend its waters with his daily meals,
> He would so love it, that in his death-hour
> Its image would survive amongst his thoughts."

It was amid a scene to which these lines might be applied that Lord Sandilands and his daughter were living, a year after the death of Gilbert Lloyd—a scene so grand, and yet so full of soft and tender beauty, that an English writer, who knew it better than any one except the native Swiss dwellers in it, declared it to be, "even amongst the wonders of the Alps, a very miracle of beauty." It was a nook in the Savoy Alps, near the Valley of the Sixt. It had needed both money and interest to enable the old English nobleman to make even a temporary "settlement" in the remote region ; but he had used both to good purpose, when he found that the wounded spirit, the mind diseased, of his daughter, were not be healed by the distractions of travelling in the busy and populous centres of European life. They had tried many places, but she had sickened of all, though she tried hard to hide from her father—whose solicitude for her increased daily, as did her affection for him—that all his efforts to procure peace and pleasure for her were to a great extent incffectual. The young English *prima donna*—whose brief and brilliant career, whose sudden, unexplained disappearance from the scene of her triumphs, had been the subject of much talk and many conjectures in London—was not identified on the Continent with the Miss Keith who kept so much to herself, but who was so very charming when she could be induced to enter into the pastime of the hour. This was the more natural, as Gertrude never exerted her greatest, her most characteristic, talent—she never sang after she left England. The last occasion on which she had "tumbled," as she had said, to a limited but critical audience at Hardriggs, was the last appearance of Miss Lambert on any stage. Miss Keith looked well when she was to be seen, and talked well when she could be heard ; but she never sang, and thus a kindly mist diffused itself over her identity.

It seemed incredible to Gertrude that the incidents which had occurred, the great emotions she had experienced, the various kinds of suffering she had undergone, could all have passed over her within so brief a period : that in so short a space of time the exterior and interior conditions of her life should be so completely changed. She had passed through many widely-varying phases of mind since she had left England with her father : the uncertainty of her life over, the necessity for personal exertion at an end, and the death of her husband—horrible and unlamented as it was —had produced a great effect upon her. It was like relief from torturing, bodily pain, exhausting and constant ; it made her feel the need of deep and prolonged rest, quite undisturbed and irresponsible. She turned impatiently in the great relief of her freedom, from men and cities ; and longed for the solitudes of nature, and the release from conventionalities, which she felt was needed to complete the sense of her emancipation. Lord Sandilands, who, though he had been very well since they left England, was sensibly older, and who had gradually come to centre all his interests in this woman—who, though a reproach, was yet a constant delight to him—instantly obeyed her wishes, and they went to Switzerland. The beaten track of the tourists did not content Gertrude, whose taste for the wild and solitary beauties of nature was thoroughly gratified in the Alp region, and at no late period of their wanderings they found themselves in the neighbourhood of the beautiful and little-known valley of the Sixt. The place had an interest for Gertrude, from association with a favourite volume which she had read many a time, wondering whether the time would ever come when the scenery of the great glacier-world should be other than a romantic, unattainable vision to her. Lord Sandilands found the air invigorating, and though he could not join Gertrude in her explorations, he made every possible arrangement for their being effected with comfort and safety ; and by means of supplying himself with a number of truly English " comforts "—most of which were entirely unintelligible to the simple people of the district, and caused him to be regarded with more than common awe—he established himself very satisfactorily at the hospitable hostelry of the Fer à Cheval, formerly the Convent of Sixt. There had always been a good deal of philosophical contentment in the disposition of Lord Sandilands, and under his present circumstances this useful mental characteristic grew stronger and more ready at call. Reflecting, as he often did now, upon the past, it had an almost amusing effect upon his mind to remember how his time had formerly been passed—the people whom he had really thought of consequence to him, the things he had cared for and taken an interest in. How far away, how along ago, it all seemed now—now that he cared for nothing but Gertrude : the memory of Gertrude's mother—ah, what a blunder his conduct to her had been, as well as what a sin! —and his dead friend's son, mysteriously involved in that sin's consequence. Who remembered him, he thought; and whom did he remember of the many who had been his associates, and had called themselves his friends? If tidings of his death were to be sent to England, how many would say or think more than—"Old Sandilands has popped off, I hear ; deuced good thing for the parson's son in Dorsetshire, nephew or cousin, isn't it?" None he knew—and the knowledge did not pain him—except Miles Challoner. And of these phantom friendships, these several associations, he had made the pabulum of his life. What utter nonsense it seemed now, to be sure, when his daughter, sedulously kept out of sight and out of mind during so many years, was now the great central truth and occupation of his life, and his books and the eternal hills the quiet company in which he most delighted! To the old man, too, the time seemed strangely short, though eventful, since the whole aspect of his existence had been changed by the revelation made to him by his daughter. Since Gilbert Lloyd's death he had watched her even more closely than before, for the purpose of making up his mind whether she should be left in entire ignorance of who the wicked man who had blighted her young life, and was now removed from it for ever, really was, or whether she should be told the truth. He decided that the latter course should be pursued if Gertrude pined for Miles Challoner's presence, if she made any persistent attempts to break through the barrier of separation which circumstances and her own consent had placed between them. If change of scene, the excitement and interest of travel, and the natural influence of her youth and her recovered liberty should produce the effect he hoped for, should lead her to remember Miles with only a soft, kindly, painless regret, he would not tell her the truth at all ; the whole mystery of Geoffrey Challoner's life should rest in his grave with him, instead of only that dark secret which now Lord Sandilands could never by any possibility be forced to divulge. The purpose which his dead friend had had in view in imparting it to him had been faithfully served so long as the unhappy man lived,—it had died with him. Neither Miles nor

Gertrude should ever learn *that* tremendous truth. Lord Sandilands took great delight in his daughter's society, and sometimes under its influence lost sight of the troubles of the past. But the future fate of Gertrude occupied his mind painfully. He had never felt very strong since the illness he had gone through at St. Leonards, and he had become sensible since then that his life was not likely to be much prolonged. He had said nothing to Gertrude of his conviction on this point, nor had he alluded to it in his communications with Miles Challoner. But in the quiet majestic region where they had now taken up their abode, Lord Sandilands found an influence which attuned his mind to very serious thought, and disposed him to the setting of his house in order. What was to become of Gertrude when he should be gone? The painful and peculiar circumstances of her former life disinclined her to seek the busy haunts of the world, and her disposition required companionship, sympathy, and affection. He could leave her in easy circumstances, to be sure,—and he was of much too practical a turn of mind to underrate the importance of such a power,—but he could not give her security or happiness for the future. His heart turned yearningly to Miles Challoner as this solicitude troubled him, and he wondered whether his daughter's heart turned in the same direction. It had not been mentioned between them for long. The death of Gilbert Lloyd had set Gertrude free, so far as she knew; but she felt that the barrier between her and Miles existed still. He had loved and wooed her under a false impression, and since he had known the truth had made no attempt to see or write to her. Lord Sandilands had not failed to discern that she suffered keenly from this cause, but he still believed that she would suffer more keenly had she known the truth—the imperative and insurmountable reason which prevented Miles from again seeking her presence. Thus on this subject—the most interesting, the most vital to the father and the daughter —there had been silence, and now Lord Sandilands wished to break it, but hardly knew how to do so.

The time since the travellers had set up their rest at the Fer à Cheval had passed tranquilly away, and Gertrude had frequently assured her father that she had never enjoyed her foreign tour so much as now, when she found herself

among the solemn and majestic beauties of the Alpine
lands, and surrounded only by associations with nature, and
people of the simplest and most primitive habits.   This
assurance, so far as it went, was strictly true, and yet
Gertrude was not quite happy.   It was not altogether the
shadow of the past which oppressed her—it was dark, and
fell chill upon her, doubtless—but there was an actual
haunting grief which was more painful even than that.
She had loved worthily a man worthy of her love, she had
loved him more than she had known or realized to herself,
and he was lost to her now,—a great gulf seemed to have
fixed itself between them, and she was perforce condemned
to stand upon the opposite shore and gaze vainly across it
with longing eyes.   What was he doing there, far away in
the distance beyond her ken ?   She did not know, and now
not to know was becoming unbearable.   Had he forgotten
her ?   How had he borne the revelation which Lord
Sandilands had made to him, and which had disclosed to
him the terrible deception of her life ?   Her father had
conveyed to her an assurance of his perfect forgiveness, and
told her that he had said, hopeless as his suit was now, and
void of expectation or happiness as his life must be, he could
not regret that he had known and loved her.   This was all
she knew, and the need, the strong, desperate desire to
know more became very potent as the time lengthened, and
the first shock of her husband's death, with the revulsion of
feeling it had caused, passed away.   Thus it happened that
by a somewhat analogous process a similar result was
wrought in the minds of the father and the daughter, and
it became imminent that Miles Challoner should be spoken
of between them.

The occasion arose on a splendid evening, late in the
summer, when the beauty of the scene amid which they
lived was at its height, when the peace and the majesty of
the mountains filled their spirits, and the turmoil of the
past in their lives seemed an impossible delusion.   A time
to think of the beloved dead with joyful hope as well as
with poignant sorrow ; a time to make eternity seem true
and near, and hardly surprising ; a time and a scene to
soften and refine every feeling, and to put far away the passions and pursuits of the common world.   Lord Sandilands
was keenly impressed by this vague and beautiful influence

of nature ; and under the impression reverted, as the old do, to the long-past scenes of youth, its pleasures, its dreams, its occupations, and its companions. He talked a great deal to his daughter that evening of her mother, and of his own. The great wrong he had done Gertrude Gauthier once frankly acknowledged, and the sincere repentance he had come to feel earnestly professed, Lord Sandilands had alluded to that no more. Gertrude's mother might have been his honoured wife for any tone of restraint or difference there was in his infrequent mention of her. Then he strayed into talk of the associates of his boyhood and his school and college days, and mentioned Mark Challoner, the "young Squire" of Rowley in those distant days. Here was Gertrude's opportunity, and she availed herself of it promptly.

"Tell me about the Squire," she said, looking up into her father's face from her low seat by his side, and laying her clasped hands upon his knee. "I should like to hear all about him. Miles Challoner used to speak of him with the greatest affection and respect."

"Yes," said Lord Sandilands, "Miles loved his father. He was a very good son."

Seeing that a thoughtful expression spread itself over his face, Gertrude was afraid he might lapse again into silence, and once more asked him eagerly to tell her about the Squire. He did so. He told her of the old times at Rowley, of the geniality, heartiness, popularity, happiness of the Squire ; of his pretty young wife, her death, the change it wrought in the friend he so loved ; of the long-unbroken confidence which had existed between them, only disturbed by death ; and as he told the story, and dwelt upon the affectionate remembrances which it revived, he felt how little death had really disturbed the tie between them, how faithfully he had kept his friend's secret, and how wonderful it was to think that his own daughter was so deeply concerned in it—quite unconsciously. As her mobile, expressive face lighted up with interest and emotion, he looked at her with deep tenderness and compassion, thinking of the common suffering which linked her with his dead friend, and made that secret more important to her than even it had been to him. For him it was over and done with for ever; for her its baleful and guilty influence lingered still.

"Is Miles like the Squire?" Gertrude asked.

"Yes," replied Lord Sandilands, "like him in face and in character, but of a milder temper. Mark Challoner was very hot-tempered in his youth, quick, and impatient. Miles is more like his mother in his ways. She was a very sweet woman, and a terrible loss to her husband."

It was a relief to them to have thus slipped into an easy and familiar mention of him whose name had been for so long unspoken between them.

"Have you heard of Miles lately, father?" said Gertrude quietly, and without removing her eyes from Lord Sandilands' face.

"I am very glad you have asked me, my dear," replied her father. "I did not like to talk of Miles to you until you should mention him first. I have heard from him lately, and I don't like the tone in which he writes about himself."

"Is he ill?" said Gertrude, with quick alarm in her face and in her voice.

"No, not at all; but he is thoroughly discontented and unhappy. He has tried his very best and hardest to live the life of a moral English squire at Rowley, but he cannot do it; he has no heart for it; and I should not be surprised any day to hear that he had given up the useless attempt. He has not forgotten you, Gertrude; and he cannot forget you."

"I am glad of that," she said in the same calm tone. "I suppose I ought to say otherwise; but it would not be true, and I cannot say it. I deceived him, and was forced to disappoint him, and bring a great cross on his life; but I *cannot* say that I should be glad to know he had forgotten me, and had found elsewhere the happiness he thought he might have had with me."

"I am glad you speak so frankly to me," said Lord Sandilands, laying his hand tenderly on the shining bands of Gertrude's dark-brown hair. "I have been thinking a great deal about you and Miles Challoner; and I should like to know exactly how you feel about him."

The answer was very plainly to be read in her face, but Gertrude did not hesitate to give it in words.

" There is no change in my feelings for him, father," she said. " I shall never cease to love him."

" Would you marry him, Gertrude, if he came to ask you, though your marriage should involve your relinquishing all connexion with England, breaking entirely, even more completely than we have done, with old associations, and making quite a new life in a new country for yourselves ? Don't start, my dear, and look so agitated ; he has not told me to ask you this. You are not required to give a decision. I have asked you for my own satisfaction, because I want to know."

" I would marry him," Gertrude answered, " to go to the other end of the world with him, if it did not mean parting with you—but that can never be—without a scruple, without a regret, without a fear. But he could not marry me—have I not deceived him ?—even supposing he cared for me now as he once did. No, no, that is over and I must not repine, blest as my life is far above my deserts."

She put her father's hand to her lips as she spoke, then laid her soft cheek tenderly upon it.

" And you think the obstacle which your hard fate raised between you and Miles is insurmountable ?" said Lord Sandilands, thinking the while of that obstacle of which she was unconscious.

" I think so," Gertrude answered sadly. " Do not you ? Have you any reason for thinking it is not so ? "

" None that I can make you understand, my child," said Lord Sandilands. " But I have a strong conviction—a feeling which may not be reasonable, but is irresistible— that all this strange riddle of your life will yet work itself out to a clear and happy solution in your becoming Miles Challoner's wife. I understand the extent and force of the objections much better than you do, and give them their full weight in the estimation of the world. But (since I have been here particularly) I have for some time ceased to set very great store by the opinions of the world, and to believe that there is much happiness or even satisfaction to be got out of conformity to them. I fancy Miles is very strongly of my opinion, and in time—not a very long time either—I have a perfect conviction that all will be well, and that when I leave you I shall do so in better hands than mine."

Gertrude's tears were falling before her father concluded these sentences, which he spoke with much earnestness, and for some time she did not speak. At length she said :

" When he writes to you, does he ever mention me ? "

" Always, and always in the same invariable tone. No other woman will ever be offered the place in his home which he once hoped would have been yours. This he has told me often, and desired I should tell you, if ever, or whenever, you should again speak of him to me."

" He knows we have not spoken of him lately ? "

" He knows that, and has been satisfied that it should be so ; the time that has elapsed since the event that set you free has not been too long for a silence dictated by propriety ; but it has expired now, Gertrude, and I think you and he might be brought to understand each other, and make up your minds, like rational people, what extent of sacrifice you are prepared to make to secure the privilege of passing the remainder of your lives together."

" I have it not in my power to make any sacrifice," said Gertrude ; " that must come from him, if it is to come at all. I wish I had ; but it is he who would have all to forgive, all to forego, all to endure."

Lord Sandilands, with his secret knowledge of the truth, felt that she had reason in her words. But he had strong faith in Miles Challoner, and confident hope in the result of a plan which he had formed, and on which this conversation with his daughter finally determined him to act. He did not prolong their conference, but bade Gertrude be of good cheer, and trust in him and in the future. She gave him her ready promise, and a fervent assurance of the happiness and contentment of her life with him, and said a few earnest words of affection to him, which her father received with a fervour which would have astonished himself almost as much as it would have surprised his London acquaintances. As the shades of evening deepened, silence fell upon Lord Sandilands and Gertrude once more, unbroken until he asked her to sing to him. She complied immediately (her father and the peasants were the only persons who now heard the glorious voice which had enchanted the most splendid, refined, and critical audience in the world), and the rich, thrilling strains soon floated out upon the pure mountain-air. Her father—lying on a couch beneath the window at the end of the long room, which commanded a glorious view of the valley leading up to the Col d'Auterne, and from whence Gertrude had watched many a sunrise, and gazed at many a moonlight scene, such as no words could convey a description of—listened to her singing, and was transported in fancy back to the long-vanished past. The last song which Gertrude sung that night was the first she had sung at the concert at Carabas House, when Miles Challoner had looked upon her to love her, and Lord Sandilands had looked at her and found Gertrude Gauthier's features in her face.

A few days later, when he had considered the matter maturely, and made up his mind that in the way which had suggested itself to him the happiness of his daughter and Miles Challoner might be secured, Lord Sandilands wrote to his dead friend's son. The letter was a long one, replying fully to the last which he had received from Miles, and giving him excellent advice, which the writer was thoroughly well qualified to offer, concerning the disposition and management of his property. It contained intelligence of Lord Sandilands' health, and a description of the *locale* and its resources. Then it continued :

"I have purposely avoided mentioning Gertrude to you until the present stage of my letter should have been reached, because I have much to say concerning her of a more serious nature than the details of her daily occupations, and a report of her health and looks. The latter are good, the former are as usual. She still retains unaltered her pleasure in the mountain scenery, the primitive people, and the flowers. She is still the same to me—an affectionate daughter and a charming companion. But some time has now passed since the death of her unhappy husband, and its influence is telling upon her. I have not been blind to the change in her ; and a few days ago, for the first time, I mentioned you, and elicited from her an avowal which I am about to disclose to you, addressing you in my double character (and of course without her knowledge) of Gertrude's father and your oldest, and I think I may add truest, friend. She is still attached to you—and in spite of all the sorrow and all the equivocal experiences which have been

hers,—with a fresh, vivid, and trusting affection, which
would suffice, or I am very much mistaken in my estimate
of both of you, to make your lives, if united, happy. I do
not entertain any doubt that your feelings towards her
remain unchanged, and it is on this supposition that I now
address you. You have known me long, my dear Miles,
and as well as a man of your age can know a man of mine;
and when I tell you that I regret more deeply, bitterly,
and unavailingly than anything else—it is my lot, the
common one of old age, to look back upon the past with
vain bitterness and regret—the having hesitated before the
opinion of the world in doing my duty by the woman I
loved, and following to a practical issue my own conviction
of the means by which my true happiness might have been
secured, you will not suspect me of unduly underrating, or
carelessly despising the opinion and the judgment of the
world. The circumstances must be very exceptional indeed under which I would counsel any man, holding a
fair position in society, and endowed with the duties and
privileges of a landed proprietor as you are, to defy the
opinion of society, and to turn his back on those duties
and privileges. But yours is a very exceptional position,
and I do counsel you to do both these things. Your
heart is not in Rowley Court, nor are you capable of fulfilling your duties as you are at present. Make new ones
for yourself, my dear Miles. Yield to the inclination which
you have partly confessed, and which I have very distinctly
perceived, and turn your back upon the scene which has
been overclouded for you since your boyhood by a sorrow
which has ever been, and must remain, a mystery to you.
Geoffrey Challoner's crime is buried in the grave of Gilbert
Lloyd; but you will never lay its ghost while you remain
at Rowley Court. I am neither a credulous nor a super-
stitious man; but I have seen more instances than one of
the passing away of the 'luck' of an old place, and I feel
that Rowley Court is one of those from which the old
'luck' has passed away. So far as leaving the place is
concerned, I believe my advice will only anticipate, if even
it does anticipate, the resolution I fully expect to hear you
have by this time taken. And now to my other point.
Society in England and English law do not recognize such
a marriage as that of yourself and Gertrude would be; and

under anything like ordinary circumstances I should be one
of the first and strongest protestants against such a union;
but as I have already said, yours are the most exceptional
circumstances conceivable out of the region of the wildest
romance. Your marriage with Gertrude could not injure
any rights, or offend any principles or prejudices, as no one
ever likely to see your faces again, or, if you did marry,
ever to be aware of the fact, has the least notion of the
existence of those circumstances. Sell the property, leave
England, and if you still love Gertrude, as she loves you,
marry her, and seek happiness and home in a foreign land.
I write now, you must bear in mind, remembering that she
is entirely ignorant of the complication in your story and
hers which sets it apart from perhaps any other human experience. She regards herself as a faulty woman, who
deceived the man she loved by an assumption which she
deems unpardonable, undeniable, even after that wretched
man's death had set her free. You regard her as still (as
I believe) the object of your truest love, but parted from
you by the fact that the man who made her miserable, and
might have made her guilty had not true love intervened
to save her, was your own brother, the author of the misery
which made the latter years of your father dark and cheerless. These are both substantial truths and phantoms,—
the first in their simple existence, the second in the effect
they ought to produce on such a mind as yours. The
misfortunes of your life are irremediable; but they are also
past and gone, and the future may still be yours—yours, too,
without a braving of opinion, a defiance of the world to which
you would probably not feel equal, if the selection of your
future course of proceeding were put before you hampered
with any such imperative condition. You might take
wealth with you to a foreign land, and the antecedents of
your wife could never be known there to any one; here,
only to me; and I am ready to give your determination
to carry out such a scheme as this my warmest approbation and support, though, if you do it, I must lose the
society of my child, which is inexpressibly dear to me.
But I owe it to Gertrude, and still more to Gertrude's
mother, that I should not rest content with a half-com-
pensation to my daughter, that she should not be only
half-happy. I know in what her true happiness would

consist, and it shall not be wanting through any failure of self-denial on my part. My time here is not to be long; perhaps it may be peaceful, and less haunted by remorse, if my daughter becomes your wife. I have sinned much towards the living and the dead; and though there does not at first sight appear to be any reparation in the scheme which I propose, there is a reparation which you will understand in part, and I entirely. If I am not in error in respect to your feelings, write to me, and say that you will join us here, when the necessary arrangement of your affairs will admit of your coming,"

When Lord Sandilands had written this letter, he did not immediately despatch it, but laid it by for a few days, during which he deliberated with himself much and secretly. But the end of all his meditations, the upshot of all his close observation of Gertrude, was a conviction that the letter was an exposition of the truth, and ought to be sent. Accordingly, on the fourth day after he had written he despatched it, and it was fortunate that he had taken and acted upon the resolution at the time he did; for Lord Sandilands was not to act upon any more resolutions, or play any active part in the affairs of this world any more.

On the evening of the day on which his letter to Miles Challoner had been sent away, and while his daughter was singing to him, Lord Sandilands was taken ill with acute gout. The attack had many features in common with that which had tried him so severely at St. Leonards, but was more severe and exhausting. The English doctor from Chamouni shook his head and looked very grave from the first,—he was naturally a gloomy practitioner, but in this instance his gravity was amply justified. There was not enough rallying-power in the constitution of the patient, it seemed, and the illness rapidly assumed a fatal aspect. The intelligence was conveyed, not without humane gentleness, to Gertrude, on whom its effect was overwhelming indeed. A kind of stupefaction came over her; she could render but little assistance, but she never left her father, and even when his exhaustion was greatest he was conscious of her presence.

One day, when the end was only a few hours off, she was sitting by Lord Sandilands' bed, holding one of his thin hands in hers, and gazing with looks expressive of such anguish as only such a vigil knows, on his sleeping face. A slight noise at the door disturbed her, but she merely raised her hand with a warning gesture, and did not turn her head. In another moment a man's form approached her with swift, noiseless strides, and she was silently clasped in the arms of Miles Challoner.

Thus sheltered, thus comforted, her father found her when he awoke, and a little while after Lord Sandilands died.

CHAPTER IX.

TWELVE MONTHS AFTER.

MORE than twelve months had rolled away since the man called Gilbert Lloyd had been found dead in his lodgings in Duke Street, when the medical journals improved the occasion and had a word of advice for the general public, and a good many words of abuse for each other, and when the affair created a little sensation; for amongst a certain set Lloyd was very well known, and on the whole very much hated for his success in life. The fact of his quarrel with Lord Ticehurst had got wind, though the cause of it was kept secret, and had been duly rejoiced over; but the man must have had extraordinary luck, every one said; for the newspapers, in their account of the inquest, published a half-written letter which was found in his room, and on which he had evidently been engaged when seized with the spasm which he sought to allay with that confounded poison, which he had evidently taken in mistake for the medicine standing by it, in which he alluded to the offer made to him by some nobleman, of an appointment exactly like that which he held with Lord Ticehurst, and which, the latter said, the state of his health made him decline. At the inquest Mrs. Jobson gave her evidence as to the fit with which her lodger had been seized on the morning previous to his death, and as to the remedy which he told her had been prescribed for him; a practical chemist gave professional evidence; Mr. Pattle produced

the letter he had received ; the coroner summed up, and
the jury returned a verdict that the deceased had died
from a dose of poison taken accidentally. But this was
more than twelve months since, and the manner of Gilbert
Lloyd's death was never spoken of ; and the fact of his
ever having lived was almost forgotten by the members of
that busy, reckless, stirring world in which he had moved
and had his being ; that world which calls but for the
"living present," and carefully closes its eyes against both
the past and the future.

That world which never makes the smallest difference in
its career whether old members drop out of it, or new
members are caught up and whirled along with it, was
pursuing its course in very much its ordinary way. The
Marchioness of Carabas still had a soul which required
male supervision, and still found somebody to supervise it ;
though Mr. Pennington's year of office had expired, another
charming creature reigned in his stead. Mr. Boulderson
Munns still drove his mail-phaeton, still told his foreign
artists that he didn't understand "their d—d palaver,"
and still managed the Grand Scandinavian Opera, though
not with so much success as formerly. There had been a
reaction after Miss Lambert's secession from the boards ;
people began to think there was something good at the
Regent, and went to see ; and the heart of Mr. Munns was
heavy under his gorgeous waistcoat, and he had half made
up his mind to retiring from management, or, as he phrased
it, "cuttin' the whole concern."

A change had come over one person who has played an
important part in this little drama—Lord Ticehurst.
Gilbert Lloyd's place in that young nobleman's establishment never was filled up, much to the disgust of Bobby
Maitland, who wrote off directly he heard of the quarrel,
volunteering his services, and being perfectly ready to throw
over his then patron, Mr. Stackborough, at a moment's
notice. But the news of his old companion's death acted
as a great shock upon the young earl, and those reflections
which had come upon him during that homeward drive
from Hastings, after his refusal by Miss Lambert, came
upon him with redoubled force. His life was purposeless,
and worse than purposeless ; was passed in a not very
elevated pursuit among very degrading surroundings. He

had a name and position to keep up ; and though his brains were not much, he knew that he might do something towards filling his station in life, and, please God, he would. From Mr. Toshington you may gather that Lord Ticehurst has carried out his intention. "God knows what has come to Etchingham, sir !" the old gentleman, who has grown very shaky and senile, will say ; "you never saw a fellow so changed. He's cut the turf and all that low lot of fellows—deuced good thing, that ; lives almost entirely at his place down in Sussex, and has gone in for farmin', and cattle-breedin', and that kind of thing. What does it mean, eh ? Well, I don't know, more than that there's never a sudden change in a man that I've ever seen, that there wasn't one thing at the bottom of it. A woman ?—of course ! They do say that Grace Belwether, niece of my old friend Sir Giles, is a devilish pretty, sensible young woman, and that Etchingham is very sweet on her."

And Miles Challoner, was he changed ? He was sobered and saddened, perhaps ; for a great deal of the gilding, which is but gum and gold-paper after all, but which makes life seem bright and alluring, had been ruthlessly rubbed off during the past two years, and he bore about with him what was at once the greatest sorrow and the greatest joy— his love for Gertrude. This absorbing feeling influenced his whole life, and so engrossed him that he gave up every-thing in which he had formerly taken interest, and passed his time in recalling fleeting recollections of the happy days he had spent in the society of his beloved and in endea-vouring to arrange the wildest and most improbable com-bination of chances under which those happy days might be renewed. Long since he had fled from the "gross mud-honey of town"—where almost every place was fraught with bitter memories not merely of the loved and lost, but of the wretched man his brother, whose career of crime had been so suddenly brought to a close—and had established himself at Rowley Court in the hope that the quiet life and the occupation which his position required, and in which he would involve himself, would bring about a surcease of that gnawing pain which was ever at his heart.

All in vain. The ghost of the dead Past was not to be

laid by change of scene ; nor in the clear air of the country did the uncompromising Future loom brighter and more rosily than it had in murky London.   Nor horse, nor dog, nor gun afforded the smallest pleasure to Miles Challoner, who said " Yes " or " No," whichever first entered his head, when his steward made suggestions or asked for instructions, and who walked about his estate with his head hanging on his breast and his hands clasped behind him, chewing the cud of his bitter fancy, and wondering whether this purposeless, useless existence would ever terminate, and whether before his death he should ever have the chance of playing a part in the great drama of life.

One day he took a sudden determination.   It was useless, he felt, remaining inert, inactive as he was, ever pursuing a vain phantom, and letting his energies rust and his opportunities of doing real good pass by.   He was a young man, and there was a life before him yet.   Not there, not in his old ancestral home, hampered by " proud laws of precedent " and conventionality, dragged down by old memories and associations with things bygone, but in the New World.   Why should he not yet make his life a source of happiness and comfort to himself and others ?   He had no sentimental notions about parting with his family acres. He should never marry, of that he was firmly convinced, and at his death they would go to some one for whom he cared not one jot.   Better to part with them at once, and take the proceeds with him to Australia, where at least he should be free from haunting memories of the past, and have the chance of making a career for himself.

This determination he at once proceeded to carry into effect, writing to his lawyer, and giving him instructions for the sale of the Rowley-Court property so soon as he could find a purchaser.   Find a purchaser !   It was difficult to make a selection.   The Wallbrooks and the Wallbrooks' friends, who had bought land in the neighbourhood on Sir Thomas Wallbrook's recommendation, and the friends who had been staying with the Wallbrooks, and thought they would like to have property in the neighbourhood—all self-made men who came up to London with half-a-crown and were then worth millions—all wanted to buy Rowley Court.   Eventually, however, Miles gave the preference to Sir Thomas himself, and the arrangement had just been concluded between them when Miles received the letter with which the reader has been made acquainted in the previous chapter.

In one of the wildest and yet most peaceful scenes of the Alpine land, the grave of the English nobleman was made, by his own desire. He had no wish that his remains should be brought to England, but desired that they should be suffered to remain where his last quiet days of life had been passed in the society of his daughter. Under the shadow of the rustic church he rested; and when all had been done, Gertrude and Miles found themselves alone. It was a solemn time and a solemn occasion; and their utter isolation from all whom they had ever previously known, the strangeness of the scene, and the urgency and uncertainty of the future, oppressed them; while the loss of the best friend either had ever possessed so darkened the horizon for them, that not even their mutual and avowed love could brighten it.

By Lord Sandilands' desire Miles Challoner had sent for his solicitor, who arrived at the Fer à Cheval in time to be present at the funeral, and to whom Gertrude confided all the papers which her father had with him. Their contents were explicit. The greater portion of Lord Sandilands' property he had had the power to dispose of, and he had left it unreservedly to his daughter. There was no mention made of any other person; and Mr. Leggatt, the solicitor, was charged by his late client with the administration of the bequest.

The evening had fallen on the day whose morning had seen Lord Sandilands' quiet and simple funeral. Mr. Leggatt had explained to Gertrude her very satisfactory position in worldly affairs, and had received the few instructions she had to give him. He then stated that he should be obliged to start on his homeward journey on the following day, and inquired Gertrude's immediate intentions with regard to her own movements. Gertrude replied that she could not tell him until the morning. Then Mr. Leggatt discreetly retired, and the lovers and mourners were left alone.

"I sent you from me because I have deceived you," said

Gertrude, when the conversation, after long lingering upon the details of the past and upon the friends they had lost, was flagging "And I thought you stayed away and made no sign because you could not forgive me."

"I stayed away because you had been deceived," said Miles, "and the time had not come when I could tell you the truth and ask you to aid me in making the best of it for us both. You know it all now." He took the letter Lord Sandilands had written to him from her hand. "You know that the miserable man who was to both of us a rock ahead through life was my brother—the shame and misfortune of our family."

Gertrude bowed her head and covered her face with her hands.

He continued : "All that can be said, except how truly and devotedly I love you, is said in this letter—the last message of your father, of my best friend. There is nothing in England for which we care ; we have no ties there ; we are bound to each other only by ties of love and sorrow in all the world. No one knows, no one can ever know, what that unhappy man was to you and to me. Will you let me try to make you forgive and forget it all in a happier marriage ? Ours is an exceptional case. The world would condemn us, if the world knew all it could, which would be only half the truth ; we know all the truth, and are free from self-condemnation. Say yes, Gertrude ; not to me only, remember, but to him whom we have lost ; and we shall never see England any more, or part again in this world."

Gertrude made him no answer in words. Her head was still bowed, and her eyes hidden by one hand ; but she placed the other in his, and he knew that she was won.

Their marriage took place at Berne, and they are lost in the crowd.

THE END.

WYMAN AND SONS, PRINTERS, GREAT QUEEN STREET, LONDON, W.C.

TINSLEYS' MAGAZINE,

An Illustrated Shilling Monthly,

CONDUCTED BY EDMUND YATES,

CONTAINS :

DEAR ANNETTE: a New Serial Story.

BREAKING A BUTTERFLY ; or, BLANCHE ELLER-SLIE'S ENDING. By the Author of " Guy Livingstone, " &c.

A HOUSE OF CARDS. A Novel. By a New Writer.

NOVELS: By EDMUND YATES, Author of " Black Sheep," &c.; and WILLIAM HOWARD RUSSELL, LL.D., of the *Times*.

ENGLISH PHOTOGRAPHS. By an American.

THE LATEST PARIS FASHIONS (*Illustrated*).

&c. &c. &c.

TINSLEY BROTHERS' TWO-SHILLING VOLUMES,

Uniformly bound in Illustrated Wrappers.

To be had at every Railway Stall and of every Bookseller in the Kingdom.

Black Sheep. By EDMUND YATES.

The Waterdale Neighbours. By JUSTIN McCARTHY, Author of " Paul Massie," &c.

The Pretty Widow. By CHARLES H. Ross.

Miss Forrester. By the Author of " Archie Lovell," " Steven Lawrence, Yeoman," &c.

Barren Honour. By the Author of " Guy Livingstone," &c.

Sword and Gown. By the same Author.

The Savage Club Papers (1867). With all the Original Illustrations ; also the Second Series for 1868.

TINSLEY BROTHERS, 18, CATHERINE STREET, STRAND.

TINSLEY BROTHERS'
CHEAP EDITIONS OF POPULAR NOVELS.

BY MRS. J. H. RIDDELL, Author of "George Geith," &c.

Far Above Rubies. 6s.	Phemie Keller. 6s.
The Race for Wealth. 6s.	Maxwell Drewitt. 6s.
George Geith. 6s.	Too Much Alone. 6s.
The Rich Husband. 6s.	City and Suburb. 6s.

BY MRS. HENRY WOOD, Author of "East Lynne," &c.

Elster's Folly. 6s.	Mildred Arkell. 6s.
St. Martin's Eve. 6s.	Trevlyn Hold. 6s.

BY THE AUTHOR OF "GUY LIVINGSTONE."

Sword and Gown. 4s. 6d.	Maurice Dering. 6s.
Barren Honour. 6s.	Guy Livingstone. 5s.
Border and Bastille, 6s.	Sans Merci, 6s.

Also, Now Ready, Uniform with the Above,

The Rock Ahead. By EDMUND YATES. 6s.

The Adventures of Dr. Brady By W. H. RUSSELL, LL.D. 6s.

Black Sheep. By EDMUND YATES, Author of "The Rock Ahead," &c.

Not Wisely, but Too Well. By the Author of "Cometh up as a Flower." 6s.

Lizzie Lorton of Greyrigg. By Mrs. LYNN LINTON, Author of "Sowing the Wind," &c. 6s.

Archie Lovell. By the Author of "The Morals of Mayfair," &c. 6s.

Miss Forrester. By the Author of "Archie Lovell," &c. 6s.

Recommended to Mercy. By the Author of "Sink or Swim?" 6s.

TINSLEY BROTHERS, 18, CATHERINE STREET, STRAND.